THE SOUND OF LIGHT

CLAIRE WALLIS

The Sound of Light

ISBN 978-0-9988259-1-5 (Printed Edition)

Editing by Jennifer Haymore

Cover design by Sarah Hansen of Okay Creations

For my bassist, John

K'ACY'S PROLOGUE

My daddy taught me how to break a mourning dove's neck when I was five years old. He'd take me and Charlie to the quarry where he worked, and we'd run around collecting the birds after he'd filled them with birdshot. Sometimes, they'd still be alive. They'd have a broken wing or a missing foot, and they'd look up at you with their shiny, round, black eyes. Like they were just waiting to die.

"If they're still alive," Daddy would say, "you've got to break their neck real quick. No use letting 'em suffer."

He showed us how to put their downy heads into the crook of skin between our first two fingers and flip their bodies backward until we heard the bones snap.

"Flick 'em fast," he'd say, "like the tongue on a snake."

By the time I was eight years old, I'd probably taken more lives than a poacher on the African savannah. They were good, too, those doves. My momma knew how to cook them so they tasted just like chicken.

In fact, the day I was born, the doctor asked my momma about the last thing she ate before labor came on. When she told him it was a dove sandwich, she said he looked right back at her like she was some kind of wild sinner, fresh outta the bayou.

So here I am, twenty-four years after my illustrious dove-fueled birth, sitting on a mattress with another living thing in my hands, just waiting to die.

Only this time, it's different.

CHAPTER 1

Some people think funk is dead. They say it because you don't hear funk on commercial radio anymore, unless you happen to catch "Super Freak" on the oldies station. But that's bullshit, because in music, nothing dies. It just waits for rediscovery or reincarnation. Funk is very much alive. And, right now, I'm about to lay some down.

Jarrod steps up to the mic and lingers there, his stare cutting into the audience. His lips are silent, and his body is still. We're *all* silent. No one on the stage moves a muscle.

But not them. *They* are wild. Bodies humming with expectation and alcohol. Their noises bounce around the room, amplifying the energy a thousand times over.

I can only see his profile from where I stand, but I know what Jarrod's doing. He's doing what he always does—he's making them want. Making them *need*. Even before a single note escapes the stage, he makes them beg, just by looking at them and doing nothing. The waiting and the anticipation will eventually turn them into a frenzied wad of beer-infused humanity, willing to scream until their throats go hoarse. Because Jarrod makes it happen. He *wills* it to happen. Every time.

He doesn't move. None of us do. And we won't...until he's ready.

Jarrod and I met six years ago, both of us fresh out of high school and desperate for something to resuscitate our rotting lives. I moved north after my father died because I needed to remove myself from the nightmare. I needed to get away from Louisiana and everything that reminded me of my daddy. Not because I didn't love him, but rather because I probably loved him too much. Otherwise I wouldn't have done what I did. But Jarrod, he's a born-and-raised Philadelphian. He's always known this was his place in the world. He loves it here. Back then, when we first met, he had yet to find his purpose. He needed to clean the shit out of his veins and figure out where he fit. Both literally and figuratively.

Turns out that when we found each other at that bus stop, we both found a home. Together. And we named it Crackerjack Townhouse.

Three full minutes pass before I see Jarrod's chest fill with a surge of air. That's my sign. That's *our* sign. A split second later, the eight of us strike a single simultaneous note, loud and crisp. It echoes around the room and is immediately followed by more silence. Just a pause really, but the pulsing in the air makes it feel like an eternity. My thumb rests on the E-string while the remainder of my fingers hover below it, ready to go to work whenever Jarrod decides it's time. The crowd flips their shit the instant they see his mouth open again.

This time, we don't stop. Stevie, Marquis, and Bryson blast their horns, and my heart starts its poetic thumping, just like it does every time the calloused fingers of my left hand press against the frets. What all those white girls out there in the audience don't know is that when they're staring at Jarrod in his tight-as-sin jeans, thinking he's the one giving them the panty-dropping feels, it's really me. I'm the one vibrating through their guts, sending them a pulse-quickening message of love. Jarrod may be what they're looking at, but once the music starts, I'm what they *feel*. My bass is what all those mascara-laden lovelies sense inside their chests. It's what they feel echoing in their souls, anchoring them to the song. Not Calvin's drums or Mark's keyboard or Stevie's sax or Jarrod's gyrating ass. It's my fingers dancing against this Music Man StingRay bass guitar that makes them want to stay.

Crackerjack Townhouse is funk personified. And it makes me happier than anything else in this world.

***

When Jarrod sings the last line of the night, "I am no man. I am dynamite," his voice is as evocative as ever. Our final note hangs in the air around us like a cloud of pesticide, light as air but heavy with purpose. He wrote the song long before Crackerjack Townhouse fell into place, back when he was more interested in what went up his nose than what came out of his mouth. "Ecce Homo" is my favorite song; it has been since the first time he sang it to me, sitting on the curb in front of the McDonald's on South Broad.

When Pontius Pilate presented Jesus, crowned with thorns and on the verge of crucifixion, to an unsympathetic horde, he said, "Ecce homo." *Behold the man!* I know the story. I've known it since I was a little girl because my momma was overly fond of reading from the Bible, terrifying me and my sister with its stories of suffering and contradiction, always just before bedtime.

Jarrod's lyrics, though, aren't biblical. They're a twisted-up version of the philosopher Friedrich Nietzsche's identically titled book, *Ecce Homo: How One Becomes What One Is*. In fact, the song's final lyrics, "I am no man. I am dynamite," are words from Nietzsche himself. And just like Nietzsche's book, all of Jarrod's lyrics are self-serving yet self-deprecating. Cocky yet sardonic. Structured yet raw. It's a funk song gone philosophical. My mother would have a nervous breakdown if she'd existed in my world long enough to hear the song's heretical and sacrilegious message about the conceit of self-faith.

My father, on the other hand, would've loved it. And not just because of the trumpet solo.

When the set ends and the applause begins, a sweet, familiar ache settles into my hands. The bones and tendons there are tired from stretching over the strings. As the audience's praise sinks into my heart, I rub the fingertips of my right hand across the cobweb painted on the StingRay's pickguard, remembering the familiar sting of death and how little it changes, no matter how much time has passed. I lift the leather strap up over my head and put the StingRay on its stand. Jarrod raises the mic into the air and pokes it at the audience, before sliding it back into the stand while making eyes at the blonde whose breasts are pressed against the edge of the stage at his feet.

His gaze is not a secret signal. It's a blatant invitation for her to stick around, and it's the only one he ever needs. She'll still be here when we come back out for the teardown. They always are. They wait for him, pretending to innocently chat with their girlfriends while we load everything into Calvin's van and the sound guy shuts down the house. At some point in the process, Jarrod will flash a smile at the woman, whoever *she* is, and the deal will be sealed. She'll be patient, lingering for as long as he needs her to. Then, when the teardown is complete, Jarrod and the woman du jour will walk out the back door hand in horny hand.

He's very unapologetic about the whole thing, as well he should be. They're two consenting adults, after all, so there's nothing to apologize for. Both are getting exactly what they want.

When we come out of the back room to start tearing down fifteen minutes after "Ecce Homo" ends, my predictions prove true yet again. As soon as most of the gear is loaded, Jarrod passes me, his arm around the blonde's waist, guiding her toward the door. He gives me a half-smile and wiggles his eyebrows up and down. She's too busy watching me to pay attention to the antics of his face. She wants to see if I'll jump on her out of jealousy. 'Cause just like all the other women Jarrod takes home after a show, she assumes that since I'm the only female in the band, I either want to be his mother hen or his Saturday-night score.

Nothing could be further from the truth. We all keep it professional. Especially Jarrod and I. Because I know where he's been, and there ain't no way I'm falling down that rabbit hole.

My amp is the last thing to go into Calvin's van, and when the doors swing closed, everyone says their goodbyes and heads off to their own worlds. I'm the only one that walks back into the bar. After I hit the restroom, I sling my gig bag over my shoulder and onto my back. The StingRay is nine pounds, five ounces of pure bliss. Twenty-one frets on a red maple neck, a Vintage Sunburst body with a white pearloid pickguard, a hardened steel bridge plate, a humbucking pickup, and stainless steel saddles. It's my flawless baby. And I use it to forget about the rest of the world, if only temporarily.

I step out onto the street again and head for the bus stop. As the streetlamps buzz their electronic drone, my thoughts uncontrollably shift from the baby on my back to Miriam Hansen and the end of her life. In death, as in life, Miriam Hansen lingers. Her last breath has not yet dissolved into memory; her words have not been forgotten. Miriam Hansen's death is fresh and painful. She is ratcheted to my heart.

The joy leaves me in an instant, and it's replaced with uncontrollable sadness. I start sobbing just as the bus pulls up to the curb.

CHAPTER 2

At 7:49 in the morning I walk into Pine Manor Assisted Living for the 1,487th time. Sunday mornings are always the easiest because, unlike all the other days, there are smiling people everywhere. They sit in their wheelchairs or on the leather wing-chairs in the lobby, waiting with a gentle smile. Sunday mornings hold so much promise. Promise that someone will visit them and make them feel important again. Make them feel loved. They're hungry for their families, for stories of the outside world, for the sweet grip of a real and much-needed hug. And for most of them, Sundays are the only days it comes. If it comes at all.

You can tell the ones who don't have any family left or family that lives far away. They seldom wear a smile. Not even on Sunday mornings. They know they're going to have to sit here all day with nothing to do but watch. They'll see all the visitors come and go, and it will make them feel like they're a little less important than the ones that "get company." But I know better. I know they're *all* important to this world. They *all* matter. They *all* mean something. Even if it's just to me.

I head through the lobby, past all the wrinkled faces, and give a bright hello to each and every one of them. I pat Mr. Rauch on the knee and ask him how his shoulder is feeling. I fix Mr.

Toftree's misbuttoned shirt. I straighten Mr. Ledbetter's tie and remove Francis Boyer's glasses to wipe the lenses clean. I do all this before my shift even starts. Then, I turn right, walk past the reception desk, and head down the hallway.

Ms. Sinclair is sitting there, her wheelchair parked just outside the door of her room. She's smiling. But with her, it's not because someone is coming to see her. It's because she doesn't know any better.

We have twenty-six residents, but Ms. Evelyn Sinclair is my favorite. Most days, she sits for hours at the picture window in the lobby, watching the birds at the feeder outside. I bought the feeder a few months ago, right after she moved in and told me about how she used to have pet birds when she was young. I buy the seed myself and refill the feeder whenever I'm scheduled to work. Sometimes Ms. Sinclair doesn't know who I am, but she always knows the names of all the birds. She points out the cardinals and the chickadees, the nuthatches and the mourning doves. I don't know about the other aides, but I always feign ignorance and pretend I'm hearing the information for the very first time. It makes her happy. And Ms. Sinclair needs that. Because she doesn't "get company" on a Sunday, or any other day, for that matter. I've never seen anyone here to visit her. Not even once.

"Would you like to go out and see the birds this morning, Ms. Sinclair?"

Her eyes brighten at the suggestion, and her hands clasp in front of her chest. "Why, that would be lovely. Yes, dear."

I release the brakes on her chair and wheel Ms. Sinclair out to the lobby. We pass Sondra on the way. She gives me a knowing little smirk and shakes her head.

Everyone knows that Evelyn Sinclair is my favorite. But Sondra is the only one who knows the reason why.

***

As the day passes, I enjoy seeing so many visitors walk in and out of Pine Manor, giving smiles and hugs as they promise to return again next Sunday. After dinner, I wheel several of the residents back to their rooms and turn on their TVs, tuning them to the local news or *Wheel of Fortune* reruns or ESPN. Just before my shift ends, I peek into Ms. Sinclair's room one last time. She's sitting in her recliner, watching a cooking show and unwrapping a peppermint candy with her slender white fingers. When she sees me standing in her doorway, she turns and smiles. It's beautiful and warm and genuine. I smile back.

"Oh my," she says, happiness filling her eyes, "you look lovely today. Your mother did such a nice job ironing your school jumper this morning. Do you happen to know when Bradley will be back?"

She's doing it again, and it tugs at my heart. She's forgetting I'm not one of her students. And that there's no Bradley. At least not anymore.

"No, Ms. Sinclair, I don't. I think he must have stepped out for a bit."

"Oh. Okay. Well, if you see him, will you let him know I'm waiting?"

"Of course."

"Thank you, dear."

"You're welcome."

"You go on and leave now. I've got things to do." She waves her hand at me dismissively and goes back to unwrapping her peppermint candy.

***

When I step off the bus, Jarrod is sitting on the steps of my apartment building, leaning back on his elbows, a cigarette pinched between the fingers of his right hand. He looks tired.

"Hey." He straightens his back and sits up when I get to the bottom of the steps.

"Hey, Jar." I sit down next to him, taking the cigarette out of his hand and sucking a flash of nicotine into my lungs. "So… how was blondie?"

He shrugs. "Half brilliant and half boring."

Jarrod leans forward and rests his right elbow on his knee, dropping his chin onto the heel of his hand in a posture that screams resignation and monotony. I don't understand why he keeps hitting repeat, screwing the-same-woman-with-a-different-face every weekend. It never gets him anywhere. It's like his life is dissatisfaction replicated over and over again, only he can't figure out why. But he's not a stupid guy. Someday he'll see it. Someday he'll see that happiness doesn't wear stilettos and leave with a stranger.

"Just like the rest of them, then?" I draw another breath of smoke into my body.

"Yeah. Pretty much." He shrugs again and takes the cigarette back. I turn my head to look at him, and he immediately switches his line of sight in the opposite direction, looking down the street instead of at me. He's avoiding eye contact, and that always means the same thing—he's afraid of showing me too much. He would never admit it, nor would I ever point it out, but it happens a lot. I always pretend not to notice, because it's easier that way. He doesn't need to know I can read his emotions like a book, whether he's looking at me or not.

"So, I guess you didn't ask for her number then?"

"Nope." He keeps staring down the street, as if something there is worth watching.

"Maybe you should find yourself a nice, quiet librarian or a kindergarten teacher or something. You know…someone who prefers *not* to have her ankles bouncing around her ears ten minutes after you meet."

"Very funny, K'acy. Very funny." He turns back to me with a snarl on his lips and a playful flicker in his eye. "You really should stick to bass playing and skip the stand-up."

"Then stop making it so easy for me to get my licks in."

"Don't think I won't kick your ass just 'cause you're a black girl. I don't mind making the six o'clock news."

"You won't kick my ass, Jar. But it isn't because I'm a black *woman.* It's because you know I'm right. Even though you're never gonna admit it."

"Admit what?" he says, lifting his palms in mock confusion. "That you're a *woman*?"

I roll my eyes at him. "Never mind. Go with the ankles-to-her-ears women for as long as you want. No skin off my back. It's probably better for the kindergarten teachers of the world anyway."

"*And* the librarians."

"Especially the librarians."

He looks away again, down the street. We sit in silence for a few minutes, passing the cigarette between us, each stuck in our own thoughts, mine focusing on why he refuses to acknowledge that he deserves more than a never-ending chain of superficial one-night stands. He deserves a perfect life. Just like I do. Just like *everyone* does. Until it's proven otherwise. Crackerjack Townhouse may have saved him from wasting away, but now he has to put his balls on and save *himself* from everything else.

"Stevie called me today," Jarrod says eventually. "He said we got the gig." He's changed the subject enough to look at me again, his light hair vibrating in the wind.

"The one at The Upstage?"

"Yep. He says the promoter's gonna set us up with an opener. Apparently the guy knows some funk players from Jersey. Says they're worth hooking up with for a show."

"We're headlining though, right?"

"I asked the exact same thing. Stevie says yes. He put in for a demo to make sure they're a good fit."

"Do you trust him to make the call?"

"Absolutely."

Jarrod drops the cigarette on the bottom step and snuffs it out with the ball of his foot. Something in the gesture makes me want to hug him and tell him everything will be all right, assure him that neither one of us will fall off the edge again. I've never said the words out loud, but he's the best friend I've ever had. Or ever *will* have. And that includes my big sister, Charlie.

"You wanna go get something to eat?" I ask.

"No, thanks. I gotta go to work. I'm pulling an eight-to-four at the call center. Cross your fingers for a slow night."

I intertwine the first two fingers of each of my hands and raise them up in front of my face. "Fingers crossed that no one's cable goes out in the next eight hours."

Jarrod lifts a pair of closed fists out in front of his chest, and a second later, a double fist-bump echoes between us, vibrating with unspoken understanding and love. Just like my bass strings.

Right after Jarrod rounds the corner onto Barberry Street and I walk inside, my cell phone rings. I don't know the number, but I do know 985 is a Louisiana area code. My heart rises in my chest.

I slide my finger against the screen and lift the phone to my ear as I close my apartment door behind me.

CHAPTER 3

Robert McGee—1990

I missed the birth of my second baby girl last night. Louise said she tried to call to tell me she was taking Charlie to her aunt's house and then going up to Terrebonne General, but the bartender didn't hear the phone ringing on account of the music being too loud. It's a jazz club, so loud is the way it's gotta be. When we get going, there's no way the bartender's ever gonna hear the phone ringing. The horns are just too loud. Unless we're playing a down-tempo piece. But Louise said she called at one in the morning, and we don't play no down-tempo pieces at one in the morning. By then, we're dropping the notes loud and hard, like the whiskey's free and there ain't no tomorrow.

So I missed it. I missed my second baby girl meeting the world for the very first time. And it hurts my insides.

When I got home at five o'clock, just before the sun lifted up over the horizon, I saw the empty beds and knew Louise must've gone to the hospital. I figured she just called herself a jitney…till I saw her car was gone from the back shed. It was then I knew she didn't take a jitney; she drove herself and Charlie to the hospital, and knowing it made me angry. Because she should've known better. She should've had more sense than to risk our little baby girl being born in a car on the side of the freeway while her big sister watched.

But then I got to thinking, and I decided I really only have myself to be mad at, 'cause I never should've gone to play last night in the first place. I never should've walked out the front door with my trumpet case in hand and the mouthpiece knockin' around in my pocket like a piece of loose change. Instead, I should've called Martin and told him they'd need to find another horn player for the night because my wife was having cramps in her stomach that more than likely came from something besides the dove sandwich she had for dinner. That's what I should've done. But I didn't. Louise didn't ask me to stay neither, 'cause she's not that kinda woman, but I should've known better. And now I'm holding my new baby girl in my arms and thinking about how much I'm gonna have to make it up to her.

For the rest of my life, I'm gonna show K'acy that she and her big sister are the most important people in the whole world. I'm gonna prove to both of them that where you come from or how much money you have in your wallet is not what makes you special. 'Cause special comes from the inside. Special comes from doing the right thing, every time. *Every. Time.* Without excuses or regrets. You always gotta do what you know is right.

Me missing the birth of my new baby girl will be the last *wrong* thing I ever do. It will be my life's one and only regret. And I'll never forgive myself for it.

Now, I'm gonna sit here—in this hospital—for the rest of the day, holding my baby girl and telling my wife over and over again how sorry I am that I wasn't here to hold her hand. 'Cause come tomorrow morning, I'll have to go back to the quarry, blasting limestone for a smidge over minimum wage so I can keep clothes on the backs of all my beautiful girls.

CHAPTER 4

My big sister is a fool. She's on the other end of the phone, asking me for money. Again. Why doesn't she believe me when I tell her I don't have a single dime to spare? She says she's calling me from a "friend's" phone, yet I hear a man's voice in the background. He's telling her what to say. No, change that. He's not *telling* her, he's *ordering* her. I don't like it.

"I'm sorry, but I told you the last time you called, Charlie, I'm barely making my rent. I want to help you, really I do, but I can't."

"What about selling Daddy's wedding ring? You still have it, don't you?"

If she thinks for one second that I'm going to sell my father's wedding ring so I can send her a couple hundred bucks for some man to gamble away, she's an even bigger fool than I thought. I hear the man's voice in the background again. He sounds even angrier than he did before.

"There's no way in hell I'm selling Daddy's ring. And whatever man you have there with you—bossing you around like you're his to boss—needs to shut up. You are not his bank, Charlie, and neither am I."

She's just like Jarrod. She doesn't see that she deserves a perfect life. Even though our daddy tried over and over again to show her she does. Charlie's just different like that. Some shrink would probably say it has something to do with low self-esteem, but I think it's just 'cause she's lost without our momma. No matter how hard Daddy tried to fill in the blank, it wasn't the same as it was when Momma was around. Not for Charlie, anyway.

"Listen," I continue before she can argue, "I love you. You know I do. But you have to stop listening to the *what's-his-face* standing next to you and start listening to your own common sense instead."

There's a long pause before she offers a reply. "I know," she says softly.

In those two words, I hear so much. I hear resignation and exhaustion. Maybe even a bit of comprehension. But I hear no bitterness or anger. Maybe I got through to her this time. Maybe she's starting to understand.

"Do yourself a favor and dump the *what's-his-face*, okay?"

"I'll talk to you later."

"Do it, Charlie. I'm serious."

"Bye."

Before I can say a goodbye of my own, she's gone.

***

Ms. Sinclair is bright-eyed when I get to work on Monday morning. In fact, she's more active than I've seen her in a long time. When I walk into her room, I'm surprised to see she's already managed to get herself dressed. She looks sweet in her bubblegum-pink sweater set with matching polyester pants. On her left side, just above her heart, is a gold brooch. It's an owl with big, sparkly eyes. It's a costume piece, but it glistens in the light as if it were made of solid gold and real diamonds, instead of gold-plated nickel and rhinestones.

"Did you hear the news, dear? He's coming to see me today." She looks at me, and I feel sad. I don't want her to be disappointed when "he" doesn't show up. Again. But I also can't bear to be the one to have to tell her "he" isn't coming because "he" probably doesn't even exist. I think for a moment about what I should say next. I need words that will neither encourage her delusion, nor tear her down.

"Would you like me to comb your hair and put some blush on your cheeks?"

"Oh, yes, dear. I would like that very much. Thank you."

"You're welcome, Ms. Sinclair." I straighten her hair with the ancient tortoiseshell comb she brought with her when the county moved her in. Then I brush a streak of pink powder across her pale cheeks from the compact in her bathroom drawer. She's wearing the biggest smile when she looks at herself in her hand mirror, and it breaks my heart to know no one is coming to visit her today.

"Would you like to go and see your birds now? I think there's been a woodpecker at the feeder the last few days. Would you be able to tell me what kind it is?" I'm trying to distract her with a change of subject. Trying to distract *myself*.

"I bet it's a downy woodpecker. Or maybe a red-bellied. They're beautiful birds, you know. Let's go see, shall we?"

I help her take a seat in her wheelchair and push her out into the lobby, situating the chair next to the front window and listening to her describe each of the birds as they come and go. I sit with her for a good ten minutes before Sondra nods at me from across the room to let me know it's time to get everyone to the cafeteria for breakfast and bingo.

***

In the afternoon, most of the residents like to take a nap. It's a good time for me and the rest of the aides to catch up on our paperwork and do a little housekeeping. I'm realigning the wingchairs in the lobby when the glass entry doors slide open. Every time I hear the familiar whir of the door, I instinctively look. Just in case one of the residents has lost their bearings, or they forgot they live here now, instead of in their two-story Colonial over on Maple Street. I want to make sure no one wanders off and gets lost. Intentionally or not.

When I look toward the door, I don't see any of our residents. Instead, there's a man there, looking back at me. He's young. And he looks a little lost himself. He's got his hands in the pockets of his jeans, and there's a small bouquet of daisies tucked into the breast pocket of his plaid button-down. I immediately think he looks like the kind of guy who listens to Death Cab for Cutie or The Shins. The kind of guy that's not overly interested in fitting in, but yet doesn't wanna step too far out of the box. The hair on his head confirms the same. Controlled bed-head, Jarrod calls it. Purposefully disheveled.

Once he's inside the door, the man looks over at the front counter as if he doesn't know what to do next. I'm guessing this is his first time at Pine Manor…or any other assisted living facility, for that matter.

"You have to sign in here, sir." Apparently Marie has noticed he's a first-timer, too.

"Ah, yes. Thank you. It's my first time visiting. I wasn't quite sure what to do." He walks over and signs his name on the clipboard sitting on the counter in front of Marie. "I'm here to see Evelyn Sinclair. Can you tell me where I might find her?"

My heart leaps into my throat.

"She's around the corner and down the hallway. Room 112." Marie's voice is as surprised as I've ever heard it. She's usually an emotionless robot, so frankly, any inflection in her voice is a surprise. Even Marie knows this is Ms. Sinclair's very first guest.

"Thanks." He puts his hands back into his pockets and walks right past me on his way to her room, smiling and nodding in greeting as he passes. As soon as he rounds the corner, I'm practically running to read the sign-in sheet.

"Is that Bradley? How did she know he was coming?" I ask, mostly to myself, because Marie's already turned her back and walked away. I look down at the most recent name on the sign-in sheet.

Adam Sinclair.

It's not Bradley, but at least he's got the right last name.

I'm glad I combed her hair.

Ms. Sinclair has a guest! After four months without a single visitor, she finally "gets company." I want to smack the guy for taking so damn long.

I know I shouldn't, but a few minutes later, I find myself walking down the hallway and stopping just outside her open door. Eavesdropping is against the house rules, but this isn't really eavesdropping; it's a safety check. I'm just making sure Adam Sinclair isn't stealing her owl brooch or something. As I stand in the hallway, completely out of their sight, all I can hear is the unwrapping of a peppermint candy. No voices. No television. No other movement. It's quiet, except for the crunchy cellophane symphony of one of Ms. Sinclair's candies.

I look down at my shoes, suddenly ashamed to have followed him back here under the guise of a safety check. The poor guy is probably just trying to visit his Great Aunt Evelyn in peace, and here I am, treating him like he's some kind of a thug. Nothing about him seemed suspicious, yet it took him so long to come see her that I can't help but be guarded. I just don't want her to get hurt.

Me and my nosiness are just about to leave when Adam Sinclair comes out of the doorway, rounding the corner like a shot of lightning and running smack into me, nearly knocking me on my ass. He grabs my upper arms to keep me from falling backward and continues holding on to them until I regain my balance. Then he lets go.

"I'm so sorry. I didn't know you were out here. Are you okay?" The daisies in his pocket have been smashed flat; their little necks broken and flopping forward, reminding me of life's frailty and causing Miriam Hansen's death to poke at my heart yet again.

"No. It's my fault, really. I'm fine. I was just coming to give Ms. Sinclair her medication. I shouldn't have been walking so close to the door." Good save, K'acy. Better than declaring it some bogus safety check.

"Are you sure you're all right?" His breath smells like peppermint.

"Yes. Thank you."

"Are you one of my gram's nurses?"

Oh. Adam Sinclair is not her nephew. He's her grandson. I didn't even know she had any children. All she ever talks about are her birds and her students. And someone named Bradley.

"No. I'm an aide."

"Oh. Well, thanks for taking such good care of her. She looks pretty comfortable in there. She's out like a light. I was gonna go get a cup of coffee or something until she wakes up. I didn't want to disturb her, but if you have to wake her for her medication…"

"No. That's all right. I can wait until later. Whenever she wakes up is fine." I'm standing in front of him, not knowing what to say next. I wish I was still out in the lobby straightening the leather wingchairs. "The coffee pot is in the back of the dining hall. You'll see it."

"Okay. Cool. I'm Adam, by the way. Adam Sinclair." He offers a hand for me to shake, and the instant our palms connect, I hear the bass riff from the bridge of "Soul to Squeeze" by the Red Hot Chili Peppers in my head. It's more thought-provoking than I want it to be.

"Nice to meet you, Adam Sinclair. I'm K'acy McGee. Chief wheelchair pusher and sponge bather." He smiles and tilts his head, looking at me as if I belong in a 1920s Ringling Brothers sideshow. Then, because I can't help myself, I shrug and add, "Someone's gotta keep these people in line."

He doesn't miss a single beat before opening his mouth and saying, "Gram always *has* been a rebel."

I'm considering asking him if it runs in the family, when I hear Ms. Sinclair's voice.

"Bradley? Is that you?"

Adam raises his eyebrows at me, quickly puts his hands in his pockets, and turns away, walking back through the doorway and into her room. "No, Gram. It's me, Adam."

"Oh, Adam!" There is unmistakable joy in those two words, and a jolt of happiness runs through me. But an instant later, when the next string of words comes out, her voice contains more confusion than joy. "Why are you here? Where's your father?"

I hear Adam sigh. "I came to visit you, Gram. Because I haven't seen you in a really long time, and I missed you."

"Where were you?" she asks. I can't believe I'm still standing in this hallway, *not eavesdropping*. There's a long pause before he answers.

"In Seattle. At grad school." His voice is tentative.

"Oh, yes. Yes. Now I remember." She seems to have forgotten her inquiry about Adam's father, and his obvious avoidance of the question gives me the impression that it's something he himself would rather not discuss.

"You can come in now," he says loudly, quickly popping his head back out of the room. Embarrassment courses through me. "She's awake." He turns back to Ms. Sinclair and adds, "K'acy is here to give you your medicine." Crap. It's not time for her medication. Before I walk into the room, I quickly pat the pockets of my scrubs, looking for an Altoid or something to serve as a placebo. I don't find anything besides a pen and a paperclip.

"But, dear, I've already taken my medicine. They give it to me first thing in the morning. Never in the afternoon." She says it just as I walk into the opening of the doorframe. I'm standing in full view of both of them, feeling a rush of hot blood creep up into my cheeks. Bad timing on the lucidity, Ms. Sinclair. Thanks.

Adam Sinclair stares at me long and hard, probably trying to decide if I almost just made a terrible mistake by overmedicating a resident or if his grandmother just totally busted me for spying on them. It doesn't really matter which one of the two he decides on because either conclusion makes me an idiot. All I can do is stand here like the moron I apparently am. First of all, I can't even administer medication. I'm not licensed. And secondly, I'm not holding a medication tray, or even one of those tiny paper cups they distribute the pills in, nor did I drop anything when he ran into me in the hallway. It doesn't take him long to figure out which conclusion is the right one.

"It's a good thing you've got such a good memory, Gram." He sits down on the edge of her bed and looks back up at me with an enormous, smug grin. "Don't you agree?"

"Yes. It's remarkable, really. Especially considering that just yesterday Ms. Sinclair thought I was a student in her fifth grade class." I regret my sassy words immediately. But not because I said them *to him*, but rather because I said them *in front of her*. I don't like to talk about the patients' memory failures within their earshot. The last thing I want to do is remind them that they're losing it. When you're eighty-five and tormented by Alzheimer's, you don't need any reminders of your brain's current inadequacies. Mentioning a patient's "wrongs" does nothing but frustrate and confuse them, so I try to keep our conversations grounded in reality without smacking them in the face with it. I usually try to tiptoe around their memory's mistakes. But the words I just said did not tiptoe around anything. They ran right over it.

"Really? She thought you were one of her students?" It's not the reply I was expecting. The look of smugness has left his face. It's been replaced by perplexity.

"I did no such thing," says Ms. Sinclair from her bed. "I know this young lady is my nurse. Why on earth would I think she was one of my students? She even helped me comb my hair today, dear."

"You're right, Ms. Sinclair. I'm sorry. I must have been confusing you with someone else," I say in true apology. I turn to walk away, but in my peripheral vision I see Adam's face. It's smothered in uncertainty. I'm beginning to wonder how long it's been since he last saw his grandmother.

Before I start walking down the hallway, I turn to him and thoughtfully add, "If you need anything while you're here, don't hesitate to come find me. I'd be happy to fill in any blanks." I don't mean for it to sound like some kind of code. I just want him to know I can probably tell him more about his grandmother's condition than anyone else here.

"I'll be going for that coffee a little later. I'll try to find you then."

"I'll be here."

I need to go check on Mr. Rauch and his shoulder, so I head down the hall, past the reception desk, through the lobby, and over into the other wing of the building.

And the whole time I'm walking, that Chili Peppers bass riff is thumping in my chest.

CHAPTER 5

Beth Salvo—Room number 126

I spent most of my life in a basement, doing laundry for two different families. When I was just sixteen years old, I started working for a family of seven. Then, when that family didn't need me anymore, I moved to a different basement. This one belonged to a family of nine. Washing, drying, folding, and ironing. All day long. Trousers, blouses, skirts, blue jeans, tablecloths, and bedsheets. I ironed just about everything 'cept for their socks and skivvies. Five days a week I did someone else's laundry. And yet, I loved it. I loved watching the children grow, right along with the size of their undershirts. I never had any children of my own, so it was always a pleasure to hear them laughing and playing in the family room above my head. I also loved the solitude of the work and the satisfaction of knowing I'd always have a job. 'Cause somebody, somewhere, was always gonna need their shirt pressed or their bedsheets laundered. Even if I lost that particular job, there'd always be another one right around the corner.

My only regret was marrying Paul. Sometimes he was a real charmer, but other times, he was meaner than a coked-up Ike Turner, hitting me with his words or his fists whenever he had a clear shot. Truth be told, it was a relief when he died. I would never have wanted him to suffer, because that's not something a God-fearing woman would ever want for anyone. But that heart attack...it was the perfect way for him to go. Quick and painless and in the middle of the night. I got to live another twenty years without him, and even though I was still in a basement for most of them, they were the best twenty years of my life.

As for me, when it was my turn to die, I wasn't sad. I was ready to go. There's only so much tiredness a person can take before they're ready to move on. There's only so much pain a body can manage before it just wants to get some rest. I worked my whole life and didn't have so much as a dime to share when the end came, nor did I think I had anyone who would care about me being gone. But that girl, the one from the nursing home, she cared. She cried about me dying like I was someone that actually mattered. She was good to me, but I can't imagine I mattered much to her. I was just a woman whose hair she washed every Tuesday and whose bedpan she changed when I couldn't get up and use the toilet anymore.

My whole life, I never really mattered to anyone. Why would it be any different at the end?

CHAPTER 6

During my break, I tell Adam Sinclair about his grandmother over a cup of coffee, and as I'm talking, I actually think I see his heart break. By the end of our conversation, I've learned he hasn't seen her in almost seventeen years, but he doesn't tell me why. And I don't ask.

Adam tells me he's fresh out of grad school, with a master's degree in finance from the University of Washington. He was born in Philly, but his father moved his family out west when Adam was eight. He moved back here last week, wanting to be closer to his grandmother. He's honest and frank and clearly shaken by Ms. Sinclair's condition.

As we talk, it's painfully obvious he had no clue she's suffering from Alzheimer's, and his voice cracks as he asks me about what will happen to her as the disease progresses. I do my best to comfort him, but I'm not her doctor or even a nurse, so all I can do, without getting myself into trouble, is share general information about the disease and tell him what I know about Ms. Sinclair's needs right now.

"What can I do for her?" he asks me at one point in the conversation. "I mean, outside of what my father's already doing with her doctors." I'm glad to know his father has been in touch with Ms. Sinclair's doctors. It's news to me, but I'm glad to hear it nevertheless.

"Well, I'm certainly not a doctor, but I can tell you our residents really enjoy visitors, and the more often she sees you, the easier it will be for her to stay connected to you in the future. It'll be frustrating sometimes; trust me, I know. But meet her wherever she is. Even if it means sitting at the window with her and talking about her birds."

"Her birds?" He looks confused again.

"Yes. She told me she used to have pet birds when she was young, so I set up a birdfeeder outside the lobby window. She loves to sit there and watch them."

He looks at me thoughtfully, but I don't think he's questioning my motivations; I think he's just trying to figure them out.

"Huh." He shrugs and looks off in the distance, over my shoulder. I'm beginning to get the impression that Adam doesn't know much about his grandmother at all. The sadness in his face deepens, and the bass riff still vibrating in my chest suddenly drops deep into my gut, forming a melancholy puddle of sympathy. For both of them.

"Your grandmother is a wonderful woman. She'll really enjoy having you around. That much I know for sure." He smiles at my words and takes a small sip of his coffee. His silence adds to the puddle in my gut. I think I see tears forming in his eyes. "I'd better get back to work," I add, wanting to give him some privacy and save him from the humiliation of crying in front of a girl.

"Thanks, K'acy. I guess I'll be seeing you around then."

"Like I said, I'll be here."

I turn away and walk out of the room.

***

I'm playing my StingRay again. This time, I'm by myself, in the back of a dive bar called The King's Court. It's my regular Wednesday-night emotional-housecleaning gig. The one I use to forget about the rest of the world. I don't get paid to stand here, slapping my fingers against the strings in a solo performance that's, more often than not, completely devoid of an audience much larger than a half dozen. I do it because I need to. Because it helps me forget.

Jarrod is sitting at the bar nursing a beer. He's the only person who's religiously here on Wednesday nights, and I like it that way. Flying under the radar is just fine with me. I don't need "regulars"; I just need music.

The StingRay sits against the perfect pocket formed by the front of my hip, tied to me with a thick strap of leather and a set of strings that go straight to my heart. I play for two solid hours, thinking of nothing but the music coming out of me. My foot presses down on the compressor pedal from time to time, serving to both balance the sound and decompress my soul.

Then, just before I finish, I start playing the bass riff that's been echoing through me nonstop since I shook Adam Sinclair's hand on Monday afternoon. The moment Jarrod recognizes the song, he looks up at me. He's never heard me play a Chili Peppers song before, and he's wearing a look of amused bewilderment. Hell, I'm confused myself. But "Soul to Squeeze" comes out of me in an unstoppable pulse of flawless notes. And, though I don't say them out loud, the lyrics roll through the inside of my head like they somehow belong there. It's disconcerting. I'm gonna catch hell from Jarrod for it, that much I'm sure of. But still… when I finish the song, I feel cleansed.

"What the fuck was that?" Jarrod asks, walking up to me just after I zip my gig bag closed. I stand, sling the StingRay over my shoulder, and turn to him. I can smell the beer on his breath.

"'Soul to Squeeze.' Why?"

"I know what song it was, smartass. I wanna know why the hell you were playing it."

"I don't know. It's just been stuck in my head for the past couple of days. I had to purge the earworm." It feels like we've undergone some kind of bizarre personality flip. This time, *I'm* the one turning away from *him*, just to keep from showing him too much. Too much of what, I'm not sure.

"Earworm? Since when do you get earworms that involve Anthony Kiedis?"

"Since Monday, I guess." I start walking toward the front door, hoping to avoid any more questions. I have no reason to feel like I have something worth hiding, but if anyone's gonna call me out on an awkward reason for playing a particular song, it's Jarrod. He knows I don't play anything without purpose.

"And what happened on Monday to get this particular earworm tunneling into your little brain far enough for it play on repeat for two entire days?"

"Nothing." I open the front door and walk out into the night, turning to the right and heading to the closest bus stop.

Jarrod coughs into his hand, spitting a rough "bullshit" out with the sound. I stop and turn on my heels, staring him down as best as I can without raising my hackles, or his. I don't say anything.

"Fine. Don't tell me then. But you have to know that if you don't, I'm gonna assume all kinds of stuff. Like maybe the Chili Peppers 'discovered' you on YouTube and want you to come on tour with them. Ooo, no…I've got it! Maybe you had a crazy sex dream about Flea. Like the kind where you're screwing on stage or something. Maybe that's what this is all about. Which is it, K'acy? The tour or the sex dream?" He nudges me on the shoulder with his outstretched hand, like a big brother would prod his little sister. I can't help but smile.

"It's neither, you big douche. It's just someone I met at work. They remind me of that song for some reason." I see the bus coming down the street. I turn away from him again and hurry toward the stop. I don't want to miss this one because another 43D isn't scheduled to come for another forty-five minutes. He follows close behind me.

"You met an old person who reminds you of the Red Hot Chili Peppers? You've gotta be kidding me."

"Maybe it isn't an old person."

A split second later, the bus meets me at the curb and the doors open. I step on, leaving him standing on the sidewalk alone. As the bus drives past Jarrod, I look out the window and see him frozen there, wearing his Kranky Records "hugs and/or drugs" T-shirt and one hell of an enormous grin.

***

I don't see Pine Manor again until my shift on Friday, the busiest day of the week. Today, we have two special programs for our residents, instead of just one. There's gentle yoga in the morning, and then a group of therapy dogs comes at 2:00. It's always chaos when the dogs are here because everyone wants a chance to see them. And then, to add to the crazy, when my shift ends, I have to head home to change and pick up my gear. Crackerjack Townhouse is playing at Bartholomew's tonight. We hit the stage there once or twice a month and tonight's one of those nights. It's always a barrel of amazing. The vibe at Bartholomew's is like nowhere else on this Earth.

I'm helping Ms. Sinclair out of her wheelchair and into her recliner for this morning's viewing of *Family Feud* when Adam walks into the room carrying a plastic grocery bag. I haven't heard a peep from Jarrod after leaving him stupefied at the bus stop, but the immaturity of our conversation leaps into my mind as soon as I see Adam's face. Thankfully, the earworm seems to have been purged. At least for now.

"Good morning," he says, taking off his jacket and tossing it onto her bed, right next to the grocery bag already resting there.

"Hello, Bradley. How are you feeling today? Are you better?"

Adam's face slumps at the sound of his grandmother's words, and he lets out a breathy sigh. I settle Ms. Sinclair into her seat and tuck a blanket over her legs, willing Adam to just run with it.

"Gram, it's me, Adam. Remember? I was here to see you yesterday. I brought you more peppermint candies today. And some of those peanut M&M's you used to like so much when I was a little boy." He picks the bag back up off the bed and holds it out to her. She looks inside and pulls out a clear package of Starlight mints, tearing it open and pouring the contents into the candy dish on the table next to her. Then, she picks up one of the mints and starts to unwrap it. Adam looks at me as his grandmother's focus instantaneously switches from him to Steve Harvey and *Family Feud*. I think he's feeling pretty lost. I tilt my head toward the door and raise my brow in suggestion. He gets the message.

"Gram, I'll be right out in the hallway if you need anything, okay? I just want to talk to K'acy about something. I'll be back in a few minutes." He pats her on the arm, but she doesn't look away from the television, nor does she respond.

Out in the hallway I tell Adam the words I think he needs to hear.

"I know it totally sucks, but please try not to get upset about her thinking you're someone else, or even that she's so focused on the TV. Ms. Sinclair has developed a routine with us over the past few months, and sometimes it's hard for someone with her issues to break out of that routine, even when they have guests. It might seem boring to you and me, but to her, the predictability is comforting. It's kind of like dealing with little kids; they do better when they know what's coming next. I'm not saying you shouldn't remind her that you're Adam and not Bradley. I'm just saying it's going to take some time. Does that make sense?"

"Yeah," he says, lifting his right hand and brushing it through his hair. The motion exudes both exasperation and reluctant acceptance. "It does."

"The thing is, *you* just have to start becoming part of her routine. It isn't going to happen overnight, but just keep coming. Keep talking to her. If you're lucky, eventually you might even become as familiar to her as Steve Harvey." I shrug at my lame attempt at lightening the mood. He doesn't look amused.

"Can you just tell me…is this Bradley person a part of her routine?" He doesn't sound angry, or even hurt. But he does sound as puzzled as I suddenly feel. Ever since Adam showed up and informed me Ms. Sinclair has a son, I just assumed Bradley was Adam's father. I guess I was wrong. "How often does *he* come to see her?"

"He's never come to see her, as far as I know. I don't even know who he is."

"Oh." Adam's expression turns into a tangled knot of uncertainty and helplessness. It takes everything in me not to reach across the empty space between us and wrap him in a hug. My chest is heavy. I don't know what to do or say next because there are no words capable of taking the sting out of what he's feeling. The thought of his grandmother wishing he was someone else—someone he doesn't even know—must hurt beyond measure. I try to find the right words.

"Keep coming. As often as you can. She's just like the rest of us, really. All she needs is time and love."

Adam Sinclair tilts his head to the side no more than the width of finger. His eyes narrow and his forehead tucks down on itself. It's a small movement, but it's one that instantly floods me with emotion.

"Then time and love it is," he says, keeping his eyes on mine for a long, heady second. Before I can breathe another breath, he reaches his right arm out toward me, extending his hand in gratitude. I hesitate before offering my own hand in return because I'm afraid of what might happen. I'm afraid of what I might feel.

This time, when our palms connect, the bass riff does not vibrate deep inside my chest. Instead, it bursts through the place where our hands touch, echoing up my arm and shattering me into a million shards of light. Filling me with exhilaration and causing Miriam Hansen's promise to ring in my ears.

I let go of Adam's hand and turn away before the smile hits my face.

Fate is amazing. My father always told me as much, but until this very second, I never really believed him.

CHAPTER 7

It's 5:30, and I'm about to lock the brakes on Mrs. Thompson's wheelchair when Sondra walks into the building to start her evening shift.

Sondra's been a nursing aide here for eighteen years, an incredibly long time for a career that's often nothing but a stepping-stone on the path to becoming an RN. She says she's done it for so long because she truly believes it's the only thing she could ever be really good at it. Kind without being condescending, she's careful with both the patients' bodies and their hearts.

Sondra's taught me so much during the past six years. She knows a lot about this job. And about the world. But, there are definitely some things she doesn't know. Things you can't learn from books or classes, or even from on-the-job experience. I'm talking about the things that come from your soul. The things that are a part of who you are.

Sondra once told me I'm too compassionate for this job. When she found me crying in the back stairwell after my first patient died, she said I shouldn't become so connected to them. She suggested I keep an emotional distance between myself and the residents because I already know how the relationship is going to end. She said it makes it easier when they go, and it'll keep my sanity intact. "It's not like they're ever going to switch into reverse," she said. "They won't get better. They'll just keep getting worse until it's over. That's why they're here." Sondra's far from a heartless person, but in her mind, connecting strongly with patients makes everything harder.

She has no idea how right she is.

I've lost six of them so far, including Miriam Hansen, and there's no doubt that the more you care for them, the harder their death becomes.

Pneumonia, diabetes, stroke, Parkinson's, heart disease, renal failure, emphysema, influenza. It. All. Sucks. But, to me, cancer is especially bitter and havoc-wreaking. Not only because it's a mean, unforgiving disease, but also because it took my father away from me and I will never forgive it.

But…cancer also gave me a gift. It taught me how to do things I never thought I'd be capable of. It made me realize how much of a difference love and compassion can make at the end of someone's life.

My father's cancer helped me figure out who I am.

In a strange way, I think Alzheimer's patients like Ms. Sinclair are the lucky ones. When someone has Alzheimer's, it seems to be far harder for the people who love them than it is for the patient themselves. Don't get me wrong, it's extremely difficult for *everyone* at the beginning. But by the end of it, the patient's ignorance of their own condition also happens to be its one saving grace. Their lack of awareness is what prevents them from truly suffering.

But, to be *aware*. To be *shockingly aware* that you are dying… there is no grace in that.

I watched my father as he listened to the doctors, understanding their every word, and it tore my heart out. Knowing you're dying well before you're ready to go—and then learning there's nothing you can do to stop it—is the worst kind of torment there could ever be. And then, when things get really bad, to not be able to end your own suffering is the biggest, most ironic kick-in-the-gut humanity could ever conceive. This is the point at which compassion should play its greatest and most important role, and yet, because of politics and religion and epic mounds of assorted bullshit, it isn't even allowed in the room.

After Mrs. Thompson's brakes are locked, I say goodbye to her and follow Sondra back to the office. I use my last half hour to fill out the shift change report so I can get out of here in time to grab something to eat before heading over to Bartholomew's to set up. When my paperwork's been handed over to the Nursing Director, I grab my bag and head down the hallway toward the lobby. I'm walking past the reception desk when I hear a voice behind me.

"Hey, K'acy. Wait up." The moment the words enter my ear, a tiny little jitter starts bouncing around in my stomach. I recognize the rush of endorphins immediately. I'm not surprised by them, just intrigued. Because I haven't felt their particular brand of insanity in a *very* long time. And I certainly have never felt them for anyone like Adam Sinclair. Clean, professionally educated, sincere, unscarred, emotionally connected...and white.

I halt my feet and turn around to see him jogging down the hallway toward me. He comes to a stop a few feet in front of me, hands on his hips and wearing a hearty lumberjack smile, like he has good news to share. He's got at least four or five inches on top of my five-eight, and from this angle I can't help but compare him to a hipster version of the Brawny paper towel man, minus the mustache and the flannel shirt. His teeth are perfectly straight, and he's rocking the controlled bed-head like a high school boy on prom night. "I'm glad I caught you before you left," he adds.

I swallow hard to keep the little jitter from churning into something more.

"Oh? Why's that?" I pause briefly, suddenly remembering the last time I saw him was at nine o'clock this morning. "Wait… have you been here all day?"

"Yep. I was just hanging out with Gram. You know, to try to fit into her routine. Mostly I just sat there while she watched TV. But we did play cards. And she totally loved it when those dogs came." She always loves it when the dogs come. The sudden mental picture of Adam and Ms. Sinclair petting a labradoodle together strikes a major *aww* chord in my heart. It also calms the jitter down a notch. "Anyway, I realized I never had the chance to thank you for your advice earlier. So…thanks."

"You're welcome." The sound of my own voice is followed by a good ten seconds of silence. No words. No movement. And, thankfully, no bass riff. Only a chasm of silence, somehow strangely devoid of discomfort or embarrassment. Even the jitter is quiet.

"I'm on my way out now, too," he says eventually, hands dropping from his hips and into his pockets. "Do you wanna go get a cup of coffee or something?"

A cup of coffee. With Adam Sinclair.

The gig at Bartholomew's clicks into my head. And then it clicks right back out again. "Sure. I'm up for a cup of coffee."

"Great." The enthusiasm in his voice shocks the jitter to life again.

"I can't stay too long, though. I have plans later." I say it in an attempt to settle the knot in my stomach, but it comes out sounding kind of assumptive. And bitchy.

"Oh. Well if you have plans, maybe I should just take a rain check." His face falls a little, along with the volume of his voice.

I actually think he's disappointed. I know just what to say to make it better.

"Life's too short for rain checks."

***

Within ten minutes of entering Wicked Mocha, I learn three things about Adam Sinclair. First, he takes his coffee with a little cream. Second, he uses one of those wallets with a loud Velcro closure. And third, he sits with his elbows on the table, something that would automatically send him right to the top of my mother's discard pile.

When she was still around, the only time Charlie and I were ever allowed to have our elbows on the table was when we were saying grace. To Louise McGee, a child with his or her elbows on the table was nothing but a heathen, soiled by the poor manners of bad parenting and the absence of Jesus. After she left us, Charlie and I *always* sat in the kitchen with our elbows on the table. We chewed with our mouths open. We ate with our fingers. We wiped our faces on our shirtsleeves. And the most hedonistic of all: we stopped saying grace. It was a nine- and eleven-year-old's version of revenge, and Daddy never said a word.

Strange as it is, the placement of Adam's elbows makes me like him even more.

"So, how long have you worked at Pine Manor?"

"About six years."

"Do you like it there?"

I nod and take a sip of my coffee, but I don't say anything.

"Oh man. I'm sorry. You probably don't want to talk about work now that you're out of there, huh?"

"It doesn't bother me." I shrug. "I'm lucky. I really love what I do. It's just that sometimes I don't like to talk about it because, frankly, most people think it's weird. I get a lot of *Wow, I could never do that. You must be a really patient person*, and stuff like that. People like to tell me I'm some kind of saint to my face, but I'm sure they're squirming beneath the surface because they're thinking about me having to change diapers and collect urine samples. A whole host of less-than-appealing duties probably pops into their heads. So, I've learned to mostly keep quiet about it. How about you? Do you like your job?"

"I don't have one. Not yet, anyway." His reply slides him down closer to the bottom of Louise McGee's imaginary discard pile. All he needs to say now is that he hates the Bible or Easter or something. A statement like that would shoot my mother straight in the heart, if she still had one. It also might make me want to run off to Vegas with him.

"Haven't found the right one yet, huh?"

"I haven't even been looking. I moved back here to be with Gram, and if I'm working, I can't do that." Apparently, food and shelter—and health insurance—are a lower priority for him than they are for the rest of us.

"As noble a reason for unemployment as I've ever heard."

"There's nothing noble about it, really. It's completely selfish. My father kept me from her for seventeen years, and now that he can't hold anything over my head anymore, I need to make it up to her. I need to show her it was *his* choice to keep us apart, not mine. And I'm sorry I let him make that decision for me. I should've fought back a long time ago. But I didn't, and I feel pretty damn guilty about it. I haven't seen her since I was eight, and now…now, she thinks I'm somebody else. Somebody I don't even know. Every time she called me Bradley today, I gently reminded her that I'm Adam, just like you said I should. Whoever the hell this Bradley is, he must've made quite an impression." He brushes his hand against the side of his head and leans back in his chair. "Even though I haven't seen her in years, I feel like she should still know me, you know? She was my best friend, and now I'm afraid it's too late. How do I tell her I'm sorry when she doesn't even know who I am?"

I don't hesitate a single second before offering an answer.

"Time and love." The words come out of my mouth quick but soft. He tilts his head, his eyes staring at mine, diving into me with more uncertainty than understanding.

He doesn't realize the answer is always the same. No matter what the question is.

"I'm just afraid there won't be enough of the former."

"There's always enough. Of *both* of them, as a matter of fact. That is…if you want there to be."

"Is that so?"

"Yes. Because in this case, it's the quality—not the quantity—that makes it enough."

He silently takes another sip of his coffee, as if he's thinking hard about my words. "You're a bundle of quality yourself, K'acy McGee. You know that?"

Embarrassment whips through me. It takes me a couple of seconds to come up with something to say to him that won't upset the delicate, awkward balance now between us. I finish my coffee and settle on my words before opening my mouth.

"Well then…I guess if I want to leave on a high note, right now would be a great time for me to get out of here." I stand up and toss my bag over my shoulder, holding my empty paper cup. I can barely look at his face because I'm afraid he may see that the nervous little jitter has now morphed into full-blown self-consciousness.

"But sometimes leaving on a low note is a lot more interesting." And with that, the balance is knocked totally off its fulcrum. One massive point in his favor. "Are you sure you have to go?"

"I have to go. I *definitely* have to go."

He raises his brow at me and smirks. "Where?"

"I have a date."

The grin leaves his face in an instant. At least I've managed to stabilize the balance again.

"Oh. Well, have fun then. And be safe," he says, dropping his gaze to his hands.

I'm a jerk.

"Well, I guess it's not a date really. More like an appointment. Work, even. My band has a gig tonight, and I've gotta help set up the house or I'm gonna catch hell."

"Your band?" He leans back in his chair again and crosses his arms over his chest. The smirk is back.

"Yep."

"Huh." His face flushes with a dusting of pink.

The balance seems to have officially shifted in my favor. By at least fifty points. I didn't think it would catch him so off guard. Score.

"Have a good night." I turn away from him and start walking toward the door.

The feet of Adam's chair scrape against the floor, and the next thing I know, he's slipping past me and opening the door. He uses his left arm to hold it open until I pass.

"Will I see you tomorrow?" he asks as I scoot by him as quickly as I can. "I mean…will *Gram* and I see you tomorrow? Do you work on Saturdays?" More points for me. Poor guy.

I stop in front of the café window and turn back to look at him. He's a few paces away, still holding the door open like he's been immobilized by the sheer weight of the now incredibly uneven balance. I should take pity on him and lighten the load. But before I can say anything, he starts talking again.

"Unless you wanna tell me where you're playing tonight. Then I won't have to wait until tomorrow."

My body is instantly flooded with more jitter-inducing endorphins than I thought one human being could ever produce. "Soul to Squeeze" fires through my synapses, completely blasting the balance to smithereens. Inside my head, five million points—all with Adam Sinclair's name on them—fall from the sky. Tiny pieces of emotional confetti in celebration of his decisive victory.

I turn my back on him and start walking down the sidewalk, outrageously aware that he's watching my every step. And waiting for a reply. When I'm ten paces out, I turn and start to walk backward. He's still holding the door open.

"Bartholomew's. On Pinkerton Street."

I don't wait for a reply. I just turn back around and keep walking toward the bus stop, his victory confetti quickly clearing in the wake of my words. When I hit the end of the block and start to cross the street, the sound of "Soul to Squeeze" still pumping through my veins quiets at the odd sight in front of me. There's a black car parked against the curb, its windows shaded darker than any I've ever seen before, so much that I can't even see if it's occupied. It feels misplaced; like it belongs in a movie instead of on a tree-lined city street. I pass behind the car's rear bumper, step up onto the sidewalk, and start running to catch the bus.

CHAPTER 8

Robert McGee—1995

My littlest girl is something peculiar. Not peculiar in a bad way, by any means. It's more like she's just odd. Only I can't manage to put my finger on exactly what it is that's odd about her. Louise thinks K'acy's just too clever for her own good, but I think it's more than that. Yes, she's outshining the other kindergarteners by a mile, but the peculiarity is more in the way her mind works than in her mere intelligence. Smart children are special for sure, but K'acy is more than that. She's a thinker of the best sort.

I see the way she looks at people. Especially older people. It's like she's trying to learn about them through their movements and the lines on their skin. She studies their faces as if they're some kind of map to the soul. I see her look at me that way sometimes, long and intense, and I don't know if I should get her a magnifying glass or turn my face in the opposite direction. She's only five, but there's something inside her that makes her seem far older than her age. There's something inside her that makes her a different kind of special. A deeper kind.

The first time I saw it was the evening she met Ronald Chapman, my boss at the quarry. I'd been taking her and Charlie hunting with me for a few weeks before that, but this was the first time we ever saw anyone else there. Ron wasn't aiming a shotgun into the air to get his dinner like we were. Instead, he was sitting in his fancy, expensive car in the parking lot with a woman who wasn't his wife. I didn't know who she was, but her lips were painted red and she had her hair done like a '50s pin-up, big waves and scalloped curls pinned across her scalp. Her hair was sprayed so stiff that no amount of wind, or mischievous behavior, would ever dishevel it. It looked like she was starring in an old movie rather than living a real life. I recognized his car the moment we pulled into the lot, and I intentionally drove real close to it so I could see if anyone was inside. I told Ron weeks ago I was hunting at the quarry in the evenings, so I knew I wouldn't be in trouble for being there. I was just hoping there wasn't some kind of emergency at the plant. As soon as I saw the woman in the car with him, I knew there wasn't an emergency. I drove clear over to the other side of the lot and parked as far away as I could. What the man did on his own time was none of my business, regardless of how awful it was. I didn't want him to have any reason to put me out of a job.

The moment I set the car in park and turned off the engine, K'acy was off and running. She whipped open the door and dashed across the lot, straight over to Ron's vehicle, motioning for the woman in the passenger seat to roll down her window. Charlie and I were on our way across the lot when I saw K'acy put her chin right up on the passenger-side windowsill and stare at the woman like she was made of black magic and bubblegum. By the time I got there, K'acy had already introduced herself. The look on Ron's face was not the bitterness I'd expected, but rather, sweetness and surprise. He introduced himself to K'acy and Charlie, and he introduced the woman to me. Her name was Lindsay, but he never said who she was or why they were there.

Ron got out and came 'round to the other side of the car. We chatted for a good ten minutes about work and this year's mourning dove harvest. He even asked Charlie if she knew any of her momma's secret recipes. While Charlie was telling him about Louise's dove divan and baked parmesan, I was watching K'acy stare at Lindsay through the open window, her chin still resting on the windowsill. Neither of them were saying a word, but K'acy's eyes moved across the woman's face, soaking it all in like she was making some kind of mental sculpture of her. My little girl was reading that woman like a living book. She may not have been able to read words yet, but I started thinking maybe K'acy could read people. That was five months ago, and she's been looking at people the same way ever since. Not all people, mind you. Just certain ones.

Ron and Lindsay drove away a few minutes later, and me and the girls went hunting. They were getting real good at retrieving the birds for me, climbing up to the top of the piles of crushed limestone to fetch them where they fell. Since the day they were old enough to understand, I'd been telling my girls it's good to know where your dinner comes from. That way you can say "thank you" for it and really mean the words. We mostly eat what I can hunt and fish, and what Louise grows in the garden; we don't need to spend what little money we got on steaks and chicken when a year's worth of venison and wild fowl costs no more than the price of the ammo and a couple of hunting licenses. We got enough real expenses to cover and food doesn't need to be one of them. Especially when our own hands are more than capable of providing for our bodies.

K'acy had always been as matter-of-fact as they come where hunting was concerned. But the day we saw Ron Chapman and his red-lipped passenger was different. K'acy cried that day when she had to break a dove's neck to end its suffering. She'd never cried over that in all the weeks before; not even the first time she did it. But I found her tucked behind a pile of rocks, petting a tattered bird with her fingertips and telling it "I'm sorry" over and over again. I watched her settle the bird's head between her fingers, just like I showed her, and put the thing out of its misery in an instant. When she was done, she wiped her eyes, stood up, and turned to face me. Her face was unsurprised, like she knew I was watching her the whole time.

"Is dying scary?" she asked me, the dead bird pressed against her chest.

"I don't think so, no. I think it is what it is. Just a part of life." I put my hand on top of her head and shook her fuzzy black curls from side to side. "What makes you ask that, peanut?"

"'Cause that lady's dying. And she's scared."

My jaw dropped open and my eyes widened. I felt thankful she was looking at the bird in her arms, rather than at my face. "What lady?"

"The one with the red lips. She's dying, and she's more scared of it than anything else in the world."

"She told you she's dying?"

"No, sir. I just knowed it." K'acy looked up at me, her clear eyes weighed down by something I couldn't see. Before I could reply, she held the bird out for me to take and ran off toward her sister.

I remember we hit the limit that day, bagging fifteen birds before the sun set below the horizon. After that, K'acy went back to being her matter-of-fact self whenever we went to the quarry. She never cried over a bird again. In fact, she asked Charlie if she could do all the neck breaking from then on. She got real good at it, putting them out of their misery in less than a heartbeat if the size 8 birdshot didn't do its job. She'd run toward the falling bird the moment she heard the blast of the gun, ending what needed to be ended, swift and sure.

CHAPTER 9

My fingers move along the frets, their calloused pads pressing down on the strings to form notes. Deep, sweet, soul-stirring notes. Notes no one notices, but everyone hears. Notes that sing through your chest with their vibrancy and resonance. Bass notes. The very best kind.

The stage lights are so bright I can't see beyond the first few rows of people, but somehow, I feel Adam Sinclair's presence. I know he's here. Somewhere. Because the look on his face as I was backing away from him a few hours ago, his hand still on the coffee shop door, told me there was no way in hell he would miss it. I don't let it change me, though. I play like I always play. With everything I've got.

By the time we finish the first set, I'm cleansed. I've gotten rid of the toxic buildup of real life.

Jarrod leads us all off the stage to a rousing blend of chatter and applause. We'll take fifteen to catch our breath and empty a glass, then head back to the stage for our final set. As I step down off the stage stairs and out of the glare of the lights, I see him. Adam's standing at the end of the bar with his left hand in the pocket of his jeans and his right hand holding a dark beer. He's wearing a light-blue T-shirt topped with a dark, unzipped hoodie.

And he's looking right at me. He lifts one eyebrow in perfect synchronization with his beer. It's a freakishly charming double toast, and it makes me glad I exist. Jitter and all. I can't help but smile at him and lift my own empty hand, now curled around an invisible glass. I dip my head as I offer a mock toast, then I lift the invisible glass to my lips and throw back a nonexistent shot.

The moment my head drops back down, I walk straight into Jarrod's chest. For some reason, he's walking toward me, like he's about to return to the stage instead of going to the back with the rest of us.

"Dude? Watch where you're going," he says. I offer Jarrod a quick apology and ask him why he's going in the wrong direction. "I left my cigarettes on top of Liam's amp."

"Oh," I say, glancing quickly over to Adam. His embarrassed wince and raised shoulders tell me he witnessed the impact. Jarrod must follow my gaze because when I turn back and look up at him, he's smirking.

"Who's the guy?"

I wait a long second before offering an answer.

"Mr. 'Soul to Squeeze.'"

I walk around Jarrod, who is frozen in place, looking out at Adam with narrowed eyes and a now-straight mouth.

"Seriously?" he asks my back as I walk away.

"Seriously."

Ten minutes later, Jarrod walks into the back room with a lit cigarette hanging out of his mouth. There's another guy behind him. A white guy wearing a light blue T-shirt topped with a dark, unzipped hoodie. Everyone is watching them, and I've got a not-so-good feeling about what's about to happen. Stevie hands Jarrod a beer.

"Gentlemen, meet Adam. He's a friend of K'acy's. I hear he's a big fan of the Red Hot Chili Peppers." Jarrod winks at me and then walks away. I roll my eyes at him before turning to Adam. He looks confused as hell.

"Was that some kind of an inside joke?" he asks.

"Just ignore him. He's drunk." Jarrod's definitely not drunk, but I can't think of anything else to say. Adam nods in understanding.

"I hope you don't mind that I'm back here. He just came over and introduced himself, then he asked if I wanted to come see you and say hey. So…hey."

"Hey."

I can't even hear my own thoughts over the freggin' bass riff currently clogging up my brain. Again. My silence must be too long because he suddenly looks nervous, like he's ready to bail.

"Okay. Well, I guess I'll head back out." He offers a sheepish wave and starts to turn away.

"You don't have to go." I put a hand on his shoulder, and he turns back around. "We've gotta go back out in a couple of minutes, but you can stick around if you want." I drop my hand, pick a full beer up off the table and pass it to him. I pick another one up for myself and offer him a real toast this time. We clink glasses and take a sip. He looks comfortable again.

"You guys have a great sound. How long have you been playing together?"

"About six years for Jarrod and I. Five years for everyone else. Except Mark. He's only been with us for two. Our last keyboard player bowed out due to some family stuff, and Mark jumped on board as a replacement."

"I've never heard live funk before. It's pretty dope."

Did he just use the word *dope*? I wanna laugh, but I'm pretty sure he's serious.

"Glad you're enjoying yourself."

"To be honest, it isn't only the music I've been enjoying. Jarrod's got a great ass." Wait. What did he just say? "I mean, at least that's what the women out there seem to think. It's been interesting listening to them swoon over him. I've never heard women talk about a man as if he were a piece of meat to be eaten alive. Must be quite a burden for him to bear." A thick dollop of sarcasm dangles from his last sentence like honey from a spoon. I can't help but smile.

"He manages just fine."

"I'm sure he does. And how about you? How do you manage?" I'm not quite sure what he means. "Seems like you've got your fair share of swooners out there, too." I listen for the sarcasm but there isn't so much as a drop, let alone a thick dollop. He can't be serious.

"Since when does *one* define a fair share?" And by *one,* I mean *him.* I hope, anyway. Adam tilts his head to the side and examines my face very carefully, as if he can't believe what I just said.

"Oh, there's more than one. Trust me. Every guy out there has his eyes on you and only you. I've been watching them almost as much as I've been watching you. Do you really not see it? You're amazing up there. Like some kind of funk-infused goddess. I'm not alone in my swooning. No way. Despite how much I wish it were true, *one* is an underestimate of epic proportions."

Holy Mother of Moses...

What do I say? Think, K'acy, think.

Somewhere in the background, I hear the sound guy tell us it's time to head back out. I catch Jarrod's stare in my peripheral vision, but I don't care. He's the one who brought Adam back here, so I might as well make it worth his effort.

"Even if what you're saying is true, none of it matters. Because, unlike Jarrod, I only really need one swooner." I put my half-full beer back onto the table and step closer to Adam, looking him dead in the eyes. I'm glad when I see joy and curiosity there. "And I choose *you*, Adam Sinclair, to be my lone swooner. That is, if you want to."

Before Adam can respond, Jarrod's hand grabs one of mine, and he starts to pull me toward the door. Marquis and Bryson have passed us and are already up on the stage. When I'm halfway up the stage stairs, I hear Adam's voice behind me.

"I want to."

I step onto the stage feeling like the funk-infused goddess I apparently am. I pick up my Music Man StingRay for the millionth time and put the leather strap over my shoulder, running my fingertips across the cobweb painted on the pickguard and thinking for a brief second about my father and what he'd say about my swooner. He'd tell me I deserve a perfect life. He'd say I need to take care of myself and watch out for my heart. Then he'd kiss me on the forehead and tell me I'm a smart girl. My heart both rejoices and aches with the thought, remembering how difficult it was to watch him go.

As Jarrod pretends to adjust his mic stand, waking the audience with renewed anticipation, he turns to me and mouths, "He's hot," wiggling his eyebrows up and down just like he does every time he leaves a gig with a new girl on his arm. I offer him only a half-smile in return. He doesn't need any more encouragement.

Bartholomew's welcomes Crackerjack Townhouse back to the stage with a fresh pulse of love and affection. Jarrod does his thing, standing silently at the mic until the crowd is at a near frenzy. He starts the second half of the show the same way he starts the first: with as much sweet expectancy as possible. He waits for them to need him. Then he inhales a sharp breath, and it's game on.

***

We finish the show with "Ecce Homo," just like always, and with his last words, "I am no man. I am dynamite," Jarrod throws his arms out to his sides as if he's Jesus himself, preparing for crucifixion. A bit overdramatic if you ask me, especially since the only thing getting nailed tonight is the brunette he's been eyeing since before Calvin's drum solo in "Break It Out," but the crowd must love it because they whoop it up long and hard. Jarrod eats up every moment, even as we leave the stage.

After the audience clears and we each down a celebratory shot and a beer, we head back to the stage to pack up the gear. The houselights are up, and I'm surprised to see Adam is still here, standing at the end of the bar, this time with both of his hands in the pockets of his jeans.

The whole time we're tearing down the equipment, Ms. Sinclair's grandson is watching me. When we're finished, I take my sweaty self over to where he's standing.

"I offered to help, but the sound guy told me to fuck off," he says.

"He's a little protective of everyone's gear. Doesn't want anything broken or stolen, I guess."

"No worries. I just thought maybe I could be a makeshift roadie and help you guys out."

"Swooners can't be roadies. It's against the rules." He looks surprised that I would say such a thing. And, frankly, I'm surprised, too.

"Good to know."

I cross my arms over my chest and wait for one of us to say something else.

"So, can I give you a ride home?" he offers eventually.

"That'd be great. Yeah. Thanks."

I go up onto the stage one last time and pick up my gig bag, swinging it over my shoulder until it sits comfortably against my back. The familiarity of the StingRay's weight calms and centers me.

A minute later, Jarrod leaves with his brunette, and I leave with my bed-headed swooner.

***

The whole way back to my place, Adam and I talk. He seems genuinely interested in the band and our music, asking me questions about this and that until we're just a few blocks away from my apartment. Then, the questions get a little more personal.

"So, do your parents live close by? Do they ever come see you play?" It's then I realize he doesn't know anything about me. All the talking we've done has been about Ms. Sinclair. I never offered him anything more.

"No. I grew up in Houma, Louisiana. I left there when I was eighteen, just after my dad died. But my sister Charlie still lives there."

"Sorry to hear about your dad. That's gotta be tough." He keeps his eyes on the road. Mine are on my hands.

"It was. He was diagnosed with lung cancer pretty late in the game. Not much they could do. He died a couple months after he got the news." I don't tell him the rest of the story.

"Ouch."

"Tell me about it."

"What about your mom? Is she still around?"

"My momma left us when I was nine and my sister was eleven. Apparently, Louise McGee loved God more than she loved her own daughters, because soon after Reverend Thompson's revival tent was pitched in Houma, she chose him over us. Said she 'found Jesus' and he told her she had a job to do. She told us to be good for our father, packed up her bags, and we haven't seen her since. I still say she was brainwashed into some kind of religious cult, but my father always insisted it was one-hundred percent her choice and no one could've brainwashed Louise McGee into anything. Regardless, I don't even know if she's still alive. Nor do I care."

"Double ouch."

I shrug my shoulders to show him it doesn't bother me anymore to know that my momma picked Reverend Thompson and his smelly white tent over us.

"It's not so bad, really. The three of us did just fine without her. My dad made a better mother than she did anyway. Except for cooking. That's a skill he never mastered. It also happens to be the only thing I've ever missed about her." I lift my gaze and smile at Adam in an attempt to lighten the mood.

"Do you ever get back to Houma to see your sister?"

"Not really. Charlie and I don't see eye to eye on a lot of things. My father didn't raise her to be a fool, but she turned into one anyway. She calls me every now and then, usually to ask me for money. She's pretty down and out. Always has 'man troubles' of some sort. I still love her, though, you know? I wish I could help. I wish there was a self-confidence fairy I could sic on her or something." He lets out a soft chuckle just as we turn onto my street. "How about you? Do you have any siblings?"

"Nah. It's just me."

I point out my building and tell him he can pull up to the curb out front. "If you don't mind my asking, how come your dad kept you from your grandmother for so long? Ms. Sinclair seems about as harmless as you can get." I'm probably violating a hundred-and-one patient information privacy rules by asking him, but I can't help myself. I blame it on the alcohol. And the swooning.

"Because he's a giant dickhead with a lot of money who enjoys controlling people." I wait for him to continue, but he doesn't say anything more. He just pulls up to the curb in silence and puts the car in park.

"A giant dickhead, huh? Do you happen to know if that's hereditary?"

"Don't worry, it's a freak mutation. My father's one in a million. Trust me." It's nice to see his smile again.

"Your father's name wouldn't happen to be Reverend Thompson, would it?"

He snort-laughs, and the sound of it fills me with something I can't put my finger on. Happiness, maybe. Or hope.

"No. His name is Winston. But, come to think of it, he does run a different sort of cult. No religion, though. Just politics."

Winston Sinclair. Sounds like the perfect name for a giant political dickhead.

"Your dad's a politician?"

"Of sorts."

"Huh. I voted a couple of times, but that's about as close to politics as I'll ever get."

"Me, too. Though at one point, he wanted me to follow in his footsteps. No chance in hell of that. The last thing on this Earth I want to be is a giant dickhead."

"When I look at you, I definitely don't see a giant dickhead." I have my fingers on the handle, ready to open the door.

"What *do* you see when you look at me?" He turns his upper body to face me and settles his hands in his lap, dropping them off the steering wheel with a small grin. It's a loaded question if there ever was one.

"I see a guy who cares about his grandmother. A lot. I also see a guy who enjoys swooning over bass players and drinking coffee with a touch of cream in all his unemployed spare time." I open the car door and start to get out.

"Spot on."

When I'm out of the car, I open the back door and take my bass out. Before I close both doors, I lean in to him and add, "I also see a guy who won't tell anyone at Pine Manor about tonight because the girl in front of him would very much like to keep her day job." I don't know how my supervisors would feel about me hanging out with a patient's family, and I'm not ready to find out.

"I wouldn't dream of it."

"Thanks," I say as I close both doors.

Then I swear I hear him add, "But I might dream about *you*," through the glass and steel.

I sling the StingRay over my shoulders and head up the stairs wearing a huge smile.

It's beginning to look like Miriam Hansen was right.

CHAPTER 10

Christopher Siewers—Room number 116

I spent most of my life in the corner office, ordering people around and proving beyond a shadow of a doubt the only way to get someone to truly respect your authority is to repeatedly show them you're the one in charge. It's especially true of women. Always has been, always will be. They need to be kept in their place. Screw women's lib. Or whatever the hell they call it these days.

When I started working for the firm in 1946, I had a secretary named Thelma. God, that woman knew how to push my buttons. She never said a nasty word out loud, but then again, she didn't really have to. She'd tell me she hated me with her eyes. For the first four months, whenever I told her to take a letter or hang up my coat or reserve a table for lunch, she'd glare up at me with that pasty face of hers, spilling silent curses out of her dark pupils. I always suspected she was spitting in my coffee and slipping hair-loss tonic into my bourbon, but I could never catch her in the act. When I asked him to get rid of her, Mr. Morgan said he wouldn't fire her. He said "demonic eyes" weren't grounds for dismissal or reassignment, and Thelma was a faster typist than any of the other girls at Breakstone and Gladshire. Plus, she'd already been with the firm for two years before I even got there.

Nowadays, they won't allow you to do what I did. They won't allow you to show a woman who's boss by banging her on the conference room table against her will. They call it sexual harassment. Rape, even. But back then, back when things were *right,* a man could put a woman in her place, even if she wasn't his wife. He could show her, in no uncertain terms and by whatever means necessary, that he was the one in charge. But not these days. These days, you got women doing all sorts of jobs built for men, jobs they have no business doing. If you ask me, that's why the world's so backward these days. That's why women are sassy and brazen. They forgot where they belong.

Thelma kept working for me for five years, only needing an occasional conference table reminder that I meant business. The one time she mustered up enough nerve to try to tell me no, I only had to tell her if she quit, I'd make sure she never worked in Philadelphia again. Her spinster ass would be moving into the church basement in the time it takes to refill the office percolator. After that one time, she kept her demonic eyes on the floor whenever I spoke.

See what I'm saying? Show a woman where she belongs, and she'll be at your heels, waiting to be dealt her next duty with nothing but a smile.

I practiced law at Breakstone and Gladshire for forty-five years, working my way up to full partner by the time I was in my late thirties. Marilyn kept the house running like a well-oiled machine, just like I told her to. I had her put Christopher Junior to bed promptly at 6:30 every night. A boy needs his sleep, a man needs his bourbon, and a husband needs an obedient wife. I was a lucky man.

Then life changed. Christopher Junior died of rheumatic fever when he was twelve. Marilyn never got over it. For years, I found solace at the office and in a parade of women hoping to climb the steno pool ladder via the slick spot between their legs. I busted my ass for that firm, but the younger partners forced me to retire at sixty-eight. They said I deserved a good, long retirement after all those years of putting in such long hours, but I think they were nothing but a bunch of pussies who couldn't handle how tightly I held the reins. It was 1991. Marilyn and I spent a couple of years together after I retired, but I lost her to a stroke in 1997. I've been alone ever since.

I was ninety-two when I died, but I was ready to go long before that. Trapped in a dense, buttery body with legs that were unable to carry my own weight, I cursed God for letting me get so damned old. I never wanted to live so long. I never wanted to be helpless. Especially not surrounded by a bunch of women. But that's precisely what happened. Everyone at that place was a woman. The nurses, the administrators, the secretaries, the aides, the cooks. All women. Sassy, brazen women who didn't know a damn thing about taking care of a man. They all but smacked my hand away the few times I was bold enough to try and pat one of them on the backside. At the end, I was confined to the damn bed, with only a bunch of women to cut my food, comb my hair, and sponge wash my dried-up pecker. There's nothing more degrading than that.

But that one girl, the one with the dark skin and the bottomless smile, she was different. She snuck me a glass of Elijah Craig Single Barrel bourbon every day for the last three weeks of my life, and sat and talked to me like I somehow mattered to her. She was good, that girl. Good at pretending like she cared.

I don't believe in the words *please* or *thank you* or *sorry*. They're a sign of weakness. Most everyone I'd ever met had a problem with that. But not that girl. She never seemed to mind me being me.

CHAPTER 11

I spend the weekend changing soiled sheets, labeling fluid samples, and helping people get dressed. Adam spends the weekend with his grandmother. They play cards and watch TV. At one point, he reads to her. I know all this because I stop by Ms. Sinclair's room several times a day, checking in on her as I go from one patient to another. I can't help myself.

Sondra calls me out on it just before my shift ends on Sunday. We're standing in the lobby, getting ready to start moving people to the dining room for dinner.

"So, you got a thing for Ms. Sinclair's grandson or what?"

"Maybe," I say, shrugging and offering her a sly smirk.

She shakes her head and crosses her arms over her chest. It's not the reaction I expected. I thought she'd be happy about it, seeing as how she's always interested in my nonexistent love life.

"I told you before, K'acy, you shouldn't get attached to the patients. And the same goes for their families. You'll only end up heartbroken. Someday, Ms. Sinclair's gonna leave us, which means her grandson's gonna leave us, which means you're gonna be a hot, sobbing mess in the back stairwell yet again, sweetheart. And this time you'll be crying over losing *two* people instead of just one." She drops her hands to her sides, relaxes her face, and blinks one long, thoughtful blink. "I know what Miriam Hansen told you before she died. I was there, remember? But don't put too much stock in that, okay? They were just words from a crazy old woman. That's all. You know that, right?"

I haven't put "too much stock" in Miriam Hansen's words—I'm laying my entire heart out on them. But only because Mrs. Hansen was right. About a lot of things.

"I don't like Ms. Sinclair's grandson because of what Miriam Hansen said." There are plenty of other reasons, too. But I keep those to myself.

"Good." Sondra smiles at me and pats me on the shoulder. "Just be careful, okay?"

I nod and smile, knowing full well there's nothing to be careful about. Everything about this is right.

"Time to get everyone rolling. Let's go," she adds.

Sondra and I part ways to shuffle everyone into the dining room for dinner service.

The last room I go to is Ms. Sinclair's.

"Hi," I say as I walk into the room. "It's time to go to dinner, Ms. Sinclair."

She and Adam are sitting at a card table with a checkerboard between them. Ms. Sinclair's face is in her hands, her elbows propped on the table. Then I notice that all the checkers are scattered on the floor, likely swept off the board by Ms. Sinclair in a fit of frustration. I've seen it happen before. Even games that have been played a thousand times over are different with Alzheimer's. "Is everything all right?" I ask.

Before either of them can answer my question, Ms. Sinclair raises her head and looks directly at me, lowering her hands onto the table at the same time. They fall with a thud.

There's something new and startling in her eyes. Something I haven't seen before.

Fear rushes through me. All the air leaves my lungs in sickeningly slow motion, knotting my stomach as it goes.

It's all there, in her eyes. The story of the end. Every second. Every detail. All the things that will happen if I'm not here to stop them.

A gurgle of apprehension ripples through me. The room is quiet as I study her. It may be five seconds, it may be five minutes. I don't know, but I can't look away.

Adam's voice cuts into the silence, jolting me back to reality. "You know what, Gram? We don't have to play checkers anymore, okay? In fact, let's get rid of them." He picks up the checkerboard, folds it in half, and dumps it into the trashcan with a clunk. Then he scrambles around, collecting all the checkers off the floor like candy at a parade. They fall into the wastebasket, bouncing off the discarded checkerboard with a disheveled clatter.

When he's finished, Adam straightens his back and takes a deep breath. He looks over at me, and there are tears in his eyes. "I never liked checkers anyway."

"Me neither," I say, trying my best to disguise the new and sudden fear in my heart. "I mean, who says pieces of plastic can't get along simply because of what color they are? It's totally ridiculous, if you ask me." His head tips to the side and a smile tugs at the corners of his mouth. I smile back, feeling instantly better, despite what I've seen.

"Come on, Ms. Sinclair. Let's get you into your wheelchair. I hear the dining staff is serving those pork chops you like so much." Ms. Sinclair tilts her chin up to look at me, but I quickly turn away. I can't handle any more.

I follow Adam as he pushes his grandmother down the hallway and into the dining room. He nestles her wheelchair up to the table, sets the brake, and tells her he'll see her in the morning. Then both of us turn to walk away.

"It was so lovely to see you. Thank you both for coming. Goodbye, Adam."

I think it's the first time she's ever called him by his real name without being reminded. He freezes in place, and his eyes close for a moment, taking it in. "Goodbye, Gram," he says, turning to kiss her on top of the head. We walk out of the room together.

***

When I leave the administration office to head home fifteen minutes later, Adam is alone, sitting on one of the lobby's leather wingchairs with one leg crossed over the other. He's looking down at his phone.

"Hey," I say, walking over to him and taking a seat in the adjacent chair. "You okay?"

He shuts his phone off and shoves it in his pocket. "Yeah. I'm okay. It was just a hard day, that's all."

Unfortunately, there's going to be a lot more of those. But he doesn't need to hear that; he already knows.

"Alzheimer's is unpredictable. You just have to roll with it as best as you can, you know? Time and love." I pause for a second, shrugging my shoulders and shifting in my chair. "It was pretty cool when she called you by the right name, though. That's stellar."

"I just wish it weren't on the heels of the checkers incident."

"You're gonna have to take what you can get." My words are true for so many things in life. Especially this.

"I'm trying."

"I know you are. And somewhere inside, she knows it, too."
I want to take his hand in mine and tell him everything is going
to be okay. I want to hug him and reassure him and say that
things are going to get better. But Sondra's voice is in my head,
reminding me of the truth. Reminding me that things are not
ever going to get better for Ms. Sinclair. They're only going to
get worse, and you don't need to see what I saw to know that.

I decide the conversation needs to change direction before
he sinks any deeper.

"So, what are you doing sitting here by yourself? I thought
you left after we took your Gram to dinner. How come you're
still here?"

"I was waiting for you."

Oh. "Well, here I am."

"I wanted to ask if you'd like a ride home or something." His
hands are fidgeting with the fabric cuffs of the chair.

And just like that, the bass riff commences.

"A ride would be great. Thanks."

"Do you wanna grab some dinner, too? My treat. Just to say
thanks for all you do for Gram." He stumbles over the words.

"Okay." I try to keep my cool and ignore the notes knocking
around inside my skull.

Adam gets up from his chair and offers me his hand, as if I
might need help to stand up. As if I were his grandmother. I'm
not sure if it's habit or if he's trying to be a gentleman. Either way,
I take it, but only after glancing at the front desk to make sure
no one is watching. I feel like I'm on the set of *Downton Abbey*.
Except I'm wearing scrubs. And I've got the wrong color skin.

My hand is connected to his for precisely 2.4 seconds.

I'm glad when Adam lets go and starts walking toward the
door because that's exactly when Sondra rounds the corner and

walks into the room. She softly shakes her head and rolls her eyes at the sight of the two of us together. I shrug, knowing Adam's back is to me.

"You off tomorrow, K'acy?" she says as I head for the door myself. Adam turns around to face us both.

"Yep. And Tuesday."

"Guess I'll see you Thursday then. I got nights this week." Sondra switches shifts sometimes to accommodate her husband's work schedule. She must be off on Wednesday.

"Okay. See you then. Good night."

"Night, K'acy. Keep out of trouble now, you hear?"

"Yes, ma'am." I give her an eye roll of my own before following Adam out the door.

I direct him to my favorite Mexican place, and the hostess seats us at a small, round table by the bar. Rather than sitting across from me, Adam sits at my side. It's another thing that would put him on Louise McGee's discard pile. I like it.

As we eat, Adam and I chat about Sondra and some of the other aides and nurses I work with. He says everyone at Pine Manor seems very nice. Except for Marie. He calls her "the grouch at the front desk." I tell him she's definitely the exception; everyone else is pretty great.

Then he asks me about Jarrod.

"So your front man...the one with the great ass...what's up with him?"

"Jarrod? He's a good friend. My best friend, actually."

"So I've heard." I furrow my brow at him, wondering who told him Jarrod is my bestie. "When he came over to me at Bartholomew's on Friday night, he introduced himself as 'K'acy's best friend, Jarrod.'"

I don't ever remember Jarrod calling me his *best* friend before, and even though I'm only hearing it through the proverbial grapevine, it feels good.

"I hope he wasn't an asshole or anything."

"Not at all. He introduced himself and then invited me to come back and see you." He pauses for a second before continuing. "Why? *Is* he an asshole sometimes?"

"Never to me. No. But sometimes to other people. I think it's probably just him being overprotective."

"Of what? You?"

"Of the band, I guess. But maybe of me, too." Though I never really thought of it that way. Until now.

"What's he protecting you from?"

It's a good question, come to think of it. I've done some protecting myself since I met Jarrod, and my best guess is that he just feels the need to return the favor.

"Swooners, apparently. Though I didn't even realize I had any until Friday night."

Adam laughs out loud. The sound is jitter-inducing and downright amazing.

"Maybe he's just jealous because you have more swooners than he does. He's trying to scare them off before you even notice they're there."

"That must be it." My gaze settles on my half-eaten enchilada because I'm too embarrassed to look at him anymore. I wish I had a shot of tequila.

"Well, I guess he won't have to worry about that anymore, now that I'm your lone swooner."

And now I wish I had a whole *bottle* of tequila. I keep looking at my enchilada because I have no idea what to say.

But then I feel his hand touch my face, and the words come to me.

"No, I guess he won't."

Adam Sinclair leans over and kisses me.

There's thumping in my ears, and at first, I think my brain must have turned up the volume on "Soul to Squeeze." But then I realize it's my heart, jackhammering against my ribcage as if it suddenly wants to be set free. He tastes like the whiskey and Coke in his glass. I'm pretty sure I taste like an enchilada. But it doesn't stop me from kissing him back. In fact, right now, I don't think *anything* could stop me from kissing him back.

Louise McGee and her discard pile can go to hell.

Adam's palm moves from my cheek to the back of my head, holding me against his mouth. I lift my hand to his jaw, touching him with my fingertips, with four separate square centimeters of my own calloused flesh. They are the same fingertips I use to make music. The same pieces of me I use to show my love to strangers. They're electric, carrying silent, awe-inspiring human music out of me and straight into him.

Adam's hand releases me just before his lips separate from mine. I open my eyes only to find his still closed. He looks peaceful. Sedate. A direct counterpoint to the craziness bouncing around in my chest. He inhales, then presses his lips closed and opens his eyes.

They're gray. I hadn't noticed before. Probably because I was too busy looking for something else.

"K'acy McGee." His voice should be muffled by the blood and bass filling my ears, but the words are loud and clear. "I think I might like you."

I suck in a slow breath before I reply.

"I think I might like you, too, Adam Sinclair. So much so, I'm considering upgrading your swooner status."

His eyebrows go up. "To?"

"Chief Executive Swooner."

***

After dinner, Adam drives me home and walks me to the door, saying nothing more than *you're welcome* when I thank him for dinner. He asks me for my number before he leaves, and I program it into his phone. He doesn't kiss me goodbye, though. I don't know what stops him, but I hope it wasn't the enchilada.

I feel better when my cell phone chimes the moment I close the apartment door behind me. I smile at the thought of Adam wanting to text me before he even sets foot off my front stoop.

Gram's gonna miss you for the next few days.

And with that, the bitter absence of a good-night kiss turns to sweetness again.

Sondra and the others will take good care of her. I promise.

What I meant was, I'M going to miss you for the next few days.

Whoa.

Trust me, you're not gonna miss me checking in on your gram every 15 minutes.

Is that what you were doing?

Yes…

Uh-huh. Sure. Right.

What else would I have been doing?

Interviewing me for the job.

I look out my apartment window. Adam's car is still sitting at the curb.

Good night, Adam.

Good night, K'acy.

Through the slats of the window blinds, I watch Adam's car pull out of its space. My silly schoolgirl grin doesn't last long, though, when I notice another car parked on my street, just a few spaces behind where Adam's was. The glow of the streetlights bounces off its too-dark windows. I watch it there, wondering if it's the same car that was parked across the street from the coffee shop on Friday. It's out of place here, too, and I wonder for a second if it's possible that the car is here because of me. When it pulls away from the curb a few moments later, makes a right at the corner and disappears into the night, my wisp of paranoia disappears, too. I dismiss it for what it likely was: nothing more than my own imagination.

CHAPTER 12

I come back from the grocery store on Tuesday evening to find Jarrod sitting on my front steps. He's got a cigarette hanging out of his mouth and a pair of Beats covering his ears. His eyes are closed, as if he's thinking hard about whatever's coming out of the headphones. I set my grocery bags down, tap him on the shoulder, and sit next to him. He pulls the Beats from his ears and drops them down around his neck. A distorted collection of horns and drums is coming out of them.

"What's that?" I ask, tilting my chin and moving my gaze from his face to the headphones.

"The demo for the gig at The Upstage. The guys from Jersey that wanna open."

"They any good?"

He takes the Beats off and puts them down over my ears. It doesn't take long for me to answer my own question.

"Looks like it's gonna be one hell of a night in Philadelphia." I take the headphones off and hand them back to Jarrod with a smile.

"Stevie says the promoter's hoping for a sell-out."

"From the sound of it, he just might get one."

Jarrod takes a drag on his cigarette, then sends the stub out to the sidewalk with a flick of his finger.

"So how'd things go with Mr. 'Soul to Squeeze' on Friday night?"

"Good. But probably not as good as things went with you and the brunette."

"Oh, I'm sure your night was far better than mine." He's still looking at the burning cigarette stump.

"Why? What happened?"

"Apparently, the brunette's roommate didn't appreciate her bringing a companion home at two in the morning."

"Oops."

"Yep. And it was especially awkward because her roommate is her father."

"No way!"

"Way. I never ran so fast in my goddamned life. The old man was pissed. I should've known no twenty-two-year-old would have a duplex that nice." He turns his head to look over at me. I can't help but laugh.

"That can't be the first time that's ever happened…"

He sits up, raises his right palm into the air, laughs a single, loud laugh, and says, "I have never been chased down the street by a half-dressed man before. I swear on all that is holy. This was the first time."

"But will it be the last?"

"Yes. Please, God. Please let it be the last." He partners his hands and pretends to pray.

"I bet the neighbors are still talking."

"I guess I'm lucky the guy didn't have a shotgun or something."

I nod in agreement but keep quiet because the same thought had already crossed my mind. I know how fathers can be when it comes to their daughters.

"So how about you?" His face switches from jovial to serious in a heartbeat. "What happened with you and The Mister?"

"He drove me home after the show, that's all."

"And?"

"And he took me to dinner on Sunday night. After I got off work."

Jarrod raises his brow and draws in a sharp breath. "What? K'acy McGee let a man take her to dinner?"

"Shut up, Jar. His grandmother is a patient. We just happened to be leaving at the same time, and he offered to take me to dinner to say thanks." Jarrod pauses and eyes me suspiciously before he speaks again.

"Kace, the dude put a Chili Peppers earworm in your head for two entire days, *and* he's the first person you've ever invited to come see us play. It was *not* just a dinner to say thanks. You can't lie for shit. Even to yourself." I'm not telling him he's right. Even though he is. "So, do you like him or what?"

"Yeah. I kinda do."

"And he likes you back?"

"So it seems."

Jarrod puts his arm around my waist and pulls me up against his side. I rest my head on his shoulder, looking at the cigarette stump that continues to burn on the sidewalk, a skinny trail of smoke wafting out of its tip. "You want me to run a credit check on him before this thing takes off?"

I'm not sure if he's serious or joking. "Nah. He's unemployed. I don't think I really wanna know."

"He doesn't look unemployed."

"He says he has a master's in finance."

"He doesn't look like he has a master's in finance either."

"I think it's the bed-head that's throwing you."

"Could be. I bet the guy listens to Death Cab for Cutie, too."

I smile against Jarrod's shoulder. "Yeah, probably."

***

I don't talk to or see Adam until Wednesday morning. I've been at work for a half hour when visiting hours start and he walks in through the sliding glass doors of Pine Manor, carrying a bouquet of daisies. Their necks are unbroken, with every petal in its perfect place. It's much bigger than the bouquet he brought the first day he came to see his grandmother. The one I accidentally smashed. Adam signs in with Marie and heads for the hallway. He doesn't see me changing the oxygen tank on the back of Mr. Ledbetter's wheelchair.

A short time later, I head back to Ms. Sinclair's to say hello. But before I can even get the word out of my mouth, Adam is putting his index finger to his lips from his seat across the room. Ms. Sinclair is asleep in the bed.

Adam gets up and walks over to my side of the room. He's wearing the same dark hoodie he was wearing on Friday night, only this time it's over a brown striped shirt instead of a blue one. The daisies are in a green plastic water pitcher on the nightstand.

There's a bright yellow tray of untouched breakfast on the bedside table. Something is going on.

The bags under Adam's eyes are hard to miss now that he's standing right next to me. His right hand reaches behind me and pushes the door closed.

"Hey," I say quietly, trying to mask my worry with a casual tone. "What's going on?"

"Let's just say it was a rough night."

"Oh." I reach out and grab one of his hands, holding it between my own. It's warm and soft and still.

"One of the nurses called at three in the morning to tell me Gram fell trying to get out of the bed. Not hard or anything, but they told me they have to report all falls immediately. I wasn't allowed to come in and see her until this morning. After they called, I couldn't get back to sleep."

"I'm so sorry. It happens sometimes. Patients lose their balance. Or their knees go out on the way to the bathroom. We have more falls than we'd like. Most places like this do. I'm sure Sondra and the night nurse made sure she was okay. If it was bad, they would've taken her to the hospital for x-rays."

"They told me Gram will be getting a lower bed today. And we should all remind her to use to call button to get help before she tries to get out of bed."

"Yeah, that's pretty standard. Other than that, there isn't much we can do."

"I'm just glad she's okay."

"Me, too." I squeeze his hand and think about how many more times this is probably going to happen. "Next time you should call me. Maybe I could come check on her for you."

"You'd do that?"

"Of course."

Adam puts his lips against my forehead. I feel his breath skim across my skin. "Thank you," he whispers, pulling his hand out of mine and caging my hips between his palms. He pulls me closer and slides one hand up to the small of my back. Then his lips drop to mine. Right here, only a few feet from his sleeping grandmother. It's not a need-fueled kiss like the one we shared on Sunday night, but rather a gentle, appreciative kiss. One that makes me feel like my whole body is wrapped in a gigantic hug. I feel a different kind of happiness this time. There is comfort and gratefulness in the kiss. From both of us.

***

There are exactly five people at The King's Court when I hit my first note. If there ever was a Wednesday night for an emotional-housecleaning, tonight's the one. I need this. Probably more than I ever have before. It's not because I'm confused about anything, or because I have to think twice about whether or not what's happening between Adam and me is right. In fact, I've never been less inclined to second-guess something in my entire life.

My need to houseclean stems more from what's happening to Ms. Sinclair than it does from Adam. She's the one who has my brain balancing on the railroad tracks. I know what's going to happen, but I don't know when. And the thought of it splits my insides right open. *This* is the sucky part, and I'm not sure this particular unfairness can ever be negated. No matter how many notes I play. But it isn't going to stop me from trying. My father would never forgive me if I did.

With every song, I'm reminded of how it's all out of my control. There's no doubt it would be easier if I was my mother. Then I could say—and believe with my whole being—that God would handle it. Because I would believe he has control and purpose and a damn good reason for everything he does. But I'm not Louise McGee, and I don't believe in all of that. I don't believe in a god that could ever watch the very things he created suffer so much. If we are all God's children, like my mother always told me we are, then he is one hell of a sadistic father.

So, instead of putting control of what happens to Ms. Sinclair into God's metaphorical hands, I'm more aware than ever of my role. Yes, what will happen, will happen. But I will definitely be there to make sure compassion fills all the empty spaces in between.

I play for two solid hours, just like last week. And the week before that. And the week before that. I want to finish where I started, with thoughts of Adam and how right we are. I finish with "Soul to Squeeze," knowing full well that Jarrod is sitting at the bar laughing at me.

When I finish the song, I pack up the StingRay and head over to the bar to have a drink with Jarrod. Just before I get there, the bartender puts a pair of Victory Wild Devil IPAs in front of him and offers me a nod. I pick one of them up and take a long, satisfying sip.

"Nice set," Jarrod declares as he lifts his beer to me. If I were any other woman, I'd assume he was talking about my breasts, but I'm me, so I know he's talking about the music. I'm surprised he hasn't made a smartass remark about my closing song. I'm sure there's one to come.

"You want us to close with that song on Saturday night?" And…there it is. "It might be a nice change to play a cover." If he weren't wearing the face of a lunatic, I might think he was serious.

"Jackass."

"I've been called worse."

"By me."

"By you, yes. And others."

"Wonder why."

Jarrod takes a sip of his beer while I give him a feigned look of utter exasperation. Even though I'm pretending to be irritated, our teasing always makes me appreciate him a little more than I did before. It's like having a twin brother who rags on you, just to keep you humble. And it goes both ways. Our relationship is a two-way street studded with endless ego-balancing jabs. Never mean, and never serious.

"You gonna invite The Mister to come see us play on Saturday night? I kinda wanna hang out with the guy a little bit. Make sure he's suitable, you know?"

"Suitable? What are you, my grandpa?"

"Just watching your back, that's all. It's what best friends do. Or so I've heard." He said *best friend*. Out loud. To me. And not through the proverbial grapevine. I can't help but smile.

"Okay, Grandpa, I'll invite him. Just don't take your teeth out in front of him, okay?"

Jarrod curls his lips in until they cover his teeth, then, in his best grandpa voice, he says, "Wouldn't dream of it, schweetheart!"

"Thanks, Gramps."

We each finish a couple of beers and have a strangely candid talk about our own grandfathers. It's a topic that, in our six-year friendship, we've never covered. Both of my paps were charmers. One played the squeezebox in a Zydeco band and the other was a school janitor. Neither is still alive. Seeing as how he's never even met his father, Jarrod only has one grandfather. And he's pretty sure the man disowned his daughter right around the same time Jarrod did. Jarrod says he should look the guy up sometime, just to see if he's still alive. I tell him I think it's a great idea, even though I don't. I'd hate to see him get hurt.

We're climbing out of our seats when my cell phone chimes. I glance at the red digital clock above the bar. It's almost one in the morning, which means it's either Charlie or Adam. My stomach drops. I tell Jarrod to hang on a second and pull my phone from my back pocket.

Hey. You awake?

It's not Charlie.

Yep. Everything ok?

Please don't let there be anything wrong with Ms. Sinclair. Pretty please.

Yeah. Just couldn't sleep again. How bout u?

Oh, good. Nothing's wrong.

Wide awake and slightly inebriated.

Jarrod tells me he's going to hit the bathroom before we head out. I tell him I'll meet him at the front door in a few minutes.

Slightly?

Played earlier. Just blowing off some steam with Jarrod.

Where are u guys?

The King's Court. But we're leaving in a minute.

U want me to come get u? Happy to see u both home safely.

Sweet. So, so sweet.

Nah. I'm good to take the bus.

Yes, but is the bus good enough to take u?

More sweetness.

If Big Al's driving, it is.

Ummm…Big Al?

He drives the 43D every Wednesday nite.

U take the 43D on a Wednesday nite often enough to know the driver?

Every week.

Every week at 1:00 in the morning?

Yep. Sometimes earlier. If I don't get slightly inebriated.

Then I guess Big Al is going to miss u.

Huh?

Meet me out front in 10.

Dude. U don't even know where The King's Court is.

Just Googled it. Not far from where I live. I'm already in the car.

U totally do not have to do this.

Can't text…driving…

He's coming to get us. At one in the morning.

Adam Sinclair is a really nice white boy. A really, *really* nice white boy. I wonder if Miriam Hansen knew about that part.

I make my way to the front door and find Jarrod standing just outside, smoking a cigarette and typing something into his phone.

"Everything cool?" he asks as I step outside.

"Yeah. Um…apparently we're getting a ride."

"What?" He looks appropriately confused.

"Adam's coming to get us."

Jarrod's eyebrows shoot up, and a gigantic shit-eating grin spreads across his face. "He's not coming to get us."

"Uh, yeah he is. He's already on his way."

"No, I mean he's not coming to get *us*. He's coming to get *you*."

"No. He said he would take us both home."

"And I'm sure he would. Probably just to make sure we both end up in our own beds and not each other's." I crinkle up my face in disgust, as if the mere idea is the grossest thing I've ever heard. "Ha-ha-ha," he mocks, tilting his head to the side with a smirk. "As if you've never fantasized about ending up in my bed."

I move my entire body in an over-exaggerated shudder of revulsion. "I love you, Jar. But that is one fantasy I'll never have. I know too much about you to ever go there."

He grabs me and squeezes me in a tight hug. It feels good. Familiar and safe. "You're a smart woman," he says, "but does The Mister know that? Wouldn't want him to get the wrong idea about us or anything." He's serious now, back to being my brother.

"I told him we're best friends. He's definitely not coming to keep me out of your bed."

"There's probably already someone in there anyway. No room for you."

"I'm sure they'll be lined up outside your door by the time you get home."

"Either that or I'll just pick one up on the way."

I feel sad because he's right. I want more for him. I want him to find the right someone and believe he deserves her, whoever she is. He lets go of the hug. I look up and shake my head at him.

"So, you don't want a ride home, then? Is that what you're saying?"

"Like I said, he's not coming to get *us*. He's coming to get *you*. I'll wait with you until he gets here, but then I'll get my own ass home."

"Suit yourself. But you know this would be a good chance for you to watch my back, Grandpa."

"Don't think I didn't consider that. But if you like this guy like you say you do, you don't need a third wheel bringing you down. I'll wait to interrogate him in public on Saturday night. It'll be more fun anyway." For him, but not for Adam, that's for sure.

We sit down on the curb together, side by side, and wait. When Adam pulls up a few minutes later, Jarrod offers me a double fist bump. A smack of love shoots from him to me when our knuckles connect. Jarrod looks at me, a coy smile filling up his face. The night we met flashes through my mind, and the memory, coupled with the alcohol, causes a wave of emotion to swell. I stuff it down inside, trying to hide how much it means. Everything is different because of that night. *Life* is different. For both of us.

I say goodbye and get into Adam's car.

CHAPTER 13

Robert McGee—1999

Louise left two weeks ago today. She packed her bags right in front of the girls, told them to be good, and walked out the door as if she was doing nothing more than visiting her sister in Shreveport for the weekend. But I know better. I know she's never coming back. 'Cause I know all about men like Reverend Thompson. Men who sweet-talk old folks into tossing their life savings into the collection basket. Men who claim to heal the sick with only a palm to the forehead and an "Oh, Lord Jesus" on the tongue. Men who convince wives to leave their hardworking husbands in order to build themselves some kind of harem of confused, baby-making disciples. Men who ruin families with false prayer and empty promises.

The girls, though, they still think their momma's coming back. I don't tell them she ain't, 'cause I think they're better off holding on to some kind of hope, at least for now. Time always makes things easier, and this is no different. Rushing reality isn't going to do them any favors.

My girls are learning about the hardest parts of life way too young, and me cursing their momma in front of them would only make it worse, so I keep my mouth shut about Louise. I don't say a single bad word about her. I only tell them I love them and I'll always be here for them. No matter what. From the day they were born, I knew I would need to protect my girls; I just never thought I'd have to protect them from the heartbreak of their own momma's departure. I'm no saint, and that's no secret. We all got our vices, after all. But every time my Charlie cries herself to sleep after praying for Reverend Thompson to bring her momma back, my sins seem a little less significant.

The day Charlie realizes she's permanently motherless is probably gonna be the hardest day of the lot. And I suspect it's coming soon. She's a fragile girl, an eleven-year-old piece of dark-skinned porcelain, and when it hits her, it's gonna hit hard. A full-on kick to the heart courtesy of a man in a white tent and her own mother, and there's nothing I can do to buffer the blow other than to assure her that her momma's leaving had nothing to do with her and her sister. Louise left because of *herself*, not because of her girls. I only hope they're strong enough to realize that someday.

I worry a little less about K'acy. She's fierce, like a scrappy little dog constantly out to prove she doesn't have any fleas. And, she's a lover, always seeing the best in people—even when the rest of us think there's nothing good to see. It's like she can look straight into a person's soul and find something decent to hang on to. K'acy's my little glass-half-full; the exact opposite of her glass-half-empty big sister. She says she doesn't hate her momma for leaving and she never will. Even if Louise never comes back, K'acy says she'll keep on loving her, because she loved her momma's biscuits and gravy and her dove casserole and her crawfish boil. Louise's cooking is the "something decent" K'acy's hanging on to. There are other things there, too, I'm sure, but K'acy's always loved her momma's cooking. I think it's the thing she'll miss the most.

But Charlie…I can say without a doubt she's gonna hate Louise something brutal when reality strikes. She's gonna be a whirlwind of hatred and fury, fingernails trying to dig in and latch on to whatever negatives she can grip. *That's* what she's gonna hang on to. And I hope it doesn't beat her down and steamroll the spirit right out of her. She's already on the edge, just waiting for me to say the words so she can excuse herself from the calm she's been trying to keep. The moment I serve up some kind of confirmation of the permanence of Louise's absence, things will change for Charlie. The only thing that might keep her from dropping completely over the edge is her little sister. K'acy has a way of keeping it real for Charlie by sharing her slightly skewed view of the world. K'acy will remind Charlie of the positives, just like she always does. Maybe, just maybe, she can make Charlie think hard enough to find one good thing to hang on to. And, Lord willing, that one good thing, among all the negatives, just might be enough to keep Charlie afloat.

I know things are gonna get worse. A lot worse. But, then they'll get better. I'll make sure they do.

It's just gonna take some time. And lots and lots of love.

CHAPTER 14

I'm looking out the window of Adam's moving car, wondering who taught him how to be so nice. It couldn't have been his father, because a giant dickhead would never think to leave his apartment in the middle of the night to pick up a slightly inebriated woman at a bar and drive her home. And a giant dickhead certainly wouldn't teach his son to sit with his grandmother in a nursing home for hours on end. It leads me to believe Adam must've learned how to be so nice from his mother. He's never mentioned her, and I'm a little afraid to ask.

What if she had nothing to do with why he's such a gentleman? What if she made like Louise McGee and cut out when he was just a kid? Or, even worse, what if his giant dickhead of a father snuffed her out of Adam's life, just like he snuffed out Ms. Sinclair?

"You okay?" he asks as my muddled mind moves from one thought to another.

"Yep."

"You're awfully quiet. You're not upset Jarrod didn't come with us, are you?"

I turn away from the window to look at him. We're pulling onto my street. "I'm so far from upset, it's ridiculous."

He smiles at me. It makes my stomach flip-flop and sends a shockwave of notes through my mind. He pulls over in front of my building, puts the car in park, and turns off the engine.

"Sounds like a pretty good place to be," he says matter-of-factly, opening his door and climbing out of the car. I do the same. Adam opens the back door and pulls my gig bag out, gently hoisting the straps up over his shoulders. He walks around the front of the car, steps up onto the sidewalk, and takes my hand. We walk together up the front stairs of my building. I twist the doorknob, thinking about how he's the first person besides Jarrod I've ever let carry my StingRay. It means something.

"If you're going to carry my bass, the next logical step is for me to invite you in," I say.

"I didn't carry your bass with any expectations." He raises his right palm. "Promise. I was just trying to be nice."

Nice. There's the word. I can't help it. "You know, your momma did a hell of a job raising such a nice boy."

"No, she didn't. All the nice parts come from my grandmother."

I shouldn't be surprised, but I am. I walk into the building and gesture for him to follow. "Don't tell me *both* of your parents are giant dickheads?"

He's behind me now, following me up the staircase. "My mother isn't a giant dickhead. She's just a too-busy-shopping-and-getting-her-nails-done-to-bother-with-her-own-child kind of mother."

"Oh." We're headed up the second flight now.

"Like I said, my grandmother was my best friend. She essentially raised me. That is, until I turned eight and my father saw fit to shut her out and head west. From then on, I had after-school nannies and summer camps to raise me."

"Why did he shut her out?" He never gave me an answer the last time I asked, and besides, it's way too late for patient privacy now.

"To be honest, I'm not sure. He never talked about it, other than to tell me I wasn't allowed to be with her anymore. He wouldn't even let me write or call her. I was just a kid, so I figured it must have been something really, really bad for him to keep me from her. He knew how much I loved her. To this day, he won't tell me why. Not that I ever talk to him anymore. He always just said it was for my own good. That's part of the reason I came here. To find out why he shut her out. But now it looks like I'll never find out." There's so much emotion in his voice. So much sadness and confusion.

I open the door to my apartment, and we go inside. Adam closes the door behind me and lays my bass on the floor. That isn't where it belongs, but at least he didn't lay it facedown, on the strings. I don't say a word, but he keeps on talking.

"I mean, I don't want to waste what's left of my time with Gram continually prying her for answers. It's bad enough that I have to stop myself from asking her who Bradley is. Whatever happened back then probably doesn't matter now anyway. It's too late." He sighs and runs his hand through his hair, down to the back of his neck. It sits there, frozen with exasperation. He's been thinking about this for a long time. Seventeen years, to be exact. It's got to be hard to let go after all that time.

"This might be totally out of line, but…maybe you're better off not knowing what happened. I mean, maybe your gram wouldn't want you to know. Like, what if it's something that would change your opinion of her? Maybe that's what your dad's been protecting you from all these years."

His brow furrows, and his hand drops down to his side. "That's a big maybe, K'acy. My dad's not that kind of guy. He doesn't protect other people. He only protects himself."

"Sounds like a giant dickhead."

"Like I said…" He's smiling at me again, and it feels good. "So, are you gonna offer me a drink now or what?" It's a clear attempt to change the subject, and his face flushes with relief when I run with it.

"Let's see…I've got beer, water, and Gatorade. What can I get you?" I'm already on my way to the kitchen as I ask.

"Beer." He takes a seat on the sofa. I can see him over the half-counter between the kitchen and the living room. Adam's head swivels from side to side; he's checking the place out. "Your apartment's really great. I like the layout."

I open two bottles of beer and walk back out. "Thanks. I've only lived here a year or so. Took me a while to save up. My place before this was a bit of a dump." He takes a beer from my outstretched hand, and I sit down on the sofa next to him. Not too close, but not too far away either. "How about you? Where's your place?"

"It's over in Mount Airy." That would be why he was only a ten-minute drive from The King's Court. "It's a decent one bedroom. I had a real estate agent find it for me so I'd have somewhere to live as soon as I got here. Someday I'll pick out my own place, but this one will do until the lease runs out."

Adam and I talk for a long time, snug against each other on the sofa, taking sips of beer in between words. I learn more about his time in Seattle and share my thoughts on growing up in Louisiana. It's easy, and before I know it, it's close to three in the morning. I'm not drunk, or even buzzed anymore, but I've got to go to work in a few hours.

Still…I don't really want to ask him to leave.

When we finally stop talking, Adam slumps down in his seat and puts his arm out along the back of the sofa, as if he doesn't want me to ask him to leave either. I move closer and put my head down on his chest, curling my legs up onto the cushions and sinking into him like he's the most familiar thing in the world. He lowers his outstretched arm down against my side and pulls me in tight.

Then, Adam Sinclair kisses the top of my head and says, "Good night."

***

I wake on Thursday morning to my cell phone alarm vibrating in my pocket. Adam and I have shifted in our sleep; we're both lying on the sofa, crammed together with his arm around my shoulder and my head still on his chest. His left foot is up on the arm of the couch, and his right is dangling off the edge. He's too tall for the sofa, and yet he's sound asleep. I do my best to get up without disturbing him. He doesn't even move.

I'm standing in my living room, looking at Adam sleeping so soundly on my sofa, and wondering, yet again, what my father would think about all this. I wonder what he would warn me about. I wonder what negatives he would see that I'm missing. My daddy was always good at tempering my bright side and giving me a dose of reality without crushing who I am. Not even a little bit. I'm not sure I would listen to him, though, even if he were here to give me advice. I think my heart's already taken the lead on this one, and there's nothing I can do to stop it.

Sorry, Daddy. Destiny, and Miriam Hansen, had it right this time.

I head to the bathroom to shower and get ready for work, and even as I detonate one squeaky floorboard after another, Adam's breathing stays steady.

***

The very-nice-boy-I-can't-stop-thinking-about drove me to work this morning, dropping me off in Pine Manor's parking lot before heading home for a shower of his own. He kissed me just before I got out of the car. A *real* kiss. *Not* a sweet kiss on the forehead. *Not* the kiss of a nice boy. A kiss that shimmied around inside my ribcage Anthony Kiedis-style. I will carry it around with me for the rest of the day. Hell, maybe even for the rest of my life.

Adam comes back to Pine Manor, freshly showered and shaved but still sporting a tuft of intentional bed-head, at 10:30, just as I'm about to start moving everyone to the community room for bingo.

Ms. Sinclair has been sitting at the front window, watching her birds, since Sondra moved her there just after breakfast. She's chatty this morning, telling me about the tiny goldfinch perched on the feeder as I straighten her blanket. She says it's a male. She can tell because the feathers are so bright. The female's feathers are drab, she tells me. Brown and drab. It startles me when our eyes connect. I catch a glimpse of something again, something in her eyes I'd rather not see. I'm thankful when Adam interrupts us with a soft hello.

"Good morning, Adam," Ms. Sinclair says, clear as a bell. Adam looks at me and sighs a small, happy sigh. "This young lady and I were just looking at the goldfinches. Do you see them out there? The ones with the yellow feathers?"

"Yes, Gram, I do. They're beautiful."

"You know, your father used to have a canary when he was a boy. He kept it in his bedroom. I wanted to get you one, too, but your mother said she didn't want such nonsense in her house."

It's the longest, most cohesive string of sentences Ms. Sinclair has said in days. Adam's expression is a combination of utter surprise and absolute pleasure. I take a step back to give them both some space as he sits down in the chair facing her.

"I would've loved to have a canary, Gram. Do you remember those fish I used to have?"

"I do. They were the only pet your mother would let you to have. She wasn't too keen on animals."

"No, she sure wasn't." Adam can't take his eyes off of her. He's clearly in a state of shock over his grandmother's clarity. As am I.

"How *is* your mother, darling? You know, I haven't seen her in quite some time."

"My mother is fine. She and Dad still live in Seattle."

"Yes. Yes. Seattle. That's right. Now, what about you, dear? How is high school?"

"Gram, I'm not in high school anymore. I'm twenty-five now. I just finished graduate school not too long ago." His face falls. He knows he's losing her.

"Well, then. You'd better get back to work. Both of you. Principal Sykes does not like our students to be tardy. You'll get scolded if you're late." Her brow furrows and she waves her hands at us, as if to send us away. It breaks my heart.

I step into the conversation in hopes of bringing her back to the present before she slips fully away. "Ms. Sinclair, why don't you let Adam take you into the community room? They're about to start a new game of bingo, and if I recall correctly, you mentioned earlier you'd like to play."

"Why, yes, dear. That would be quite nice." Nice. Like all the parts of Adam that came from her and not from his animal-hating mother.

"Come on, Gram. Let's get rolling." Adam stands up and walks around to the back of Ms. Sinclair's wheelchair. As he releases her brake, he nods at me and quietly adds, "How 'bout that. I never would've pictured my dad as a canary type. Vulture, yes. But canary…"

I can't stop myself from smiling.

***

The following two days fly by uneventfully. Ms. Sinclair enjoys a few more fleeting moments of semi-lucidity, but nothing like the canary conversation. Nothing that gives Adam a reason to hope for more. By the time the end of Saturday's shift arrives, I'm in need of another housecleaning.

Crackerjack Townhouse is playing at a bar in South Philly tonight, and Adam has enthusiastically agreed to come swoon, even though I warned him of the pending inquisition from Jarrod. When he said, "Bring it on," I told him he has no idea what he's in for. The truth is, though, I don't think he has much to worry about. I think Jarrod is well-enough freaked out about me seeing someone that he won't want to scare the poor guy away.

Just before I leave work to head home, Adam tells me he'll pick me up at my place at 7:15 so I don't have to take my bass on the bus. I've lugged the StingRay on and off of a bus a million times before, but it doesn't stop me from accepting his offer without a second thought. I already can't wait to see him again, even when he's still standing right in front of me.

On the bus ride home, I think about tonight and how Jarrod and Adam will be together, with me as their common thread. I'm both excited and, admittedly, a little nervous.

The bus drops me at my stop and passes with a belch of exhaust as I walk the last block to my building. In its wake, a black car races past me, one with dark, shaded windows. It's the same car I've seen twice before; I'm sure of it now. But why is it here? Is it possible that someone's watching me? A sinking feeling quickens my pulse when a few possible reasons why someone would be following me flicker through my mind. I climb the stairs of my apartment building and immediately head inside.

***

As we're setting up the stage in South Philly a few hours later, my mind is reeling with more questions about the car. I don't owe the man on Latham Street anything, but that doesn't mean he doesn't think I do. Nor does it mean he didn't sell me out. Maybe one of his "associates" is in that car. Or maybe the cops are watching me, hoping to catch me with whatever it is he told them I have. I won't know why the car is following me, of course, unless I know who's driving it.

Just before we start the sound check, my thoughts turn to what I should do about it. Knocking on the car window and asking the driver what they want is definitely a bad idea, no matter who's behind the wheel. If I ignore the car and make sure I don't give the driver any new reasons to stick around, maybe they'll eventually give up. It's a big maybe, for sure, so the thought doesn't offer me much comfort.

The whole thing ties my insides into a thick, contorted knot. Too much is at stake. Too much could be lost.

As the bar doors open and Jarrod, Marquis, Bryson, and the rest of us head backstage to wait for showtime to arrive, I shut down my worry as much as I can. I close it out and prepare to let the notes scrub my mind and my soul clean once again.

Despite all of my uncertainty about the car, the gig is downright amazing. The music flows out of my fingers like a rousing symphony, clean and warm and luscious. There are women, so many women, crowded against the front of the stage. All of them watching Jarrod's every move, but feeling *my* every note. Feeling the echo of the song in their chest. It makes me happy to see them happy. Just like always. But better. *Way* better. Because I know my lone swooner is out there somewhere, feeling the very same thing.

A few minutes after we finish the first set and head to the back for a break, Adam comes in to see us. He says hello and briefly shakes hands with Stevie and the rest of the guys as he passes them on his way to where Jarrod and I are standing. By the time he gets to us, a lump of excitement has clogged my throat. Adam extends a hand, and Jarrod takes it firmly into his own. It's a solid handshake, from one man to another. Full of respect and acceptance. Even though I'm not the one touching Adam's skin, "Soul to Squeeze" is there, low and resonating and wonderful. The handshake makes me giddy.

"Good to see you again, man." Jarrod is the first to break the silence, just as their hands release. "Thanks for coming."

"I wouldn't miss it." Adam steps over to me, puts a hand on the small of my back, and bends down to kiss me on the temple. It's simple and electric. A nice-boy kiss, full of promise. "You guys sure know how to put on one hell of a show."

I look up to find Adam's gray eyes connected directly to mine.

"That's because Kace is one hell of a bassist," Jarrod says, breaking Adam's stare with his words. Jarrod's wearing a half-cocked smile, one that tells me he took note of Adam's kiss and he's trying to talk me up in front of my swooner.

"And Jarrod is one hell of an ass shaker," I add, talking *him* up in return. Mostly to show him how ridiculous it sounds. But also because the whole idea of someone talking me up makes me a little uncomfortable.

"Exceptional bass playing and ass shaking aside, you guys really do sound great. K'acy tells me you've been playing together for like six years. How'd you two meet?" The question is aimed at Jarrod, not me, and it's clear from Jarrod's expression he did not expect to be on the receiving end of the inquisition. He thought he'd be the one asking all the questions.

I wonder how much of the story he'll tell.

"We met at a bus stop. I was high out of my fucking mind, nearly ready to claw my own eyes out, and some stranger named K'acy sat down next to me and fixed everything." His face is relaxed, full of peace and gratitude. We've talked about that night before, lots of times, but he's never put it quite like that. He's never made me feel like I was his savior. Until now.

I'm not quite sure what to say. The emotion wells up inside of me. I swallow hard.

Adam is silent at my side, knowing he's just gotten way more than he bargained for. It takes me a second to come up with the right words.

"All I did was remind you that you're in charge of your own future." I shrug and shake my head. "The rest was Crackerjack Townhouse's doing, not mine." I hear Adam's exhalation.

"Whatevs, Kace. Fine. Don't take credit for my current state of epic ass shaking then. But it's the truth." He switches his attention to Adam, turning the tables as he goes. "And how about you? I hear your grandmother's a patient at Pine Manor. How'd you manage to hook up with one of her nurses?"

"For the millionth time, I'm not a nurse, Jar. I'm an aide."

"Oh yeah. Right. An *aide*. So, how'd you hook up with her *aide* then?"

"I guess I got lucky," Adam answers. "She was coming to give Gram her medicine, and we literally ran into each other in the hallway."

I don't think Jarrod knows I'm not licensed to medicate patients, so thankfully, my eavesdropping will remain a secret.

"Well, not to give too much away about the girl, but..." I have the sudden feeling my best friend is about to throw me to the wolves, "...unless she's lying to me, I know K'acy better than anyone else ever has, and I gotta say, she seems to be a little more relaxed since you started hanging out with her. She's taking it a little easier on the rest of us." Jarrod moves his hand to indicate the other guys in the room.

It never dawned on me until now, but he's right. I haven't been overly involved in band stuff since Adam showed up. I haven't been texting Jarrod twenty times a day, asking for extra rehearsals and writing sessions. It makes me wonder how Jarrod *really* feels about it. He hasn't said a word, until tonight. I hope he doesn't think I stopped caring.

"You *do* know I'm standing right here?" I say with a lift of my brow, trying to keep things from getting too serious.

"I'm just trying to let Adam know that your relationship—or whatever it is—has been beneficial to all of us. I wouldn't want him to think we disapprove of it or something."

"All very good to know," Adam chimes in with enough lilt in his voice to sink a ship. "I'll do my best to keep her off your back."

I turn to Adam just as the stage manager comes in to tell us it's time to head out for the final set. "How noble of you," I declare.

"No problem." Adam is smiling from ear to ear.

"In the meantime, we've got some funk to play," Jarrod says. "Come on, Kace. Kiss The Mister adieu, and I'll see you out there." He reaches over to shake Adam's hand again, and I can see the mischief on both of their faces. They've just had a male bonding moment. Cute.

Jarrod walks away, and I issue an unnecessary apology to Adam, telling him I'm sorry for all the foolishness. He tells me he loved every second. I kiss him on the mouth and walk out onto the stage.

***

When the show ends and we start the teardown, Adam watches us from across the room. I guess he doesn't want another rebuke from a sound guy, so this time he keeps his distance.

Despite the emaciated woman with a pixie cut who can't take her eyes off of him, Jarrod is talking to me as we pack up. He glances at her from time to time, silently telling her to hang tight. "So, you going home with The Mister tonight?" he asks. "I see he's still here."

"Yeah, I guess. He'll probably offer me a ride."

"A ride on his love stick?"

What? "Oh my God, Jar. You're so weird."

"What?" He lifts his palms and shoulders to the sky. I shake my head at him and roll my eyes. "Don't tell me you guys haven't done it yet…"

"That would be none of your business."

He narrows his eyes at me. "You haven't, have you?"

"Like I said, none of your business."

Jarrod tosses his arm around my shoulders and puts his mouth against my ear. "Good for you," he says in a near whisper. There's no sarcasm in his voice. Two seconds later, his arm drops off my shoulder and he offers me another double fist-bump. He turns to wink at me just before he jumps off the stage, heading toward the Pixie Princess and her promise of easy, temporary "love."

For some reason, as I turn away from Jarrod and the Princess to put the StingRay into its bag, my momma pops into my head. She never taught me a lick about sex. In fact, she bailed on us just a few months before my big sister was christened into womanhood in sixth-grade gym class. Charlie thought she was dying. Mrs. Krick had to take her into the locker room and explain the situation.

The gym teacher had to tell my sister how to be a woman because her own momma decided she'd rather be somewhere else. The controlled descent of Charlie's self-esteem spooled out about a mile of rope that day. And I don't think it's stopped unraveling since.

Lucky for me, I had a big sister to teach me how to be a woman. The day Mrs. Krick told Charlie about "her friend" was the very same day Charlie shared the information with me. Probably a bit much for a nine-year-old, but useful nonetheless. Eventually, I heard about everything from Charlie. She showed me how to kiss a boy three years before one even took interest in me. I learned about sex by listening to my own sister recall, in great detail, her encounter with Treyvon Rail under the football bleachers. She showed me how to buy a bra and how to deal with my period when the time came for both. Charlie said she didn't want me to be as lost as her. She said she was watching out for me.

'

But then I grew up, and I started thinking maybe I should've been watching out for her instead.

Thinking about all of this makes me wonder who taught Adam about sex. He didn't have a big brother, and I can't imagine his animal-hating mother sitting him down with a book or something. He was too young for it to have been his grandmother. Maybe it was *his* gym teacher or a camp counselor or, God forbid, one of his nannies. It certainly couldn't have been his giant dickhead of a father. Giant dickheads don't care enough to teach their sons about stuff like love and sex.

Whoever it was, I hope they did it justice.

CHAPTER 15

Mary DiPetro—Room number 107

I spent most of my life on the telephone, talking to friends or neighbors or relatives, just to avoid feeling alone. And when I couldn't reach someone I knew, I'd call someone I didn't. I spent a collection of long hours over my lifetime talking to assorted catalog representatives, pretending to be interested in placing an order and asking question after question about their products. It started with Sears and Roebuck in 1949, the year I turned thirty and Donald was forced to take his sales team on the road for days at a time. I was alone a lot, for many years. Yes, I had the children, but it wasn't the same as having another adult to talk to. Plus, they were always at school or out playing in the woods. The three of them could disappear for hours at a time, only to return at the clang of the dinner bell. Donald used our only car for work, and so I was stuck. It was just me. And the telephone.

The Lana Lobell dress catalog was my favorite, and then came J.C. Penney and Radio Shack. I would spend hours looking at the pages, deriving a list of questions about a particular product and then telephoning to ask them all my questions. I'd end the call, sometimes an hour later, with a promise to place my order in the mail the following day. I never placed the orders, though;

I just called a different catalog and asked another long string of pointless questions.

Then Dottie moved into the cottage down the lane, and she was as lonely as I was. Her husband, Jim, was a long-haul trucker, and he was gone almost as much as Donald. We'd talk on the phone every day, sometimes three or four times. And we'd get together for coffee and cards a few afternoons a week. But in between our conversations and visits, I was even more desperate for company than before. It was like I would have a long drink of water, only to be followed by hours upon hours of drought.

In many ways, Dottie's friendship made the lonely times all the more lonely. When she moved away in 1973, my children were long gone, out of the house and off living lives of their own. I had no one left to talk to except for a few church friends, my sister in New York, and the catalog call center operators. Donald spent weeks at a time away from home, driving cross-country to sell industrial steel. It was just me again. And the telephone.

I watched the years roll by courtesy of the catalogs whose pages I turned over and over again. Lillian Vernon, Plow & Hearth, Macy's, Lands' End, Toys "R" Us. I studied them all, watching house and toy and fashion trends come and go. I watched them until I stopped being lonely.

I'll never forget the day it happened. March 15, 2004. I was an eighty-six-year-old widow with no one to talk to. My kids and grandkids were too busy for much more than a weekly phone call, and all my church friends—and my sister—had long since passed. Tommy, my eldest and most practical son, decided it was time for me to move out of my house. He said I couldn't take care of myself anymore. He said he was scared I would hurt myself worse than I did the day I fell off the ladder changing the battery in the kitchen clock. I didn't fight him because, truth be told, I was tired of taking care of that house. And I was tired of being alone.

But once I moved into Pine Manor, things were different. There was always someone to talk to. I could have my pick. Sometimes the conversation might not go as planned because someone's mind would slip, but by and large, I could talk all day if I wanted. I was *never* lonely there. I *never* ate another meal by myself, and I *never* again had to call a catalog representative just to hear a voice. They were the sweetest ten years of my life. I made many good friends at Pine Manor, both men and women. It turns out I wasn't the only one that spent far too many years with no one to talk to but telemarketers and the Meals on Wheels driver.

A place like Pine Manor is proof that loneliness is a soul-smashing thing. After so many years, it wears you down, and some people never get over it. They showed up there and didn't know how *not* to be lonely anymore, so they stayed in their rooms and refused to make friends and denied themselves the chance to feel again. Those were the people I was drawn to the most. Those were the people I wrapped in my folds. I talked with them until they talked back. I listened to the story of their life and told them all about mine. We talked about what we'd seen of the world. Wars, births, sorrow, fortune, deaths, happiness, loss. At one time or another, each of us had felt both the heart-lifting joy of the world's goodness and the stinging touch of its bitter evils. But there, in Pine Manor, we were all the same. Just a bunch of old, lonely widows and widowers who, at long last, didn't have to be lonely anymore. And it felt good. It felt really good.

When it was time for me to go, I only had one wish. In the last moments of my life, I wanted a phone against my ear. I wanted to listen to a voice, any voice, and I wanted to remember what it was like to be lonely. Somehow, knowing loneliness was only a memory and not a reality, made the pleasure of the last ten years feel all the more sweet. So, in the middle of the night, when my sons and daughter were asleep in a nearby hotel room, it happened. My children knew it wouldn't be long until I left. That's why they came to be with me. But that girl, the dark-skinned one that put the phone to my ear, she knew *exactly* when it was time. So she dialed a number, settled the phone against my cheek, and held my hand until it was over.

CHAPTER 16

The tendons in my forearms are aching and sore; it's the best kind of tired for a bass player. On our way out of the bar, I quickly scan the street, looking for the black car. It's nowhere in sight, but that doesn't stop the worry from squirming its way back in. As I swallow it down, Adam opens his car door and I climb in. I rub my arms gently the whole drive home, trying to massage the ache out of them, and by the time we reach the landing outside of my apartment door, I want to fall straight into bed.

Adam is standing next to me, watching me put the key into the lock. When the door swings open, I turn and give him a soft smile of thanks. For tonight's swooning and for the ride. He looks down at me, and I see something new on his face. It isn't appreciation or tenderness or admiration. It's want. Plain and simple and undeniable. My eyes lock on to his, and the moment he touches the back of my neck, I forget all about the black car and my tired forearms. I forget about *everything* except Adam's lips on mine and the sudden music inside my head.

This kiss replaces the one in the parking lot at Pine Manor, knocking it out of First Place in an instant. With his lips on mine, and the StingRay still slung over his back, Adam pushes us both inside, closing and locking the door behind him. The hand now at the back of my head holds me against him as if he's afraid I might pull away. The other is sitting on my hip, fingertips pressing into the bone, holding on for dear life. Holding on as if separating from me at this moment would end everything he's ever known.

The intensity of this kiss, this not-such-a-nice-boy-kiss, sinks deep into me. This kiss means something. Adam is sandwiched between me and my bass. He's surrounded by *us* and apparently wanting nothing but more. His tongue sends a jolt of happiness straight into me every time it brushes against mine.

Adam's hands drop away from me when, a few moments later, we separate. He slides the straps of the StingRay's gig bag down off his shoulders, propping it against the wall behind him without taking his eyes off of mine. He's motionless now, standing in front of me, bright and electrified. Full of light.

"Thanks." His voice is charged. And apparently connected straight to the lump now rising in my throat.

"For?"

He doesn't answer. Instead, he rushes at me, wrapping his arms around my waist and sliding his hands up my back, underneath my shirt. His mouth connects to mine, and the endorphins jolt through my body, kicking and screaming and lighting a fire everywhere his skin touches mine. The wildness of it is like nothing I've ever felt before.

His hands move down to my backside and push me against him with their solid grip, his fingertips again holding me as if to keep me from pulling away. I melt my body into his, removing the space between us and wordlessly assuring him that pulling away is the last thing I want to do.

This is *exactly* where I want to be.

We don't make it to the bedroom, or even to the couch, before our clothes are off. They litter the floor in a circle around our feet, as if they are soft, colorful statues frozen in dance. I imagine them revolving around us in time with the music in my head. *We* are the bonfire, and they are the pagans.

His hands touch my flesh, surveying it with skill and temperance, as if to absorb each detail. The lightness of his skin against mine is shockingly beautiful, and because of it, I don't want to close my eyes. Not now, or ever again. He kisses my neck, tilting my head to the side and running his lips across my collarbone. His mouth moves over the front of my shoulders, and he sweeps his hands across my breasts, sending a heady stream of anticipation through me. Then his hands move downward, along the sides of my waist, squeezing and molding me. They grasp my hips and tug me closer just before they skim over my stomach, light as a feather, as his lips meet mine again. One hand wraps around my waist, holding on to me. Holding me still. The other drops lower, down between my legs.

Adam Sinclair is touching me, turning me into his light. He circles his fingers against my skin, teasing my flesh with his, feeding his want and mine. My knees buckle just enough to make the arm around my waist hold me a little tighter, as if to catch me before I fall. I won't fall, though, because my heart is holding me up. Just like it always does. Adam doesn't stop touching me until, a few minutes later, a remarkable, fiery release litters my brain with another flurry of pyromaniacal endorphins. This time, they ignite a string of deafening bass notes and "Soul to Squeeze" burns in my ears and over my skin. Louder than ever.

Together, we drop to the floor of my living room, and with the carpet against my back, I wrap my legs around his hips. Our bodies fuse together; his rhythmical hips push into me, deep and steady. It feels just like I knew it would. Perfect.

Adam's face hovers above mine, studying me for signs hesitation or regret. But he won't find any, because there's not a single morsel of either. There's only desire, the memory of Miriam Hansen's words, and destiny.

**

I'm snuggled up against Adam's side, my head resting in the cradle of his shoulder. My left hand is splayed out on his chest, the lightness of his skin shining out from between my fingers, making four perfect Vs of light. It's like I'm shooting rays of sun out from the crook of skin between each of my fingers. Out from a place that has brought so much music into this world.

And taken so many lives out of it.

"That's hotter than it should be." Adam's voice breaks the silence, and I tilt my head up to look at him. He's staring at the same place I was, examining my hand on his chest.

"It's beautiful," I say in agreement. His gaze moves to my face.

"This is going to sound totally weird after what just happened, but…" He stops as if he's not sure he should say whatever he was going to say. I have a feeling I already know what it is.

"If it makes it any less awkward, you're my first white boy, too, you know."

His face cracks into a huge smile, and his cheeks flush with embarrassment. I was right.

"How'd you know what I was going to say?"

"Just a good guess."

He pulls me in a little closer and kisses my temple. "Well, I for one liked it. A whole damn lot. Black or white or pink or yellow or upside down and inside out, K'acy McGee—this is going to sound a hundred-and-one kinds of cheesy—but everything about you is right."

There are a few seconds of silence before I find my response. "Copy that, and send it back."

I'm too embarrassed myself to say anything more. He kisses my temple again and exhales the breath he'd been holding since the end of his last heart-on-your-sleeve sentence.

"Come on," he says, sitting up. "Let's go to bed."

Adam helps me to my feet, and we walk to my bedroom hand-in-hand, leaving the colorful pagans alone to dance in silent celebration on my living room floor.

***

For the next four weeks, Jarrod is no longer alone at the bar at The King's Court on Wednesday nights. Adam sits there with him, each of them nursing a beer as they listen to me clean my soul. They don't talk much, but I know they like each other because their body language tells me so. One of them will occasionally smile or wink at me as I play. And Jarrod's face lights up when I end each week's set with "Soul to Squeeze." I think he likes knowing we still have secrets between us, even though "Soul to Squeeze" is the most trivial of the bunch. Jarrod's told me things I would never share with anyone, things he had to do to survive before we met, things we've talked about in the dead of night. And then there are the things *I've* told *him*. Things I don't think I'll ever tell Adam. Because he doesn't need to know. These secrets connect Jarrod and me, and that's never going away. No matter where life takes us.

Tonight, the three of us leave The King's Court together, but once we're out the door, Jarrod heads to the left to hop on a bus, and Adam and I cross the street to where his car is parked. I sometimes wonder if Big Al on the 43D misses me, but I'm not about to argue with having my own personal chauffeur/swooner. Plus, the car rides offer me and Adam a great opportunity to connect somewhere outside of the emotionally unpredictable confines of Ms. Sinclair's room. We never ride in silence. We share and joke and laugh and learn. A few more car rides and Adam will know more about me than anyone else in the world, except for my father and Jarrod.

Adam walks me to my apartment door, but he never stays on Wednesday nights. He knows I have to be at work by 8:00 the following morning, and he knows how exhausted I always am after so much mental housecleaning. He graciously leaves me at the door with a kiss and the promise of tomorrow, the pale skin of his palm brushing against the darkness of my cheek, filling me with its light.

Looking out the window, I watch Adam's car pull away from the curb just like always, thinking about how beautifully comfortable things have become for us. I don't want it to ever end.

The black car is there, lurking against the curb a block or so from my building, its driver still invisible behind the dark glass. I've seen it a handful of times over the last few weeks, always watching in perfect stillness from just far enough away. Each time I see it, my fear grows stronger, and when I think about the possibility of it being the police, panic rushes in, replacing my worry with something far more visceral. Could they be watching me because of something more than my visits to Latham Street? Did I miss some small detail?

Did I make a mistake?

To protect myself from all of the possible answers, I take the small wooden box out of the back of my closet, wrap its contents in a thick layer of paper towels, and toss them down the hallway trash chute.

***

Soon after I walk through the glass doors of Pine Manor the next morning, I learn from the shift change report that Ms. Sinclair got out of her bed four times last night. And all four times, when someone went in to help her, she was angry and very confused, yelling and telling everyone to stay away from her. She's been doing it a lot lately, and as a result, at the bottom of the page is a note from the Director of Nursing about possibly changing Ms. Sinclair's medication to keep her calmer and more compliant at night. It's often a sad necessity for Alzheimer's patients; it reduces a lot of dangers. I don't like the thought of Ms. Sinclair being in a medicated haze, but I understand.

I'm sure Dr. Kopsey will soon be talking with Adam about it. It won't be an easy conversation; it never is. The day nurse will tell Adam about Ms. Sinclair's night when he comes in today, if she hasn't called him about it already.

All I can do is make sure Ms. Sinclair is safe and comfortable, just like always. Outside of Sondra, no one here knows about Adam and me. But he knows I'm here for him, if he needs me to be.

A few minutes after Adam arrives at 10:30, I see the day nurse head back the hallway to Ms. Sinclair's room. I watch her go in, and then I watch Adam follow her back out. Together, they go into the family conference room. I wish I could be there to hold his hand.

I'm staring at the conference room door like a hawk when they come back out twenty minutes later. As he walks back to his grandmother's room, Adam wipes his face with the sleeve of his shirt. It breaks my heart.

After lunch, I wheel Ms. Sinclair back to her room. I haven't been able to talk to Adam all day, and the mass of emotion in my throat is getting harder and harder to swallow. When we round the corner into Ms. Sinclair's room, Adam is standing at her window, looking out over the parking lot. There's an empty Subway bag and a bottle of Sprite on the side table.

"Hey."

He turns at the sound of my voice, dropping his shoulders and offering us a small smile.

"Hey, ladies. How was lunch?" He walks across the room until he's standing right in front of his grandmother.

"Uninspiring," says Ms. Sinclair, looking up at him with admiration. "It's a good thing there was chocolate pudding for dessert. It may have been the only redeeming thing about that meal."

Sudden surprise hits Adam's face, as if a distant, lovely memory has flooded in. "Do you remember how you used to pack chocolate pudding in my lunch every day, Gram?"

I see what he's doing. He's hoping to dig up a scrap of her memory, something to connect them together again. Over the past few weeks, he's learned to take whatever he can get. Small bits at a time. Tiny pieces of the Evelyn Sinclair who raised him.

"Yes, dear. I do. It's really too bad you never ate it."

Adam looks confused. "But I always ate it. That was my favorite part of lunch."

"Don't be foolish, Bradley. I know you didn't eat it because I dumped it into the garbage every day. Such a waste." It's the first time she's confused him for the mysterious Bradley in many days. It must be destroying him inside to hear the name again.

Adam lifts his gaze away from her face and up to mine. All I can do is shrug and offer a nod of understanding.

"Gram, I'm Adam. Remember?"

"I don't care who you are, young man, we don't waste food."

He sighs and offers a resigned, "Yes, ma'am."

Ms. Sinclair doesn't say another word as we help her out of her wheelchair and into the recliner next to her bed. As she twists the cellophane off of a Starlight mint, Adam switches on the television, tuning it to a cooking show. She watches it contently as her grandson gives me a small kiss on the cheek just before I walk out the door.

***

Over dinner, Adam and I talk about his meeting with the day nurse. Just like I knew she would, she suggested he make an appointment with the doctor to discuss his gram's medication. He's already scheduled one for the middle of next week.

We're at the same Mexican place where he kissed me for the very first time, and just like that night, Adam isn't sitting across the table from me. He's sitting right next to me, as close as he can get. With his hand on my thigh. Louise McGee's imaginary discard pile has long since been burned to ashes. The only card I cared to hold on to was Adam's. Still, every time he puts his elbows on the table, I can't help but think of her and feel the last bits of bitterness slip away.

It seems I'm falling hard for Adam Sinclair. Just like Miriam Hansen knew I would. I can't help myself. He's the one.

***

It's 1:30 in the morning when Adam's cell phone rings. We're both sound asleep, our naked bodies curled around each other like some kind of oft-clichéd yin and yang. Dark and light. Opposite and yet interdependent. Each of us has now dipped one toe into the other, leaving a small dot of ourselves on the other one's soul.

Adam grabs the phone from the nightstand and clears his throat before offering a timid, "Hello?"

I only hear one-half of the conversation, but I know what's happened. We're out the door five minutes after he hangs up.

CHAPTER 17

In 2008, the floor at Terrebonne General consisted of alternating blue and white squares, highly polished and smelling of floor wax and disinfectant. For as long as I live, I'll never forget that floor. I watched the wheels of my father's wheelchair roll across it more times than I could count. I've never looked at that shade of blue quite the same way again.

But tonight, the floor in Penn Presbyterian is a mellow tan, and as Adam and I walk into the emergency center, his hand tenses in mine.

The nurse at the front desk asks Adam a slew of questions and then tells us his grandmother has suffered a concussion and, perhaps, a fractured hip. The doctor just sent her down to radiology for confirmation. Ms. Sinclair fell again while trying to navigate her way to the bathroom at Pine Manor. One of the night nurses found her and called an ambulance immediately.

Two hours pass before we learn Ms. Sinclair's hip does not appear to be fractured. Her wrist, however, is sprained, and they're going to keep her here for a few days because of the concussion. The doctor has also ordered an MRI of both her head and her hip, just to confirm the extent of the damage. They tell us they plan to do the MRIs later this morning.

As we sit in the family center, waiting for Ms. Sinclair to be put into a regular room, Adam is clearly shaken. His voice is unsure and unsteady. I wait with him until I have to head to the bus stop to go home and get ready for work. He wants to drive me, but I won't accept his ride knowing how much he needs to be here. Saying goodbye is far from easy, especially because of how vulnerable I know he's feeling. He looks exhausted, both physically and mentally. For a brief time I consider calling in sick, but I know my absence on this particular day might appear to be something more than a coincidence to my supervisors. I'm not ready to take the chance.

***

I don't hear a single peep from Adam until four o'clock in the afternoon. I've been on pins and needles all day, walking around with my phone on vibrate in the pocket of my scrubs. Personal phone use is completely prohibited while on duty, but I can't help myself.

The moment I feel my pocketed phone kick to life, I shuffle myself into a stall in the ladies' room.

Gram's finally in a room. She's sleeping.

Any news from the MRIs?

Concussion is minor. She's lucky.

Yes, she is. In many ways.

And not so lucky in many others.

Focus on the positives.

I'm trying, but it's hard. She looks so frail.

It's tough to see someone you love looking so vulnerable. Trust me, I understand.

I could use a friend tonight, if you don't have plans.

No plans. Want me to come to the hospital after work?

No. I'll come to your place when they kick me out of here.

Okay. Tell your gram I hope she gets back to Pine Manor real soon. Everyone's been asking about her today.

Really?

Yep. Any time an ambulance comes, it's a big deal, but night visits are particularly hard on everyone. She's got a lot of people thinking about her right now.

She'll appreciate that. I'll tell her when she wakes up.

Sounds good. I'll see you soon, Adam.

Not soon enough.

Those three words momentarily make me forget about the beautiful old woman asleep in a bed in Penn Presbyterian. They sing with promise. Because I feel exactly the same way.

Copy that, and send it back.

***

Ms. Sinclair and her grandson spend the weekend at Penn Presbyterian. And K'acy McGee spends her day off there, too. We're quite the trio, hanging out and watching television like we're at home in the living room on a Sunday afternoon.

Ms. Sinclair seems comfortable, though she doesn't seem to be fully aware of where she is. I'm certain she recognizes me, but it's like she can't pinpoint exactly where she knows me from. Regardless, she talks to Adam and me about whatever topic strikes her fancy at any given moment. I'm surprised at how often she laughs. I don't recall her ever laughing at Pine Manor, and I wonder if this new happiness is the result of Adam's presence. Or maybe mine. Or maybe it's the concussion. Or the medication. Regardless of the reason, it's nice to see her so content.

Sometime after lunch, we're told Ms. Sinclair can go back to Pine Manor in the morning. The social worker assigned to her case will take care of setting up an ambulance transport. She also tells us the doctor has already approved the change in Ms. Sinclair's medication in hopes of reducing her inclination to climb out of bed by herself again. Adam looks almost too relieved, as if changing her meds and taking her back to Pine Manor means his grandmother will somehow be okay.

About ten minutes into the drive home, Adam turns left where he should've turned right. Worry sinks into me immediately, and I can't help but turn and peek out the car's rear window, in search of the dark sedan. Maybe it's following us. Maybe Adam has seen it, too, and I'm going to have to explain it away. But, thankfully, the rear view is free of black cars, and my worry is exchanged for confusion. When I ask him where he's going, Adam smiles at me and tells me we're going to his place. It'll be the first time I've ever been there. My place is closer to Pine Manor, and since I have to go to work in the mornings and he doesn't, it's always made sense for us to hang out at my place instead of his. I wonder why he's decided today is the day.

Mount Airy is a beautiful community, especially in the dusky light of a sunset. But when Adam pulls into a driveway, I'm a bit confused. He once described his place as "a decent one bedroom," but the driveway belongs to a big-ass house, not an apartment building. The house is gorgeous, a gray stone facade with white trim. The landscaping is impeccable, and there are three other cars at the end of the driveway, all parked in front of the accompanying four-car garage. One is a Lexus sedan, the other is a Range Rover, and the third is a Cadillac Escalade. Adam parks his Passat in front of the last garage door on the right. I turn my head to find him smiling back at me. He looks a bit nervous.

"Dude. This is where you live?"

"Yep."

"Then why the hell have we been hanging out at my place for all this time?"

Adam laughs out loud as he opens his car door and gets out. I follow suit.

"I guess because your place is closer to Gram. And also because the walls here are surprisingly thin. Not to mention the fact that everyone who lives here is a little...let's just say... less-than-hip."

I raise my eyebrows at the notion of anyone living in this house being described as "less-than-hip," but when we walk in the front door, I see what he means.

An older gentleman, maybe around fifty-five or sixty, is standing in the foyer, sorting through his mail. He's wearing a three-piece suit and very shiny shoes. I immediately match him up with the Cadillac Escalade. Adam says a brief hello in passing, and I see the man's gaze quickly dart to our clasped hands. His eyes widen slightly, as if he's surprised such a nice white boy would have a black girlfriend on his arm. The man then offers me a close-mouthed smile and a sheepish nod. I say a bright "hello" and greet him with more charm than he probably deserves. Adam pulls me up the stairs.

Adam Sinclair's apartment is the entire third floor of what's essentially a mansion. But when he unlocks and opens the door, it isn't the closed-off, segmented floor plan I'd expected from an old house. It's totally open, save for a few exposed columns covered in stone. Someone clearly tore down walls and completely rebuilt the space into something more reminiscent of an artist's flat than a manor house. The hardwood flooring is polished to the nines, and a two-sided stone fireplace stands to the right-center of the room, with living-room furniture stationed on the side closest to the door and a bedroom suite stationed on the other. It's hard not to notice the bed is unmade.

Once the door closes behind us, Adam lets go of my hand and walks off to the left, toward the kitchen area. I purposefully cross my arms over my chest and slump my bodyweight down over one hip, like I'm perturbed about something. Even though I'm not.

When he gets to the kitchen, he turns around to find me still standing by the door, looking like a mother who's about to scold her child for lying to the teacher about what happened on the playground.

"What?" he asks, cocking his head to the side in flirtatious confusion.

"Thin walls and less-than-hip neighbors are no longer a valid excuse." I hold my stance, waiting for his response. He turns and opens the fridge, taking out a couple of beers and placing them on the granite countertop. The whoosh of carbonation when he pops their caps is the only sound in the room. He carries the open beers over to me and tries to hand me one. I keep my arms crossed and raise my brow in question. He smiles.

"Is embarrassment a valid excuse?" he asks.

"Embarrassment? Seriously? This place is beautiful. What in God's name do you have to be embarrassed about?"

He sighs and drops his shoulders at the sound of my words. "The fact that you've busted your ass taking care of people like my grandmother for the past six years and were only recently able to move out of an apartment you yourself described as 'a dump.' And here I am, unemployed and living in an apartment that costs eighteen hundred dollars a month. Trust me; it's embarrassing."

"This place costs eighteen hundred dollars a month?" I only say it because I have no idea what else to say.

"Yep." He holds the beer out to me again, and this time, I take it. He turns on his heels, and I follow him over to the sofa.

"Wow. So…if you don't work, how do you manage to pay that kind of money?" As soon as the question is out, I regret it. It's not only none of my business, but the answer is also obviously the true source of his embarrassment. As we sit down on the sofa, he looks only at the floor, watching the tip of his sneaker scuff against the hardwood. "I'm sorry. That's none of my business. I shouldn't have asked," I add. Besides, I think I may already know the answer.

"I wish I could say I invented some patented, eco-friendly water filter that's saving lives in the third world, or even that I invested in some creative dot-com startup, but nope. It's nothing like that." He pauses for a long time, clearly uncomfortable with the truth. "I recently aged into an embarrassingly huge trust fund. And the fact that it's courtesy of my giant dickhead of a father makes it even more humiliating."

"Oh." All other words escape me. Except judgmental ones he doesn't deserve.

"I *am* going to do something important with it someday, something way beyond spending it on an unnecessarily expensive flat some self-inflated commission-based Realtor found for me. I just haven't figured out what it is quite yet, and in the meantime, I want to be able to be with Gram. I guess I just didn't want you to see me differently because of it." He's genuinely worried about this changing my opinion of him. But it won't. Because Adam is still Adam, and I am still me.

I put my free hand on top of his knee. "I have no doubt important things will happen in this world because of you. But it won't be because of some water filter or a dot-com investment or even a trust fund. It will be because of your heart."

The embarrassment leaves his body in a surge of visible relief. Everything about him softens as I lean over and kiss him on the cheek.

"Thanks for the faith," he says, tilting his face to line up with mine.

"Anytime."

My mouth is six inches away from his and it takes less than a second for him to close the gap, smothering my lips with his. The kiss is not only fierce and lust-driven, it's also bursting with confidence and sexy, soul-affirming relief. His mouth is warm and sure, and though we've now kissed countless times since the day he showed up at Pine Manor, something about this kiss tells me he has more to share, more information to reveal. And I have more to discover.

But the truth is, just like his trust fund, whatever else he shares won't change a damn thing about how I feel. He may be embarrassed about who he is and what he has, but I'm not. Because I already know everything worth knowing about Adam Sinclair. I already know what's right.

As we kiss, my hands move across Adam's back and tug his shirt up and over his head. His skin is warm against my palms, and when he takes my shirt off and presses his chest to mine, a heady concoction of happiness and bass notes bubble around inside of me. I pull away from him, drop off the edge of the couch, and kneel on the floor, scooting myself between his open knees as I unbuckle his belt and open his zipper. When my mouth slides down over him, he lets out a small, throaty grunt. My head rises and falls in a rhythmic and arousing cadence while my palms grip the tops of his thighs. The soft slickness of my mouth hardens him, and it isn't long before he gathers my dark hair in one of his hands and slouches down in his seat, settling into my cadence by lifting his hips to meet my mouth. A few minutes later, I hear his voice asking me to come to the bed with him; it's quiet and gritty, filled with expectation. I lift my head and stand up. Before he rises to his feet, he leans forward and unfastens my jeans, sliding them to the floor. He pulls me forward and his mouth meets my stomach, covering my skin with soft, wet kisses. Adam's hands latch on to my hips, and as he stands, his lips and tongue glide up my body, enticing me as they go.

The unmade bed is soft and welcoming, and Adam doesn't waste a single second of our time there. He touches me for what feels like forever, teasing and seducing me until I can't hold back any longer. He's in complete control of my body, of every nerve ending in my skin, of every note in my head. Even before the rapid, euphoric pulse of my own happy release leaves my body, Adam is on his back, lifting me on top of him and entering me as if he's been given full and exclusive rights. We move together for a long time, flexing and arching and bending. I look down at the place where our bodies meet, where dark melts into light, and I realize the perfection of us, together.

I fall asleep snuggled into Adam's side, staring at my own hand splayed out on his chest until my breath steadies and my eyes drift closed. I don't sleep for long, though, because the sound of my phone ringing startles me awake a short time later. I look up at Adam who's now turned toward the digital clock on his bedside table. It says 12:56 a.m.

"Sorry," I say, climbing out of bed and heading out to the living room with a knot of curiosity and apprehension in my chest. I pick up my jeans and pull the phone from my pocket.

It's Jarrod.

"Hey. What's up? Everything okay?" I try to mask it, but I'm sure he can hear the concern in my voice. Late-night calls from Jarrod are seldom a good thing.

"Hey, Kace. Sorry to bother you." He's drunk. Actually, from the sound of it, he's *super* drunk. "But I've got a problem."

"What is it?"

"You're not home."

What's he talking about? "What makes you think that?"

"Because I've been ringing your door buzzer for like fifteen minutes."

"Oh. Why? What are you doing there?"

"Are you *finally* having a sleepover at The Mister's? It's about time, woman." The lilt in his voice is telling me he's quite pleased with his own little joke.

"Very funny. Seriously, why are you at my place?"

"Because I have some news to share with my best friend. It's good shit. But you're not here. So…I guess it's gonna have to wait."

What is he talking about? "The hell it is. Spill it."

Adam, wearing only his boxer briefs, walks into the room and narrows his eyes at me in confusion. I mouth "Jarrod" and "he's drunk," and he nods his head in understanding.

"Nope. And you can't make me."

"Jarrod, you do know that if you don't tell me, I'll sneak into your apartment and stab you in your sleep, right?" Adam's face recoils in surprise and a light smile touches both of our lips. I can hear a smile in Jarrod's response, too.

"The gig at The Upstage is an official sell-out, *and* Stevie says a rep from Naysayer Records is gonna be there."

"Seriously?"

"Seriously. It's awesome, right?"

I don't even know how to respond, because I don't quite know how to feel. I don't want to get my hopes up. A prolonged silence is all I can give him.

"Anyway, so…me and Stevie went out to celebrate, and I wanted to tell you in person, but you weren't here. So I called. But now I have another problem."

"And what's that?"

"Buses stop running at one o'clock on a Sunday night, and I don't have enough cash for a taxi."

"Drank up all your money, did you?"

"I blame it on Stevie."

"I'm sure you do." Adam walks up behind me and slides his hands around my waist. "Key's taped behind the picture on the landing. And please don't leave the toilet seat up." I feel Adam's chest shaking with light laughter against my back.

"You're a doll, Kace."

"I'll be home at seven to grab a quick shower and a change of clothes on my way to work so sleep with your clothes on, okay? Please."

"Yes, ma'am. Oh, and tell The Mister I said hello."

"Good night, Jar."

"Night."

I press the end icon and drop the phone onto the couch. Adam unwraps his arms, takes me by the hand, and leads me back to the bedroom. Just minutes after I share Jarrod's news with Adam, we're both sound asleep.

***

Ms. Sinclair is back at Pine Manor just before noon on Monday. She's bright-eyed and bushy-tailed during lunch. I overhear her talking about her hospital stay to the other ladies at the table. Some of what she says is true, but most of it is muddled. She tells them she was there because of a bee sting. Apparently, she's allergic. Still, despite her confusion over the details, I'm glad she remembers being in the hospital at all. It makes me wonder if she'll remember me being there with Adam.

Later in the day, it's clear Ms. Sinclair is in need of some rest. As I'm wheeling Mrs. Thompson through the lobby on the way back to her room for a nap of her own, I see Adam taking his grandmother from her bird-watching spot by the front window to her room. He winks at me on his way past. It makes me happy inside.

After Mrs. Thompson is settled in her bed, I head back out to the lobby to straighten up, hoping I might see Adam. He often heads out to get his own lunch while his grandmother naps. I'm collecting and organizing the pile of magazines and newspapers on the lobby table when a car pulls up and parks just outside the glass doors. I can tell from the hood emblem it's an old Jaguar.

My father was quite keen on pointing out fancy cars whenever we'd see one driving around Houma. Every time he'd spot an expensive classic car like this one, he'd declare that "a man can dream." His boss at the quarry, Ronald Chapman, drove an old Mercedes, and my father would sometimes talk about it as if it were his own. I remember seeing that car parked outside the funeral home the day Mr. Chapman buried his daughter, Lindsay. Daddy didn't even know the man had a grown daughter until he'd heard she died from an inoperable brain tumor.

My father made all of us go to the funeral, saying we needed to pay our respects as a family. After all, Charlie and I had met the young woman in the quarry parking lot just a few months before. I was five, and it was the first time I'd ever been to a funeral. I'll never forget her carefully pinned-up hair and bright red lipstick, and how "alive" she still looked, even lying in that glossy casket.

I'll also never forget the way my daddy looked at me that day. It was like he was frightened for me. Maybe even *of* me. Later that night, I heard him talking to Momma about how I must've overheard Lindsay telling her father she was dying the day we saw them in the quarry parking lot. He told my momma what I'd said that day, trying to explain it to himself as much as he was to her, I suppose.

I never told my father about those sorts of things after that. Because I didn't want him to look at me that way ever again.

A man in a suit gets out of the rear passenger door of the Jaguar and starts walking toward the entrance. The glass doors slide open just as the car pulls away from the curb. The man walks in and heads straight over to Marie who is shuffling papers on the reception desk, her sour face aimed down. The man does not make eye contact with me or anyone else in the room. He coughs lightly to get Marie's attention. They talk quietly for a few seconds, and he writes his name on the sign-in sheet. I can tell from Marie's gestures she's directing him to someone's room.

Just as the man is about to head back the hallway, Adam rounds the corner and stops in his tracks the moment his feet hit the lobby carpet. He's face-to-face with the man. The instant their eyes connect, Adam's posture changes. He straightens himself, puffs his chest, and raises his chin, as if he's preparing himself for a punch to the gut.

"Adam," the man says flatly. "So this is where you've been."

CHAPTER 18

Robert McGee—2004

There's nothing in this world more unpredictable than a teenaged girl. One minute she's looking at you all doe-eyed and sugar-tinged, and the next, she's scowling at you like you just ate her best friend for breakfast. There ain't nothing in the world that can prepare a man for life with a teenaged girl. I got two of 'em living under my roof right now, and when I walk up to the door after a full day working at the quarry, I'm never sure what's waiting for me inside.

Today is my fortieth birthday, which seems kinda funny because, most days, I don't feel a lick over twenty-five. And here I am, a single father of two girls who are nearly women themselves. Charlie's aiming to get her driver's license in a few weeks, and K'acy's already taller than her big sister. The two of them together are trouble-on-a-stick: beautiful and spirited and uninhibited by the rules of the grown-up world.

Charlie's boy-crazy and impervious to parental advice, even though I sure would like to give her some. I was exactly like those boys she runs around with when I was sixteen. I know what they want. And it ain't a conversation. It's a real shame her momma's departure left Charlie so wounded. I know she's turning to those boys for artificial affection. I try my best to give her love and tell her how much she deserves a perfect life, but I don't think she cares to aim that high. I think she's managed to convince herself she doesn't deserve one.

K'acy, on the other hand, is trouble for entirely different reasons. She can't keep her fingers off the Music Man StingRay bass guitar I got her for Christmas. She's got her heart set on being a musician, practicing every second she isn't in school or doing homework. Mr. Simpson, the music teacher at Terrebonne High, gives her lessons twice a week. I pay for them by tuning, repairing, and polishing the school's instruments once a month. K'acy's getting pretty good, and someday soon, the guys and I are gonna invite her to play with us down at Jackson's on a Saturday night. It'll be her first gig, and I'm gonna be about as proud as a man can be when she lays down her first riff. The girl's got a light around her that'll just about blind you, especially if you don't see her coming.

It's nearly seven o'clock by the time I get home from work, and when I open the front door, K'acy's standing there, wearing a smile the size of the entire bayou. We haven't been to church since Louise left, but the girl is dressed in her Sunday best. Behind her, on the dining room table, are a pair of lit candles and three empty plates. They're flanked by a bunch of Louise's fancy silverware and crystal that hasn't seen the light of day in over six years. From the smell wafting out of the kitchen, I'm guessing my girls made me a pot of Creole jambalaya for my birthday dinner.

My mouth is watering before I even get my boots off.

When I hug K'acy and thank her and her sister for the surprise, she rolls her eyes at me, all dramatic and sassy, and tells me Charlie didn't have anything to do with the jambalaya. She says her sister never even came home from school today. Granted, not coming home until nine or ten at night is pretty par for the course with Charlie, but still…she knows it's my birthday. And she knows we always celebrate together. Just usually not with candlelight and crystal.

After we eat, I tell K'acy her sister missed one hell of a meal and the credit is all hers. The jambalaya tasted just like her momma's, but she doesn't look happy when I point it out. Instead, she tells me she seasoned it differently and used better sausage than Louise ever did. I apologize for my error and tell her again how delicious it was.

She sings happy birthday, and I blow out the candle on a single chocolate cupcake, wishing yet again that my girls would quit growing up so fast. Then K'acy slides a small package across the table toward me. It's wrapped in blue paper and topped with a light green bow. She's smiling another bayou-sized smile, silently telling me how proud she is of whatever's in this box. I pull off the bow and tear open the paper.

Inside the box is a man's ring. My wedding ring, to be exact. It's another thing that hasn't seen the light of day in over six years. At least I didn't think it had. I pick up the ring and examine it carefully. K'acy's had it polished smooth and then re-engraved. On the inside of the ring, where a circle of words used to say *Louise & Robert 5/22/89*, it now says *Love You Daddy 9/14/04*. On the outside of the ring, a string of tiny musical notes are etched into the metal. I look at K'acy, and she confirms they're from the chorus of a song I've been singing to my girls since the day they were born, Otis Redding's "That's How Strong My Love Is."

I can't stop the emotion from coming out of me, and before I know it, I'm a grown man who's crying like a sappy granny and hugging on his teenage daughter like she's the Lord Jesus himself. I'm grateful to K'acy for hugging me back. And for confirming that the shot-in-the-dark fathering I've been doing for all these years has worked on at least one of my girls.

I put the ring on my finger, and tell my beautiful, soulful daughter how much I love it. And her.

CHAPTER 19

No one moves. Not even Marie. We're all frozen, holding our collective breaths and waiting for someone else to move first. Adam doesn't reply to the man, at least not with his voice. It's his posture and facial expression that are screaming back at him. The anger and bitterness are undeniable, but there's also fear and vulnerability in his stance. It's almost as if Adam is holding something in and letting something out at the very same time.

A thick smirk quickly settles across the man's face. And it's not a friendly or sheepish or sassy smirk. It's one that says he's proud to have just opened some kind of personal Pandora's box and tossed a dense slab of complication into Adam's world. The word *diabolical* pops into my head. I don't know who the man is, but I have a feeling something is about to change for Adam. I have a feeling the man is about to mess with everything.

"What are you doing here?" Adam's voice is a mixture of disdain and acrimony. He's trying to steady his voice, but I can hear the anger and fear in it. The smirk leaves the man's face as he thrusts his hands into his pockets, as if he's suddenly in need of something important housed inside of them. Only he doesn't pull anything out. Instead, his hands sit motionless inside the pockets. The posture exudes cockiness and self-importance.

"I'm here to see my mother. Why else would I be here?" He shrugs. It's Winston Sinclair, the giant dickhead, up close and in person. Wow. "It seems to me the better question would be, what are *you* doing here?" Adam glances over at me for the briefest fraction of a second before his father adds something else. "Your mother and I have been looking for you. You could've called."

Just then, Sondra walks into the room with Mrs. Rupert on her arm. They're chatting about yesterday's worship service. Pastor Glickson comes every Sunday morning to provide for our residents who can't make it to church anymore. Mrs. Rupert is hard of hearing so Sondra's voice is even louder than usual. I hear her say something about Daniel and the lions as they walk across the lobby. I look over and offer Sondra a quiet nod. She and I both turn toward Adam and his father at the same time. Mrs. Rupert starts talking. It's the only noise in the room.

Winston Sinclair turns and looks at Sondra first. Then, a second later, he looks at me. Our eyes meet, and I almost drop to my knees when I see it. He looks just like Adam, only older and more worn, and there is a deep stillness in his eyes. Like he's lost.

But that's not what makes my knees want to buckle. It's what I see *inside* that does that.

It's going to be bad, an ending no one deserves. *No one.* Not even a giant dickhead.

Winston Sinclair is going to die soon. And he's going to suffer. A lot.

***

Adam and his father disappeared down the hallway and into Ms. Sinclair's room over a half hour ago. The door is closed, and despite my best efforts at repeatedly sauntering down the hallway to eavesdrop, I hear only muffled voices.

Another ten minutes pass before the door opens and Adam's father walks out. I'm loitering near Ms. Sinclair's room, folding Mr. Rauch's blanket for the fifth time, when he walks past me. Winston Sinclair keeps his chin up and his eyes straight ahead. He doesn't acknowledge my existence with a smile or a nod or even a sideways glance. Once he turns left at the end of the hallway, presumably to head back to the lobby or the exit, I walk over to Ms. Sinclair's room and peek into the now open door.

Adam's back is to me, and he's looking out the window, leaning forward with his hands resting on the windowsill. Ms. Sinclair is sitting in her recliner watching a cooking show on the television. She looks over at me as I walk into the room.

"Why hello, dear! It's lovely to see you again."

Adam turns around at the sound of her voice.

"It's lovely to see you, too, Ms. Sinclair. I just stopped in to see if there's anything you need." I clasp my hands in front of me and smile at both of the Sinclairs in the room. Adam does not smile back.

"No, dear, I'm fine. My son was here a few minutes ago, you know."

"You must be very happy to see him."

A huge grin settles across her face. Adam, on the other hand, is wearing a scowl.

"I haven't seen him in quite some time. He lives very far away."

"Yes, I understand he lives in Seattle. How nice of him to come visit with you and Adam." I ignore Adam's continued scowl and walk over and sit down on the corner of the bed. I want to see her closer, to make sure she's really okay.

"Oh Adam!" she says, turning to face him, her eyes lit with a surprising amount of emotion. "You should go now. You know how your father is. He's not going to be very happy if you're still here when he comes back."

"I'm not going anywhere, Gram." Adam steps over to us and puts his hand on his grandmother's shoulder, as if to reassure her about something. "Remember? I'm going to stay right here."

"Oh, yes, well...then you'd better at least get your homework done."

Adam's eyes close briefly in frustrated acceptance. The scowl drops off his face and is replaced by sadness. "Yes, ma'am," he says with resignation. He inhales a deep breath and looks straight at me. "Gram, do you mind if I step into the hallway with K'acy for a moment? I have something I need to ask her."

"Go ahead, dear." Ms. Sinclair's attention returns to the television as Adam and I head out into the hallway. He closes the door behind us as he runs a hand through his hair.

"So, that was your dad, huh?"

"The one and only."

"You look a lot like him."

"So I've been told." Adam's shoulders slump, and he looks down at his feet. "He wants to separate us again."

"What do you mean?"

"He wants to move her to Seattle. He says it's so he can monitor her care better, but I know that isn't the real reason."

Move her to Seattle? Seriously? Winston Sinclair just kicked "giant dickhead" up another notch. Anger wells in my chest, but I try my best to hide it.

"What do you think the real reason is?"

"I can guarantee you that, until he saw me here, there was no way in hell he wanted to take her back to Seattle with him.

He probably came here to settle her affairs and make sure her will was in order or something. Then he was going to go back to Seattle and forget all about her again. But then he saw me here, and now, since he can't control what *I* do anymore, he's trying to control *her* instead."

I want to say something to make him feel better. I want to tell him Ms. Sinclair is not going anywhere. "If it helps, I doubt your gram's doctors would approve of a relocation right now. She's pretty fragile. Plus, patients like your grandmother need consistency in their care and seldom do well with relocations. With any luck, the doctors' judgment will be all the convincing your father needs to let her stay right where she is."

"It takes more than luck when it comes to my father." Adam crosses his arms over his chest and takes a deep breath. "He actually tried to kick me out of the room this afternoon. He said he wanted to talk with Gram alone, but I said I wasn't going anywhere. I told him whatever he has to say to her, he can say to me, too. He walked out of here all pissed off, saying that when he gets back, I'd better be gone. I told him he can go to hell."

We're both silent for a few moments while I carefully chose every word I'm about to say. "Just do me a favor with all this, please. Try not to upset your gram. I totally understand why you're pissed off at your dad, but please don't argue with him in front of her. Please try to keep things calm. She doesn't need any more turmoil than what's already happening inside of her own body. And, just as a heads-up, if any of the doctors or nurses ever hear or see you doing anything that disturbs a patient, they'll kick you out of here in a heartbeat. Ms. Sinclair needs you here. Just please try to remember that."

He looks embarrassed, as if he knows he's gotten a well-deserved scolding. Adam's obvious shame makes me want to wrap my arms around him and assure him I know he's just trying to do the right thing.

"You're absolutely right. I won't do it again. And I won't let *him* do it again either. I promise. And I'm sorry."

I nod in understanding, but I don't say anything else. Instead, I think about what it will be like for Adam when the losses strike.

It will be two this time; one that's loved and one that's not. But loss is loss, and it's never easy, not even where there's no love. It will be the first time in a long time I've been this close to it. But when the time comes, I'll do what's right. I'll find a way around whoever is in that black car and make a trip to Latham Street, no matter how risky it is. I'll handle what needs to be handled. Because I made that promise to myself a long time ago, and I'll never forget it.

**

The rest of the afternoon passes without another appearance from Winston Sinclair, but when I walk into Pine Manor first thing on Tuesday morning, I see him sitting with Dr. Kopsey through the tiny, rectangular window in the family conference room's door. He's wearing a suit and tie, as if he's at some kind of business meeting instead of a nursing home. Before I even take my jacket off, my phone is out of my purse and I'm sending a text to Adam.

Your dad's here.

WHAT?

He's talking to Dr. Kopsey.

What are they talking about?

I don't know. They're in the conference room.

I'm on my way.

Ok. Drive safe.

Mr. Sinclair and Dr. Kopsey are in the conference room for another fifteen minutes before they come out, shake hands in the hallway, and go their separate ways. Dr. Kopsey says hello as he passes me. Winston Sinclair does not. Instead, he strides by me quickly and heads straight for his mother's room. I follow him into the open door and immediately begin to busy myself by pulling a clean sweater set out of her closet. Ms. Sinclair is still in her nightgown, sitting in her chair and watching the morning news. Mr. Sinclair stands in the corner of the room, watching us both.

"Good morning, Ms. Sinclair. How was your night?"

"Just fine," she says, waving her hand at me dismissively. I lay the sweater set down on the bed and walk over to Adam's father. As I offer him my hand and introduce myself, I try not to look at his eyes, keeping my focus on the tip of his nose. I don't want to see it again.

"Hi, I'm K'acy. I'm one of Ms. Sinclair's nursing aides. You must be her son. She told me yesterday you're here for a visit." His grip is lighter than I expected, like he doesn't really want to touch me. I don't really want to touch him either, so it doesn't bother me one bit.

"Winston Sinclair," he says. "And, yes, I'm her son."

"It's nice to meet you. Your mother is a wonderful patient. We all enjoy having her here at Pine Manor." I turn around and walk back over to the closet, pulling out a pair of pants as I talk. "She's mentioned you're from Seattle. How long are you in town for?"

He's unmoving and unfriendly. "I'm not quite sure yet."

"Well, welcome to Philadelphia. Is it your first time here?" I already know the answer, but I ask him anyway, just to kill some time until Adam gets here.

"No." One word is all he offers. So much for killing time.

"I'm going to help your mom get dressed now. Do you want to wait in the hallway?" His brow furrows and his eyes narrow as if he's suspicious of something. "Ms. Sinclair might be more comfortable that way."

"Yes, of course. Mother," he says, directing his attention toward Ms. Sinclair, "I'm going to step into the hallway while this young woman helps you get dressed." She waves her hand dismissively again, as if to shoo him off. He nods at me and steps out of the room, closing the door behind him. I'd bet any money he's already forgotten my name.

As I help Ms. Sinclair out of her nightgown, I hear voices outside the door. I can't hear what they're saying, but I can tell one voice is Adam's and the other is his father's. The voices are low, and the tone is telling me there's anger in both of them. I take my time getting Ms. Sinclair dressed and into her wheelchair, talking to her the whole time so there's no chance of her hearing the discussion taking place on the other side of the door. I put her socks and shoes on last, retying them multiple times until I hear the voices settle. Before I wheel her out of the room, I brush her hair and fasten the gold owl brooch with the big, sparkly eyes to her sweater. On our way to the door, I tell her how beautiful she looks.

I push Ms. Sinclair's chair out the door, passing between Adam and his father, turn left, and start heading for the dining room, but the moment she sees Adam standing there, Ms. Sinclair brightens into a million shades of excitement. "Bradley! You're here! I'm so thrilled. Did you hear the good news? He's come back! Winston's come back."

It only takes an instant for everything to change. Adam's expression falls at the sound of Bradley's name, and his father, who's now standing behind me, begins to charge forward. He rushes past me in a burst of purpose and power, heading straight toward Adam. But before he gets there, Winston Sinclair turns on his heels to face Ms. Sinclair. He's filled with some unknown rage, and as he bends forward to line his face up with hers, words come out of his mouth. They're harsh and acidic.

"*That* is Adam, Mother. *Not* Bradley. Jesus, do you really not remember?"

I've changed my mind. Winston Sinclair does deserve the ending he's going to get. He deserves every single second of what's to come.

I can't stop myself.

"Your mother has Alzheimer's, Mr. Sinclair. There are a lot of things she doesn't remember, and if you can't understand that, then maybe it's best for you to go back to Seattle sooner rather than later."

Adam's mouth drops open. It takes everything in me not to say anything else.

Mr. Sinclair straightens himself and stares at me for a long, intense moment. This time, I don't look at the tip of his nose, I look straight into his eyes. Because this time, I *want* to see it. This time, I don't want to miss a single detail. I want to see *all* of it.

My gut rises up into my throat when Winston Sinclair turns his back on me and comes face-to-face with his son.

"I will see *you* later," he says, poking an angry finger at Adam's face. "And don't be late." Mr. Sinclair rushes down the hallway and out the door without so much as a single backward glance.

"Sorry, Gram." Adam is now the one bending down to meet Ms. Sinclair's face, only his expression is sympathetic rather than infuriated. I walk around the side of the wheelchair and stand next to him.

"I don't understand." Ms. Sinclair's face droops and her brow creases. Her hands fidget in her lap. Their movement sends specks of reflected light off her brooch and onto the walls and ceiling around us. They're dancing and twitching and flickering like little, heatless dots of fire. Adam drops to his haunches in front of his grandmother and tries to meet her gaze. She lifts her hand and puts it against Adam's cheek, softly shaking her head and pursing her lips as she shrugs her shoulders. "You're not Bradley?"

"No, Gram. I'm Adam."

"Where is he then?" She drops her hand from Adam's face and looks down at her lap.

"I don't know. Because I don't know who Bradley is."

Ms. Sinclair's head quickly rises, and she lifts her chin proudly into the air. She speaks as if she can't believe what Adam has just said. "Why, Bradley is Winston's son, of course."

I can feel the weight of her words pressing down on Adam's heart.

"No, Gram. *I'm* Winston's son."

"Yes, and Bradley is his *other* son."

CHAPTER 20

Gerald Shrewsbury—Room number 101

    I spent most of my life next to a pond, searching for needles of red darting amongst the reeds. The Eastern Red Damselfly, *Amphiagrion saucium*, was my life's work. An insect as long as a pinky finger and as slender as a poppy stalk may not seem very intriguing at first, but let me assure you, the moment you see the multifaceted eyes of such a creature through a magnifying glass, or watch it fly gracefully through the air while attached to its partner in a heart-shaped mating wheel, wonder and amazement will strike. It's hard not to be rendered speechless by nature's stunning beauty and complexity when looking at an insect as wondrous as the Eastern Red.

    For many years, each and every time I saw a flicker of crimson settle on a blade of grass and fold its graceful wings down over its body, my heart would warm and fascination would take hold. Some people dedicate their lives to understanding the human body; I dedicated mine to understanding an insect's.

    Midair dips and dives that evoke thoughts of alien flight; four wings that work together in perfect, mind-blowingly complex harmony; a complete metamorphosis that rivals caterpillar-to-butterfly or grub-to-beetle; aquatic larvae that use harpoon-like jaws to capture prey—these are the things that made the Eastern Red Damselfly the love of my life. And these are the things I dreamed about every single night, until the day I died. The Eastern Red was my everything.

When the Pennsylvania Entomological Society honored me with their Entomologist of the Year Award in 1980, I saw my life's biggest goal realized. I had published three studies and was rightfully admired by many researchers in the international entomological community. To celebrate, I took to the wetlands, immersing myself in even more research and observations. I loved the steady buzz of wings beating through the air, the tickle of six tiny legs climbing over my skin, the soggy taste of the marsh constantly settled in the back of my throat.

By the time I was fifty-five, I had taken more notes than Darwin himself and I set my sights on writing a book about damselflies. A book the average Joe could appreciate, one that avoided scientific jargon and focused instead on my passion for this charismatic insect. I wanted to write a book that spoke about the importance of nature to human beings themselves. I wanted to connect people to the Eastern Red with a trail of passionate and thought-provoking words about nature herself. I wanted everyone to have the chance to feel what I felt every time I saw a flash of red skimming across a pond.

But it didn't work out that way. I had my first stroke before a single word ever hit the paper. Without any family to help, my recovery was long and arduous. It was months before I could walk well enough to return to the wetlands. A speech therapist visited twice a week to teach me how to talk again, and an occupational therapist helped me relearn how to write. By the time I could hold a pencil and form written words correctly, nearly a year had passed. But, as soon as I felt I could, I started writing. I wrote fast and fevered, putting words to paper as quickly as I could, as if I was on a mission from Mother Nature herself. I spent long hours hunched over my desk, sorting through my notes, looking for ways to link people with nature through stories about the Eastern Red. I was halfway done with the manuscript when my second stroke hit. The blood thinners failed to do their job, and I was struck hard. My ability to write—and walk—was completely gone.

From that day on, the words came out all wrong. I called girls, boys and cats, dogs. My brain knew what to say, but it couldn't make my mouth form the right words. And it couldn't make my hand hold a pencil anymore either. The Eastern Red's lessons got tangled up in knots inside of me and no amount of therapeutic cajoling was ever able to get them out.

I lived in Pine Manor for the last twenty years of my life, the right side of my body frozen and stiff, unyielding and useless. I chewed on the left, scratched on the left, breathed on the left. But when I dreamed, I dreamed with both sides of me. I dreamed about the Eastern Reds, rising up out of the reeds and surrounding me every single night. Observing me as I had observed them. They had so much to tell me, and I'll forever be disappointed I wasn't able to share their message with the world.

On the night I died, my left hand held my last polyresin-encased damselfly against my chest. I had given the rest of my collection to the Natural History Museum years ago, but I couldn't bear to part with my Eastern Red. He was my only comfort, aside from the young lady at my side. She was the one who handed him to me when the time came. And she was the one who listened to the last breath of air leave my body.

She was the one who gave me peace.

CHAPTER 21

Adam and I are sitting in Wicked Mocha, each of us nursing a warm cup of coffee. His with a touch of cream, mine black. His elbows are on the table.

We walked here together after my workday ended and he said goodbye to his grandmother. Winston Sinclair stayed away from Pine Manor for the rest of the day. I'm certain that in doing so, he made what was probably the smartest decision of his life. I think if he had come back, his own son would've smacked him in the face with the closest bedpan.

Either that, or I would have.

After I took Ms. Sinclair to breakfast this morning, Adam left. He walked right out the door of Pine Manor without saying another word. I spent the morning worrying about what he was doing, and wondering if there really is a Bradley and whether or not Dr. Kopsey agreed to let Mr. Sinclair take his mother back to Seattle.

When Adam returned to Pine Manor just after lunch, his grandmother was napping, and when I asked him where he went, he would only say he had to get out of there for a while. He said he had to think about what it all meant. His uncertainty and hurt was—and is—undeniable.

Adam spent the rest of the afternoon with his grandmother, treating her no differently than he ever has. I checked in on them several times, and they followed their usual routine to a T, playing cards and watching the cooking channel until it was time for dinner.

I'm not sure what he's going to do or say in this coffee shop, but I'm not going to press him for anything. I'm just going to sit here and take whatever he's willing to give.

"Crazy morning, huh?" He takes a sip of his coffee after the words are out.

"Yep." I take a sip of mine, too.

"Sure was fun to meet my father, wasn't it?"

"Not so much."

"Good thing I warned you about the giant dickhead part."

"Yep. And now that I've met him, I can think of a few other appropriate descriptors, too."

"I'll bet you can." His joking tone turns serious with the next sentence. "I've got a few new ones myself."

I don't know what to say, so I just take another sip of my coffee.

"I'm going to see him tonight." Adam looks down at the table, as if he's ashamed of his words.

"Oh." I pause for a moment before I continue. "I bet that's going to be one hell of an interesting conversation."

"I agreed to have dinner with him before Gram even called me Bradley, so it was going to be an interesting conversation in the first place, but now... Now, *interesting* doesn't even begin to describe the conversation we're going to have."

No one can blame him for being pissed off. His grandmother might be taken away from him again, and he might have a brother he never even knew existed. He's obviously pained by all the lies he suspects he's been told his whole life. It's like watching him put together a puzzle, knowing all the while that the resulting picture is going to be nothing but a heartbreaking portrait of lies and deceit.

"Do you think he'll give you any answers?"

"I'm not going to give him a choice. I'm not walking away until I have every answer I deserve."

I nod in agreement and silently hope he isn't making a mistake by going to see his father while the wound is so fresh.

"Where are you meeting him?"

"Dante's on Fifth. Whatever that is."

"It's a restaurant." Which means it's a public place. Good.

"Want me to kick him in the shins for you?" He's back to joking again, and a small smile crosses his lips.

"That'd be nice."

"I'll see what I can do."

And with that, my bed-headed swooner and I finish our coffee without another word about Winston Sinclair and his giant dickheaded ways.

Adam kisses me goodbye in front of the coffee shop twenty minutes later. I wish him good luck, knowing tonight is probably going to change everything for him.

***

I'm sitting on the couch, eating takeout from The Golden Duck and watching a rerun of *Castle*, when my phone rings. I'm expecting it to be Adam with news about the dinner with his father, but what I see on the screen instead is a 985 area code.

Charlie.

"Hello?"

"K'acy? Are you there?" She's whispering. No, I think maybe she's crying.

"Yeah, I'm here. Charlie? Is that you?"

"I…um…yes, it's me." She sniffs and coughs, and her voice gets a bit clearer. She's pulling herself together. "Hey. How are you, little sis?"

"What's wrong? Are you crying? What's going on?" Something flutters around in the pit of my stomach, churning up my insides.

"It's okay. I'm just…it's just a little crazy here right now, that's all." I hear voices in the background. Lots of voices.

"Where are you? What do you mean it's a little crazy?"

"I'm at a bar. A restaurant, I mean. I just wanted to say hey and find out how you are."

"I'm fine. I'm great, actually. But you're not. I can tell by your voice. Please tell me what's going on. Are you in trouble?"

"Kinda. Yeah. I mean, I know you're tired of me asking, but I really need some money right now."

She's asked me for money a million and one times before, but this time something is different. This time my heart is racing because her voice is all wrong. It isn't Charlie on the other end of the phone. It's panic.

"You have to promise me you aren't gonna give it to someone else. Promise me you're not gonna let some *what's-his-face* gamble it away."

"It isn't like that this time," she says, her quivering voice revealing a different kind of angst, one I've not heard before. "I promise. Really. I promise."

"And you also have to promise you're gonna call me every week from now on, so I know you're okay. I don't like not knowing if you're safe. Okay?"

There's more sniffling on the other end of the phone. "Yes. Yes. I promise. Just please…"

For the first time in a long time, I believe every word she's saying. It's like a desperate beggar is pushing the words out of her mouth; I think my sister is quietly pleading for something that will save her life. I know instantly that the trouble she's in is not the same as all the times before. "How much do you need?"

"Like eight hundred."

Eight hundred? That's a month's rent. Half a month's salary.

"I'll see what I can do. Which Western Union?"

"Number 697. On Barrow Street," she says, obvious relief behind the words. "Promise you'll send it?"

"I promise."

"When?"

"Tomorrow. By ten. Okay?"

"Good. Okay." She sucks in a deep breath and then exhales it slowly, as if to steady herself. I nod in understanding even though I know she can't see me. "Thank you, K'acy. Thank you so much. I'll pay you back someday. Seriously. As soon as I can, I'll pay you back. And this is all I'm gonna ask for ever again. Really. This is gonna fix things for me, you know? Like, for real. This is gonna help me get it all back together."

"I believe you," I say.

"I mean it."

"Just be safe, Charlie. Okay?"

"Okay," she replies. "I'll talk to you later. Next week."

"Sounds good."

"Love you, sis."

"Love you, too, Charlie."

"Bye." The phone goes silent and my fluttering gut turns over on itself. All I can do is hope we both just made promises we can actually keep.

After I use my phone to Google "24-hour pawnshops in Philadelphia," I head back to my bedroom to find my father's wedding ring.

***

It's nearly midnight by the time I hear from Adam. I expected him to text or call, but instead, he's ringing my doorbell. I'm suddenly thankful to still be in my street clothes and not in my pajamas. I'm also thankful tomorrow is my day off. I head across the room to let him in.

"Hey." I open the door and see an exhausted Adam standing there with his arms slack at his sides.

"Hey."

"Are you okay?" *Because you don't look okay.* I step aside and motion for him to come in.

"Funny you should ask that." He walks into the room, and I close the door behind him. "Because 'okay' is not one of the words I would use to describe myself right now." He turns to look at me.

"Then what words would you use?"

"Number one: tired." He starts walking toward me.

"Yeah, I can kinda see that."

"Number two: angry." He stops and stands right in front of me.

"Totally understandable."

"Number three: confused." He puts his hands on my hips and looks me square in the eye.

"Also, totally understandable."

"Number four: in love."

I must look confused as hell myself, standing still as a stone with my mouth hanging open. A second later he adds, "With you."

"Umm… Have you been drinking?" I narrow my eyes, but he doesn't move a muscle.

"Number five: completely sober."

I shake my head in disbelief at what's happening. Struck again by the astounding accuracy of Miriam Hansen's words. I put on a smile so he knows I'm not about to trample on his heart. "Man, your father must've done a real number on you tonight."

He presses his thumbs against the front of my hips, but his face doesn't change.

"That he did. And it made me realize something. The whole time I was sitting there, listening to his bullshit, all I could think about was you. Yes, I'm desperate to know if Gram was telling the truth about who Bradley is, but I realized all my confusion and anger is because of *my father's* life, not mine. I'm clear as a bell when it comes to *my* life right now. And that's because of *you*."

Notes start to throttle around in my brain, bouncing and echoing and singing. They fill my heart with "Soul to Squeeze" and "That's How Strong My Love Is" and "Ecce Homo" and every other song I've ever heard in my entire life. Before he can say another word, I stretch up onto my tiptoes and kiss him. My tongue dances against his, following the rhythms in my head. It's like the music inside me is melting us together.

Adam wraps his arms around my back and holds me tight as the kiss sinks deeper. A shockwave of emotion shudders through me at the idea of someone—no, of *Adam Sinclair*—being in love with me. It's stupendous and terrifying all at once. It means all the love I've been sending out for all these years has finally been received. And, most importantly, returned. To be loved is a far more significant thing than anything else in this world, and to be loved by someone who doesn't share your blood is something to be treasured even more. Because *that* kind of love isn't given. It's earned.

When our lips separate, Adam tilts his head down. There's a new energy on his face. I don't see anger and confusion anymore. I only see strength and purpose. He lets go of my waist, and his hands fall to his sides.

"My father is not a good person," he says, with a voice full of clarity. "I've sensed it my whole life, but now I know it for sure. He refused to tell me anything when I told him what Gram said about Bradley. All he would say was she was mistaken. I fought for answers, but he gave me nothing. Nothing." He takes a step backward, putting some distance between us.

"I know you don't want to hear this again, but maybe it's better that way. I mean, maybe it's better not to know the truth." I put my hand in my pocket, fidgeting with the folded stack of crinkled twenty-dollar bills from the pawnbroker. A burst of sadness ripples through me like a rapid flash of ignited gunpowder. Here and gone in a heartbeat. "It might be something that hurts."

"Maybe." He takes a breath and cracks a small smile.

"I hear there's a lot to be said for the whole *ignorance is bliss* thing."

"I'm not sure I'm ever gonna believe that. Not when it comes to the possibility of me having a brother out there somewhere."

I nod my head in understanding, sensing he's already mourning the loss of something he's not even sure he's ever had. I need to pull him back into what's real. "Do you wanna know something that's definitely the truth?"

"Yes. Please."

"I'm in love with you, too."

Adam Sinclair's mouth stretches into a sea of happiness, teeth shining between a pair of dimples deep enough to sink in. "Now that's what I'm talking about," he says. He steps up to me and hitches his hands back onto my hips. His smile fades as his lips move to connect with mine. The kiss is rushed and needy, sending my endorphins into another lust-induced frenzy. My veins throb with energy, and all I can do is return the kiss and hope he understands the importance of this new "us."

As my fingers work to unbutton his shirt, his hand moves to the back of my neck, cradling my head and holding me against him. I run my palms across his bare chest and down to the zipper of his jeans as his tongue explores my mouth, reaching into it as if searching for more truth. For more words he can trust. We don't disconnect until we fall into my bed, naked and wrapped around each other, both of us hanging on to the last small fragments of self-control.

I lie on my back, Adam's mouth leaving mine to pepper kisses down my neck and then onto my stomach, tickling and enticing as they go. He gently spreads my thighs and settles his head between them. My body is tossed into a cyclone of bliss with every warm, wet stroke of his tongue. A symphony of desire spills out of him and seeps into me, crushing me with its meaning and making me realize that all I want from him is everything he has. All of his light and all of his love. And in return, I'll give him peace. I'll give him me.

Just before I reach the edge, he's gone, pulling away and flipping my body over. Adam lifts my hips until I'm up on my knees, facedown in the pillow. A few minutes after he comes inside, he exhales a jagged sigh. The sound of it makes me lose all my words, all my thoughts. His hands and lips continue to march across my body, moving wherever they want and taking whatever they need, until I'm shouting Adam Sinclair's name with a jagged breath of my own and hoping this feeling never stops.

***

I'm exhausted, nearly asleep against Adam's chest, when he offers me something else. Something surprising.

"I wasn't being entirely honest with you when I said my father gave me nothing tonight." His voice is solid and unemotional. Like what he's about to say is anything but important. "He did give me something."

"Oh yeah? And what did he give you?"

"He told me he's not going to take Gram back to Seattle."

CHAPTER 22

My daddy took me and Charlie to the Louisiana State Fair the summer I turned sixteen. It was a five-hour drive up to Shreveport on I-49, and I just about threw myself out of the car numerous times during the trip. Charlie sass-talked my father the entire way, second-guessing his every move and regularly accusing him of embarrassing her for one reason or another. I remember her griping to him about the broken air conditioner in the Buick. She said the wind was going to make her hair look like a hickory horned devil by the time we got there. When she wondered out loud how she was gonna nab herself one of those cute rodeo boys with her hair all wild and crazy, he passed her the bandana from his pocket and told her to tie it over her head like Bret Michaels. For a hot second, I thought Charlie might literally explode with fury.

She gritted her teeth for the rest of drive, and the moment my father parked the car in the fairgrounds parking lot, she was out the door. We didn't see her again until we came back to the car ourselves, nearly eight hours later, and found her leaning against the fender with a rodeo boy's tongue shoved down her throat. Daddy didn't cuss at Charlie or lay a single hand on the boy. He just asked her if he could please have his bandana back. Then he got in the car and drove the three us to a motel for the night. Neither one of them said a single word to each other for the rest of the trip.

I always wondered why he didn't yell at her that night. And about a million other nights. Maybe if he would've yelled, she wouldn't have ended up where she is, waiting at some Western Union for her little sister to bail her out of trouble. Maybe yelling would've proved to her that she's worth more than that. Maybe yelling would've gotten the message through.

It's too late for yelling, though. Way too late. Now it's just a matter of keeping Charlie afloat.

Adam holds the door open for me as I walk into the Western Union on Chestnut Street. He was a patient listener this morning when I told him about my phone conversation with Charlie. He didn't judge or question my motives; he just said he'd be happy to drive me wherever I needed to go before heading in to see his grandmother. So after a quick shower, we stopped for breakfast and then hit the ATM. Between the pawnbroker's cash and my checking account, I have just enough money to cover Charlie's request. The clerk at Western Union counts it carefully as I fill out the paperwork with Adam's hand resting against the small of my back. Charlie's eight hundred dollars will be at the Houma location in an instant. Now all I can do is mentally cross my fingers and hope it gets her what she needs.

On the drive back to my place, I think about Adam's words from last night. I'm grateful his father changed his mind about moving Ms. Sinclair, but I do wonder what caused it. Maybe Dr. Kopsey managed to work some magic in the conference room yesterday morning after all. Or maybe it was my harsh reminder about his mother's condition that convinced him to let her stay put. Regardless of the reason, Adam is obviously taking a fair amount of comfort in the fact that his gram isn't going anywhere.

He's chatting about his plans to take her outside today so she can see her birds a little closer. He asks me about Pine Manor's rules for such "field trips," and I tell him as long as they stay on the grounds, he can push her wheelchair wherever he'd like. He seems excited by the possibilities. It feels good to see him this way, especially after the emotional turmoil of yesterday.

A few minutes later, we pull up to the curb in front of my building. Before I hop out and head upstairs to use the rest of my day off to request bill deferrals and clean the bathroom, I ask Adam if I'll be seeing him at The King's Court tonight.

"I'll be there," he says with a smile. "Of course I'll be there."

"Good. Oh, and tell your gram I said hello." I open the car door and start to climb out. "And enjoy your walk."

"Will do." There's a long pause while I close the door behind me. I turn to look back at him through the open car window. "Bye, K'acy. Love you."

A familiar bass riff resonates deep in my chest, summoning a smile to my lips and a flutter to my heart. My lungs release a silent sigh, one filled with sweetness and contentment. Happiness.

"Copy that, and send it back."

***

Jarrod's already at The King's Court when I carry the StingRay off the bus and walk into the bar. By the time I've unpacked and set up, he's finished his first beer. I walk over to the bar to say hello and have a drink of my own before I start my set. I haven't talked to Jarrod since the brief conversation we had on Monday morning when I came back from Adam's to get ready for work and found him sprawled across my bed. The only words his hung-over brain managed to form that morning were a quick "thanks for the crash pad" and a sarcastic cocktail of comments hoping my night at The Mister's was worth the wait. When I sit down on the barstool next to him, he hands me a full beer and raises his own in a toast.

"To us," he says, his voice completely devoid of its usual sarcasm.

"To us," I return. We clink glasses and each down a few sips of beer. I wonder what has him in such a generous mood. We've never toasted to ourselves before.

"I've got two bits of good news, though neither of them is as miraculous as the sell-out at The Upstage."

"Little could be." There's no sarcasm in my voice either. I'm damn proud of Crackerjack Townhouse for filling up the place nearly two weeks before the gig's arrival. Jarrod puts his hand on my shoulder and squeezes it in agreement.

"True. But you're gonna hear about them anyway."

"Well then, go on. Tell me."

After he takes another swig of his beer, he says, "One: I've managed to fully recover from having to spend a night in your bed. Alone, fully clothed, and with the toilet seat down. And two: I have a date."

Whoa. Is he serious? "Really? With who?"

"Geez. Try not to sound so surprised, Kace."

"Sorry. But, you can't blame me for being surprised. Dating isn't usually your thing. I mean…this is good. This is *really* good. Who is she? Wait. Wait." I hold my hands up in front of me, fingers spread and palms out. "Please tell me she's a librarian. Or a kindergarten teacher."

"Neither. She works at the call center with me." He shrugs. "Actually, she's a manager."

"Seriously? What's her name?"

"Grace." The epic ass shaker Jarrod Wilcox is blushing over a woman named Grace. The obvious irony of someone with such a pious name going out with the man doesn't escape either one of us.

"Well, isn't that just a kicker? Is she as holy as her name?"

"With any luck, I'll get to find out on Friday night." The sarcasm is back. He wiggles his eyebrows up and down, just like he does every time he's planning to take someone home.

I shake my head in exasperation. "Jesus, Jar. Keep it in your pants. At least for the first date, okay?"

"I can't promise anything. The ones with the biblical names are usually the kinkiest."

"Totally TMI." I roll my eyes and contort my face. He gets a few chuckles in at my expense and then turns the tables.

"And how about you and your biblical boy? Anything kinky happening in the Garden of Eden?"

Now I'm the one who's blushing. "No kink. Sorry to disappoint you." I hesitate for a second, deciding if I should tell him any more. But isn't sharing good news what best friends do? "Just a lot of 'falling in love' stuff, that's all." I shrug it off as if my words are no big deal.

Jarrod's mouth drops open, and his eyes widen. "Are you serious? You put your cards on the table already? It's only been like, what, two months since you met the guy?" He clasps his hands in front of his chest and closes his eyes as if in prayer. "Just please tell me you didn't say it first."

"I didn't say it first."

He opens his eyes and drops his hands. "Wow. That dude is a brave, brave man. What'd you do when he said it?"

"I asked him if he'd been drinking."

"And?"

"Completely sober."

Jarrod shakes his head and smooths one of his hands against the front of his mouth, as if it might help him think.

"Did you say it back? I mean...do you love him back?"

"Yeah. I did. 'Cause I kinda do."

"Damn." Jarrod's head tilts up and he leans back in his seat, resting his spine against the bar and crossing his arms over his chest. A huge smile jets across his face. "*That* is stellar, Kace. But I knew it already. I see the way he looks at you. And the way you look at him. I'm happy for you. *Both* of you. You deserve it."

I don't say anything in reply because no sooner are Jarrod's words out when I see Adam approaching us from across the room.

"Speak of the devil..." Jarrod adds, winking at me just before Adam comes into earshot.

"Hey," Adam says as he nestles up to my barstool and slides his arm around my waist, kissing me on top of the head. He smells like Pine Manor mixed with Melio's Pizza. "Sorry I'm a little late. I had to get something to eat on the way. I was starving."

"No worries, man. She was just about to get started." Jarrod stands up, grabs my hand, and pulls me off my barstool. He guides me toward the stage as if he has important private business to conduct with my swooner. As I lift the leather guitar strap up over my head and lightly stroke the cobweb painted on the pickguard, I turn back to see Adam now sitting in my vacant barstool, finishing my beer. The mischievous look in his eyes makes me wonder what the two of them talk about every Wednesday night while I'm chasing the worries out of my soul with a chain of songs. But my wonder only lasts a moment because once I start playing, Jarrod and Adam and Mr. Sinclair and the driver of the black car—and everyone else for that matter—leave my thoughts.

It's just me and the StingRay, tossing our love out into the air, note by beautiful note. With each flick of my fingers, the sins of these two hands are forgotten. The memories I have of the last breaths of life are temporarily set free, if only for a few hours.

As long as I'm playing, I can forget. I can shut it out. My mind is quiet.

Tonight, I start my chain of songs with "Soul to Squeeze," instead of finishing with it. I do it, because now that I know how Adam feels, I'm not worried about giving too much away.

***

When I get to Pine Manor on Thursday morning, Sondra's already there, putting her lunch bag in the break room refrigerator.

"So, I'm gonna go ahead and take a guess that things are a little tense now that Ms. Sinclair's son is here," she says, closing the refrigerator door behind her.

"What makes you say that?" She's certainly right, but I wonder what drove her to make such an appropriate conclusion.

"'Cause yesterday, when I went to get Ms. Sinclair for lunch, her grandson was in the room talking to his father and neither one of them looked happy." Sondra's words remind me I never even asked Adam how his day was after we left The King's Court last night. In fact, I didn't even ask about Ms. Sinclair. I was too exhausted to function, so he dropped me off at my door, just like every other Wednesday night.

"Let's just say they don't get along very well."

She crosses her arms over her chest and shakes her head at me. "Just watch what you're getting yourself into, girl. This is the last time I'm gonna say it, but patients and personal lives don't mix. I know it's too late now, 'cause you and that boy are probably already in it too deep, but just be careful. Especially if his father is as nasty as I hear he is."

"Nasty?"

"I heard Marie talking to Ellis about Dr. Kopsey's notes, saying that Mr. Sinclair was a belligerent and bossy son of a bitch. His words, not mine."

"Sounds about right."

Sondra doesn't say another word. She just purses her lips and shakes her head at me again before turning and walking out of the room. She's right about me being in too deep, but the truth is, I wouldn't have it any other way. I may not trust Winston Sinclair, but I do trust his son. And Miriam Hansen.

A few minutes later I find myself standing outside Ms. Sinclair's room, looking at her through the open door. She's sitting in her wheelchair watching *The Today Show*, her bony fingers unwrapping a Starlight mint. She looks so sweet. I try not to think about what I saw in her eyes the day the checkerboard found its way into the trash can because I don't want to be reminded of the sorrow that will come with it. There will be sadness, and plenty of it, but at least there won't be pain. That much I know for sure. Because I will make sure of it.

"How's Gram doing this morning?" I turn my head to see Adam walking down the hallway toward me.

"Good. She's already dressed." I step away from her door to meet Adam a few paces away. He's wearing a blue T-shirt, jeans, and a smile. I want to hug him, but I can't. So instead, I ask him what I should've asked him last night. "I just realized I never asked you about yesterday. How was your day? Did you have a nice walk with your gram?" I'm hoping he offers me more than just an answer to my questions.

"It was okay. The walk was great; she loved it. But my dad showed up, so that made it a little challenging."

"How come you didn't say anything about it last night?"

He shrugs. "Because, frankly, I'd like to forget he even exists and bringing him up wasn't going to make me feel better. It was just gonna piss me off. It felt good to not have to think about it for a little while." Light dances in his eyes, as if he's about to say something really special. "Plus, I knew I'd be seeing you today—and hopefully every other day for the rest of my life—so I figured I could just tell you about it some other time."

Embarrassment and elation course through my veins, weakening and strengthening me at the same time. "I won't be distracted by your charm, Adam Sinclair, though I do understand why you didn't want to talk about it last night. But today is a new day, and I just want you to know that I'm here for you, *whenever* you want to talk. Okay?"

"Okay. But the truth is, there was nothing revolutionary about yesterday. My dad was just his prickly self, ordering people around and treating Gram like she's an idiot for having Alzheimer's. I don't even know why he bothered to show up. He was only here for an hour. He couldn't get out of here fast enough."

"Sounds like his quick departure was for the best."

"It was definitely for the best." He reaches for me, putting his hands behind my neck and pulling me in for a kiss. It's super quick; just a peck, really. But I wasn't ready for it. I wasn't ready to take the chance. When he pulls away, Adam must see the look of shock on my face because he apologizes. And then he hurries into his grandmother's room before I can say another word.

I sigh to myself and put my hands into my pockets before heading back to the nurse's station. When I turn the corner at the end of the hallway, Winston Sinclair is standing there, still as stone. I nearly walk right into him.

"How's my mother doing this morning?" His voice is raw and cold. He pauses for a second before he adds, "It's K'acy, isn't it?"

I'm surprised as sin he remembered my name. "She's quite well, Mr. Sinclair. And, yes. It's K'acy." He doesn't so much as blink, let alone step out of my way. I focus on the tip of his nose, even though I'd very much like to look him in the eye. "Your son just got here. I saw him heading back to her room."

"Is that so?"

I don't quite know what to do because he isn't budging. He's just blocking the hallway with his overdressed, overconfident body.

"Yep. Well, I've got to run. Have a nice day, Mr. Sinclair," I say, internally hoping he has a lousy day instead. I step to the side of the hallway and turn my body so my back is flush with the wall. Making room for him to pass seems like it might be the only thing that'll encourage him to get out of the way.

He doesn't return my nicety or even say goodbye. He just starts walking.

***

I spend the rest of Thursday and Friday working, and Adam spends them at his grandmother's side. His father doesn't bother to show up at all on Friday, and his Thursday-morning visit lasted only an hour, just like Wednesday's. Adam will not leave his gram's room when his father is here. He's like a papa bear protecting his cub.

Ms. Sinclair's become less and less lucid over the last few days. The effects of her medication change are starting to settle in, and she's more confused than ever. She's even gotten mildly aggressive a few times, yelling at Adam or one of the staff members for doing some small thing that annoyed her. Adam's distress is apparent every time she lashes out. I do my best to explain to him there's nothing unusual about her behavior. Everyone here understands it's the medication and the Alzheimer's talking, not his grandmother.

After work on Friday, Adam and I meet in the parking lot. The dark sedan, backed into a spot in the far corner of the lot, unsettles me with its presence yet again. As Adam and I pull out of the lot, I watch the reflection of the dark sedan in the passenger's side mirror. Relief comes only when the car doesn't leave its parking space.

On the drive back to my place, Adam tells me his father wants to meet with him again tonight. Apparently, the giant dickhead said he has some important things to discuss with his son.

"I hope to hell one of those things is that he's going back to Seattle." Adam's words are confident, but doubt and skepticism seep through in his voice. "I really don't want to meet him, but I kind of feel like this might be my last chance to press him for answers." He's still hoping his father will give him more information about who Bradley is. He was right; the whole *ignorance is bliss* thing is never going to work for him.

"Just be careful how hard you press. He seems like the kind of guy who might press back."

Adam drops me at my door and promises to text me later. Then he kisses me goodbye. When our lips connect, the music in my heart is as loud as always, but something about it is different. Because this time, it's distorted with worry.

CHAPTER 23

Robert McGee—2008

Charlie moved out of the house three weeks ago, said she got herself an apartment with two of her friends. Ever since she graduated from high school, Charlie's been working at a hair salon, washing hair and answering the phones, and she seems to really like it. Now she wants to start taking classes to get her cosmetology license. I told her I'd pay for her schooling, not just because it's part of my responsibility as her father, but because I think it's something she can be good at. Something she can feel proud of. Ever since Louise left, I've been saving a little money every month, hoping at least one of my girls would head off to college someday. Charlie's already been accepted at Blue Cliff, and I couldn't be prouder of my first baby girl for getting herself on the track to success. Classes start in the fall. My Charlie finally seems happy.

It destroys me to know that's gonna change. Because of me.

Dr. Bryson told me about the cancer last Wednesday. She said it started in my lungs, but now it's gone to my liver. It's why I've been so short of breath lately. And why the whites of my eyes are the same color as my morning piss. But the cancer's also in my bones and my lymph nodes. She pretty much said I'm screwed, only she didn't use those exact words. Instead, she used words like *incurable* and *inoperable* and *metastasis* and *prognosis* and *palliative care.* She said I'm stage four. I asked her how the hell I could be stage four when I didn't know one, two, or three even existed. All she said was, "Cancer can be like that."

I haven't told either of the girls yet, and I have no idea how I'm gonna. I told Ron and the rest of the guys at the quarry just this morning, and the way this town works, everyone that's ever crossed paths with Houma, Louisiana is gonna know by dawn tomorrow. Which means I've got to tell my girls tonight. The idea of hurting them pains me more than cancer ever could.

Ron promised my job would still be waiting for me when I'm done kicking cancer's ass. I didn't have the heart to tell him cancer isn't the one who's gonna get his ass kicked. I couldn't bring myself to tell him that once I'm down for the count, I'm never getting back up again. Ron's already gone through this with his daughter, Lindsay. He doesn't need to do it again with me. Plus, Dr. Bryson said surgery would only cause me pain, not cure anything. Medication can help manage things, if I want it to, but there'll be no chemo. No radiation. No experimental therapies. No clinical trials. No miracles. I stopped praying for one of those nine years ago. Ain't no use in starting again now.

And so here I am, sitting on the couch, waiting for K'acy to come home from school. She'll be surprised to see me here because I'm always at the quarry this time of day. No more, though. I guess twenty-eight years of blasting limestone was enough. Dr. Bryson suspects I only have a couple of months, and a good portion of them will be spent in a bed. I need to get everything in order before things get bad. I need to make sure my girls are gonna be all right without me.

K'acy walks in the door at 2:43 with her backpack slung over her shoulder, wearing a skirt that's way too short for an eighteen-year-old with legs as long as hers. It's hard to believe my smart little girl is already a woman. She'll be graduating from Terrebonne High in a couple months, and with any luck, I'll be sitting in the audience cheering her on. The idea that I might not be hits me straight in the heart, making the conversation we're about to have all the more difficult.

K'acy closes the door behind her and starts heading for the stairs, no doubt to go up and practice her bass. When she sees me sitting on the couch, she freezes and asks me what I'm doing here. I tell her we have to talk.

As I tell K'acy about the cancer, her face doesn't change. She doesn't look surprised or sad or angry or confused or any of the things I expected her to be. She just looks resigned. Like she already knew what was coming. Like she knew stage four was here. Because, unlike the rest of us, she already knew about one, two, and three.

When I tell her I only have a few months left, all she says is that she'd like to be with me when I tell Charlie.

CHAPTER 24

Jarrod's text arrives at 11:04.

I kept it in my pants.

I cross my fingers and hope his much-deserved perfect life started tonight. With a woman named Grace.

I knew you could do it.

It wasn't easy. The woman is H.O.T.

I take it the date went well?

Damn straight.

You gonna see her again? Outside of work, I mean.

I hope so.

I'm sure she hopes so, too.

Thanks, Mom.

You're welcome, Grandpa.

A long minute passes before I get another text.

C u tomorrow. 7:30ish?

We're playing at Bartholomew's tomorrow night. It'll be our last big show before The Upstage.

I'll be there. Adam, too. I think.

Cool. How are things in Eden, BTW?

A bit tense. His father's in from Seattle.

Nice guy?

The exact opposite.

Oh. That sucks.

Sure does. Adam's been dealing with some family stuff. Plus, his gram isn't doing so well.

Yeah, he mentioned that on Wednesday night. Sounds pretty much like hell.

Yep.

Good thing he's got your shoulder to lean on.

Not sure my shoulder's strong enough when it comes to his father.

It is. I've tested it myself. Strongest shoulder I know.

:)

C u tomorrow, Kace.

Later.

I'm happy for Jarrod. Really happy. I hope this Grace is everything he needs her to be.

Not long after I send my last text, I decide to go to bed, despite the fact that I haven't heard from Adam yet. I'm worried about him, but tomorrow's going to be a long day, and I need to get some sleep. I keep the ringer turned on, knowing it'll wake me no matter what time his text arrives.

My last thoughts, before sleep comes, are of Ms. Sinclair and her birds. I picture the woodpeckers and goldfinches, the cardinals and chickadees, all flying around her like little living versions of Alzheimer's, protecting her from the harsh reality of her life as they fly off with her memories. They flutter over her, carrying tiny pieces of her former self in their beaks. But they also shield her. They make her blissfully unaware of her own tragedy.

Just as I drift off to sleep, the last bird comes. It's a mourning dove. It lands on Ms. Sinclair's lap, nestling into her waiting hands and leaving her memories to the other birds. It looks up at her with its round, dark eyes, asking only for comfort and mercy. She smiles at the bird and then promises it everything will be okay.

***

I wake up Saturday morning to the sound of my alarm, but when I roll over to turn it off, something's blocking my way. I open my eyes to find a shirtless Adam lying on his back, halfway between me and the alarm clock. He grins, lifts his right arm, and smacks the snooze button.

"Hey." I'm sure he can hear my surprise as I snuggle against him and lay my head on his shoulder.

"Hey."

"When did you get here?" I can't see his face, but the hesitation before his answer gives me all the information I need.

"Late. Too late to wake you." He brushes his hand against my cheek and down my neck to my shoulder. It's gentle and sincere. "I remembered you telling Jarrod about the key taped behind the picture. Hope you're not mad."

"I'm not mad." How could I be? His arm wraps around my shoulders and holds me against him.

"I know I promised to text, but I figured you were already asleep, and I didn't want to wake you. So I just came over and let myself in." Something is wrong with his voice. It sounds like it's been wrung out. It's twisted and contorted. Broken.

"No worries." I spread the fingers of my left hand against his chest, looking at the perfect alternating Vs of light and dark, and hoping the weariness in his voice isn't telling me what I think it is. "Did everything go all right with your dad?"

He inhales and then releases the breath in a deep, long sigh, confirming my fears about last night. "I should've known better."

He's silent for a few seconds, as if he's thinking about what to say next. "It'll be a cold day in hell before I ever do that again."

"Do what again?"

"Willingly talk to my father."

"That bad, huh?"

"That bad." He releases my shoulders and kisses me on the forehead. My hand drops off his chest. "He's just so damn manipulative." He doesn't offer anything more. But I have to ask.

"Did he tell you anything else about Bradley?"

"No. And he told me if I bring it up again, he'll change his mind and take Gram back to Seattle."

"Seriously?"

"Yep. And that, my dear, pretty much sums up the entire night." His voice is still broken. And now I know why.

"I'm sorry, Adam." I kiss his chest, and he runs the tips of his fingers down my spine, causing a ripple of notes to burst through my skin.

"Me, too." We're both quiet for a few minutes before the alarm sounds again, shocking us back into reality. "You'd better get ready for work," he says. "Gram will get upset if you're late, you know." A little lightness has seeped back into his voice.

"She isn't the only one. Mr. Rauch doesn't like anyone else to touch his colostomy bag, let alone empty it." I sit up and start to climb out of bed, suddenly conscious of the old T-shirt I slept in, not knowing Adam would be in my bed this morning.

"Lucky you."

He thinks I'm joking, but I'm not.

"I *am* lucky. Really. Because I adore that man, colostomy bag and all." I stand up and shrug. Adam's head tilts to the side. He eyes me with intense curiosity.

"Your patients are the lucky ones, K'acy McGee. Them and me."

I don't agree or disagree with him. I just smile, walk into the bathroom, and close the door behind me.

***

Thankfully, the rest of Saturday is a beautiful day, with lots of sunshine and no sign of Winston Sinclair. By the time I finish filling out the shift change report at the end of the day, I'm more than ready to crank out some funk with Jarrod, Marquis, Bryson, and the rest of Crackerjack Townhouse. After grabbing a quick dinner together, Adam drives me to Bartholomew's.

It's an amazing night. Full of everything that makes the world perfect: loud music, an incredible audience, epic ass shaking, and my lone swooner. And for the first time ever, when the show's over, Jarrod doesn't leave with a blonde. Or a brunette. Or a redhead. He leaves alone, with only the clothes on his back. I know he and Grace have only had one date, but I think it's already helping him understand how much he deserves happiness. I think it's given him a small taste of the hope he's been looking for.

After the stage is torn down and the equipment is loaded into Calvin's van, Adam takes me home. I can't help but notice the black car is suspiciously absent from both the street in front of Bartholomew's and the street in front of my apartment building. Its absence, however, doesn't bring me the comfort I was hoping it would. It doesn't make me feel better; it just makes me feel a different kind of nervous.

Eventually, though, I find myself falling asleep in Adam's arms, thinking again of his grandmother and her birds. Only tonight, he's there, too. Standing next to her wheelchair, holding her hand.

***

I leave Adam in my apartment, asleep in my bed, and walk out into the sunshine. The Sunday-morning quiet is familiar and comforting. As usual, it's only me and the driver on the 61A. I walk into Pine Manor to find many of the patients are already sitting in the lobby, fully dressed and waiting for their Sunday-morning company to arrive. Or for Pastor Glickson's service to start.

Sondra's here, too, setting the brake on Mr. Ledbetter's wheelchair. After a brief hello, to her, as well as to some of the patients, I head back to the nurses' station to drop off my bag and read the report from last night. But before I get there, Susan Campbell, our Director of Nursing, meets me in the hallway and asks me to come into her office. Instead of greeting me with her usual warm smile, Susan's mouth is a straight line. Her gaze barely connects with mine, and there's no small talk, no friendly banter. She doesn't say another word as we walk into her office. She closes the door behind us, and I take a seat in the chair across from her desk.

Something is wrong.

My mouth goes dry. Susan sits in her desk chair and her lips start moving; they're telling me something, but my ears don't want to hear. My brain rejects the words as soon as it registers them. A flush of sadness envelops me as more words come tumbling out of her mouth. Wrong words. Hurtful words. Words I never thought I'd hear. I swallow back my tears, wanting more than anything for this conversation to be a mistake. For Susan to have the wrong person.

Her hands are clasped together, resting on the desk. Her body is tilted forward, as if she's leaning into me to make sure I'm hearing what she's saying. Her final three words are *I'm so sorry.* I hear them. And I also feel them.

I've worked here for six years, and until this very moment, Susan has never had a single negative thing to say about me. She's only ever given me glowing evaluations. She knows me as well as anyone else here. And yet, she has to follow company policy. Her hands are tied.

She told me she can't share details, but someone has filed a complaint. They said I mistreated a patient. They said I'm not fit to take care of the people I love. I'm sick inside because everything this person said about me is everything I am not. I know it. And Susan does, too. It's why she said she's sorry.

I'm not allowed to say goodbye. Not to Mrs. Thompson or Mr. Reizenstein or Mr. Rauch. Not even to Sondra or Marie or Dr. Kopsey. I have to walk straight out the door, and I can't come back until the investigation is over and my name has been cleared. If it's cleared at all.

As I leave the building, the possibility of never being able to set foot in Pine Manor again saddles my soul with its crushing weight, breaking my heart and filling my eyes with tears.

Losing them to death is always hard, but this… Losing them to *this* would be far crueler than death could ever be.

The more you care for them, the harder it becomes.

Sondra's words have now become the harshest gospel I'll ever have to swallow. Because not only am *I* being forced to leave *them*, but with me goes their last chance for compassion. Their last chance for peace.

And that's how it will be for Evelyn Sinclair, if I'm not allowed to come back. Knowing she's going to suffer makes my heart weep. Not just for her, but also for her grandson. Because he will have to watch it happen, desperate and hopeless and crippled by his own helplessness.

I walk through the parking lot to the bus stop, sucking in a deep breath through my tears and thinking about Winston Sinclair. I think about why he did this, and what I'm going to have to do to make him take it back.

I'm going to have to fix this myself. And I can't wait to look him straight in the eye when I do.

***

A second after I step into my apartment, my cell phone rings. It's Adam. I'm surprised it took him so long.

"Hey. I just got here. Where are you? They said you left." The pitch of his voice is far higher than usual. It's filled with confusion.

"I'm at home."

"But you left early this morning. I thought you had to work today?"

"I did. But I had to leave."

"Why? What's going on?"

"I'm not allowed to go into details, but I made a mistake. It got me suspended for a couple of days."

"What mistake?"

"I said something I shouldn't have."

"What?" The pitch of his voice has dropped. Anger has replaced his confusion.

"Like I said, I'm not allowed to share any details." I can hear him breathing on the other end of the line. It's heavy and fast, like he's walking somewhere in a hurry. "But, please know it's being handled. Everything's going to be all right." I don't tell him how I'm going to handle it.

"The hell it is." There's more breathing. For several seconds, it's the only sound coming through my phone. "I can't believe he did this. I can't believe he... Yes, I can. I can believe it."

I take a second to collect my thoughts before trying to reassure him. "Everyone at Pine Manor knows me. They know I didn't do anything wrong. They've dealt with people like your father before. They're just going through the motions to appease him. I'll be back at work in a few days."

"Don't be so sure of that."

I'm struck by the strength of his words. They tell me immediately he knows something I don't. I wish I could see his face. "That doesn't make me feel any better."

"Sorry, but it's the truth. I know exactly what he's doing. He's using you to get to me." I don't understand. A long second passes before Adam adds, "He knows about us, K'acy."

"*What?*" My stomach drops and my chest tightens. What the hell is going on?

"That's the real reason he wanted to talk to me on Friday night." He's gathering his thoughts, carefully choosing his words. The resulting silence sends my mind reeling into a fit of apprehension. What if I can't fix this? What if I never get to see them again? What if Adam is right, and I won't be back at work in a few days? "I'm sorry I didn't tell you, but I didn't think he'd take it this far."

"Take *what* this far?"

"He saw me kiss you in the hallway on Thursday. And he had his driver sit in the parking lot on Friday. He saw us talking. He saw us leave together."

I immediately think of the dark sedan, backed into its spot in the far corner of the lot, quiet and watchful and still.

Maybe that car has nothing to do with Latham Street after all.

I hear Adam shuffling his cell phone around as he talks. Then I hear a car start.

"Adam…" I don't even know what to say next.

"I'm not going to let him hurt you—and Gram—in some kind of stupid attempt to prove something to me."

"Prove what?"

"That he still has control."

"Over what?"

"Over everything. My life. What I do. Where I live. Who I love. Everything." It only takes me an instant to understand. Now I know the real reason why his voice sounded so broken on Saturday morning.

"Oh." I nod in acknowledgement, as if he can see me through the phone. This whole thing has nothing to do with the sassy words I said to Winston Sinclair about his mother's Alzheimer's. In fact, it has nothing to do with my behavior toward him at all.

Instead, it has everything to do with my behavior toward his son.

"I'm not gonna let him do this." A siren sounds in the background. Adam's driving somewhere. Worry streaks through me.

"Where are you going?"

"I'm going to see my father."

No. No. No. "Don't. Just…let's talk about this first, okay? Let's figure it out together."

"There's nothing to figure out here, K'acy. I'm gonna take care of it." His words are hot and angry, as if he's turned into somebody new. Somebody with a point to get across.

Adam doesn't even wait for me to respond before he says a

quick, "I'll see you later," and hangs up. I'm left standing alone in my living room with a silent phone at my ear, wondering what the hell he's going to do.

***

A few minutes later, I'm sitting at my table, folding laundry and thinking about what's about to happen in Winston Sinclair's hotel room. Just as I fold a pair of jeans down over my forearm, the doorbell rings. I quickly finish folding the jeans, set them down on the table, and walk over to the door. Relief swells in my chest at the thought of Adam coming here instead of heading to his father's.

But when I open the door, Adam isn't the one standing there.

CHAPTER 25

Harlan Webber—Room number 122

I spent most of my life in prison. I checked into the place a few days after my twenty-second birthday and wasn't paroled until I was sixty-eight. My sentence was fifty years. I served forty-six of them before they let me out. And truth be told, I wish they never had.

The day I walked outta there was the scariest day of my life. I spent forty-six years having three square meals a day and living with absolute structure. Then I got out. For the next eight years, I was lucky if I managed to eat six meals in a whole week. Nobody would hire me once they found out about my conviction. I had no skills, no decent clothes, and no address. Plus, I was old. I wouldn't have hired me either.

The Curran-Fromhold Correctional Facility was my home. The real world was not.

There were days when I thought I should've done it again, just to get back inside, where life was predictable and I had friends. It was easy the first time, so I always figured the second time would've been easier still. Those young girls were always talking to each other, never paying attention to what was happening around them. I could've grabbed one of them on their way out of the community rec center and landed myself back in lock-up by dusk of the same day. Sometimes I'd sit on the curb across the street and watch them walking in and outta there, wearing outfits that showed off their little girl bodies in all the right ways. But I never could bring myself to do it again. Maybe it was my seventy-year-old pecker that stopped me, or maybe it was 'cause of the prison therapist. The reason why doesn't matter; I let them be and just kept living under the Barkley Street overpass, begging for the occasional dollar and sleeping on a cardboard mat.

When I was seventy-six, I got run over. I was crossing the street, on my way to nowhere, when some drunk lady ran the red light and damn near killed me. I was in the hospital for a long time. Head injury, broken pelvis, internal bleeding. But I survived. As soon as I could, I called myself a lawyer and filed a personal injury case.

All the reading I did at the Curran-Fromhold Correctional Facility's law library finally got me something besides a failed appeal. It got me a settlement.

Even after paying all my medical bills, I had enough money left to spend the rest of my life sleeping on a mattress, instead of on a cardboard mat. The only trouble was, the mattress I slept on wasn't in a house or even in an apartment. It was in a nursing home.

After the accident, I couldn't walk without a walker, and I couldn't make my hands work right anymore. Buttoning my shirt and wiping my own ass became the two biggest challenges of my life. The head injury messed me up more than anything else. I knew I couldn't take care of myself, so I had the social worker assigned to my case find me a nice place to live.

She did a good job when she picked Pine Manor. I started getting three squares again, and the scheduled structure of the place wasn't that different from the penitentiary's. I spent seven years at Pine Manor, playing checkers, reading the newspaper, yelling *bingo!*, and watching all the pretty little great-granddaughters who came to visit every Sunday afternoon.

I wasn't an "inmate" anymore; I was a "resident." And it was a damn good seven years.

I died when I was eighty-four. I got pneumonia and told the doctor I didn't want any treatment for it. I told him to just let me alone. He did.

But *she* didn't. She kept coming around. All the time. She never tried to give me any medicine or talk me into going to the hospital. She just sat with me and talked. A lot. I tried to shoo her away, but she wouldn't have it. So, one day, when I'd had enough of her chit-chat, I told her about me. I told her what I'd done on a summer night sixty-two years ago. I gave her every detail, hoping she'd despise me like everyone else who knew what I'd done. I confessed my sins and told her the secrets I'd been holding in for all those years. I told her so she'd go away and let me die by myself.

But it didn't work. In fact, she seemed to want to sit with me even more after that. Her talking stopped, though, and she'd just sit there, silent and stone-faced, probably thinking about how I deserved every second of the ugly death headed my way.

I hate to admit it, but eventually, her presence became more comforting than it was annoying. Sometimes she'd hold my hand while she was there, something no one had ever done in my whole life. Not even my mother. Or she'd comb my hair or give me a shave. But it wasn't like she was doing it as part of her job. It was like she was doing it 'cause she cared.

There are lots of people in this world who would've enjoyed watching me suffer, but she wasn't one of them. I ended up suffering way less than those two little girls did all those years ago. Some would say there was no justice in my death, that I deserved to suffer more, but maybe my accident was enough penance for what I'd done. Maybe the years of pain it caused were enough for God to call it even. I don't know.

All I know is, at the end, when I left the world, she was there with me, silent and stone-faced and giving me the compassion I never deserved.

CHAPTER 26

Winston Sinclair is wearing a dark suit with a crimson tie. His hair is perfectly in place, and the gray at his temples looks far more extensive here than it does under the fluorescent lights of Pine Manor. The man is well over six feet tall, and if I didn't already know what a horrible person he is, I'd actually think he seems like a decent guy. He looks fit and well-groomed and smart, just like his son. But, I know better. I know, in this case, looks are incredibly deceiving.

The smirk on his face is a good indication of what's underneath the slick facade.

At first, I'm at a loss. I just stand in the doorway, not knowing what to do or say. Of course, I know what I *want* to do and say, but now that I'm alone with him in the doorway of my apartment, I'm not sure either would be the best idea. My stomach jumps into my throat, choking me with fear. A hit of fight-or-flight-invoking adrenaline surges through my veins. And yet, I don't let it take over my body. I don't move a single muscle. I just stand here, trying to process the hows and whys of his unexpected visit and what I'm going to do about it.

"May I come in?"

This is it. This is the only chance I'll probably ever have to make him take it back. It isn't the way I planned, but I swallow my fear and buckle up for the ride. To hell with the risks.

"Certainly," I answer, but I don't step aside. I plant my feet into the floor. He hesitates for a moment, examining my face carefully before turning himself sideways and sliding in between my body and the doorframe. I look straight into his eyes as he walks past, catching a quick, intense flash of what's to come.

I close the door and turn around to find him checking out my apartment. His back is to me as his head pivots and examines the place from top to bottom. He puts his hands in his pockets and turns to face me. "Not exactly Buckingham Palace, is it?"

My stare is unyielding, absorbing every detail his eyes will share. I'm watching his future—studying it—with an energy unlike anything I've ever felt before.

"Is there something I can help you with, Mr. Sinclair?" I move one step closer to him.

"I know what you two are doing, and I want it to stop. I know everything about you, young lady, and I'm here to ask you nicely to walk away from my son."

He's here to *what*?

"I'm certain you don't know *everything* about me, Mr. Sinclair."

"Ahh…but I *do* know everything." He nods his head and narrows his eyes. "A man in my position has a very easy time discovering such things. All I have to do is ask the right people, and I can get whatever information I need."

If his driver is the one who's been watching me from the black car, then Mr. Sinclair knew Adam was in Philadelphia long before he decided to show up at Pine Manor. Apparently *that's* what being a giant political dickhead will get you. The ability to know what you don't deserve to.

"Even if you did know everything there is to know about me, what would any of it have to do with Adam?"

"Everything," he says. "He deserves far better than what you have to offer."

"Is that why you filed the complaint? To get rid of me?"

"I filed the complaint to get your attention." He takes his hands out of his pockets and runs one of them against the back edge of my sofa. "And if you don't walk away from him, I'm capable of doing far worse."

"You don't get to decide who your son loves."

"Who he loves? *Loves?*" His face splits into a gigantic smile. "He doesn't love you. He only thinks he does because you're the exact opposite of what his family wants for him. *You* are his way of getting back at us for whatever he thinks we've done wrong. And, while we're at it, you don't love him, either. You only love his multimillion-dollar trust fund because you've got nothing to your name but a couple sets of scrubs and a guitar."

I want to kick him in the crotch. "Your informant seems to have missed a few details when they told you about me, Mr. Sinclair." I sound calm and sweet, even though inside I am spitting fire. "Your son's trust fund means nothing to me. I don't care about money. I only care about happiness."

"Thank you for the refresher course in childish idealism, sweetheart." He picks his hand up off the back edge of the couch and crosses his arms over his chest. "But I'm willing to give you the benefit of the doubt. It's just that, if what you say is true, I'm going to need some proof." His words are slow. Calculated. "So how about this…how about I give you a choice between money and happiness, and see which one you pick?"

Winston Sinclair steps up to me, lowering his face to mine. My gaze drills into his eyes, unwavering and watchful and deep. It's like a movie, and I'm going to watch it until the end. I won't look away until I've memorized every single detail. I'm absorbing it all.

"You have two choices," he continues. "One: you can do what I say and walk away from Adam. If you do, I'll give you twenty thousand dollars, and I'll let you keep your so-called career. But you'll have to leave Pine Manor and work somewhere else. End of story. Or, two: you can stay with my son and have your happiness. But if you do, I'll file a lawsuit against Pine Manor and have your license revoked. I'll pay one of your coworkers whatever the hell they want to testify they saw you hurt my mother. And when that happens, I have no doubt Adam will be the one leaving *you*." He smiles and tilts his head to the side, as if he's the cleverest thing to ever set foot on the planet. "When I'm done, you'll never work in this state again. But then, I'm sure your sister would love to have you back in Houma."

Anger surges through me, ripping apart my self-control. I'm sorting out what to say when he adds, "And if you tell Adam about any of this, you won't have a choice at all. Everything will be gone. I'll take it all away. I will ruin any chance you've ever had for happiness *or* money." He uncrosses his arms and puts his hands back in his pockets, rocking back on his heels as he does. "You and I both know people who hurt the elderly never fare well in the prison system, K'acy."

The words don't come to me fast enough. Nothing does. I'm frozen. But in that moment of absolute stillness, I finally see it. I see everything there is to see. The movie in his eyes ends, and all the bitterness and fear instantly drain from my body because I know something Winston Sinclair does not.

"I'll take the twenty thousand dollars."

After the words are out, a huge smile settles across my face. And his.

"So much for childish idealism. Looks like money wins again."

"Imagine that."

"You're smarter than you look, young lady, I'll give you that." He nods in smug satisfaction. "I'll withdraw my complaint first thing tomorrow morning, and my driver will drop off half of your cash at noon. You'll get the other half at week's end, just to be sure you're holding up your end of the bargain." He offers his hand to me, and I take it, knowing what will happen when I do. The instant our palms connect, fire pulses though my veins, initiating a jacked-up, menacing version of "Soul to Squeeze." Raw and aggressive bass notes burn through me, igniting my soul with strength and purpose. Confirming that I've made the right choice. "I'll give you a week to leave Pine Manor. *And* my son. But you might not want to wait until the last minute. In my experience, quicker is always better."

"I'll do my best."

He lets go of my hand, and the music inside my head instantly falls silent. "It's been a pleasure doing business with you." When he reaches the door, Winston Sinclair turns and faces me before twisting the knob. "You probably wouldn't have wanted to be with Adam for much longer anyway. He's going to be a very different man as soon as he manages to grow up. One that doesn't give a damn about happiness."

"A man like his father?"

He smiles at me one last time before walking out the door.

***

Jarrod is on his way to work when he answers the phone.

"Hey, Kace."

"Hey."

"What's up?" I hear skepticism in his voice. He's clearly wondering why I called. There's no real reason; I just needed someone to calm my nerves until I hear from Adam.

"Great gig last night, wasn't it?"

"Yep." He pauses for a second before he asks, "Is everything all right? You never call me from work." He knows Sundays are a busy day at Pine Manor because we've talked about it on many occasions.

"I got suspended."

"From work? Why?" His surprise is front and center. Unmistakable.

"Adam's father didn't like something I said so he filed a complaint."

"Are you kidding me? The dude had you suspended because of something you said? Who does that kind of shit?"

"Guys like Winston Sinclair. I told you he was not a / nice man."

"Wow. What the hell did you say that pissed him off so much?"

"He was being a jerk to his mother, so I reminded him that she has Alzheimer's. And then I told him he should probably go back to Seattle sooner rather than later."

"Aww, man!" He chuckles under his breath, as if he finds it funny. "That's awesome!"

"No, it's not. I must've really made him angry because the guy lied and said that not only did I talk disrespectfully to him, but I also mistreated his mother."

"That's a hell of a thing to lie about."

"Yep. And now I've been suspended until the investigation is complete." A lump of sadness rises into my throat, causing my voice to choke with emotion, even though I know for a fact all of this will be over by the week's end.

Jarrod must hear my sadness because he abruptly changes from playfulness to sincerity and understanding. "They know you there, Kace. They know you would never hurt anyone. I bet you'll be back to work by the end of the week."

"I hope you're right."

"Do you want me to call off work and come over to your place? We can drink beer and plot your revenge all day long."

It doesn't sound like a half-bad idea.

"You know I'd love to, but Adam is already on his way. He went over to his dad's this morning to try to talk some sense into the man. I doubt he had any success, but it was sweet of him to try." In reality, I hope Adam was completely unsuccessful. Because I hope he was long gone by the time his father even got back to the hotel room.

I don't tell Jarrod about Mr. Sinclair's visit, of course. He doesn't need to know about what else Mr. Sinclair has done. He doesn't need to know about the man's ultimatum. Because it doesn't matter anyway.

"Well, I hope Adam manages to fix this for you." We're both quiet for a few seconds before he thoughtfully adds, "Be safe, okay?"

"Okay. Thanks, Jar."

"You bet. Talk to you soon."

"Bye."

"Bye."

I wait for two full hours, folding laundry and nervously organizing my apartment, before I finally hear from Adam. He calls to ask me if he can come over because he doesn't want to tell me what happened over the phone. My gut sinks low when I realize he did, in fact, talk to his father today. I listen for hints in his words and his voice, but I get no indication of what transpired.

Adam rings my doorbell a little after three o'clock. He's borderline chipper when he kisses me on the head and says hello. He looks energized and content. Both bode well for the outcome of the story he's about to tell.

The first thing he does after greeting me is apologize for taking so long. Apparently he stopped back in to see his grandmother for a quick visit before he came to see me. He says he felt badly about leaving her in such a hurry this morning. She was fine, though. In fact, he doesn't think she even realized he was gone.

As Adam talks, he walks across the room and sits down on my couch. When he gets there, he motions for me to sit down next to him. The moment my bottom hits the cushion, his arm is around me, pulling me in close. I rest my head on Adam's shoulder, wondering what he's going to say.

"You'll be happy to know my father has changed his mind. He's going to drop the complaint tomorrow."

I sit bolt upright, as if I've just heard the biggest surprise of my life.

"Really?" I pour as much enthusiasm into my voice as possible. I hate lying to him, but for now at least, it's my only option.

"Yes, really." Adam leans back against the couch, props his feet up on the coffee table, and puts his hands behind his head.

He's obviously quite proud of his perceived victory. I might as well stroke his ego while I have the chance. He's a pretty modest guy, so who knows when I'll get another opportunity. "My hero," I say as I lay my head on his chest, on top of his heart, and listen to it beat. It's strong and reassuring.

"I sat on the floor outside his hotel room for an hour and a half before he showed up. And when he finally got there, I just started talking and I didn't stop until I got what I wanted. I can't believe the man actually listened to reason, but he did. I told him either he accepts you, or he loses me. I told him the ball was in his court because *you* aren't going anywhere."

I'm proud of him for standing up to his father, even if the outcome was predetermined. "That's amazing. Really. I can't thank you enough." I snuggle in closer, enjoying his happiness. And mine.

"You'll be back with Gram, and everyone else, in no time at all." He pulls one of his hands out from behind his head and starts playing with my hair. His silence tells me he's thinking hard about something. After inhaling a deep breath he adds, "I'm sorry, K'acy."

"For what?"

"I'm sorry my father is the kind of asshole who would do something like this. And I'm sorry you got hurt."

"The things that hurt the most are always the things that make you stronger." Words I hope he remembers himself in a few days, when it's his turn to hurt.

He twists his fingers through my hair. They work their way to the base of my neck and then gently tilt my head upward until my gaze meets his.

"You're incredible, you know that?"

I smile at his words. "Copy that, and send it back."

His mouth covers mine, and for a moment, I forget about what the next few days will bring. I forget about his father and his grandmother and all the complications of life. It's just his mouth kissing mine, devouring me with thoughtfulness and love. Each time his tongue meets mine, a chorus of notes flits between us, inciting my body and rousing my senses. As his hands wander across my skin, they conjure Miriam Hansen's promise and remind me of the importance of *us*.

Adam lifts my shirt up over my head and lays me down on the sofa, covering my lips and neck with kisses. He tugs my bra straps down off my shoulders and reaches around my back to unhook the clasp. His hands are smooth and sure as they pull my jeans and panties down over my hips and drop them onto the floor. He's hovering over me, caressing me with his eyes and his fingers, tempting me with his light. Adam kneels on the floor and takes off his shirt, using his mouth to tease my breasts as his hand glides down my stomach and between my legs. I lift my hips to meet his hand, relishing every stroke of his fingers, wishing they could go deeper into me. Light sliding into dark. Yang disappearing into yin.

An orchestra of sound weaves its way through my body, every note echoing through my nerve endings and lifting me higher. I am vibrating with want, wrapped in Adam's song—his symphony—and silently asking him to never stop.

I reach down and unfasten his jeans, taking him into my hand and feeling his stiff warmth in my palm. His hips push forward against my hand as I sit up on the sofa. He rises to his feet and cups my head in his hands, guiding himself into my mouth and filling it with his hard flesh. My mouth latches onto him, sucking and teasing until I know he's aching for release.

But before release comes, Adam steps back and drops out of my mouth. He pulls me up off the couch, grabs my hips, and lifts me until my legs are wrapped around his waist. He turns and puts my back against the wall, entering me and taking what is his to take, what's *always* been his to take.

Our souls dance together as our bodies fall into a vibrant and chaotic syncopation. Eventually, release spreads through us, one in chorus with the other, our minds littered with euphoria and ecstasy. Love.

Adam carries me to the bedroom and we lie there together, each of us lost in our own mind. But after the endorphins fade, my thoughts only bring questions, doubts.

For a brief moment, I wonder what will happen if I'm wrong. What if what I saw in Winston Sinclair's eyes isn't the truth? What if Adam somehow finds out about our deal before *it* happens? He won't understand how things are. He won't understand my choice. Or my gift. Everything will change if he finds out.

But then I remember I've never been wrong before. I've always seen the truth.

Why would this time be any different?

Chapter 27

When my father first told Charlie about his cancer, she said she didn't believe him. She accused him of trying to get out of paying her beauty school tuition. She said he was making it up because he didn't want her to be happy. Daddy broke down in tears and fell to the floor right in front of us, swearing to God all he ever wanted was for his girls to be happy. For *Charlie* to be happy. It was the second time I'd ever seen him cry. The first was on his fortieth birthday, when I gave him the refurbished wedding ring I just pawned for Charlie. The third was on the day he died.

As my daddy wept at our feet, my sister stood there, staring at me in disbelief. When I nodded at her to let her know he wasn't making the cancer up, her eyes fluttered closed and she knelt on the floor next to him, wrapping her arms around him and telling him again and again how sorry she was for being so selfish.

Right before I moved to Philadelphia, Charlie told me she'd never forgive herself for that moment. She said his death would be her motivation to make something of herself. She said she wouldn't let him down. I suppose that's why I keep giving her so many second chances. Because I want to believe she's still capable of making him proud.

Truth be told, I feel a little like Charlie right now, having just done something so opposite of everything my father ever taught us about living an honest life. I've essentially brokered a deal with the devil; it's one that, if I'm right, won't come to full fruition, but it's still one worth being ashamed of. If my father was alive, and he found out about my agreement with Winston Sinclair, he'd probably knock me over the head with a sack of crawdads until I came to my senses. I always thought that's what he should've done with Charlie, but now I realize he always knew better. He knew Charlie was, and is, too fragile to handle those kinds of hits.

But then again, maybe he wouldn't sack me. Maybe my father would be proud of me for taking Winston Sinclair to the table on this one. Maybe he'd say *good for you* when I said I wanted the twenty thousand dollars. Maybe he'd tell me I should've asked for fifty.

Regardless, I'm sure he'd have plenty to say about what I'm going to do with the money.

As I lie in bed, staring at the ceiling and thinking about my father, I hear Adam making coffee in my pint-sized kitchen. A cabinet door clunks closed as he searches for the filters. A few minutes later, when the smell of freshly brewed coffee finally wafts under the bedroom door, I drag myself out of bed and pull on my clothes. The alarm clock tells me it's 10:15 already. My work suspension is a nightmare, but sleeping in certainly is not. I can't remember the last time I slept this late, even on a day off.

I walk out into the kitchen, where I'm greeted by a freshly showered Adam and a full pot of coffee. He's wearing the same clothes as yesterday, but I can smell the soapiness of his skin. His wet hair is combed to perfect, bed-headed attention. Adam hugs me, and I hug him back, sinking my face into his chest and inhaling his fresh, clean scent. He pours us both a cup of coffee, and as we're making plans for him to pick me up for an early dinner after he visits with his grandmother, my phone rings.

It's Susan Campbell. But this time she's not the bearer of bad news, and she doesn't feel the need to apologize. Instead, she tells me the complaint was withdrawn. She doesn't tell me the name of the person who filed the complaint of course, but she does say that "he" informed her via telephone first thing this morning that the whole thing was a big misunderstanding. At her request, he's heading in to Pine Manor as we speak to fill out the appropriate paperwork. Susan says management needs a few days to clear things up on their end, but it looks like I'll be back to work by the end of the week.

As Adam listens to my half of the conversation, his face grows lighter and lighter. It's as if I'm watching a gigantic burden being slowly lifted from his shoulders with every word I say. I'm guessing that, until this very moment, he doubted his father would actually do what he said he would. By the time I hang up, he's wearing an enthusiastic grin and beaming with pride.

I fill Adam in on all the details of the conversation, and soon after, I manage to convince him to stick around and hang out with me a little longer. I remind him rushing off to Pine Manor right now means a definite run-in with his father, but if he waits here for a bit, their paths are less likely to cross. He doesn't like to leave his father alone with Ms. Sinclair, so I know he considers staying here with me to be a substantial gamble, but his newfound confidence kicks in and he agrees to stay for a little while longer.

I'm keenly aware that I'm walking a fine line, wanting them to avoid each other, but needing Adam to be gone by the time Mr. Sinclair's driver comes at noon. I offer to make us omelets. It seems to do the trick.

Soon after the breakfast dishes are washed, Adam's out the door, planting another not-such-a-nice-boy kiss on my mouth just before he goes. It makes my blood—now infused with a fevered rush of notes—pound through my ears. I ask him to give my best to his grandmother and tell her I'll be seeing her in a few days. I don't know if she'll understand or not, or even if she's noticed I'm gone, but it somehow makes me feel better.

So does the knowledge that after all of this is over, after *everything* is over, there will only be us. Me and Adam. And there will be love and compassion and music filling us both, holding us up and keeping us connected.

***

My doorbell rings at precisely 12:00. When I open it, I find a huge, smartly dressed black man standing in the hallway. He introduces himself as Perry Devine, Mr. Sinclair's driver, and asks if he can come in. He's holding a thick envelope in his right hand and in his left earlobe is one of the biggest diamonds I've ever seen. Under any other circumstances, I'd give him a big, fat *no* for an answer, but our transaction is one I'd rather keep private. The neighbors already consider my bass practicing annoying; I can only imagine what they'd think if they overheard the conversation I'm about to have with this massive man in a suit and aviator sunglasses. I open the door and step aside.

Perry Devine walks into my apartment and turns to face me as I close the door. I have a sharp and sudden memory of Winston Sinclair standing in the exact same place just yesterday. This guy, though…this guy is different. He's more physically intimidating than Mr. Sinclair, but there's something softer about him. He takes off his aviators with his free hand and tosses the envelope onto the coffee table behind him, watching it fall onto the wooden surface. When he faces me again, I see a pair of deep brown eyes, long-lashed and fierce, yet full of something warm and familiar. There's no longer a lens of shaded glass between his eyes and mine, but I don't see his death. I don't see anything.

Perry Devine will not be there when it happens.

"If I might be so bold, I'd like to give you some advice, Miss McGee." He crosses his arms over his chest and tilts his head to the side. Just by a hair.

"Please do."

"I've been Mr. Sinclair's driver for seventeen years. I've driven him to the State Legislature Building and the senate offices more times than I can count. I've taken his wife to tea at the Governor's Mansion the first Tuesday of every month for the past ten years. I've watched his son stumble through puberty—hell, I drove the boy to the prom for God's sake—and I shook his hand after every graduation, from grade school to grad school." He stops talking for a second, as if to let his words sink in. I keep quiet but don't take my eyes off of his. "This family is my business, Miss McGee, and I take serving them very seriously. Loyalty is not something I take lightly, so I suggest you take that ten grand and sever yourself from the Sinclairs immediately. You wait too long, and it'll be too late. Mr. Sinclair is a man of his word. Has been since my first day on the job."

"He gave me until the end of the week."

Perry Devine's eyebrows rise, as if he can't believe I've said something other than *Yes, sir. Right away, sir.*

"I'm aware of that. But, I'm trying to be nice. I'm telling you, the sooner, the better. For everyone. Just make my job easier, Miss McGee. Following people like you around is not what I was hired for."

And there you have it. Confirmation that my Latham Street visits had nothing to do with the black car. I'm both relieved and mortified by the knowledge that *this* is who's been watching me so closely.

He uncrosses his arms and points to the envelope on the table. "Be smart. Take that money and go back to Louisiana. Or wherever. Leave Adam alone. I'll see that you get the rest of your money. Like I said, Mr. Sinclair is a man of his word."

"May I ask you a question, Mr. Devine?"

His eyes narrow as his hands clasp just in front of the lowest button of his suit jacket. I'd bet the ten grand sitting on my coffee table he's former military.

He doesn't answer, but I ask my question anyway. "Have you seen anything that would lead you to believe I don't love Adam?"

There's not a single breath of time between my question and his answer. "Love has nothing to do with this. But that ten grand over there sure has a lot to say about it."

"Mr. Sinclair didn't give me much of a choice."

"He's like that sometimes." He shrugs his shoulders coyly.

We stand in my living room for a few silent moments, neither of us moving or opening our mouths. Thoughts of Adam's light skin against my dark sneak into my thoughts, introducing both a sharp blast of love and a slip of fear.

I'm suddenly second-guessing the risk I've taken, regretting nothing and everything all at the same time.

But, it's true…I don't have a choice. I have to follow through and hope Mr. Sinclair's eyes held the truth.

And I have to pray to Louise McGee's god that Adam doesn't find out about it.

Perry Devine takes a deep breath before unclasping his hands and walking over to me. He stops in front of me, my forehead level with his chest. Looking down, he says, "Find yourself someone else to love." He walks around me and opens the door, a trail of expensive cologne following his footsteps. Just as he steps out into the hallway he adds, "You'll be better off. Trust me."

A hundred questions slam into me with the click of the knob, every one of them casting a shadow. Every one of them generating a dozen more.

Wednesday cannot come fast enough.

***

At dinner, Adam tells me Gram had a pretty bad day. She fell again this afternoon, in the bathroom, but he caught her just before she hit the floor. After he helped Ms. Sinclair back onto her feet, she told him she'd have to report him to Principal Sykes for his unacceptable behavior. She scolded him for touching her in an inappropriate manner. He said he apologized profusely, and by the time she finished using the bathroom, she'd already forgotten the whole thing and was talking about the lack of chalk for the school chalkboards.

We talk a little more about his grandmother and about the conversation he had with Dr. Kopsey concerning her upcoming dental appointment. But, what Adam doesn't mention is his father. From the sound of it, this morning's omelet tactic worked.

***

I take a gamble and make a phone call Tuesday morning, just after Adam leaves to visit his gram. Since I no longer need to be up and out the door by 7:30, we spent last night at his place. We watched a movie on his cushy couch, had sex in his big bed, and ate breakfast at his granite countertop—each moment perfect and amazing. And probably under the watchful eye of Perry Devine.

I'm not sure if it's the right number, but I dial it anyway, hoping for the best. A man answers after four rings. I've obviously woken him. It's 10:30 here; 9:30 Louisiana time. I don't feel bad for waking the *what's-his-face*. His lazy ass should be working anyway.

"What'd you want?"

I steady my voice to steady my nerves. "May I please speak to Charlie?"

"Who is this?"

"Her sister. Is she there?"

"Hell no. Is that why you woke me up? Jesus. I haven't seen that bitch in a week. I'm done with her ass. Ain't got no use for her no more. She prolly livin' over at Tasha's place." Good. "Don't call me again, you hear?"

"I hear." I turn on the syrupy sweetness. "Thank you. You've been a big help. Enjoy your day."

"Fuck you." Click.

Tasha Pearson was my sister's roommate before my father got sick. They lived with another girl in a flat in a high rise on Gravelston Street. It wasn't a big place, but it was theirs. I used to love going over there when I was a junior in high school; they'd give me cigarettes and let me watch *The Vampire Diaries* with them every Thursday night. Tasha and Charlie were supposed to go to Blue Cliff cosmetology school together, but just before my father died, Charlie withdrew her application. Tasha went without her.

I use my iPhone to Google Tasha's number. It rings twice before a woman answers. I can hear a baby babbling in the background.

"Hello?"

"Hi. Is this Tasha?"

"No. She's at work right now. Can I take a message?" It's Charlie. I recognize her voice immediately. This time, though, it doesn't sound panicked. It sounds like Charlie. Maybe my eight hundred dollars actually meant something.

"Hey. It's me."

"K'acy?"

"Yep."

"I was gonna call you tomorrow, I swear."

"It's okay. I'm just glad you're all right. The *what's-his-face* told me you're living with Tasha now. So, it's true?" Inside, I'm bursting with hope. Hope that she's finally found her way. Hope that my daddy and I have a reason to be proud.

"Yeah. It's just temporary. I'm watching her kid in exchange for a place to stay so she can save a little on daycare. You won't believe it, but she still lives in the place on Gravelston. Looks the same. Only now she's got a little kid. A baby named Elijah. She still works at the salon, too."

"That's great, Charlie. I'm glad to hear it."

"I'm looking for a real job. So I can pay you back. For real this time. I swear."

"It's okay. Don't worry about it. In fact, I have something else I'd like to send you—no strings attached. I didn't know your address, but now I do."

"You don't have to send me anything."

"I know I don't have to. But I want to. I just...I picked up some extra work."

A small sniffle eventually breaks the long silence on the other end of the line. "I won't waste it," she says.

My heart swells with the knowledge that she's telling me the truth again. I can feel it. "I know."

Soon after we hang up, I call a taxi. First, it takes me to my place. Then, it takes me to the bank. I get a cashier's check for $9,500 made out to Charlie McGee. The taxi driver's last stop is the post office. As I slide the envelope into the slot, I think about what it's going to mean to Charlie, and how she's going to feel when she tears the envelope open and sees what's inside.

Fifteen minutes later, the taxi driver pulls up to the curb in front of my apartment. I pay the driver with some of the remaining Sinclair cash and wave to the dark sedan now parked across the street. I can't see him through the shaded windows, but I'm pretty sure Perry Devine does not wave back.

***

I wait for sleep to arrive on Tuesday night with Adam wrapped around me, his warm body holding me snug. Trepidation over the day to come has burned a small, smoldering hole in my heart, sending a flutter of notes—atonal and harsh—out into my bloodstream. They settle against my nerves and cause nausea to simmer in my stomach. I want to warn him about tomorrow. I want to tell him what's to come. But I can't, because he'll feel the same fear and horror my father felt when he looked at me after Ronald Chapman's daughter died. When he realized what I said had come true.

I never want someone to look at me like that again.

I can't believe I'm saying this, but a small part of me actually hopes I'm wrong. Maybe tomorrow will not be the night. Maybe the date on the bank sign wasn't right. Maybe Winston Sinclair is an anomaly in my fate, and for the first time ever, I'll be wrong. I think this not because I care about what happens to Winston Sinclair, but because of his son. The possibility of Adam somehow suffering is what's ignited the smoldering hole in my heart because I can't see what he will feel. I can only see the torturous end of his father's life.

My eyes do not close for a long time, even as Adam's breath falls into the soft, rhythmic pattern of sleep. As I stare at my hand resting on his chest, tracing the perfect alternating Vs of light and dark with my stare, I think about the gift I've been given. About what I can see and do. And, even in moments like this, moments where some might consider it a curse, I know what a miracle it is. I know how lucky I am.

Still…not for the first time, I wish I couldn't see death. I wish I couldn't see human loss, right down to the very last detail, if I care to look hard enough. It only happens when their time is close. A few months at most.

But, right now…I wish it didn't happen at all.

CHAPTER 28

Robert McGee—2008

I'm in a wheelchair and hooked up to an IV, but I'm here.

I made it.

It's 7:14 on the evening of May 21st, and I'm watching my baby girl walk down the center aisle of the Terrebonne Civic Center. She left the house two hours ago, looking like a million bucks in the white dress Charlie picked out for her at the Goodwill Store, her dark skin freshly dusted with some kind of shimmery powder and her neck graced by a set of pearls that once belonged to my mother. All of it's covered up now, though, by a long, white robe and a gold honors stole.

My little girl is graduating.

K'acy looks at me and Charlie from across the aisle, and it takes my breath away. She's wearing a smile, but there are tears running down her cheeks. I don't know if the tears are happy or sad, but they sure are quiet. For a sharp second, I feel bad for Louise. I feel bad she's missing such an important moment. But the pity passes quickly because I don't think too much about Louise anymore. I don't like to waste my time. Especially since I don't have much of it left.

When the school superintendent calls K'acy to the stage and hands her the diploma, my chest fills with pride. But, it's not the same kind of pride all the other daddies in the room are feeling. It's not because she passed AP English with flying colors, or even because she won the County Jazz Band's "Musician of the Year" award. I'm so damn proud of her because she already knows *exactly* who she is. Not many freshly minted eighteen-year-olds have a clue how to be authentic to themselves. They're too busy putting on a show for everyone else to pay attention to who they really are on the inside. But K'acy…she shines with light and self-love. She knows precisely who she is, and she's not afraid to show it to the world. And, of all the things I love about my girls, that's the one that fills me with the most pride.

But, even knowing all that—even knowing how *real* she is—I also know there's more to her than what the world can see. I never could put my finger on it, but there's something profound about K'acy's kind of special. It's like she's meant for something bigger than the rest of us. I don't know what it is, but I know she's gonna do big things. I've been telling my girls their whole lives that you always gotta do the right thing, even when it hurts, and I truly believe K'acy heard my message loud and clear. She *gets* it. Now if I could only live long enough to see where it takes her.

After the ceremony ends, Charlie takes me home. K'acy's supposed to go out to celebrate with her friends, but no sooner does Charlie get me back in the rented hospital bed in our living room, when K'acy comes traipsing in the door carrying her cap and gown like they're nothing that matters. When Charlie asks her how she got home, K'acy says her friend Jessica's father dropped her off. She says she doesn't much feel like celebrating, and she'd rather be home with us. She smiles at me when she says the last part, and I can see on her face she's telling the God's honest truth.

It makes me feel good and bad at the same time. She wants to be with me, but I know why.

While K'acy tosses her cap and gown into the hall closet, Charlie runs upstairs to get something. She comes back down holding a shoebox-sized package wrapped in colorful paper and topped with a bow. I'm instantly glad she thought enough to get her sister a graduation gift, especially since I couldn't leave the house to get one of my own. Charlie moved back home a few weeks ago, saying she wanted to save money on rent. I'm happy to have her here again, even if she lied about the reason. Having my two girls together is real, real nice.

K'acy thanks her sister for the gift and opens the box. Inside is a pile of hair-care products from the salon where Charlie works. As her sister is explaining how to use them all one-by-one, K'acy looks over at me with a devilish twinkle in her eye. We both know she finds the gift ridiculous, but at the same time, she doesn't want to seem ungrateful. Charlie loves working at the salon with Tasha, and she's forever talking about the day she gets to do more than answer the phone and wash people's hair. I'm afraid of what's going to happen when I tell her I can't pay for her schooling anymore. She's going to have to do it on her own now because the hospital bills are overwhelming. There's one right after another, and it'll only get worse. Hell, it'll be a miracle if the house is still in my name on the day I die. That's the worst thing about this disease; cancer doesn't just take your body and your spirit, it takes your wallet, too.

When Charlie finishes her hair care lesson, K'acy gives her a hug and says a genuine "thank you." There's real love there; I can see it.

A little while later, just after Charlie heads upstairs to get my pajamas, K'acy comes into the room with her Music Man

StingRay bass. The one I got her for Christmas when she was thirteen. I remember the day I went to pick it out. I chose the one with the Vintage Sunburst body and the white pearloid pickguard because it reminded me of her—all shiny and eager to fill the world with song. Turns out it was a good choice. She loves that thing more than life itself. It's become a veritable "third arm" for her these past five years. After she slings the shoulder strap over her head, she plugs the cord into a small amp and starts playing for me. For us.

I don't know when she learned to play it, or how long she's practiced, but she's got "That's How Strong My Love Is" down pat. She's not playing the bass line; she's playing the melody. I listen to every note, singing silently in my head, the lyrics sitting heavy on my heart. As the words roll through my mind, I push down the valves of an imaginary trumpet right along with her, note for note. We're making beautiful music together, my baby and I. And it nearly makes me cry.

When she finishes the song, I ask her to hand me the guitar. Then, I send her out to the shed to get my paint box, the one I used to use to touch things up around the house every now and then. In the box I find a small bottle of black acrylic lacquer.

I dip a slender-tipped brush into the bottle and start painting on the pickguard. I paint a cobweb there; a delicate and complex series of lines, woven together with love. With every stroke of my brush, I create a miniature safety net that will forever be attached to her hip. One that will remind her of me long after I'm gone. One she can rely on to see her through life without a father.

As I paint, K'acy sits down on the bed next to me, and out of the corner of my eye, I see her watching the brush as the picture takes shape. When I finish and put the brush down on the living-room table, she asks me what it means. I tell her it means I love her, and I'll always be there to catch her, even after I'm gone. I tell her every time she touches it, it's gonna remind her of how I'm watching over her, making sure she doesn't fall.

K'acy doesn't say a word. She just closes her eyes, puts her arms around me, and cries.

Chapter 29

A shot of fear flashes through my sleeping mind like a lightning bolt, causing me to sit straight up in the bed and gasp for breath. My nervous heart knocks against my ribcage, waking me with its urgency. It takes me a moment to remember what this feeling is for.

Adam is lying next to me, staring at me in startled confusion. I don't say anything. I only try to catch my breath. And remind myself it was just a dream.

Adam lifts his arm and touches me on the shoulder. His hand is warm and dry. It makes me feel safe. It's like a new version of home.

"Hey," he says, his voice full of sleep. "Are you okay?"

I nod.

"Bad dream?"

I nod again, still unsure of myself.

"You scared the crap out of me."

"Sorry," I say, not taking my eyes off of his.

"Must have been a pretty brutal dream. You wanna talk about it?" There's nothing I'd like to do more. But I can't. Because I'm pretty sure having your secretly clairvoyant girlfriend tell you she dreamed about your father's death is a definite deal breaker.

"Not really."

"Come on," he says, tugging on my arm and coaxing me back down next to him, "let's just try to go back to sleep for a little while. It's early."

"I don't think I can." Nor do I want to.

"You sure you don't want to talk about it?"

"I'm sure."

He turns onto his side and lifts his hand to my face. His thumb skims the crest of my cheek as his palm rests on the side of my jaw. It's such a little thing, but full of meaning. Masculine and caring. As the corners of his mouth lift with a small, understanding smile, the dream melts away and takes a sliver of fear along with it. There's a morsel of comfort there now. Calm.

"When I was a kid, Gram used to tell me bad dreams were a sign of a charmed life. She said it was your brain's way of balancing things out. If life was full of good things during the day, the bad stuff would have to come out at night." Sadness seeps into his sleepy voice. He tries to stuff it back down as he talks, but it's undeniable. "I'd call for her whenever I'd have a nightmare, and she'd always come running. She'd sit on the side of my bed and rub my back until I fell asleep again." He stares off at the pillow behind me, lost in a memory. "I remember the moment I realized my life was no longer charmed. I had a nightmare one night in Seattle and no one came running when I called."

I lift his hand off my cheek and put it to my lips, planting a small kiss on his fingertips.

"I bet she thought about you every single day."

"Maybe." He sighs deeply, wraps his arms around me, and pulls me in close. Together, our bodies form another seamless *taijitu*; two parts of a whole. Opposite, yet perfect. Each with a drop of themselves inside the other. I can tell he's thinking hard about something. Maybe Bradley. Or perhaps his grandmother. "What about you? What happened when you had a nightmare?"

"My mother would read from the Bible. She'd read to us before bed, too, and I think that's what probably caused my nightmares in the first place. Let's just say the passages she picked weren't very comforting. I'm sure there were greater lessons in them somewhere, but the deeper meaning was lost on me and Charlie. My mother never gave us context, just direct quotes. Needless to say, we stopped calling for her after a while. Instead, whenever one of us would have a nightmare, we'd just hop into each other's bed. Up until Momma left, Charlie was a great big sister. Then she just kinda lost herself." I shrug as if it doesn't really matter. Even though we both know it does.

Adam nods in understanding. As if he, too, had once been lost. We lie in silence, and I think again about Charlie opening the envelope I mailed her yesterday. The hope I now have for her future fills me with nervous anticipation. I will her, once again, to make our daddy proud.

A few more moments of quiet pass between us before Adam's voice settles in my ears. "Can I ask you a favor?"

"Sure."

"If I ever have a bad dream, will you sit on the side of the bed and rub my back until I fall asleep again?"

My smile must be a mile wide.

"Absolutely."

"I love you, K'acy McGee."

"I love you, too."

***

Watching the minutes slip by on the microwave clock is torture. After Adam heads to Pine Manor, I spend the day doing the only thing capable of taking my worry away. I practice my bass, my ears covered by headphones filled with amplified notes. I play song after song until my fingers buzz with electric satisfaction and my heart falls back into its own steady beat.

When early evening arrives, with deep, heart-steadying music still echoing in my ears, I lift the StingRay's strap up over my head and put it back in its stand. I skim the pickguard's painted cobweb with the tips of my fingers, feeling the delicate, glossy lines and thinking for a moment about its meaning. The security of my father's promise somehow reassures me Adam and I will survive whatever the rest of this life has to offer. We will still be standing when everything is over, even if we stumble along the way. Adam will not break. And neither will I.

I have more than enough time to eat and grab a shower before I have to slip the StingRay into its gig bag and hop on the 43D. Tonight's King's Court soul-cleansing is going to be different. But not because I've practiced all day.

It'll be different because at 10:46 p.m., I'll know what's happening six miles away, in front of the Star City National Bank. I'll know, but Adam will not.

Just before I walk out the door my cell phone vibrates with an incoming text. The gig bag is already slung over my back and my shoes are half on. I reach into my pocket and pull the phone out.

Hey.

It's Adam.

Hey. How was your gram today?

Pretty good.

I wonder if it's the truth, or if he's just trying to make me feel better about not being there. I wish I could see his face.

Glad to hear she had a decent day.

Ran into your supervisor Susan. Pretended I didn't know why you were gone and asked when you'd be back. She said she thought by the end of the week.

Here's hoping. I haven't heard from anyone about it yet.

She sounded pretty positive. Maybe you should call her tomorrow.

Probably a good idea.

Gram's ready to have you back. Mr. Rauch's colostomy bag probably needs you, too.

LOL. I'll bet.

Also got some good news from the giant dickhead. He called me earlier and said he's going back to Seattle tonight. Taking the red-eye. Says he won't be back.

What? I look at the text again, just to be sure I read it correctly.

Seriously?

That's what he says.

Wow.

Yep.

My mind starts racing. Mr. Sinclair will be headed back to Seattle when it happens.

How do you feel about that?

Happy as hell, of course. He asked me to take him to the airport.

My heart drops to my core as the gig bag slides down my shoulders and crashes onto the carpet. I press my back against the wall and sink down until I meet the floor. My guts shuffle around inside me, causing a sudden streak of nausea to fill up my insides.

Shit.

Doesn't he have a driver to take him?

The absence of death in Perry Devine's eyes hits me hard. He isn't going to be driving Mr. Sinclair tonight because Adam is.

The possibility of Adam's pain being physical, and not emotional, never entered my mind. Until now.

I asked him the same thing. He said he wanted me to take him instead. He said he wants to clear things up between us before he goes.

No no no no…

But I thought you were coming to The King's Court?

Please. Please. Please say you are…

I am.

So you told him no?

I told him I already had plans.

Cautious relief breaks through the rush of nauseating adrenaline. My fingers shake as I text my reply.

So you're definitely coming tonight?

Yes. I'll be there. Gonna stay with Gram until visiting hours are over, then I'll head out.

My racing mind skitters to a halt, and before I can text a reply, my phone vibrates with the arrival of more words from Adam.

The man is insane to think a ride to the airport will clear things up between us.

I can't catch my breath, let alone think of what to say next. My fingers fumble against the phone.

I'm glad you're coming tonight. Really glad.

Wouldn't want you to have to play without your lone swooner there to cheer you on.

Me neither.

See you in a bit.

I love you.

Copy that and send it back. :)

Now that I know Adam will not be injured in a crumpled car in front of the Star City National Bank later tonight, I'm left with a strange, post-torture sense of peace. As I sit on the living-room floor, my back to the wall and knees folded up against my chest, questions start to jump through my mind. Why is Mr. Sinclair leaving so suddenly? Doesn't he want to make sure I follow through with my end of our arrangement? Why did he tell Adam he wouldn't be back? How will Adam handle what's going to happen tonight now that he knows he could've been there, too?

I wipe my hands against my face, running my fingers up my forehead and through my hair. They stop when they reach the back of my neck. I'm frozen, filled with questions and wishing Adam were here with me right now so I could see his face and wrap myself around him. I close my eyes and inhale a deep breath.

***

The bus drops me off a block from The King's Court, and as I'm walking up to the side door, I see him standing across the street. He's leaning on the front fender of the black car, arms crossed over his chest and dressed in a dark suit. I can tell from here that his white shirt has been ironed to crisp perfection. There's no tie today; I guess this is his version of casual. I can't see his eyes from here, but I'm sure nothing inside of them has changed.

I'm not nervous about him being here. In fact, I hope he comes inside and sees Adam and me together. I hope he hears me play and feels my music vibrating through his chest as it sends its message of love and compassion out into the world. Maybe it would change his mind, make him wonder whose side he should really be on. But I know even if he does come inside and see and hear and feel everything I want him to, it will be too late to change things. Too late to make a difference.

None of it will matter in a few hours anyway.

Perry Devine lifts his chin to me as I open the door to The King's Court and slip inside. I give him a small nod in return, feeling a quick bite of sympathy for the man despite his boss's intentions. After all, he's about to lose someone who might have mattered to him. Seventeen years is a long time to drive someone around and not care about them at least a little bit. It's now obvious why he won't be in the Jag tonight. Instead of driving Mr. Sinclair to the airport, he'll be spying on me. I guess he's the one who's sticking around to make sure I hold up my end of the bargain.

Perry Devine's point is clear. He wanted me to see him tonight, so I'd know he's still watching. But I'm sure the second the bar's door closes behind me, he'll be back inside that car, behind its tinted glass and out of sight. He won't risk being seen by Adam because he knows exactly what will happen if the boss's son catches sight of him spying on his girlfriend. He's played Mr. Sinclair's games for seventeen years; he knows which secrets to keep.

Once my eyes adjust to the bar's dim lighting, I spy Jarrod perched on a stool at the end of the bar. There are only six other people here, and one of them is sitting right next to him. It's a woman, wispy and dark-haired, with bright pink lips and kohl-rimmed eyes. Her slender legs are snug against his, and she's smiling and looking at him as if he's everything that matters in the world. As I walk a little closer, I see a name tattooed on her right shoulder blade, its large, curled cursive creeping out from under the strap of her shirt.

Grace.

I watch them for a few minutes from several paces away, hoping to catch a glimpse of the perfect life Jarrod deserves. She touches his arm and laughs. He puts his hand on her knee. They talk and drink and look more comfortable than they should for being so new. I smile at the thought of her being his supervisor. Together, their body language tells me I like her already.

If Grace is going to be my best friend's girl, I'd better go introduce myself.

"Hey kids," I chirp as I approach them and signal for the bartender to bring us another round of beers. Jarrod takes care of the introductions, and as the small talk commences, I watch Jarrod's face closely for signs of embarrassment or disapproval. I wait for him to look away, but I only see affection and happiness there. For both of the women next to him.

It takes a mere ten minutes of conversation for me to determine Grace is downright lovely; her name suits her perfectly. She's soft and funny and really, really into Jarrod. When I look in her eyes, I see nothing. No sadness, no suffering, no death. I'm relieved.

A short while later, I head to the stage to set up, and for the first time ever, Jarrod follows me. As I take the StingRay out of its bag and start to get myself organized, he pretends to be helping. But I know he's really here to find out what I think of Grace. I don't make him ask, I offer my thoughts without being prodded.

"Isn't she a little young for you, Grandpa?" I plug my bass into the amp and lay out the cord.

"Very funny, Kace."

"Did you take your teeth out for her yet?" I'm trying not to smile. I don't want Grace to think this is anything but a normal conversation between two friends.

"Not yet, but I'm thinking maybe tonight's the night. If your playing puts us in the mood."

"So I should play some Barry Manilow then?" I ask as I prop the StingRay up on the house's stand.

"Maybe Barry White would be better. We're a few dates in, after all. I like to hit it heavy right out the gate." He's trying not to smile, too, but his eyes are giving him away.

"Anything for you, Jar." I put my hand on his shoulder and give him a friendly pat. I'd rather hug him, of course, but I won't. Because of Grace. "In all seriousness, she seems great. And you seem happy." I drop my hand from his shoulder and twist the cap off a bottle of water. "I'll let Adam ask her all the hard questions. Only seems fair."

"So, he's coming tonight?" He looks a little surprised.

"Of course. Why wouldn't he?" I'm confused.

His brow goes up as he shrugs. "Well, I didn't know how things worked out with his old man. Was he able to talk some sense into the guy?"

"Kind of, yes. Adam convinced him to withdraw the complaint. And now it looks like his dad's going back to Seattle tonight."

"He is?" More surprise.

"Yep."

"I guess your sassy comment worked then?"

"I guess so."

"Sounds like things are gonna go back to normal for you and The Mister. That's good."

I don't say anything in return. I don't tell him "normal" is not how it's going to be. Instead, I smile and nod as I sling the StingRay's leather strap up over my head and switch on the amp. Jarrod turns away and starts walking toward the bar. As he steps off the stage, he turns back and adds, "Oh, Jesus. I almost forgot. Calvin's gonna pick you up at seven on Saturday. Make sure you wear something that shows a little skin for the Naysayer rep, will you?" He wiggles his eyebrows up and down, and just like that, a dull ache presses down on my heart.

I know I'm never going to set foot in The Upstage on Saturday night. Because I'll be elsewhere, fixing someone.

"Soul to Squeeze" is not the first song to come out of me. Instead, I play "Ecce Homo" for Jarrod, to let him know he's worth beholding, just like his song says. He deserves Grace's affection and attention, and I want to remind him he deserves a perfect life, too, even if he's going to live it without me. I play the song to let him know I think he really is an epic ass shaker. He *is* dynamite. And hopefully, after Saturday, the rest of the world will think so, too.

Soon after I start playing, the electric buzz returns to my fingers, raising me up and clearing out my insides. The satisfaction is instant and grounding. I keep playing, song after song rolling out of my brain and off of my fingertips. Each note washes a small piece of me until I am glowing and clean again. I am at peace.

As my string of songs continues, I watch Jarrod and Grace together, sitting side by side at the bar, each drinking their beer. I can't help but smile when I notice Jarrod's foot tapping against the leg of the barstool in perfect time with each song I play. He can't help it. It's inside him, too.

At first, I'm too wrapped up in soul-cleansing notes for Adam's absence to be shocking. But then, when the clock over the bar suddenly shouts at me in between songs, everything changes. In fact, the red neon 10:43 does more than shout at me; it wraps its hands around my neck and squeezes, its tightness so strong and sudden that I can't breathe. Fear gnaws at me, quick and fierce, like an oilman eating up the bayou.

I don't start playing another song. Instead, I stand on the stage, unmoving and silent, frozen with sudden doubt and fear and dread.

Seven faces turn and stare at me, all of them wondering why the music has stopped.

CHAPTER 30

Miriam Hansen—Room number 112

I spent most of my life telling people what they didn't want to hear. When I registered for nursing school in 1948 I had no idea how much bad news I would have to bring to people's lives. If I'd have known it, I might've become a teacher instead.

It isn't easy telling a mother her child isn't going to survive a bout with scarlet fever. Or informing a husband his wife's MS is only going to get worse. Bringing bad news to the family of someone who had so much potential only a few days before will forever be the ugliest part of being a nurse.

Don't get me wrong, my job was filled with lots of good things, too. I got to see babies being born, red-faced and full of promise. I got to see people with life-threatening injuries walk out of the hospital months later with nothing more than a Band-Aid on the inside of their elbow. I got to see beautiful young women with breast cancer leave the hospital in full remission. There was plenty of good, for sure. But, telling people about the bad things was always the part that haunted me the most.

It takes a special person to care for a stranger deeply enough to want to heal them. Compassion is a human trait that's innate in nearly everyone, but there's a particular level of empathy required to be constantly surrounded by sick people and still see each one of them as a person, rather than an illness. Doctors have it to some extent, but it's different with them. They can separate themselves because their hands aren't physically connected to sickness every single day. They aren't catching the vomit, holding the needle, or washing the bedsores. That's what nurses are for.

It used to keep me from sleeping, thinking about a particular patient and wondering if the second-shift nurse was caring for them as much as I did. At first, I thought I was the only one who worried about what happened to my patients after I walked out the hospital door at night. But it didn't take me long to figure out I was far from alone. Every nurse I've ever known worries about their patients, some just show it more than others. For certain nurses, it's easier to pretend to build an emotional wall between themselves and their patients. For whatever reason, they think it'll make it easier on them if things go awry.

But it never does. It just makes them better at hiding how they feel.

I retired from nursing after working for forty-five years, but I stayed at the Sisters of Mercy Hospital as a volunteer until I was seventy-nine. Instead of doing the hard stuff, I got to bring people magazines and books. I got to sit at their bedside and talk with them. When I was a nurse, I always *listened* my patients, but it took becoming a volunteer to truly be able to *hear* them. Once I started volunteering, it didn't take long for me to discover the difference between listening and hearing. *Listening* involves receiving a request and doing something to satisfy it. *Hearing*, however, isn't quite so literal. It doesn't require any action. Instead, it requires only time and attention. *Hearing* someone means letting them give you a piece of their soul through a story or a thought. It doesn't mean you have to fix something, it just means you have to open your ears and your heart and try to understand who they are on the inside. I got real good at hearing people in the last twenty years of my life, and I learned a lot about the world as a result.

The sad truth is that most people are too busy to hear these days. They just go about their business, listening to the requests of their boss, their child, their spouse, their neighbor, and trying to fulfill those requests with some kind of action. But they don't really hear anything in the process. They don't have the chance to open their hearts to someone else's life. There's no time for it. Their own life is moving too fast. But what they fail to see is that it only takes a minute to open your heart wide enough to hear someone. It only takes a single question to spark a story that takes but a moment to be heard.

There's so much to be learned from even the quickest glimpse into someone else's life. This is especially true of children. Our children deserve to be heard more than anyone else. I wish parents wouldn't just listen to their child's requests and try to fulfill them with mindless immediacy. Instead, I wish they would stop and really *hear* their child. Hear the desires of their child's heart, hear about her accomplishments, her struggles and fears, no matter how small or trivial they might seem to grown-up ears. Because to a child, these things are the world, and the only way you can learn what a child is like on the inside is to *hear* them talk about their world.

But most people can't do it. They can't hear because they're too busy listening.

In all my days on this Earth, the only other person I found who understood how to hear people as well as me was K'acy McGee. From the moment they wheeled me into Pine Manor, I watched her hear people. She could take the smallest moment and fill it with a tiny slice of someone's life by asking a simple question that would invoke a memory. She did it to me countless times, without me even realizing what she was doing. Later, I'd get to thinking about our conversation and realize what she'd done, and it would always make me smile. For the first time in my life, I was the one who felt heard.

That girl was special to me, and I like to think I was special to her, too. Not only did she hear about my life, but I heard about hers as well. She told me about her father and her sister and everything they'd been through. Sometimes, she'd come in on her days off and play her bass guitar for me, its deep notes echoing off the walls of my tiny room. When it got close to the end, she'd stay with me, long into the night. She'd read to me, or we'd watch TV together, or she'd share some special memory, usually about her momma's cooking.

I knew about her and she knew about me. We *heard* each other in equal measure. I don't know why God made her like he did, but I sure was glad to be a part of it.

The night I died, I told her how important she is and that the world is lucky to have her walking around on it. I asked her not to be sad about me dying, but to be happy for the chance to know the next person who's going to sleep in my bed. I assured her they'll have a different story to tell, and their story will somehow bring her all of the happiness she deserves.

I promised her the next person to fill my room will offer her the one thing she needs but doesn't yet have: love.

I told her all this without a second's hesitation because you never know when and how love will come into your life. And, sometimes, if someone tells you it's coming, it's easier for you to find.

I saw the displeasure in Sondra's eyes that night as she stood behind K'acy only long enough to hear my promise. But it didn't matter, because Sondra is one of those wall builders who never puts faith in her own emotions. She just tries to hide behind the wall and ignore how she feels. She offered me nothing but a small, disapproving shake of the head before turning her back on us and walking out of the room, no doubt to pretend she didn't care.

An hour later, I was gone. K'acy ushered me out with all the compassion any human being could ever ask for. I saw it and I felt it. And I understood.

CHAPTER 31

I've had this feeling before. Just over six years ago. The day after my father died. When Charlie didn't show up at the funeral home to help me plan the service. I hadn't seen anything different in her eyes when I left her a few hours before, and yet, when she didn't come, I knew something was wrong. It feels that way again, like a giant sinkhole has opened up beneath my feet and swallowed me whole, closing over on itself and trapping me inside. Charlie wears the physical scars of that night, slashes of scar tissue across her wrists. But tonight, it's my invisible scars that are humming with fear. They remember this feeling.

I watch the numbers on the clock, willing 10:46 to never arrive.

Out of the corner of my eye, I see Jarrod's head tilt with curiosity and his eyes narrow as he slides off his barstool and starts walking toward me. He seems to be moving in slow motion, with Grace in the background, her hands resting on her lap. As Jarrod moves closer to the stage, my mind snaps to attention, and I reach behind me to pull my cell phone from the back pocket of my jeans.

There is no message from Adam.

Jarrod steps onto the stage in front of me, and I hear the low din of bar noises start to fill the room. Before I can even raise my head to look up at him, I hear him talking.

"Kace. What's up, girl? You okay?" His hands are on my shoulders.

The moment I lift my head, I see it behind him.

10:44. In neon red. Screaming at me.

After sliding my phone back into my pocket, I lift the Sting-Ray's leather strap up over my head, knocking Jarrod's hands off my shoulders. As I walk over to the stand and put it down, I brush my father's cobweb with the tips of my fingers, feeling absolutely nothing through the numbness of my skin. The sinkhole squeezes me tighter, gripping my heart and stealing my breath. I want to cry.

One of Jarrod's hands is on my shoulder again, gently turning me around until we're face-to-face.

"What's going on?" His expression is soft.

I don't know what makes me say it, but I do.

"I think something bad is about to happen to Adam." Jarrod lifts his hand from my shoulder and brushes it against the side of his chin. "He's supposed to be here right now, and he's not." My tears are stuck in the bundle of nerves now clogging the back of my throat. I swallow hard, hoping to keep them from rushing out.

"The man's just late, that's all. There's nothing to worry about."

Words come out of me, faster than I can control them. I'm surprised at how angry they sound. "He's not just late, Jar. Something is happening."

"What are you talking about?"

"I can't... Just forget it." I cross my arms over my chest and look away.

Grace is next to him then, putting her arm around his waist and asking us both if everything is okay. Jarrod tells her everything is fine. He tells her I'm just worried because Adam is running late. She mentions that traffic might be bad because of some ballgame. It doesn't make me feel any better.

10:45.

I turn to pack up the StingRay, holding in my tears and wondering how in God's name I'm going to do this.

Then, from behind me, I hear Jarrod's voice.

"Told you the man was just running late."

The tension leaves my body the instant I see him. The sinkhole opens wide and spits me back out again, the force of it filling my lungs with a new, full breath of air. I can't help myself. I'm at a near run when I slam into Adam, jumping into his arms and wrapping my entire body around his. Dark folded around light, covering it with love.

A few seconds later, I let go. Trepidation sinks its bitter claws into me when I realize he isn't squeezing me back. He is just standing there, letting me hug him but giving me nothing in return. I look up to find his face solid and unemotional.

"What's going on? Are you okay?" My voice is on the edge of tears again, ripped apart by a muddled concoction of confusion and cautious relief.

In the second of silence before he speaks, the red neon switches to 10:46.

"He told me about your deal, K'acy. He said you took the money."

The sinkhole bursts open again, this time filling with a surging tidal wave of disgust and fear. It washes over me and drags me under as searing bubbles of hatred scorch my skin.

I picture Winston Sinclair's body bursting into flames. His flesh melting away at the hands of the hottest fires of hell. His nerve endings blistering with pain so intense it would make the devil himself shudder. His eyes shriveling into burned-up bits of flesh, leaving him blind to everything but the charred memories of a life he'll no longer have. I picture the pain. *His* pain. And I relish the knowledge that *it is real*. It is happening. Right now. Even as my own heart is being ripped out of my chest, Winston Sinclair's suffering is all I can see. It's all I want. Wrong or right, I'm heady with elation at the thought of it. I want him to experience every single second of the agony to come. I want his pain to be as intense as a billion atom bombs.

I want him to suffer.

I watch the movie—*his* movie—inside my head, remembering every detail and watching them all unfold in my mind exactly as it's happening in real life. Six miles away. In front of the Star City National Bank.

I don't know what words to say to Adam, so I don't say anything at all. I just stare at him as the movie inside of my head comes to its climax. Winston Sinclair's burning body stumbles out of his crumpled, flame-engulfed car. He drops to the asphalt as a bystander throws a jacket over him to smother the flames. Black smoke wafts from his body. He's screaming.

The bank sign behind the car glows a brilliant green. *10:46, 58 F, September 20, Refinance TODAY.*

As soon as I see the sirens, I deliberately stop the movie in its tracks. I know the rest already. I know what happens next, and I don't need to see anything else to know how the story ends.

Adam's voice snaps me back to reality and out of Mr. Sinclair's movie.

"I meant it, you know…every time I said I love you."

I can only look at him, my eyes open wide, struck with the knowledge that fixing this is impossible. Winston Sinclair will never be able to take it back. And I will never be able to explain it. There is nothing I can tell Adam—no reason for doing what I did—that will be good enough to fix this. Except maybe for the truth. And I can never tell him that. Because he won't understand.

He stands in front of me, in all his bed-headed glory, wounded and heartbroken. Mystified.

Adam turns on his heels and starts walking toward the door.

I say the only thing that feels right, even though I don't think he can hear me.

"Copy that and send it back."

As soon as the door closes behind him, Jarrod and Grace are at my side. My tears burst free in a rush of salty anger and grief. I bury my face in my hands, damning myself for being stupid enough to take Winston Sinclair's money. Foolishness and regret stab at my heart, tearing it open and filling my veins with a whirlwind of disjointed, reckless notes, all of them out of tune and full of despair.

I've broken us, and there's no turning back. Destiny—and Miriam Hansen—had it wrong after all.

"What the hell is going on?" Jarrod asks through my sobs, rubbing my hunched back in small, comforting circles. I can't answer his question. I can only tell him I need to leave. I walk back to the stage, grab the StingRay, and head for the door, leaving Jarrod and his wispy, dark-haired savior slack-jawed with confusion.

Just as the door to The King's Court closes behind me, I see Adam's Passat turn the corner onto Cohosh Street, the brake lights signaling his departure with another unwelcome jolt of neon red. I want to run after him, to chase his car until I fall over with exhaustion, screaming my apology and begging him to forgive me for what I've done.

A new burst of sadness rips through me just as I hear the squeal of car tires from across the street. I turn around to see Perry Devine's car peel out of its parking space and tear off down the street, no doubt after receiving word about what happened six miles away. In front of the Star City National Bank.

***

By the time I'm standing in front of the glass doors, it's nearly midnight. I slide my keycard through the slot, never believing for one second it will work. But, when the doors glide open and I see the leather wingchairs arranged in their perfect rows, I know Susan Campbell never believed him in the first place. Because if she did, she would've deactivated my keycard.

I walk past Ms. Sinclair's vacant seat at the lobby window, the exterior floodlights illuminating her birdfeeder. It's empty and quiet, and it hurts me to know no one has paid attention to filling it for her while I've been gone.

Like every other night, the front desk is unstaffed. The skeleton crew of night-shift nurses and aides are either busy helping someone to the bathroom, changing a soiled bed linen, or conversing about something in the back room. I hurry down the hallway, my gig bag in tow, and quietly open Evelyn Sinclair's door.

She's sound asleep, blissfully unaware of the tragedy that's happened to her son. Her breathing is steady and quiet. The bathroom light is on, no doubt to serve as a reminder for her to pull her call cord for help if she needs to get out of bed. The small pile of empty cellophane candy wrappers on her bedside table glints in the bathroom's dull light. I walk across the room, past the foot of her bed, and place my gig bag on the floor before taking a seat in her recliner. More tears come then, when I see the framed photo someone has placed on her dresser. It's an image of Adam as a young boy, perhaps five or six. She's standing behind him with her hands on his shoulders. Her hair is in a bun; a clump of his is standing straight up in a little kid version of bed-head. They're both smiling, filled with joy and obvious love. I can only guess Adam put it there to help her remember. My tears are silent, but they keep coming. I don't think I could stop them if I wanted to, so I let them fall until my face is puffed with exhaustion. When they finally stop, I wipe them away with the back of my hand and rise to my feet. I straighten Ms. Sinclair's covers before sitting down on the edge of her bed. I don't know why, but I start talking.

In my quietest whisper, I tell her everything that's happened. I tell her I fell in love with her grandson and he loves me back. I tell her about what happened when he found out about my deal with his father and how much hope I have for Charlie now that she has enough money to get back on her feet. The whole time I'm talking, Ms. Sinclair's breath is unwavering and her eyes stay closed. She sleeps through every word, but it feels good to get it out, even if my words fall only on her deaf ears.

The last thing I tell Ms. Sinclair is the story of her son. I tell her about the accident and how difficult it's going to be for him for the next few days. She doesn't stir, so I just keep talking until I've said everything I need to say.

Then, I ask her what I should do next. I ask her if there's anything I can do to make Adam understand. But she doesn't answer. No one does.

I sit on the edge of her bed for a few more minutes, watching her sleep and thinking about how quickly life can change. I touch her hair with the tips of my fingers, remembering how many times I sat on the edge of my father's bed, just like this. When he got too weak to eat, I would sit with a glass of chalky nutrition drink, holding the straw to his mouth and begging him to take a sip.

Just one sip. Please.

On "good" days, I would sit and read to him, but not from the Bible. From *Louis Armstrong: In His Own Words*. Sometimes, I'd give him a shave or brush his teeth from my place on the edge of his bed. He never once asked me to leave him alone. Even when he couldn't tell me so, I knew he was glad I was there.

I've sat on the edge of lots of other beds over the past six years, too, offering my compassion and comfort when no one else could.

It's what I do. It's who I am.

A smack of sudden shame barrels through me when I realize taking pleasure in Winston Sinclair's suffering is against everything I am. Even if he isn't the kind of person who deserves forgiveness, he's still a human being, and no human being deserves to endure the pain that's been thrust upon him. Wanting him to hurt is *not* a part of me; it's a part of my anger, and I'm embarrassed to have embraced it, even temporarily. I've given meaning to my life by using my gift to care for people, and I can't let Winston Sinclair change that. I can't let him change *me*.

My father would never forgive me if I did.

I touch Ms. Sinclair's hair one last time, and tell her goodbye. Then, I promise her I'll take care of her son.

I'm just about to stand up and leave when the door opens.

Sondra is there, holding the door handle in her right hand and a clipboard in her left. A lick of surprise streaks across her face the moment she sees me.

"Jesus, Mary, and Joseph! What the hell are you doing here?" Her voice may be at a near whisper, but her shock is loud and clear. Before I can answer, she turns and glances down the hallway then quickly steps into the room and closes the door behind her.

"I'm sorry. I was just leaving." I stand and bend over to pick up my gig bag. When she sees it, she nods in understanding, obviously thinking I came to play for Ms. Sinclair, just like I used to play for Miriam Hansen.

"This woman has already had enough activity for one day," Sondra whispers as she crosses her arms over her chest. "I've already had to kick two people out of her room tonight, don't make me kick you out, too, girl."

I shake my head and furrow my brow. "You had to what?"

We start walking toward each other, meeting at the foot of Ms. Sinclair's bed. The whispers between us continue as soon as we're within arm's distance. "Your boyfriend and his father were in here arguing like a couple of fools in front of the poor woman. I could hear them all the way down in Mr. Rauch's room. I had to tell them both to leave."

"When?"

"I don't know. Maybe like eight o'clock? Just before visiting hours were supposed to end. Marie said your boy was here all day and things were fine. But when the father showed up tonight, I guess the shit hit the fan. Hell, they kept going at it in the parking lot, too. We were watching them out the staff room window."

"Could you tell what they were arguing about?"

"Sounded to me like Ms. Sinclair's grandson is about done with his father's bossiness." She glances over at Ms. Sinclair to make sure she's still asleep. I do the same. "All I can tell you is that they were out in the parking lot for a long time after they walked out of here, and it looked like they were both really angry. When the father's car ripped out of the lot like his ass was on fire, your boy sat down on the asphalt and buried his face in his hands. If I didn't know any better, I'd say he was crying. Must've sat out there for a good ten minutes before he left."

I shake my head, trying to fathom the words said between Adam and his father. More sadness rises in my throat. Sondra starts whispering again.

"Listen, I'm not gonna tell you what to do, 'cause clearly you're not gonna listen to me anyway. You never do. But here's the one thing I'm begging you to remember, girl…you've got to protect yourself from whatever's happening between the two of them. Don't get caught up in it."

"I already am."

Sondra sighs, dropping her shoulders and straightening her mouth into a hard line. She steps over and puts her arms around me, clipboard and all, wrapping me in a caring and thoughtful hug. "Oh, Lord," she says into my ear. "I'm telling you, you're gonna get your heart broken."

I don't tell her it already is.

She squeezes tighter and holds me there for a long minute. By the time she lets go, I've managed to choke back the tears without letting any more of them fall. I'm building a wall, just like hers.

"You'll get through this," she says. "Whatever it is." She looks over at Ms. Sinclair and touches the end of the bed with her fingertips. "These people need you, K'acy. Don't forget that."

"I won't," I whisper.

Sondra nods and snuggles the clipboard close to her chest. "I'm leaving now, and I'll make sure the hallway is clear, but you'd better get yourself out of here in a hurry, you hear? Before anyone else sees you."

I offer her a small smile as I pick up my gig bag.

On her way out the door, Sondra passes the photograph sitting on Ms. Sinclair's dresser. She stops and looks at it for a second before turning back to me. In a hushed voice she adds, "Mr. Sinclair brought that in for her today. Might be the only nice thing the man's ever done. It's amazing how much Adam's little brother looks like him." She starts walking again. "Those Sinclairs must have some potent genes."

She's out in the hallway before I can think fast enough to stop her. Her words echo in my ears as I rush over to the photograph. I flip it over on the dresser and open the frame, pulling the picture out from behind the glass. There's writing on the back.

Bradley, Spring 2004.

My broken heart shatters for Adam.

***

When I get off the bus just after one o'clock in the morning, Jarrod is sitting on the steps of my building. He has a lit cigarette pinched between his fingers, and he's leaning back on the step behind him, looking every bit the epic ass shaker. I take the cigarette from him as I put the StingRay on the bottom step and sit down next to him. I suck in a single breath of hot, unfiltered smoke before handing it back to him. The rush of nicotine hits me hard, unwinding my brain and temporarily settling my nerves. He takes a drag of his own and looks off down the street. I don't have to ask him why he's here because I already know.

We sit together for a long time, side by side, each lost in our own thoughts. My exhausted mind is sifting through the remains of the night, trying to process what it all means, when he finally speaks.

"Hope you don't mind. I had to let myself in to take a piss. I've been waiting a long time."

"Sorry," I say, rubbing my palms against the top of my thighs.

"Where've you been?"

"I went to see her." He knows how much I care for Evelyn Sinclair. Everyone does. Except for her son.

"In the middle of the night?"

I quietly nod.

"Why?"

"Because I might not get to see her again."

"But you told me he withdrew the complaint?"

"He did."

"Then why wouldn't you get to see her again?"

I shrug, not sure if I should tell him the truth.

"I was worried about you, Kace. Grace was, too. You rushed out of there like some junkie stole your baby. Not to mention the whole emotional breakdown thing. I've never seen you like that before. You gonna tell me what's going on?"

"Adam says we're over."

"*What?* Why?"

I take the cigarette from him and inhale another hit. "Let's just say I made a deal with the devil, and I should've known it would bite me in the ass."

"Meaning?"

"I took money from Mr. Sinclair, and Adam found out about it." The truth sounds even worse when I say it out loud.

He looks properly bewildered. "Why'd you take money from that asshole?"

"He didn't give me a choice. He said if I didn't take it and stay away from his son, he'd get my work license revoked and accuse me of far worse than what he already has."

"Jesus. Are you serious? That's like movie-worthy blackmail, right there."

I suck in more smoke and tap off the ashes. They float like snowflakes down to the concrete. "He thinks I only want to be with Adam because of his trust fund. And now Adam thinks I picked his father's money over him."

"Trust fund?"

I look at him and roll my eyes.

"That sucks, Kace, That *really* sucks." Jarrod's arm reaches around my shoulders, pulling me tight against him. "Looks like you got yourself into a real pickle, schweetheart. Why didn't you tell me all this before?"

"Because none of it was supposed to matter." I take a deep breath and focus my eyes on the snowflake ashes at my feet. "The man was supposed to die before Adam could ever find out about our deal."

"You saw it?"

"Yeah. The very first time I met the man."

"Do you know when?"

"It started tonight. At 10:46. A car accident."

He recoils in surprise, then nods in understanding. "I guess that explains the emotional breakdown."

"Yep."

Jarrod is the only one who will ever know. It's one of the precious secrets we hold between us. The deepest one. He's known since the day we met, because I saw death in his eyes that night, six years ago, at that bus stop. He was too high to function, and something inside me made me want to stop him from staggering out into the street and getting crushed by a moving truck with "AQUARIUS" spray-painted on the side in bright yellow graffiti. I never thought I would see him again. He seemed so lost, and

I just wanted to help him find himself. I wanted to give him a second chance. So, to save his life, I told him about what I can see in people's eyes. I told him it was going to be his day. Unless he didn't want it to be. I told him about the "AQUARIUS" truck and how the driver was going to swerve to miss a pothole, lose control, and crash into the building on the corner. I told him his body would be wedged between the truck and the brick wall. Right there. At the end of the street.

Then, I asked him to stay next to me until the truck with a bright yellow "AQUARIUS" spray-painted on the side crashed into the corner building and I couldn't see death in his eyes anymore.

He sat with me until we heard the crunch of metal. And for a long time after.

It was the first time I stopped an accidental death from happening.

But it wasn't the first time I changed the ending of someone's life.

CHAPTER 32

The toilet seat is up and the bathroom light is on. It makes me smile because it offers proof of Jarrod's patience and concern. Even though it's been a few minutes since he walked off into the darkness, leaving me standing alone on my front stoop, the remnants of our double fist bump are still echoing up my arms. I feel better. A little less lost.

I walk back to my bedroom and start to undress. My exhausted muscles are screaming at me to let them rest. They've had enough for one day. Maybe for a lifetime.

My apartment is quiet as I sink down onto my bed, but the night's events continue to sort themselves out inside my brain, like a bunch of restless kindergarteners jostling to find their place in the schoolyard rank. I search for reasons and predictions among them, but they're moving too fast, scattering around, only making more confusion. The one solid thought I can find among them is my promise to Ms. Sinclair. I grab hold of it, knowing it's the only thing I can control. I will not let the promise be empty. I tell myself that somehow, I will find a way to take care of her son.

As sleep comes, the rest of my thoughts—the ones still left fluttering in confusion—change into birds. Ms. Sinclair's birds. Chickadees, blue jays, finches, swifts. She's there with them, watching them circle around her as they carry more of her memories away in their slender beaks and protect her from the pain of tomorrow. This time, though, Adam isn't the only one standing next to her, holding her hand.

I'm there, too. And there's a mourning dove nestled like a downy baby in the soft cradle of my arms.

***

The accident is all over the morning news, but the images on the television are ones I've seen before. The bank sign. The burned-out car. The discarded jacket lying on the street. The flashing lights bouncing off the dark asphalt. It's daylight now, but the darkness of last night is all I see on the screen.

The reporter announces the victim of this one-car crash, Washington state lobbyist Winston Sinclair, is in critical condition at Penn Presbyterian. She says he's the principal partner of the most contentious and influential lobbying firm in the state, and ends the segment with, "But at this time, police suspect no foul play was involved in the accident. As we understand, Mr. Sinclair was in Philadelphia to attend to a family matter."

I feel sick to my stomach.

I turn it off, hoping and praying Ms. Sinclair's television is tuned to the cooking channel. I should have checked before I left her last night. I want her to learn about her son's accident from someone who loves her, rather than from a television screen. I'm not sure she'll fully understand what's happened anyway, but still...

As I shower and dress, I think hard about what to do and say. I won't be welcome, but I need to go to the hospital in order to keep my promise to Ms. Sinclair. I need Adam to know I care, and more importantly, I need to see exactly where Mr. Sinclair is. Because when the time comes for me to fulfill my promise, I'll need to be able to find him quickly.

I don't know how Adam will react when I walk into that hospital, and the last thing I want to do is make this harder on him than it already is. But I love him. And somehow, I'm going to have to prove it to him all over again by showing kindness and compassion to a man who's done nothing but try to manipulate and control us both. It won't make Adam love me again, but at least my presence there today might show him how much I care, in spite of the horrible mistake I made when I took his father's money.

It takes me a little over forty-five minutes to get to Penn Presbyterian. By the time I step off the bus and onto the hospital's mellow tan floor, it's nearly lunchtime. The volunteer at the information desk directs me to the trauma ICU, sending me up the elevator and down a long corridor. At the end is a set of double doors. I push through them and into a waiting area.

The air is warm and dry, and the crisp smell of disinfectant hangs in the air. The room is empty except for a dozen chairs, a few magazine-laden end tables, and a middle-aged woman sitting behind the reception desk. She's bent forward, carefully examining something on the computer screen in front of her. Her reading glasses sit low on her nose, and she sighs as she types something into the keypad. I walk over and stand in front of the desk. A few seconds pass before she talks.

"Patient name?" She's sour and unfriendly, only making visual contact with her computer screen.

"Winston Sinclair." The moment his name hits her ears, the woman's gaze instantly lifts to meet mine and her eyebrows rise in a silent inquiry. She gives me a quick once-over, as if she's wondering why someone *like me* is coming to see someone *like him*.

One of her pudgy hands whisks the glasses off her face and sets them down next to the computer's keyboard. She folds her arms together and leans her forearms down on the desk as she tilts forward, toward me.

"Are you…family?" The unfriendliness is gone from her voice. It's been replaced with snarky cynicism. Great.

"Not yet." I flash a shining, teeth-filled smile at her. Her mouth puckers in response.

"Young lady," she says, "this is an intensive care unit. It is not the place for jokes and insolence."

I straighten my back and plump out my chest, standing tall. "I wasn't aware that smiling was considered disrespectful, ma'am."

Her eyes narrow. "Only family is permitted to see Mr. Sinclair. At the request of his security detail."

"Ahh," I sigh, tilting my head back and glancing at the ceiling before continuing. "Well, then I'd like to change my answer to yes. Yes, I'm family." If she wants insolence, then insolence she shall have. And, with any luck, that insolence will get me exactly what I want.

She rolls her eyes and asks my name.

"K'acy McGee."

"You sure you don't want to change that to K'acy Sinclair?" More conceited sass from a woman whose over-inflated sense of self-worth comes solely from her ability to control who walks through a hospital door. I don't want them to, but her words hit hard and deep. The sound of my first name followed by the second half of Adam's pricks me with an intense sting of sadness.

"Maybe someday." I smile at her again, this one even bigger than the one before.

The woman picks up the telephone on her desk and dials a number that's handwritten on a piece of paper taped to the desktop. Someone answers quickly.

"Mr. Devine? This is Lois at reception. There's a young woman here to see Mr. Sinclair." She stares wryly at me as she talks. "She says she's family."

A second of silence passes while Perry Devine asks her my name.

"K'acy McGee."

More silence as he tells her he'll be right out.

"Yes, sir. Thank you." She puts the phone down in its cradle, and I instantly know I've gotten what I want: a conversation with Perry Devine, and hopefully, a visit with the Sinclairs. "You can have a seat, Miss McGee. Someone will be with you in a minute." There is so much snark in her voice, it makes me want to laugh. She thinks Perry Devine is going to come out here and kick me out. But instead, Perry Devine is going to come out here and *let me in*.

A minute later, he comes through the set of double crash doors at the opposite end of the waiting room. He's wearing the same dark suit as last night, only his crisply ironed, white shirt isn't so crisply ironed anymore. He tucks his cell phone into the breast pocket of his suit coat as he walks over to me. He doesn't look at the reception desk as he passes, nor does he say a single word to the woman sitting there. I stay planted in my seat, even as he stops and stands directly in front of me.

"What can I do for you, Miss McGee?" The diamond in his left earlobe looks smaller than it did before.

"I need to see him."

"He's not here right now."

If Adam's not here, then where is he? I hope he's with this grandmother, gently telling her about the accident before she sees it on the news.

I immediately switch my focus to finding another way to see Mr. Sinclair.

"I'm not talking about Adam."

He crosses his arms over his chest, and the smell of now-stale cologne wafts through the air. I stand up in the snug space between his body and the chair behind me. Over his shoulder, I see the receptionist staring at us from across the room, no doubt straining to hear our conversation. I glance over at her before looking straight into Perry Devine's fierce-yet-familiar long-lashed eyes.

"After seeing Adam walk out of the bar last night looking so deflated," he says, "I'll assume you followed through with your end of the deal. Is that why you're here today? For the rest of your money?" He looks peeved. Like he's upset that he might be correct.

"No. That's not why I'm here." My voice is solid and sure.

"Then why are you?"

"I'm here because I heard about the accident on the news and thought I might be able to help."

A look of intense surprise flashes across his face. "You want to *help*? You're kidding, right?"

"No. I'm not kidding."

Perry Devine's loud, clear laugh causes the receptionist to nearly jump out of her seat. "You're not here to help, Miss McGee. You're here to see how bad it is. 'Cause you think if he dies, you won't get the rest of your money. Or you think you might be able to get Adam—and his trust fund—back." He uncrosses his arms and puts his hands into his pockets. I don't argue with him, or even disagree. Even though none of it is true.

Obviously he doesn't know Mr. Sinclair already told Adam about our deal.

"I tell you what…if you really wanna see how bad it is," he continues, "I'll show you. But don't tell me you're here to help, 'cause you and I both know you ain't here to help."

"Yes, sir." I say it because it's what he wants me to say.

He turns and starts walking toward the reception desk. I follow close behind. When we get to the sour woman sitting there, Perry Devine doesn't stop. He doesn't even blink. He says nothing and keeps on walking. I do the same.

The beeps and blips of medical equipment start as soon as we set foot through the crash doors. Glass-fronted rooms line both sides of the hallway, allowing a brief view of the patients housed inside as we walk past. Outside of each room, in the hallway, is a nurse's station. Some are staffed while others are not. We walk farther down the corridor, past a large central area where several nurses and doctors are collected, discussing something in a hushed tone. They pause and watch Perry Devine as we walk past. He doesn't look at them, but I do. And I offer a small, sheltered smile in greeting. Some of them nod back at me before returning to their conversation. At the end of the hall, in the far left corner, is Winston Sinclair's room. I draw a map inside my head, so I won't forget. Mr. Devine holds the door open for me as I walk inside.

A burnt, metallic odor—like used fireworks—infuses the air, twisting my stomach and walloping my senses. It sticks on the back of my tongue, along with the smell of scorched hair and antiseptic. Mr. Sinclair is lying in the bed, the stiff whoosh-and-hum of a respirator causing his chest to rise and fall. Most of his skin is covered in gauze, except for the inside of his left forearm, where the IV enters. The skin there is thick and leathery. Soon, they'll cut it away. They'll scour his body and get rid of all the burned, dead tissue. When they pull him out of sedation, the pain will be shockingly relentless. Intense and unending. He'll suffer through it, but in the end, he won't survive. His organs will fail, and despite a surge of antibiotics, an infection will turn septic. All of his pain will be for nothing.

I close my eyes at the sound of my own quiet voice. "How is Adam?"

There's a pause before Perry Devine offers an answer. "I don't know."

"What do you mean, you don't know?"

"He won't talk to me. He won't talk to anyone. All he did last night was sit here."

"Where is he now?" I ask, willing Mr. Devine to confirm my hope that Adam is with his grandmother.

"I'm not sure."

I inhale a single cleansing breath and open my eyes to look at Mr. Sinclair, swaddled in gauze and temporarily blind to his own intense pain, thanks to the miracles of opiates and modern medicine. I want to sit on the edge of his bed and take the useless hurt of his future away. For how intensely I wanted the man to suffer less than twenty-four hours ago, I now feel equally as passionate about taking it all away and giving him peace. But it's not just because I promised Evelyn Sinclair I would take care of her son. It's also because I'm me.

My daddy taught me the difference between outside pain and inside pain a few weeks after Momma left us. When he finally told me and Charlie she wasn't coming back from Reverend Thompson's revival tent, he said there was nothing a person could do about certain kinds of pain. He said you can fix most kinds outside pain with medicine and Band-Aids and kisses, but inside pain was different. He said there's no way a doctor can fix that kind of pain; only time and love can.

After that night, Charlie stopped crying herself to sleep and praying for Reverend Thompson to bring our momma back. It's like she accepted it and decided to wear her pain like a badge, letting it lead her life to all the wrong places. I don't want Adam to do the same. I don't want his inside pain to do the same thing Charlie's did to her. I don't want it to chew him up and change him into something he's not.

If I take away Mr. Sinclair's pain, maybe it will wipe Adam's away, too. Maybe it will fix him.

"You've seen what you wanted to see. Time to go now, Miss McGee. And don't come back. There's nothing you can do to help."

"Will you let Adam know I was here? Please." *Please.*

He doesn't pause before giving his answer. "I don't think so. No."

"Why not?" I turn to face him.

"Because I don't think Mr. Sinclair would like that very much." His expression is hard and stern, even as quiet tears begin to spill out of my eyes. I nod my head and follow him as he walks out of the room and down the long glass-lined corridor.

***

By the time I get to the elevator my tears are flowing, steady and seemingly unstoppable. I don't even try to rein them in. I just let them fall, accepting them as part of my story. They deserve to be here, and I deserve to feel this way. My regret is cavernous and hollow. Mr. Sinclair's money has emptied me, despite the good I hope it brings to Charlie. It wasn't supposed to happen this way, but it did. And now my heart is scrambling to find its way back home, still unaware that home has burned to the ground, hand in hand with Winston Sinclair. My head knows it already, but my heart is so far behind.

The elevator arrives, and I ride back down to the first floor alone, surrounded only by the hospital's stale air. When the doors open, I step out onto the lobby floor and head for the exit. As I walk toward the information desk, the sight of a well-dressed woman standing in front of it stops me in my tracks. She's wearing a peacock-blue tailored suit. Her hair is side-swept and sprayed, classic Jackie-O style, and her pointy-toe beige pumps are polished and completely unmarred, as if today was the very first time they've ever seen the light of day. Wrapped through the bend of her right arm is a large handbag. Chanel, I think. My tears stop immediately, and I swallow hard as I use the back of my hand to wipe them away.

The woman says something to the desk attendant and turns to face me. I'm thirty feet away, standing stock still in the middle of the room, staring straight at her. She walks toward me, each step crossing over her midline, her slender hips swinging like a runway model. One foot snakes forward after the other, almost in slow motion. It's a practiced walk. Deliberately attention-grabbing. She approaches me on my left, and as she does, we make eye contact. The electrified sound of "Soul to Squeeze" flutters through my mind, note by breathtaking note. It comes from a lone cello this time, each note in perfect tune and rhythm. The sound is classic and refined. She smiles at me, her impeccable teeth and frosty pink lipstick shine under the fluorescent lights.

"Hello, dear," she says as she passes. Evelyn Sinclair flashes into my brain when I hear it. The voice isn't the same, but the words are.

"Hello," I reply, somehow hating the sound of my own meekness and wishing I could say more. She continues to walk, and I can't help but turn around and watch her go. The click of her heels against the hospital floor causes a rush of nervous adrenaline to kick in. I take in a shot of disinfectant-infused air and close my eyes in a long, doubt-filled blink. When I open them, I can't stop the words from coming out. "Mrs. Sinclair?"

The woman stops and turns around slowly, as if she thinks the whole world is watching. Her perfectly coiffed head tilts on its axis, sending the weight of her body over to one hip. Her hands clasp together in front of her waist. "I'm sorry, dear. Do I know you?"

My feet stay where they are, but my shattered heart starts pounding its way up into my throat. "No, ma'am." Her gaze narrows in question. "We haven't met, but I'm...I'm a friend of Adam's."

"Oh," she says, looking skeptical and perhaps even nervous. I wonder if Mr. Sinclair told her about me. And our deal. "Is he here?"

"No. Not right now." She nods at me, her face giving nothing more away. "I'm sorry to have bothered you," I continue, "but I recognized you from a photo." Lie. "I just stopped by to check on Adam, but like I said, he's not here. I heard about your husband's accident. I hope he has a speedy recovery." I know he won't, but it's the polite thing to say. And it seems to make her relax a little.

"Thank you, dear."

"Will you let Adam know I was here?" If Perry Devine won't tell him I still care, maybe she will.

"Certainly."

"It was nice to meet you, Mrs. Sinclair."

"And you as well." Her words and body language tell me she doesn't know about me. I don't think Mr. Sinclair told her a single thing about what's happened here.

I offer a small smile, turn around, and start walking toward the exit.

"Excuse me," she shouts behind me. "Tell me your name, please."

I pretend not to hear her as I push through the doors and out into the bright sunshine.

***

Halfway through the bus ride home, my cell phone rings. It's Susan Campbell. She tells me I've been cleared, and I'm to return to Pine Manor first thing tomorrow. I thank her and tell her I'm looking forward to seeing everyone in the morning. She says they're all thrilled to have me back; the place hasn't been the same without me. Her words make me happy, because they let me know the work I do there is appreciated. The news of tomorrow's return fills some of the emptiness and provides a touch of sweetness to an otherwise awful day. I can't wait to see everyone again. I can't wait to straighten Mrs. Thompson's afghan, fix Mr. Ledbetter's tie, and refill Ms. Sinclair's birdfeeders. I'm even looking forward to emptying Mr. Rauch's colostomy bag. It's been a long five days without the people I love.

As I watch the city blocks roll by outside the bus windows, a sliver of apprehension pokes at my happiness. I'm worried Ms. Sinclair may not recognize me anymore. At her stage of Alzheimer's, patients often quickly forget the people and things that don't fit into their daily routine. Even five days without me may have been enough for her to forget how much I care. I'm worried about everyone, of course, but I'm worried about her the most. Her mind and body are so fragile; I just want her to remember she's safe and loved when I'm around.

More worry strikes when I think about what will happen when Adam is there. Everything is different now, but I hope he knows it won't affect how I care for his grandmother. Aside from Sondra, no one at Pine Manor knows about us, so somehow, I'm going to have to swallow it all down and pretend he's nothing more than a patient's grandson. As the bus turns onto my street, I decide I'm going to carry on as if none of this has happened. I'm going to love Ms. Sinclair just like I always have, and I'm going to treat Adam just like I treat all the other family members I encounter on a daily basis. It might kill me, but it's the only thing I can do.

Tomorrow is going to be a challenging day. For everyone.

***

I walk into Pine Manor at precisely 7:53. The sliding glass doors open without hesitation or fanfare. It's a workday like any other, yet it's so full of personal significance that, inside my head, trumpets sound and confetti falls. Mr. Toftree greets me from his leather wingchair with a brisk hello, asking me where I went on my vacation. He's wearing his favorite Phillies shirt, and once again, it's misbuttoned. As I bend down to adjust it, I tell him I didn't go anywhere, I just took a few days to attend to a personal matter. He tells me I was missed, reaches for my hand, and kisses the back of it. My broken heart sings. It's brief but so very meaningful.

As soon as I stand back up again, Mr. Ledbetter rolls by in his wheelchair and asks me if I know where the morning paper is. He says he needs to read about last night's baseball game because he "fell asleep before the damn thing was over." Mr. Toftree immediately starts giving him a play-by-play of the last few innings of the game. As the two of them start to chat, I give them each a hearty pat on the shoulder and walk back to the staff room to put my bag away and check the shift change report. It feels good to have some semblance of normalcy back again, even if it's only for today. When I walk into the room, Susan Campbell is there. She gives me a bright hello, shakes my hand, and welcomes me back. Dr. Kopsey and Marie are also there, looking at a patient folder. Dr. Kopsey gives me a nod, but Marie says nothing. I sign in, read the shift change report, and start my workday the same way I always do. With Ms. Sinclair.

A massive lump sits in my throat as I head back to her room. The hallway seems endless this morning. Much longer than it did on Wednesday night. There's no need for sneaking today, so I take my time, saying hello to other patients as I pass by their open doors. I'm so happy I get to see her again, and the butterflies in my stomach are busy celebrating.

When I step into the frame of her door, I see her, sitting in her recliner. The same one I sat in just two nights ago. She isn't dressed yet, but the television is on, tuned to *Good Morning America*. Robin Roberts is chatting with someone about pet care equipment, and Ms. Sinclair's eyes are glued to the television. She laughs when they show a wiggly Pomeranian getting brushed with a red glove that has some kind of vibrating electric bristles coming out of it. The dog yelps on the television, and she laughs again. I stand in the doorway watching her, wondering what her memory will bring today. I wonder if she'll remember me. And I wonder if she'll know what's happened to her son.

Across the room, a bouquet of fresh daisies fills her green plastic water pitcher. There's a new bag of Starlight mints on her dresser, along with an unopened bag of peanut M&M's. All three confirm Adam's presence here yesterday. The sight of them nearly makes me lose it. I swallow hard, knowing I can't cry here. I have to keep myself together, even though my emotions want to cripple me from the inside out. I remind myself that today is not about me. It's about Ms. Sinclair and all my other patients. It's about making life better for them. Just like it's always been.

Regardless of how Ms. Sinclair handled the news of her son's accident yesterday, today she seems content. I knock on the frame of her door and ask her if I can come in and help her get dressed.

"Certainly, dear," she says. A glimmer of recognition in her eyes offers me hope that it's going to be a good day. "I'd like to wear my blue blouse today, if I could."

I know exactly which blouse she's referring to. I step into the room and head for her closet, shifting through the hangers until I find it. "Is this the right one, Ms. Sinclair?"

"Yes, of course. Has it been pressed?"

I hold it up in front of me so she can have a better look. "I believe so, yes. Would you like to wear your gray pants with it, or your brown ones?"

"The brown ones. They look better with those silly shoes."

"What silly shoes?"

"The ones they make me wear so my feet don't swell." She's coherent. At least for the time being.

"Ahh," I say, nodding and walking around her bed with the clothes in my hands. As I pass the dresser, I see the photograph there, now slightly crooked in the frame. I try not to look at it, but I can't help myself. It's only a second's glance, but she notices.

"That's me and my grandson," she says, her eyes twinkling as she, too, stares at the picture, probably remembering something about the day it was taken. "He was six."

"He's very handsome."

"Yes, he is." She pauses for a long second, thinking hard before continuing. "He's in love, you know. With a girl." She whispers the last part, as if it's some kind of secret.

"How old is he now?" I tell myself I'm not prying, I'm just trying to engage her in an active conversation.

She looks very confused. I shouldn't have asked her something so difficult. She puts her fingers to her forehead and bows her chin.

"Oh my. Why, I'm not sure. He's a grown-up now. He just got out of school." She drops her hands back down into her lap as I finish walking over to her side of the bed. "Graduate school, I believe." She's not talking about Bradley. She's talking about Adam.

And she said he was in love. With a girl. My broken heart skips a beat.

"So, he's probably in his mid-twenties by now." I take the blue blouse off the hanger and lay it down on the bed. My fumbling fingers struggle to unfasten the buttons.

"Yes. I believe you're right. He comes to see me quite a bit, you know. You've probably seen him here before. His name is Bradley."

I take the pants off their hanger and lay them down next to the blouse. Then I kneel down in front of her to take off her bed slippers and socks.

"Do you mean Adam?" I try not to look at her so she doesn't see the tears gathering in my eyes.

"Yes, yes. Adam. You've met him before, right?"

"Yes, ma'am. He comes to see you every day. He's a very nice man." I get up and put her slippers in the closet in an attempt to hide all the deep breaths I'm taking. I steady myself and come back to help her dress. "You mentioned one time that Bradley is Adam's little brother. Do you ever get to see him, too?"

"No. No…" She bows her head again and stares at her fingers as they fidget with a Kleenex in her lap. "He died a long time ago."

My breath leaves me in a hot rush. "Oh. I'm so sorry to hear that, Ms. Sinclair. That must've been very difficult for your family."

She raises her chin to look at me. "It was only difficult for *me*."

A few seconds pass as I think about how far I should take this. "What happened to him?"

"There was a car accident. An *awful* accident. His mother died, too." There's a softness in her face now; it's telling the story of all she's lost. Grief and sorrow are bubbling up through the Alzheimer's as the birds bring back scraps of her memory and drop them into her waiting hands. I should chase them away before they hurt her, but I think she's welcoming them. I think she wants them to come. "She shouldn't have even had him in the car with her. But I let him go. Because she was his mother…" She trails off to a long, difficult silence.

"Ms. Sinclair, does Adam know he had a brother?"

She softly shakes her head. "Winston said it was to protect him."

"From what?" I ask her, already answering my own question with *"from the sins of his father"* inside the silence of my head.

"I don't know. But he gets mad when I talk about it. He yells at me."

"Who yells at you?"

"Winston. He gets mad and tells me to shut my mouth." Her voice is quiet as she says the words. Her chin drops to her chest, and she starts twisting the Kleenex around itself.

Winston Sinclair has made his own mother feel humiliated. He's made her ashamed of her inability to keep *his* secrets. He's made her feel guilty for having Alzheimer's. I think of him then, in the hospital's soaking tub, getting scrubbed with a stiff brush, the nurses sloughing off all his dead, burned-up skin as his nerve endings scream out with pain. I think of it and consider negating my promise.

But then, I wonder if Adam is watching his father suffer. And what he's thinking as he does.

I decide to ask Ms. Sinclair one more question before I chase the birds away.

"Ms. Sinclair, when did Adam tell you he's in love?"

"Let's see…" she says, "…it was when he brought me those flowers." She turns and points at the daisies in the green plastic pitcher. I can't help but smile. "He also said Winston's gone home. And he's never coming back here again."

CHAPTER 33

Robert McGee—2008

I spent most of my life blasting limestone for a smidge over minimum wage just so I could keep clothes on the backs of all my beautiful girls. Working for Ronald Chapman was a pretty good gig, especially for a guy who barely got his high-school diploma. In fact, the only reason I got that diploma was 'cause of Ron. I started working at the quarry on the day I turned sixteen. I'd work weekdays after school, shoveling stone and cleaning equipment. Ron told me I could move up the ranks, but to do that, I had to graduate. He said my education had to come first; the quarry would wait. It really wasn't so bad, outside of the dust and the noise. I know how lucky I was to have a steady job for twenty-eight years. It was hard work, but it was a privilege.

The best parts of my life, though, had nothing to do with that quarry. The best parts were my music and my girls. Growing up, all I ever wanted to do was play my trumpet. My pop played the squeezebox in a zydeco band, and he used to let me play with them on Saturday nights. I wasn't half as good as Timmy Melton, their regular trumpet player, but they always knew how to make me feel like I was.

The only downside to those nights was my pop letting me start to drink whiskey when I was fifteen. He said it made my lips looser, and I could hit the high notes without going all red in the face. I drank way too much, for too many years. But when Charlie came along, I cut it out. 'Cause I knew by then drinking didn't make me a better man.

Louise was a wild li'l thing when we first met. She made eyes at me while I was playing at Scrimshaw's one Saturday night, and I just couldn't say no to such a pretty face.

She'd steal cigarettes from the Piggly Wiggly where she worked, and every Friday night we'd sneak down to the swamp to smoke and drink the beer she'd take outta her father's fridge. We'd stay there all night long, making mayhem and love until the sun came up. It was always a good feeling to have Louise's hand in mine.

She got pregnant with Charlie before we had the chance to do much growing up. Louise was barely nineteen when Charlie was born. I was going on twenty-five. Neither one of us was ready to be that kind of responsible, but we did it. We got married at City Hall and brought Charlie into this world the right way. As a family.

It wasn't until after K'acy was born that Louise got real religious. At first, she'd only pray at night and thank God for her life, but then she started reading from the Bible all the time and taking everything so seriously. By the time K'acy was four, Louise was spending more time at the church than she was at home. When Reverend Thompson and his revival tent came to Houma, it was almost too easy for her to leave—she'd been "gone" for a long time before that. Still, I never could get over her picking religion over her girls. It just didn't make sense.

The girls, though, grew up real good, despite my fumble-infused fathering. Charlie's gonna make a spectacular beautician someday, and K'acy...well, she's gonna shine no matter what she picks for her life.

On the day I died, K'acy was the one sitting on the side of my bed. Charlie was asleep upstairs, but K'acy wouldn't leave my side until she knew my suffering was over. Things were real bad. There was so much pain, I'd spend my days hoping and wishing death would come and put a stop to it all. But it never did.

For a good three weeks before I died, I was hurting so bad I'd spend hours praying to Louise's God to just end it. I'd silently beg Him to let me go. The insurance only paid for so much pain medicine, and every day, I'd hear the chubby hospice nurse telling the girls there wasn't anything else she could do. It broke my heart knowing they were watching me suffer. I hated seeing them cry. But there was nothing I could do about it but keep praying for the end.

I would never have asked K'acy to do what she did; I wasn't a brave enough man for that. Nor would I have ever willfully wanted to put that kind of burden on my own daughter. She did it all on her own. Somehow, she knew what to do, without me ever having to ask. She knew when I'd had enough. She knew when it was time. I cried that night, from the pain, and she wiped away my tears with strength and purpose, humming "That's How Strong My Love Is" as her fingers brushed against my cheek. And when it was over, I was nothing but grateful to her for being courageous and caring and compassionate enough to give her own father the peace he so desperately needed.

I'd been telling my girls for years that you always gotta do the right thing, even when it hurts, and when it came down to it, that's exactly what K'acy did. I looked up at her face the moment the needle entered my vein and saw nothing but love in her eyes. So much love.

She didn't do it because she wanted to. She did it because I needed her to.

CHAPTER 34

Adam doesn't come to Pine Manor at all on Friday. He's not there for gentle yoga or for the therapy dog session. Ms. Sinclair enjoys her visit with Heidi the labradoodle as much as ever, but Adam isn't there to laugh with her when a glass of water is accidentally knocked over by an overzealous tail. It's the first time he hasn't come to see his grandmother since the day we met.

During my afternoon break, Marie tells me about Mr. Sinclair's accident, as if it hasn't been all over the news. She talks to me in a low whisper, like she's gossiping about someone's love affair instead of a car accident. She says Ms. Sinclair's grandson was here yesterday, and that he and Dr. Kopsey decided not to tell Ms. Sinclair about the accident. They thought it might be too much for her to handle, and they asked the nursing staff to please not discuss it in front of her.

I'm relieved to hear Marie's words. Not only because it confirms that Ms. Sinclair is still blissfully in the dark about her son's suffering, but also because Adam talked to Dr. Kopsey about it first. I think they made a smart decision, regardless of how difficult it probably was for Adam to lie to his grandmother about his father's imaginary return to Seattle.

I spend the rest of my workday tending to the people I love. Ms. Sinclair enjoys some time watching her birdfeeder while Mr. Reizenstein naps in a wingchair. Apart from Adam's absence, it's a day like any other. In fact, it's pretty much like all the days were before Adam arrived.

But despite the calmness of the day, in the back of my mind thoughts are clamoring around, introducing new questions and doubts, and making me wonder, yet again, if there's any way Adam will ever forgive me for taking his father's money. I wonder if his mother told him I was there. And if she did, I wonder what he told her about me.

Every time I step into Ms. Sinclair's room, the daisies look back at me, giving me hope and reminding me that maybe there's still a chance. My lone swooner may still love me. And, after tomorrow, maybe he'll be willing to forgive.

***

I step off the bus and walk up the stairs to my apartment feeling both tired and happy. It was so very good to return to Pine Manor. Today, I got back a good portion of my reason for being, and some of my patients got back their last remaining chance for peace. Ms. Sinclair doesn't know it, but someday very soon, she's going to need that chance. I saw it again today, in her blue eyes. It didn't take my breath away this time, though, because I'm not afraid anymore. I know now everything will be all right.

I unlock my apartment door and step inside, tossing my bag down onto the floor and closing the door behind me. When I turn around, I see the top of someone's head sticking up above the back of my sofa. I recognize the intentional bed-head immediately. The familiar bass riff of "Soul to Squeeze" blasts through my veins and a fresh jitter starts to dance around inside of me. He sits up and turns around to look at me over the back of the couch, scanning me from head to toe before offering any words.

"Looks like you're back to work."

Not for the first time in my life, my scrubs are speaking on my behalf.

I nod, still standing by the door, music pounding inside my head.

"How was Gram's day?" His expression stays solid. Unfazed. Though I know he isn't.

"Good. But I think she missed you." More surging notes.

His mouth flexes into a small, closed grin at the thought of her. "I missed her, too."

"How's your dad?"

He shakes his head and the small grin drops away. There's a long pause before he says, "My mom told me a friend of mine stopped by the hospital yesterday."

Oh… "I heard about the accident on the news. I just wanted to make sure you were okay."

"Really?" He shrugs with exaggerated disbelief. "That's funny, 'cause Perry, my father's driver, told me you came for the rest of your money."

Perry Devine needs a punch in the throat. The music's pacing picks up as my heart starts racing in my chest.

"Then Perry's a liar."

Adam shakes his head and stands up. He crosses his arms over his chest and glares at me. "Perry's worked for my family for my whole life. I'm pretty sure he's not a liar, K'acy."

I walk over to the sofa and stand in front of him. The key from behind the hall picture is sitting on the coffee table. "Adam, why are you here?"

"I'm here because I want you to tell me the truth." His face reddens as the words come out. "I want to hear it from you."

I stare at him, knowing no matter what I say, it's going to hurt him. I scramble for the right words. "I never wanted your father's money in the first place."

"So, you're not denying that you took money from him to end things with me?" His arms tighten across his chest. The bass line rolls on, deep and resonant.

"I took money from your father, yes. But not because I wanted to end *us*. I took it because he didn't give me a choice." It certainly isn't a lie, but I have to tread carefully.

"What are you talking about?" His hands drop against his sides.

"He told me if I didn't take his deal and leave you by the end of the week, he would file more complaints, just like the one he already had." My stare moves from his eyes to the floor at my feet. The music instantly quiets.

He's unmoving and silent for a long time. When I look up at him, his gaze shifts to a spot on the wall behind me. "What the hell is happening?" I don't think the question is aimed at me, so I don't answer it. Something hardens inside of him, and his jaw tightens. "So…you're telling me that because he couldn't convince me to dump you, he was trying to force *you* to leave *me* instead?"

I nod. "He told me you deserve far better than what I have to offer. He thinks I'm only interested in your trust fund."

He looks down at me and relaxes his jaw. "So, he decides to blackmail you? And you just do it? Without talking to me about it first?"

"I thought it would be easier…"

"Easier? Are you kidding me?" His sarcasm and scorn are front and center.

"He said he would do something worse if I told you about it."

"Worse?" Hearing the extent of his father's manipulation is not going to be easy for him. I know that, and yet, I don't have a choice. I'm in too deep. And this may be my only way out.

"He told me he would pay one of my coworkers whatever they wanted to go to the police and tell them I abused my patients, including your gram. And, if that happened, I wouldn't just lose my job, Adam. I'd go to jail." I close my eyes and suck in a fresh gulp of air, relaxing my shoulders with my exhalation. When I open my eyes again, the hard line of his mouth has softened a bit. "I knew if I didn't take his money, he would make you believe things about me that weren't true. He would make you—and a lot of other people—think I hurt your grandmother. The idea of you believing *that* is worse than having to walk away from us. It would hurt you even more than this mess, and I couldn't do it. I couldn't risk you thinking I'm the kind of person who would intentionally hurt someone I'm supposed to be taking care of."

He looks worn down and injured, inside and out. There's a long pause before he speaks again. "Did my father withdraw that complaint because you took his deal, or because I talked to him about it?"

I don't have to say a word because he already knows the answer.

"Jesus." His brow wrinkles, and his chest deflates. He runs his right hand up through his hair. It stops on the back of his neck. He waits like that, for a long time, obviously trying to process everything I've said. "It's bad," he says finally. "Really bad."

"I'm so sorry." I want to hug him, but I don't think he'd let me.

"They don't know if he's going to make it."

I don't know what to say.

"My mother's a wreck, I had to lie to my gram, and now…I don't even know what the hell to think." He covers his face with his hands and smudges his fingertips against his forehead.

I say the only thing I can think of. "You did the right thing by not telling your gram about the accident. She's better off believing your father's back in Seattle."

"That's what Dr. Kopsey thought, too."

I stand in front of him, again not knowing what to do or say next. More than anything, I want *us* to be okay. I want him to say he believes me and he understands why I took his father's money. I want him to forgive me. Without me having to tell him anything more.

"I…I need to go," he says, tossing the words into the air between us like they don't mean what I think they do. He's leaving, and I think it's for the last time. I don't know if he believes me or Perry Devine. I don't know anything anymore.

He turns his back on me and walks over to the door. As his hand twists the knob, he pauses and adds, "Take care of Gram tomorrow, please. Take her outside, if you can. I don't think I'll make it in to see her."

He opens the door and steps out.

"Adam," I call, before he closes the door behind him, "even if you don't believe anything else I've said, *please* believe I will always take care of your gram."

He turns around and looks at me, delivering no physical or verbal indication of whether or not he believes me. He just stands there and stares at me for several seconds before closing the door between us.

***

Since Adam left a few hours ago, I haven't stopped thinking about what everything means. I can't get the argument he had with his father on Wednesday night out of my thoughts. Obviously there was anger when Mr. Sinclair left the parking lot; it was the one thing Sondra was positive about. I hope Adam doesn't think he was in any way responsible for his father's accident. Argument-inspired road rage is a thing, and maybe Adam's feeling guilty about the tone between them when his father left Pine Manor. He may also be second-guessing his decision not to drive his father to the airport. Maybe there's guilt that he wasn't in the car, too.

Or…maybe there isn't.

Maybe there's absolutely no guilt. Because, maybe, Adam learned the truth about Bradley on Wednesday from the photograph in his grandmother's room. And maybe it only served to deepen his mistrust of his father. Maybe Adam is only feeling *grateful* he wasn't in the car.

I wish I could ask him about all the maybes.

I'm in bed, trying to settle my spinning mind enough to get some sleep, when my cell phone rings. It's Tasha's number. The flat on Gravelston Street.

"Hello?"

"Hey, sis." There's a long pause, during which I wait for her to say more. The silence is awkward and yet expectant. When she doesn't continue, I start talking. I need to make sure she's okay.

"Charlie. Hey. It's good to hear from you. Is everything all right?"

"You should've kept this money for yourself," she says, her voice more tender than I've heard it in years. "I don't deserve all the chances you keep givin' me."

"You deserve every one of them, Charlie. And you need to stop telling yourself you don't."

I hear her breathing, soft and thoughtful. "You sound like Daddy." The emotion in her voice is overwhelming.

Another long pause, only this time it's mine. I close my eyes and press the phone tighter to my ear, as if doing so means I won't miss a single moment of my sister. "He believed in you, and I do, too."

More silence. Maybe tears. A light sniffle escapes her body and enters my ear like a tiny Cupid's arrow meant to mend what's broken.

"I registered for the spring semester at Blue Cliff," she says finally. "And Tasha got me a job at the salon again. Starting tomorrow, I'll be the oldest shampoo girl in the history of Houma. But I'm gonna make it happen this time, K'acy. For real."

When our daddy died, Charlie totally lost it. First, she landed in a hospital; the doctors had to stitch up her wrists. And then, I made her check herself into a mental health facility. She said the guilt she felt about all the trouble she'd given him over the years since our momma left made her feel undeserving of any life at all. Especially since he lost his in such a horrible way. She said watching him suffer was like watching a puppy drown while your hands are tied behind your back and your feet are nailed to the floor.

Charlie stayed in therapy for a few months after the funeral, but all these years later, she's somehow still incapable of seeing the perfect life my father always told her she deserves. I don't know what she and her psychologist talked about in all of those therapy sessions, but when they ended and she was discharged, Charlie went back to the real world and instantly started thinking she was nothing important all over again. She started abusing herself in different ways, and I couldn't stand to see it. *She* became the puppy in the water, and I had to get out of there before I stopped believing she could pull herself back out. I was young and I was angry and I left her. Probably when she needed me the most. But I couldn't do it. I couldn't stay in Houma and watch her self-destruct. So I left for Philadelphia with her parting promise to use my father's death as motivation to make something of herself ringing in my ears.

But, from the sound of the voice on the other end of the line today, the puppy must still be afloat. And maybe, just maybe, she's finally nearing the shore.

"I know you will," I say, pride swelling in my chest. The broken pieces of my heart rearrange themselves back into some semblance of order, the tiny Cupid's arrow now holding them loosely together like a toothpick through a sandwich. Precarious and teetering, but together.

My deal with Winston Sinclair may bring some good to this world after all.

"There's something else I need to tell you," she adds, a quiet tremor in her voice vibrating between us and causing a flutter in my heart.

I open my eyes and stare at the dark ceiling, waiting for more words and wondering why she sounds so raw.

"I'm pregnant."

I slowly close my eyes again and let her revelation sink in.

"But, don't worry," she continues. "Tasha's gonna let us live with her and Elijah until I can get my own place. The classes I'm gonna take at Blue Cliff are at night. I'll watch both babies during the day, and Tasha will have them in the evening, until my classes are over."

I sit up in the bed and put my free hand on top of my head. This baby has the ability to either be Charlie's savior or her sword to fall on. What a huge weight for such small shoulders to bear.

"How pregnant are you?"

"Nine weeks."

Nine weeks. The reason for her eight-hundred-dollar phone call a few weeks ago is clear now. She was either going to end the pregnancy and has since changed her mind, or she needed the money to get away from the *what's-his-face* and start a life of her own. I'm not going to ask her which one is the right answer.

"The money that came in the mail today…" she adds, "… it's incredible. Did you know about the baby? Did Tasha call and tell you?"

"No. No. I just…I picked up some extra work, and I thought it might help you out." It's the same lie I told her before. "I'm doing okay here, and I wanted you to have it. Sounds like my timing was pretty good though, huh?"

"It definitely was." She sounds so unsure, like she doesn't believe she can do this.

"You're going to make a good momma, Charlie. A much better mother than Louise McGee ever was, that's for sure."

"Thanks, K'acy. That means a lot."

Neither of us says anything for a long time. We just listen to each other breathe and think our own thoughts. I'm going to be an aunt. And my daddy is going to be a grandpa. If he were alive, he would be singing at the top of his lungs, filled with hope and promise and love.

After she gives me her new cell phone number, I say good night to my big sister. Before we hang up, she promises to call me again next week.

I tell her how much I'm already looking forward to it.

***

When I leave for work on Saturday morning, I see Perry Devine's dark sedan parked across the street from my apartment building yet again. But this time, the moment he sees me step off the stoop, he climbs out of the car and starts walking across the street toward me. As usual, he's wearing a dark suit. His crisply ironed shirt is Oxford blue. He's decidedly uncasual this morning, with a bright yellow tie wrapped snugly around his brawny neck. I keep walking to the bus stop, as if I don't even see him. I have no idea why he's here, and since all I want to do is punch him in the throat, I think it's better for us both if I pretend he doesn't exist. He calls after me, but I just keep walking.

The next thing I know, Perry Devine is jogging past me, and when he cuts me off and blocks my way, not only do I want to punch him in the throat, I also want to kick him in the groin. Hard. He stops right in front of me and turns around. I can see my reflection in his mirrored aviators. I look stronger than I feel.

"Where is he?" he says, his voice a mixture of sadness and anger. It takes a moment for me to realize he's talking about Adam.

"I don't know. Thanks to you and your boss, he wants nothing to do with me. Congratulations."

"So, you're telling me he's not in your apartment right now?"

"No, Mr. Devine, he's not." I cross my arms over my chest and sling my weight down over one hip. A fire starts smoldering in my gut. "Why did you lie to him? Why did you tell him I only came to the hospital for my money when you know that isn't true?"

"Because it's my job to protect him. And he needs to be with his mother and father right now."

"It's your job to protect him, and yet you've somehow managed to lose him? Please tell me you see as much irony in that as I do." I try to push past him, but he stands firm, stepping in front of me each time I try to walk forward. Flames start to lick up out of the smoldering fire inside my gut. "He's probably asleep at his place. Or on his way to see his father."

Perry Devine shakes his head and eyes me cautiously. "He never came home last night. I sat outside his place until morning, and he never came home." The flames in my belly cause it to tumble over on itself. "I thought he might have come here last night, while I was driving his mother back to her hotel."

"He did come here last night," I say, my voice full of contempt. "But, thanks to your lie, he left quickly. He was only here to say goodbye." Grief and rage and confusion pump my veins full of bile and suffocate me with their intensity. I want to scream and cry, but more than anything, I want to lift a fist and swing it hard and fast, straight into him.

As he nods in understanding, his expression changes ever so slightly. It softens into something closer to worry than anger. It reminds me he's known Adam since he was just a small boy. He's watched him grow and seen how his parents have treated him. Perry Devine has seen Adam's mother choose shopping over spending time with her son. He's seen the full extent of Mr. Sinclair's need for control. He's seen Adam at his best and his worst. He probably knows Adam better than his own parents do. I'm sure he cares about him.

Hell, Mr. Devine probably cares about Adam more than his own family does.

He reaches into his breast pocket and pulls out a business card, holding it out for me to take. "I know you don't like me much, Miss McGee, and I get that. Really, I do. But would you just text or call me if you happen to find him before I do? I just wanna make sure he's safe." There's something else in his voice now, beyond the worry and concern. Compassion, perhaps. Maybe even love.

Today, Perry Devine isn't just doing his job. He's trying to find someone he cares about.

I take the card from him and tuck it into the pocket of my scrubs.

He steps aside then, and lets me pass. I keep walking to the bus stop and see him drive by soon after I take a seat on the bench. As I wait for the 61A, I think about the possibility of him being wrong. Maybe Adam did go home last night and Mr. Devine just never saw him. He couldn't have spent the night in the hospital or at Pine Manor because overnight visits aren't permitted. I sort through the reasons why Adam may not have gone home last night, and they cause a bullet of worry to burrow its way into me. Maybe there's something else going on. What if Mr. Sinclair's accident wasn't an accident at all? The newscaster mentioned that foul play wasn't suspected, but maybe that's changed. Is Mr. Devine worried something's happened to Adam, too? Has he tried calling or texting him? Does Perry Devine even have Adam's number? Panic starts to set in just as the bus pulls up to the curb.

I climb the stairs and find a seat in the front as I fumble for my phone. Once it's out of my purse, I open up my texts. The moment I do, it rings in my hand.

The ringtone is sharp and familiar.

CHAPTER 35

Back when Crackerjack Townhouse was new, we'd spend most of our practice sessions either jamming or playing cover songs, but eventually, we started writing our own music. Liam, Calvin, and I would build the base of the song, and then the horn players would come in and blow it all out into something really special. Jarrod's words would be added last. He's always had a knack for stringing a bunch of syllables together and making them sound like they were created to spread the very message he turned them into. We all play a part in piecing everything together, and watching a song come into existence is nothing short of magic.

Over the years, we've played a lot of live shows, made two albums of original music, and knocked out a few dozen extra songs that didn't make the cut. But "Ecce Homo" and "Break It Out" are the songs we've always hoped would take us somewhere. They're the ones we've wanted a recording exec to hear us play live for the past few years. And, at long last, one of them is going to get the chance to hear those songs. Tonight, at The Upstage.

As "Ecce Homo" blares out of my phone on the 61A, I have to take a second to catch myself. After all these years of making music together, I won't be there for what might be the biggest night Crackerjack Townhouse has ever seen. I won't be there because someone else needs me more than they do. No matter where Adam is, and what's happening at The Upstage, I'll need to be with Mr. Sinclair. Because if I'm not there, tomorrow—and every other day for the next three weeks—will be filled with misery beyond what any human should ever have to bear. It will bring eventual death, yes, but a seemingly endless parade of agony will come first. My promise to Ms. Sinclair has to be fulfilled tonight. If it isn't, then I've lost everything that makes me, *me*.

Before the song can continue beyond the intro, I answer the phone, lifting it to my ear and saying a soft hello. When I look up, the man across the aisle is staring at me in disapproval, as if my ringtone didn't play well with his sensible shoes and leather briefcase. He quickly looks away as Jarrod's voice comes through the phone.

"Good morning, schweetheart," he says in a whisper.

"Hey, Jar. What's with the whispering?"

"Someone's still asleep."

"Grace?" I ask, hoping to hell it's her and not some ankles-to-her-ears woman. I don't want him to mess anything up.

"No, it's not Grace." My eyes close as I release a silent, disappointed exhale. "Your Mister is passed out on my couch," he adds.

My eyes pop back open, and I lean forward in my seat. "What?"

"He called and asked me to go get a couple drinks with him last night. I guess I can handle my liquor a little better than he can because, next thing I know, I'm taking his stumbling ass home with me and prodding him to sleep on his side so he doesn't choke on his own puke."

"Really?"

"Yep. The man was shit-face drunk. He downed half a bottle of bourbon and bought like five rounds for the entire bar. Must be trying to spend some of his trust fund."

That explains why Perry Devine couldn't find him all night.

"Thanks for taking care of him."

Jarrod doesn't reply for a few seconds, and when he does, he sounds different. He's still whispering, but there's more sentiment behind his voice than there was before. "He told me he went over to see you last night. He said walking out of your apartment was the hardest thing he's ever done."

"The whole thing sucked."

"He was a fucking wreck about it, in all honesty. I couldn't keep pretending I didn't know what was going on with you guys, so I told him everything I know about your deal with his dad. He didn't seem all that surprised."

"Well, he couldn't have been *too* wrecked about it, or else he wouldn't have walked away."

"Yeah, but here's the thing, Kace...he didn't *want* to walk away. He believes what you told him, but he's terrified of what else his father is willing to do if he stays with you and the man lives long enough to find out about it."

My lungs deflate and my chin drops to my chest. I can't believe what he's saying.

"Adam told you all this?"

"Yeah, but like I said, he was pretty shit-faced. I'm not sure he'll remember, but that's definitely what he said. Sure seems to me like the guy's trying to protect you." My head is spinning. I can't even think straight. "Do you know exactly when this is going to be over? I hope it's soon. I really feel for the guy."

I was going to call and tell him later, but I might as well tell him now. "You're gonna need to get Stevie to play for me tonight."

"*What?* Why? Jesus…wait…is it going to happen tonight?"

"Yes. And I need to be there."

He sighs and pauses, obviously unhappy with what I've said. "We can't play without you. Stevie needs to be on sax, not bass. You and I both know he's a second-rate bassist. Come on, Kace. Don't bail on us. You've worked too hard to jump ship on this show. The man's gonna die whether you're there or not."

I can't tell him that isn't the truth.

"I'm sorry, Jarrod. You can be mad at me if you want, but just… Please don't tell Adam we talked this morning, okay?"

Another long pause. "I can't believe this."

"With all the epic ass shaking going on tonight, no one's even gonna notice I'm not there."

"I will."

I wonder if he can hear me smile.

"Will you call me tomorrow?" he adds. "Just to let me know you're okay."

If he were here now, on this bus, I would reach over and give him a big hug. "Yeah. Of course."

"And you'll let me know if you change your mind, right?"

"I won't change my mind, Jar," I say with as much conviction as I can muster. "Good luck tonight. And tell the guys I'm sorry, okay?"

"Okay."

I hang up as soon as we say our goodbyes. My heart is heavy knowing Crackerjack Townhouse isn't going to be quite as epic tonight, on the one night it matters the most. I might be shooting all of us in the foot by not being there. It sucks.

I pull Perry Devine's business card out of my pocket.

Perry W. Devine, Head of Security
Sinclair & Associates

Seattle, Washington

I turn the card around over and over again, flipping it between my fingers until the bus arrives at my stop. As I walk the block to work, I send Perry Devine a single text message.

Adam is safe. He spent the night with a friend.

***

Pine Manor is quiet today, too quiet for a weekend. The weather is starting to change, and this time of year, it always seems like everyone tries to enjoy every last bit of sunshine they can get. Autumn is officially here, and for the first few weeks of the season, visitation is always down. People want to spend their weekends outside, instead of in a stuffy place like this. It's a tough time of year for the residents. They know the holidays are coming in a few short months, and many of them won't be able to be with their families. Some of them can't leave the facility. Others don't "get company" at the holidays because their families are too far away or they don't seem to think they have the time to make a visit. It's difficult to see.

Our social coordinator is always looking for extra resident activities this time of year, and today is no exception. After breakfast, we're hosting a cookie-decorating contest in the community room with a local bakery. It's a fun September tradition, and I spend my morning getting the residents ready by helping them put on aprons and wash their hands. Once everyone else is settled in the community room, I head back to Ms. Sinclair's room to see if she wants to join the fun.

According to this morning's shift change report, Ms. Sinclair had another rough night. She had a night terror and woke several of the residents with her screams. The nurse who filled out the report said it took them a long time to get her settled. Apparently Ms. Sinclair didn't know where she was, and she thought the nurses were there to hurt her, instead of help her. She physically fought with them, and it was a struggle to get her to calm down. They didn't get her back to bed until nearly five o'clock this morning.

My precariously pinned-together heart aches at the thought of her being so afraid and confused. I'm not sure my presence would've made a difference, but I wish I had been here last night to try to comfort her. I wish I could've held her hand and told her everything would be okay. I suspect her nights are going to become even more difficult over the coming weeks, even if Dr. Kopsey convinces Adam to up her medication yet again. They didn't call him last night because Ms. Sinclair wasn't injured, but protocol says Sue Campbell will be calling and telling Adam about the incident sometime this morning, if she hasn't already.

As I walk back to Ms. Sinclair's room, I think of Adam, hung-over and confused, and hope he finds some comfort knowing I'm here with her today, making sure she's all right. It can't be easy on him, being with his mother and father when I'm sure he'd rather be with his gram.

I hope when tomorrow comes, things will be different.

I open the door to Ms. Sinclair's room to find her sound asleep in the bed. There's a bright yellow tray of untouched breakfast on her bedside table, just like there was the morning after she fell for the first time. Only today, Adam isn't sitting in her recliner with his index finger to his lips like he was that morning. He isn't here, but his bouquet of daisies is. Their smiling faces are tucked into her green plastic water pitcher, offering their happiness and cheer. Just like a different bouquet of them did that morning, all those weeks ago.

I watch Ms. Sinclair sleep from my place in the doorway, her pale hands tucked together against the side of her face. Her breathing is shallow and rhythmic as I step into her room, letting the door close quietly behind me. I sit down on the edge of her bed, staring at her translucent skin and lightly sweeping the hair off her face with my index finger. I think of my daddy then, and how fragile he was at the end of his life. I think of him crying on the day he died. And how I wiped away his tears, humming Otis Redding into his ear. He handed me his wedding ring that night, even though he barely had enough strength to tug it off his finger. He put it in my hand and told me he loved me.

I wonder if Winston Sinclair has anything to give *his* child before he dies.

I wonder if he'd say *I love you* to Adam, if he could.

I tuck Ms. Sinclair's blanket up against her chin and leave the room as quietly as I entered it.

On my way back to the cookie-filled community room, I stop in the break room and grab my phone from my bag. I send Adam a quick text. I think he might need to hear what I have to say.

I'll take care of her. I promise.

A few short seconds pass before I get a reply.

I know.

It makes me smile.

***

The rest of the day passes in a blur. After she wakes up, Ms. Sinclair has a decent afternoon, spending most of it watching her birds from the lobby sofa. She's pretty lucid, but the day is a busy one for me and we don't have much time to talk. By the time the second shift arrives, Ms. Sinclair is back in her room, watching the cooking channel and sucking on a Starlight mint. I say goodbye to her on my way out, but I don't tell her I'm going to see her son tonight. I don't tell her anything other than *goodbye* and *have a good night*. Because there's nothing else she needs to know.

On the bus ride to Latham Street, I carefully consider all the steps I'll have to take tonight. I walk through every scenario, working through any possible glitches before they happen. Tonight, focus and caution will be as necessary as compassion and empathy and love. It's different this time, because it'll happen somewhere new. Somewhere far more public than Pine Manor. Somewhere I don't belong.

After I find the man on Latham Street and get what I need, I take the 57B home. When I get to my apartment, I don't take off my scrubs. I don't even take off my shoes. I just sit down on my sofa and wait for night to come. I wait for visiting hours to end and for the bare bones of night-shift hospital workers to start replacing the second shift.

Even though I'm miles away from The Upstage when darkness comes, I see Crackerjack Townhouse on the stage. I see Jarrod standing at the mic, silent and still, filling the audience with want. I see *them* there, hundreds of people humming with expectation and alcohol as Bryson's lips press into the trombone's mouthpiece and Mark's fingertips hover above the piano keys. I watch Jarrod's chest fill with air, and a heartbeat later, I hear Crackerjack Townhouse strike its first note, crisp and brilliant, and I listen to it echo around the pulsating room like a buzzing bee, filled with sweetness and energy. I feel Stevie's bass notes throbbing inside my chest, their slap and pop causing a lump to rise up into my throat.

The sound of funk infuses the air around me, vibrating through my gut and sending me its message of love as if I were there, on the stage with them. I see the audience in front of me, their hearts filled with poetic thumping, and more than anything, I wish I were there for real. I wish I were the one giving those mascara-laden lovelies the panty-dropping feels. I wish I were the one vibrating inside them.

And I wish my bed-headed swooner were there, too, watching it all.

Just after 11:00, I step out into the night and walk to the bus stop, the soles of my shoes scuffing the concrete in perfect time with the electronic hum of the streetlights and the song inside my head. The memory of Miriam Hansen's words settles over me again. She said the next person to fill her room would bring me all the happiness I deserve. She said love would come, and it did. I only wish she would've warned me about how hard it would be to see it go.

The symphony of funk continues to flow through my arteries, just as it crackles through the air at The Upstage. I feel the beat jostle around inside of me as I walk into the doors of Penn Presbyterian a few minutes before midnight, each song coming and going in synchronization with the set list they're using on the other side of the city. The volunteer at the lobby information desk nods at me, no doubt thinking I'm part of the crew of night shift employees now coming to work. I see a few of them walking through the lobby, purses and lunch bags slung over their shoulders, ID lanyards around their necks. Mine is flipped over so you can't see the Pine Manor logo. You can only see my face smiling back at you.

As I walk toward the elevator, I pass the exact spot where I met Adam's mother. When I step across the same mellow tan hospital floor that was once beneath her polished, pointy-toe beige pumps, the funk inside of me calms for a moment, settling to a dull roar and refining itself for a few measures. But the moment my finger meets the elevator button, it rushes back at me, full and loud and ceaseless.

It's "Break It Out." One more song until the end.

The elevator carries me up to the trauma ICU and closer to the raw, charred skin of Winston Sinclair. I walk down the corridor and through the double doors to find the desk in the waiting area vacant. This time, it's just me and the magazine-filled end tables under the fluorescent lights. The sour, middle-aged woman with pudgy hands is at home, probably dreaming about some slick romance-novel hero coming to sweep her off her feet. I bend over her desk, looking for her self-worth-validating button; the one that opens the door. The paper with Perry Devine's handwritten number is still taped next to the phone. When I see it, my stomach twists over on itself, sending more surging notes out into my blood. The bridge of "Break It Out" rushes through me, hot and quick, its contrasting key sharpening my senses and filling me with purpose. My hand shakes as I reach down and press the door release button tucked underneath the lip of the desk. I hear a hollow click and see the light on the wall switch from red to green.

Curtains are drawn across most of the glass windows as I walk silently down the corridor. I can't see anyone inside the rooms, but I can sense their presence. I can feel their stories. The disinfectant-infused air is still, save for the occasional soft blip of a piece of medical equipment. I pass the large, central staff area where three women are busy looking back and forth between their computer screens and the various contents of manila file folders. None of them look up at me as I pass, but I know they see me. They must see me. How could they not.

I open the door—the one at the far left corner of the hallway—just as "Ecce Homo" begins. Jarrod's voice shuttles a wave of emotion through me as the words come out of his mouth. They're the same as always: self-serving yet self-deprecating. Cocky yet sardonic. Structured yet raw. It's a funk song gone philosophical. And its message is more powerful than ever. The conceit of self-faith will always exist. "I am no man. I am dynamite," will always be said, in seriousness rather than in song, inside the heads of people like Winston Sinclair. People who thrive on power and control, and who think their own importance belittles everyone else's. Even the people they're supposed to love.

But tonight, Mr. Sinclair cannot say those words. Or any other words, for that matter. Because he's in the bed in front of me, medicated and powerless, his skin wrapped in gauze and a catheter funneling his manhood away right along with his piss.

The smell of greasy ointment sinks into my nostrils as Marquis's trumpet blasts out a series of bright, staccato notes in time with Bryson's trombone. More bass notes ripple through me. I walk across the room and sit down on the edge of Mr. Sinclair's bed, the door drifting closed behind me. The stiff whoosh-and-hum of the respirator is gone; they must have removed it when he regained consciousness. There are only IV stands around him now, their bags half-filled with saline, antibiotics, and painkillers.

As I lift Mr. Sinclair's arm and gently place it vein-side-up across my lap, I think of my daddy and what he taught me about death and all the pain that can go with it. If you're not willing to stop it, the torture can be relentless, both inside and out. Nothing on this Earth should have to suffer before a foreseeable, inevitable death. Nothing. That's why we're born with empathy and understanding already inside. It's a part of being human, and my daddy taught me not to be afraid of it.

He taught me that I always need to do the right thing. Every time. Even when it hurts.

My daddy taught me how to break a mourning dove's neck when I was five years old. He'd take me and Charlie to the quarry where he worked, and we'd run around collecting the birds after he'd filled them with birdshot. Sometimes, they'd still be alive. They'd have a broken wing or a missing foot, and they'd look up at you with their shiny, round, black eyes. Like they were just waiting to die.

"If they're still alive," Daddy would say, "you've got to break their neck real quick. No use letting 'em suffer."

He showed us how to put their downy heads into the crook of skin between our first two fingers and flip their bodies backward until we heard the bones snap.

"Flick 'em fast," he'd say, "like the tongue on a snake."

By the time I was eight years old, I'd probably taken more lives than a poacher on the African savannah. They were good, too, those doves. My momma knew how to cook them so they tasted just like chicken.

In fact, the day I was born, the doctor asked my momma about the last thing she ate before labor came on. When she told him it was a dove sandwich, she said he looked right back at her like she was some kind of wild sinner, fresh outta the bayou.

So here I am, twenty-four years after my illustrious dove-fueled birth, sitting on a mattress with another living thing in my hands, just waiting to die.

Only this time, it's different.

Because this time, he's already dead.

CHAPTER 36

Winston Sinclair—Room number 736

I spent most of my life trying to hide my secrets. Some of those secrets were bigger than others, but every one of them started with a lie. One simple lie that eventually morphed into either a tragedy or a gem of good fortune. There were secrets threaded throughout my life. Too many to keep track of. Most of my lies made me a lot of money, but a few of them cost me millions.

It started when I was six. My mother got me a canary. I hated that thing, but she insisted I keep it in my room. She said it was good for me to learn how to take care of something besides myself. That damn bird would scatter birdseed and feathers all over, and start chirping at the break of dawn. Every day, for months, I wanted to break the bird's puffy, yellow neck.

Then one day, I did.

It was 5:30 in the morning on a summer's day. I should've been sleeping in, but it wouldn't shut up. So, when I couldn't take the chatter anymore, I whipped open the cage door, grabbed the little motherfucker, and tried to twist off one of its wings. It pecked and squawked at me until I dropped it on the floor. I watched it flop around on the carpet, dragging its broken wing around in some kind of frantic dance.

I broke the other wing next, just to see what it would do.

When I put the bird back down on the carpet, both of its wings dangling off its tiny body like lopsided, feathery pendants, it didn't dance or squawk. It just looked at me. We stared at each other until I heard my mother walking down the hallway outside my door. I quickly opened the window and threw the bird out, watching it flutter down like a falling leaf until it smacked head-first into a rhododendron branch and landed crooked-necked in the dirt below. When my mother came into the room and saw the open cage and window, I began my first secret. I told her the bird flew out the window while I was cleaning its cage. I cried. I apologized. I lied and told her I was sad. And, forever the schoolteacher, she told me it was a good lesson. When I pretended to beg her for another canary, as expected, she said pets weren't replaceable. She said I wasn't responsible enough yet and blamed herself for trusting me when I was still so young.

As I grew, I learned that lies could just as easily get you out of trouble as they could get you into it. When I was a teenager, my mother thought I spent a lot of time at the library, when instead, I was out making mayhem with my friends and spinning lies to cover it up. In college, I lied about my grandfather dying to get out of taking finals. I lied to girls all the time, telling them they were "the one" just so they would fuck me before I said goodbye. I even lied about graduating. I told my mother not to come for my college graduation ceremony because I had strep throat and couldn't even go myself. She was in Philadelphia and I was in Indiana, at Notre Dame. She never knew I didn't actually graduate because I didn't pass enough classes to get my diploma.

But the lies that led to my life's biggest secret were the ones I told my wife. Heather and I met when I was working at Strahan Partners. I was twenty-two, with a new job at the state's most respectable lobbying firm, thanks to a handsomely fabricated résumé. Five days a week, I was a runner. I'd deliver documents wherever they needed to go, all over town. They gave me a company car and a promise that I could eventually work my way up if I worked hard enough. Heather was a secretary for one of the state senators. I must've convinced her I was something special because after three or four visits to her office, we had our first date. She quit her job soon after we got engaged, and we were married a year later.

I met Marissa at a bar when Adam was four years old. She was very different from my wife. She didn't want to spend her life shopping and getting her nails done and having tea with some senator's wife. Marissa just wanted to have fun. A lot of fun. She was my deliverance from reality for four solid years, and she was by far my biggest secret. By the time we met, I'd already made my first million, having worked my way up the ranks at Strahan before jumping over to Murray and Associates. I got Marissa an apartment, and I'd spend a few afternoons a week sharing her bed.

But everything changed when she got pregnant. She refused to get rid of it. She started teasing me about the baby being leverage, telling me she'd have one hell of a bargaining chip the moment our child was born. She was trying to make a joke out of it, but I knew from the start there was nothing funny about it. I knew she was serious.

Two months after Bradley was born, Marissa started asking me to leave Heather. When I told her I'd do no such thing, she threatened to tell Heather about us. She knew there was no pre-nup and Heather would get half of everything if we divorced. To keep Marissa quiet, I gave her more money. But, she started doing foolishly risky things. She'd take Bradley to the park and strike up a conversation with my mother as she sat and watched

Adam on the swings. Marissa once showed me a picture of my mother holding a chubby-faced Bradley, as if she already knew he was her grandson. There was even a picture of Adam holding Bradley's tiny hand as he sat in his stroller at the park. I had to stop it, before I lost my wife and son—and money—for good.

So, I told another lie in order to keep my secret. I told my wife I wanted to move out west and open my own firm. I told her I had connections there and moving Adam away from his grandmother, whom he loved more than anything, was no big deal. She said she trusted me, and a few days later, the moving truck showed up at our front door.

I didn't tell Marissa we were moving until Heather and Adam were already on the other side of the country. She was angrier than I'd ever seen a person, and I was fresh out of lies. There was nothing I could do or say to make it better. She threatened to drop Bradley at an orphanage. Or over a bridge. She said if she couldn't have me, she didn't want him either.

I did the only thing I could think of. I hired a lawyer.

For the next few weeks, I stayed in Philadelphia, "tying up some loose ends" while my wife and son were in Seattle. The lawyer drafted the documents for Marissa to sign, and I gave her a briefcase filled with more cash than I'd ever seen in my life.

She signed away full custodial rights to her own son for two million under-the-table dollars. For her guaranteed silence, she got another quarter million and a one-way ticket to Europe.

And I was left with a baby I didn't want.

I took him to my mother's house and told new lies. I said he was the product of a one-night stand, and his mother was emotionally unstable. I said I had full custody of him because she was addicted to drugs. I said Heather and Adam could never find out because I couldn't bear to lose them. I cried and apologized for my horrible mistake, just like I did the morning I killed that damn canary. I wept in my mother's arms and begged her to take care of Bradley for me. I tugged and manipulated her heartstrings as if she were a marionette, eventually convincing her Bradley needed her more than Adam did. I promised her we would hire the finest nanny for Adam, and he would be loved just as she had loved him. We cried together, though my mother's tears were the only real ones to fall. She was mourning Adam as if he had died because she knew she would never see him again.

I never said the words out loud, but I think she always knew I would keep him from her in order to protect my secret. She knew I wouldn't risk losing everything I had for a baby I barely knew.

And it worked. Mother raised Bradley just as she had raised me. And Adam. He slept in my old bed and got the same damn chocolate pudding in his lunch I did. She'd send me pictures from time to time, always to my office so Heather couldn't see them. I kept them all in a locked desk drawer. Occasionally I would look at them, always surprised at how much Bradley looked like his half-brother.

I can't say I loved him, but Bradley was my son, and he deserved a better fate than the one my mother handed him.

I privately grieved when he died. Marissa knocked on my mother's door one day, showing her a picture of the two of us together she'd taken before Bradley was even born. She said she was Bradley's mother, and she just wanted to take him out for lunch to celebrate his ninth birthday. My mother invited her in, and then, after only a brief conversation, she let Bradley go with Marissa. They were supposed to go to Ruby Tuesday's, but instead, they ended up wrapped around a phone pole.

If he were still alive, he'd be seventeen years old.

Every day since, I've wondered why my mother let him go. I've never forgiven her for it. And I never will.

Even after Bradley died, I refused to let her back into our lives. She didn't deserve to be a part of my life. Or Adam's. Not only was my mother holding my biggest secret in her careless hands, but her mistake was beyond pardon. Having her in my life was too risky. It was easier to continue to shut her out.

I didn't expect Adam to understand. When I took the picture of Bradley to my mother's room at that godforsaken nursing home and told him the half-truth about his brother, I wasn't doing it to make him understand. I was doing it because I knew if I didn't, he'd keep pushing my mother. And the facts she might eventually give him would be far more damaging than any lie I could tell. I told Adam everything about Bradley, except for the truth about why I kept him a secret. I admitted to a one-night stand and told him about the car accident. But, I told him I kept Bradley's existence from him only to protect his mother. I told him it would destroy her to know she wasn't the only one. Even now, all these years later. I couldn't risk losing her. I said he could hate me if he wants to, but he would only be hurting his mother by dredging up the past and telling her about Bradley.

He was angry and confused, calling me an asshole for keeping it from them for all these years. After that smug nurse kicked us out of Pine Manor for arguing, we took our conversation out to the parking lot. There, Adam accused me, yet again, of trying to control his life. He was furious, saying I'm always manipulating everyone to my own favor and asking me why the hell I just can't stay away from him. When he brought that little girlfriend of his up as an example, I totally lost it. I screamed at him, telling him he was a fool for thinking she was in love with him and not his trust fund. I told him he deserved a better fuck than some minimum-wage loser from the mosquito-ridden backwoods of Louisiana.

He stood there staring at me, his eyes burning with a fire I've never seen before. His lips pressed closed, and his hands clenched into fists. I saw it coming, but before he could raise a hand, I dropped the bomb. I told him about my deal with her. I told him she picked my money over him. His mouth didn't open again, but his eyes kept burning. Even as I climbed into my car and drove away, I could feel his stare scorching through me.

I don't regret telling him any of it. I only regret I didn't live long enough to see how it would all play out.

The irony of my car accident was not lost on me. Though the Jag didn't end up wrapped around a phone pole—and I didn't die instantly like they did—it's a biting twist of fate that Bradley, Marissa, and I all left this world because of a crumpled-up hunk of metal. I'm glad, though, that he wasn't the one to suffer. His death was quick and straightforward; Marissa's, too, they said.

Mine, though...mine was far from straightforward.

My death was agonizing and infinite. He let it go on far longer than he should've, mostly because I think he enjoyed watching me suffer. When they brought me out of sedation and I was conscious enough to see his face, I already knew what he was thinking. I saw the flatness of his expression, the lack of empathy when I cried out in agony. And I knew what it meant. He was reveling in my misery. Taking pleasure in my pain.

He waited for three days—*three days*—just to see me squirm. When he finally saw fit to put that pillow over my face, my last breath was filled with far more than relief. If my death is not blamed on my own burned-out lungs, it might seem a justifiable murder; death to end suffering. But, it was far more than that. It was deceit and betrayal, the likes of which I've never seen. Even in all my years of politics.

I once told him, a long time ago, that life is full of hard choices. I told him he could tackle those choices head-on, like a man, or he could second-guess his every decision and end up being nothing more than a powerless over-thinker.

Tonight, he chose manhood. And, despite the sting of his betrayal, I'm proud of him for it.

CHAPTER 37

I touch the syringe of pentobarbital in the pocket of my scrubs. It's slender and rigid; full of mercy by the milliliter. And, for the first time ever, it's unnecessary.

Winston Sinclair's lifeless arm sits in my lap, dense and gauze-covered, save for the IV entry site. I look at it there, limply resting across my legs, and I wonder what happened. What did I not see?

The last note of "Ecce Homo" slams through me then, and inside my head, Jarrod throws his arms out to his sides, crucifixion-style, as a haze of music and lights and smoke fills the air around him. He's frozen there, his last words lingering in my ears. "I am no man. I am dynamite." The room around him pulsates with a new energy. It buzzes with life.

I carefully lift Mr. Sinclair's arm to put it back on the bed, and when I brush a small patch of his exposed skin, a hot slurry of new notes rips into me. It's "Soul to Squeeze," and it's way faster and louder than it should be. The bass line climbs up my body like a still-clawed kitten, digging into my skin with its pricks and jabs, and causing a shiver to shimmy its way up my spine. Inside my head, it's dark now. Crackerjack Townhouse is gone.

"Soul to Squeeze" is coming out of *me*, not them.

I leave Winston Sinclair's room—and Penn Presbyterian—with a mixture of fear and wonder and celebration fumbling around in the darkness of my brain, each looking for a reason to exist. I've never been wrong before, and I don't quite know how to feel about it. Winston Sinclair was definitely dead. And I definitely had nothing to do with it. Questions dance through me. Hows and whys and whats power across my synapses as the Chili Peppers set fire to my skin.

By the time the bus pulls up to the curb, "Soul to Squeeze" has ended, leaving me numb and stupefied.

Somewhere inside, I know it's the last time I'll hear it.

My apartment is quiet and calm, a perfect partner to my confusion. I leave my shoes at the door and head back to my bedroom. I take the vial and needle out of my pocket and put them carefully into the small, empty wooden box tucked in the back of my closet. I tug off my scrubs, tossing them into the wash basket with my socks, and drop a clean T-shirt over my head. I sink into bed, clicking off the light switch and wishing I could turn my brain off with the same kind of abruptness.

In the dark stillness of my bedroom, the lights and colors return to my mind, kicking up thoughts as if they were dust. Behind my closed eyelids, I watch Winston Sinclair's movie unfold from my memory yet again. It's the same as it was before. Nothing has changed. There are no missed details, no moments of clarity. Nothing that tells me why the man was already gone.

Mr. Sinclair's movie hasn't changed. Instead, someone has edited it. They've severed the film before the final frame could turn into real life. And they did it without even knowing what that final frame would be.

A thought bites into me.

Maybe they didn't do it because they knew Winston Sinclair would die. Maybe they did it because they thought he might live.

***

The sound of my alarm rouses me from sleep well before my body is ready. I swat it off as I stretch and roll onto my side. My eyes flash open the moment I hear a soft scuffle against the floor.

Adam is standing in the corner of my room. He's wearing jeans and a plaid button-down. His arms are slack at his sides, and there's a massive, convenience-store bouquet of daisies in his breast pocket. His bed-head is screaming at me.

I sit up in bed, scrambling to collect my thoughts before he speaks.

"My mother called me last night. She said my father's dead."

I stare at him blankly, as if his words come as a surprise. "I…I'm sorry."

"Don't be," he says. "I'm not." He walks a few steps closer to me. "Actually, I'm relieved. I mean…my mother's a wreck, but I think everything's going to be all right."

An unwanted nervous jitter starts wiggling its way into me. It's a different kind of jitter this time. Darker. Filled with doubt and suspicion instead of hope.

I brush my fingers through my hair and swing my legs over the side of the bed. I look up at him and see a strange sort of cautious optimism in his eyes.

"What happened to him?" I ask, not sure I really want to know the truth.

"They said his body just couldn't handle the injuries. His organs shut down around eleven last night. Someone from the hospital called my mother to tell her." That means Mrs. Sinclair knew her husband was dead even before I got to Penn Presbyterian; the hospital morgue just hadn't come to collect his body yet.

I nod my head in understanding, even though I know that what Adam just said about the cause of his father's death can't be true. I listen carefully for any regret or transparency in his voice. I hear nothing but his words.

"I know it makes *me* a giant dickhead," he continues, "but I'm kind of glad he's gone." He pauses for a second, inhaling a shallow breath. When he talks again, his voice seems to be choking on itself. "It was really tough to see him in so much pain. I can't imagine what his life would've been like, if he would've lived. My mother's, too. There would've been surgeries and skin grafts and years of therapy, and he probably wouldn't have ever been the same again. I mean, who knows? Maybe he would've been a vegetable or something." He shrugs and stares at the floor near my feet. "I didn't like my father very much, but I didn't want to see him go through all that. *No one* should have to go through all that." He swallows hard. The transparency I was looking for suddenly comes screaming out at me via a small line of tears and a crack in his voice. "My mom…she's ruined. She loved him so much. I don't know why, but she did. She might not be the greatest mom, but she was the perfect wife for him. I don't know what she's gonna do now." The emotion in his voice is striking and pure. It extinguishes the jitter of doubt and suspicion immediately, wiping away all the uncertainty.

If Adam was the one who edited his father's movie, I think his motive was sincere. Just as mine would've been.

I stand up in front of him, and he lifts his gaze to meet mine. Love rushes through my veins again, igniting a new spark of hope.

Adam's head tilts to the side as if he's carefully memorizing my face. He pulls the bouquet of daisies from his pocket and sets it down carefully on my nightstand. A moment later, he steps over to me, wrapping his arms around my shoulders and pulling me into him. The broken pieces of my heart collide, zippering themselves back together again. My cheek rests against his chest as my arms slide around his waist. I fold myself into him, and a new song begins—an unnamed love song—and it brings sweetness and forgiveness and peace. The notes glue the zippers closed until my heart is whole again, the tiny Cupid's arrow now permanently fused into the healed muscle. I hear his heart, too, beneath his shirt and skin. It's singing to me. Thumping out a song of its own.

"I believe you," he says, his breath skimming across the top of my head. "I always believed you."

"I'm sorry I made you doubt me."

"*You* didn't make me doubt you. My father did." His arms wrap around me tighter, and as they do, the rhythm of his heart picks up tempo. "I should've known there was more than what he was telling me. When you told me *why* you took his money, all I could think about was how much further he might be willing to go in order to keep us apart. I walked away because I didn't want him to hurt you any more than he already had."

Yesterday morning's conversation with Jarrod replays in my mind, offering me an extra dose of comfort and confirmation.

"It's okay, Adam. I understand." And I do.

"He told me other things that day, too, things that completely ripped me apart. And then when he told me you took his money… it was like one final knife to the heart. I just lost it." He's quiet for a minute, his hand circling my back over and over again. "I was totally blindsided."

I hug him harder, to let him know everything's going to be all right.

He tells me how he felt as his father told him the truth about Bradley. He tells me how angry he was to hear about this missing piece of his life and how powerless all of it made him feel.

"It's like he's put this horrible burden on me," Adam says, his tone a hearty dose of exhaustion and disdain. "And I think that's what pissed me off the most. He told me this terrible thing, and then smugly reminded me why I could never tell my mother—the one person who deserves to know about Bradley the most. He made me a part of his sin, and I really want to hate him for it." Adam's arms unfold from my body, releasing me until I can no longer hear the song inside of him. His chin drops down, and he lets out a long, thoughtful sigh. "And now...now I have to carry around a little brother I never even met for the rest of my life."

I pause for a moment, thinking about Charlie and how sometimes siblings can be burdens. But, they're ones worth carrying. Adam just doesn't know it yet.

"Your gram's been carrying him around for seventeen years already." He looks at me with surprise, his soul suddenly visible through his watery eyes. "I'm sure she'd love to tell you more about him, if you ask. It might help if you have each other to share the load." I shrug and raise my brow before adding, "Maybe your father gave you a gift by telling you about your brother before his accident."

He slowly nods his head in understanding and wipes his cheeks with the back of his hand. "It's just like I said in Wicked Mocha right after we met: you're a bundle of quality, K'acy McGee. I knew it even then."

I rise on my toes and lift my hands to his face. My mouth presses against his and everything that matters comes back to me. His lips are warm and soft, and as his tongue dances against mine, I feel the lightness return. My hands cup his face as his grab on to my hips, drawing me closer to him. As our kiss deepens, his fingers work their way up under the hem of my T-shirt and dance across my skin. A new surge of endorphins push their way through my flesh, and I celebrate their sweet, familiar burn. I'm immediately drunk with the desire to hear Miriam Hansen repeat her words in person, to hear her voice tell me love will come. If she were to say the words again, this time I would hold them in my hands as a fragile, but very real, truth. I would cradle them like a precious dove, one that isn't afraid of death because it knows about rebirth and forgiveness. It knows love never dies.

I raise my arms so Adam can take off my shirt. His hands lightly skim over me before his thumbs tuck under the top rim of my panties and push them down. When they drop to the floor, he steps back and stands in front of me with his arms flaccid at his sides. His stare travels leisurely across my skin, stopping only to linger on my face. It feels right to be so exposed. Everything I am is right here in front of him, laid bare. The secret part doesn't matter anymore. What I can see in peoples' eyes, and what I choose to do with it, has everything to do with who I am. But, it has nothing to do with *us*. It's irrelevant to who we are together.

Adam reaches out and takes hold of me again, surrounding my nakedness with his arms, pressing his chest to mine and covering my mouth with another kiss. My hands work to unfasten his shirt and jeans as my nerves snap to attention. The contrast of his skin against mine fills me with want as we fall onto the bed behind me. Adam lies on his back, and I take my time and touch him with reverence and appreciation and understanding, stroking every square centimeter of him with every square centimeter of me. When my fingertips graze his lips, I see happiness in his eyes. I hope he sees the same in mine.

324 | Claire Wallis

I bend down and take him into the warmth of my mouth, using my lips and tongue to tease and pleasure him. When his breath starts to twitch and catch, I sit up and straddle his hips, absorbing his light into my dark before he can find release. My body bends and flexes in time with the sharp rise of his hips until we're both breathless and slick with sweat. A moment after his hand reaches down to rub the place where my body meets his, the added friction sends me over the edge like a shot of thick lightning. My brain fills with light and crashes over on itself until I can't see anything but Adam's face looking up at mine. His eyes close, and he lets out a deep, throaty grunt when he grabs my waist and lifts his hips sharply so he can sink himself into me deeper. All the way up to my heart.

A few minutes later, snuggled up to Adam's side with a morning full of sunlight filling my bedroom, I stare again at my dark fingers splayed against his pale chest. The alternating Vs of light and dark are just as breathtaking as ever, only now they're different. They aren't two separate parts anymore. There's no more yin and yang. No more dark and light. No more opposite yet interdependent pieces. Instead, we've been stirred through each other until the dark and light have become the same thing. We've been blended together into one whole.

"I have something for you," he says, breaking the long silence with his raspy voice.

"Oh yeah? What's that?" I prop myself up on an elbow, so I can see his face.

Adam turns away from me and reaches out toward my night-stand. He carefully picks up the bunch of daisies sitting there and splits the cluster of stems in half. He puts one half back on the table and hands the other half to me.

"These are for you," he says with a smile, lowering his head back onto the pillow.

I smile back at him as I take the flowers from his hand, joy welling up inside of me and filling me with a brilliance I've never known before.

I'm glowing from the inside out.

"I love you," Adam adds, his hand lightly touching one of my curls.

Just like that, every note from every song I've ever heard rips through my veins and jets out of my body. They whirl around me, like a melodious tornado, enveloping me with their comfort and protection. Nothing can stop us again. No doubt. No lies. No giant dickhead.

It's just us. Together. Unstoppable and ceaseless.

"Copy that and send it back."

***

I don't know if it's genuine, but Ms. Sinclair seems very happy to see me when I walk into her room an hour or so later. Adam dropped me off at Pine Manor before heading back to his place for a quick shower and a change of clothes. He asked me to tell his gram he'd be in to see her before lunch, and when I do, she asks me if his father will be coming in with him. Obviously, Ms. Sinclair has already forgotten she was told her son went back home to Seattle.

I don't know what else to say, so I just tell her I don't know and promptly change the subject.

I help her dress and fix her hair, fastening the gold owl brooch with the big, sparkly eyes to the left side of her beige sweater, just above her heart.

After I wheel Ms. Sinclair to the community room for Pastor Glickson's Sunday-morning service, I busy myself taking care of my other loves. I clean Mrs. Boyer's glasses, swap out Mr. Rauch's bedsheets, and help change Mr. Ledbetter's portable oxygen tank. I say hello to an afghan-draped Mrs. Thompson as she sits in the lobby waiting for her daughter's weekly visit. She's wearing her usual Sunday-morning smile.

As I work, a fresh and overwhelming bout of gratefulness soaks into me. I've spent the last six years doing exactly what I was meant to do. I've shared my compassion with the people who've needed it most. I've shown them love and mercy, and when things got bad, they've allowed me to give them the peace they deserve. Sondra might be able to stay disconnected from these people and their suffering, but I cannot. And, as hard as it is sometimes, I'm thankful for it. I'm glad there's not an inch of emotional distance between me and the people I take care of. Because it makes it *real*. It makes it *right*.

I hear Sondra's words inside my head again: *the more you care for them, the harder it is.*

I know filling their last living moments with kindness, especially when other parts of their life have been so cruel, is precisely why this gift of mine is so important. Every human being deserves to live—and die—surrounded by *too much* compassion and grace. Even men like Mr. Sinclair.

Part of me wishes I could ask Adam how it was for his father at the end. I want to know if Mr. Sinclair left this world peacefully, if he understood why his son did what he did. I want to know if Mr. Sinclair felt any love for Adam, and if his son found it in him to feel something in return. I want to know if there was as much compassion and emotion in that hospital room last night as I hope there was. I want to know if what Adam did was as *real* and *right* as it would have been if I were the one ending his father's life. Because if it wasn't, then Adam didn't send his father out of this world with everything he deserved. He didn't do it with compassion and forgiveness in his heart.

But I can't ask Adam any of these things. I can't ask him what he was feeling. I can't confirm what I hope is true. It won't stop me from loving him; nothing could. But for the rest of my life, I'll be wondering.

The church service ends forty-five minutes after it starts, and when it does, I wheel Ms. Sinclair out to the lobby window so she can watch her birds. She's contentedly telling the very hard-of-hearing Mrs. Rupert all about the chickadees at the feeders. Mrs. Rupert is leaning over toward Ms. Sinclair with her head tilted to the side, as if she's actually interested in learning about the balls of feathery fluff outside the window. I smile as I leave them on my way to the staff room.

Sondra is here today, working the daylight shift. She's sitting at a desk filling out a transportation form when I walk into the room.

"I heard about Winston Sinclair dying on the news this morning," she says, looking up at me. "Everything okay?"

"I think so, yes. Adam came over to tell me this morning."

"How's he doing? It's too bad they were so mad at each other when I kicked them out of here the other night. I know they didn't get along, but there's nothing worse than losing someone when you're angry at them."

"Things weren't good between them for a long time, so I think that argument was just like lots of others." It's far from the truth, but Sondra doesn't need to know that. "Adam's doing all right. Mr. Sinclair was in really bad shape. I think it was a blessing."

She purses her lips and crosses her arms over her chest. "Um-hum. Probably a blessing in more ways than one."

I don't respond with words. I only shrug and try to pretend I don't know what she's talking about.

"I think it's time you come clean," she says, standing up from her desk and stepping over to me. "You gotta tell Susan about you and that boy. She needs to hear it from you, before she hears it from someone else. By which I mean, if you don't tell her, then I'm going to. I don't like holding on to someone else's secrets. They ain't good for your health." She winks at me and puts her hands on my shoulders. "And I'm pretty sure there's nothing in the employee handbook that says you can't date a patient's grandson."

"I'll tell her. I promise. But give me a few days, okay?" When I do tell Susan about Adam and me, she'll know immediately why Mr. Sinclair filed that abuse claim against me. She'll know Adam's father didn't want us to be together. I'm okay with her knowing it. Just not yet.

"Okay," Sondra says, suddenly putting her arms around me and wrapping me in a tight hug. I squeeze back, feeling grateful for her friendship and wanting her to know how much I appreciate having her in my life, walls and all.

When I head back out to the lobby a few minutes later, Adam is sitting on the sofa, in between his grandmother's wheelchair and Mrs. Rupert. He's repeating everything his grandmother says to Mrs. Rupert, only in a much louder voice. There's half a bouquet of daisies sticking out of his shirt pocket. Every element of the scene is sweet and adorable. I walk over to say hello. Ms. Sinclair sees me first.

"Well, hello there, dear. Guess who's come to see me today." She looks from me over to Adam. Her expression softens. There's love there. So much love. "Bradley, have you met my nurse yet?"

Adam looks up at me, but this time there's no sadness on his face at the sound of Bradley's name. No confusion or uncertainty. "What was your name again, young lady? I'm afraid I've forgotten," she adds, shifting her gaze back to me.

"K'acy," I say with a smile. "And, yes, your grandson and I have met." I look at Adam's gray eyes. They're shining back at me. "It's nice to see you again."

"You, too." There's coyness behind his words. I think he's finally learned to roll with it.

Adam gets up from the sofa and walks around to the back of his gram's wheelchair. I take it as a cue.

"Mrs. Rupert, why don't you and I go get a cup of tea? I think the kettle's on in the dining room."

As Mrs. Rupert and I shuffle off for her cup of tea, I hear Adam behind me as he pushes his gram's wheelchair toward the hallway.

"So, Gram, what was I like when I was little?"

"Stubborn," she says. "Like your father. Only you were also sweet as pie. You could charm the fur off a puppy when you wanted to."

Their voices trail off as the distance between us grows. I'm amazed and humbled by the affection between them.

***

During my lunch break, I text Jarrod. I don't know if he'll be awake yet, but I have to let him know I'm okay and ask how things went at The Upstage last night. If I could cross my fingers while I type, I would.

How'd the epic ass shaking go?

Amazing. The bass playing, however, was totally second rate.

I wonder if Grace is with him. I want to ask if she enjoyed the show, but then I think better of it. Because maybe there's someone else in his bed today.

And the openers from Jersey?

Also second rate.

Sorry to hear it.

Yeah, but they made us sound extra good, so there's always that.

Any word from the Naysayer rep?

They didn't show.

My heart skitters inside my chest.

What happened?

They called and left a voicemail. Apologized and said someone had the flu or something.

That sucks.

Not really. They're coming to Bartholomew's next month instead.

I let out a single, awkward laugh.

For real?

Just please promise me there will never be second-rate bass playing ever again.

Promise.

Good. All well with you? Did it happen?

Yes.

Is The Mister okay?

He will be.

You too?

Me too.

Grace says hi.

I picture the two of them together, and it makes me happy.

Tell her I said hi back.

Will do.

See you Wednesday night?
Yep.
Bye, Jar.
Later.

A sense of relief rises in my gut, knowing I didn't shoot Crackerjack Townhouse in the foot after all. I don't have to forgive myself for anything more than one night of Stevie's second-rate bass playing.

***

The rest of the day passes quickly. Adam leaves for a few hours in the afternoon to go see his mother, but he comes back just before my shift ends. When I see him walking down the hallway, straight toward me as I push his grandmother to the dining room, tiny fires erupt all over my body, inciting another desirous riot beneath my skin. Notes begin playing inside my head. Only it's not "Soul to Squeeze" anymore. It's the new, unnamed love song from last night. The melody is quiet yet fierce. Soft yet sinful. It's perfect. Just like us.

It takes everything inside me not to kiss him when he reaches us. And as he stops in front of his grandmother's wheelchair, I see it in his eyes, too. The same sly, ill-hidden pangs of need are there, staring right back at me.

Without a word, Adam takes over the driving and pushes his gram to the dining hall. After she's situated at the table, he kisses her forehead and tells her he'll see her tomorrow.

"Goodbye, Adam," she chirps, bringing an immediate grin to his face. "And don't you forget to bring your homework tomorrow, okay?"

"Yes ma'am."

I come back out of the staff room a few minutes later, after I finish compiling the shift change report. Adam is waiting for me in one of the lobby's leather wingchairs. His shoulders are relaxed, and he's got one leg crossed over the other, looking like he was born to sit in that very chair.

The moment we step outside the glass doors together, his hand grasps mine, wrapping it up in a nice little package.

"How's your mom?" I ask as we head across the parking lot.

"Not good. We had to make arrangements to have my dad's body flown back to Seattle tomorrow. She wants to charter a private jet so the casket doesn't have to ride in the cargo hold. She says she wants him to be with her, not the luggage. It's weird to see her this way, you know. She's so broken. I just keep wondering if she would be less sad if she knew about Bradley. I kinda want to tell her about him because I keep thinking seeing her angry would somehow be better than seeing her so damn sad."

"I think telling her would just make her twice as sad."

In my peripheral vision, I see Adam nod and swallow hard. His feet scuff against the asphalt, and his hand squeezes mine a little bit tighter.

"Someone once told me there's a lot to be said for the whole *ignorance is bliss* thing," he says, his voice brimming with emotion as he repeats the words I once said to him. "Maybe I should stick with that. For my gram *and* my mom."

Before I can reply, I see his car one row away. Adam's eyes are still aimed at the ground, but mine are looking straight ahead.

Right at Perry Devine.

He's leaning against the front fender of Adam's car. His crisply ironed white shirt is glowing in the pale light of dusk, a folded pair of aviators hooked over the top button. His expression is stern and dry. I think for a moment that my knees might fold up beneath me.

"Adam," I say softly. When he looks over at me, I lift my chin in the direction of his car. The moment he sees Mr. Devine, Adam's expression changes. It lightens, as if he's seeing an old friend.

"Perry," he says, striding right up to the man and extending his hand in greeting. I stand a few paces behind him, unsure of what this is all about.

"Adam." Mr. Devine doesn't take Adam's hand. Instead, he throws his arms around him and wraps Adam in a gigantic hug. One that beats Sondra's to a pulp. "You okay?"

They let go of each other before Adam offers an answer. "Yeah. I'm okay." He steps back and lifts a palm up in front of me. "I believe you two have already met. K'acy McGee, Perry Devine. Perry Devine, K'acy McGee."

I'm completely stunned. I don't know what to say.

"Yes. We've met." Mr. Devine looks at me, this time with something other than intimidation. "I only wish it had been under better circumstances."

What the hell is going on?

Perry Devine reaches into his pants pocket and pulls out an envelope. He holds it out in front of me. "I believe this is yours."

I look at Adam before I take the envelope. He shrugs in ignorance.

"What is it?" I inquire, reaching for whatever's in Mr. Devine's extended hand.

"It's the rest of your money." There's no mockery in his voice. No scorn. He's dead serious. "From what I understand, your sister's gonna need this half, too."

I glance at Adam for answers, but he's as surprised as I am.

"I'm not leaving Adam," I say, the words falling from my mouth with more confidence than I feel.

"Look," Mr. Devine continues, "I'm not giving you this so you'll leave him. I'm not the same kind of man as Winston Sinclair. I know what love is when I see it." His familiar, long-lashed eyes harden. "I did a lot of things I didn't want to do in the last seventeen years, and following you around for the last few months was one of them."

Adam's expression is ripe with bewilderment, and my jaw is almost on the ground.

"You've been following her around?" The pitch of Adam's voice is almost pre-pubescent.

Mr. Devine turns to Adam, his hands sinking into his pockets again as he nods his answer. "I don't know if you know how your father and I met, and why I started working for him. But now that he's gone, I think you should know," he says.

I hear Adam suck in a gulp of air. I'm unsure of whether or not I should leave the two of them alone. Before I can decide, Mr. Devine starts talking again.

"He caught me breaking into his car. I had the wire wedged down in the doorframe when he grabbed me from behind and knocked me flat on the ground with some god-awful jujitsu move he must've learned at the gym. I was twenty-three years old, fresh off a four-year deployment. I had no money and no place to sleep, other than on a buddy's couch. I needed a car, and your father's was right there for the taking. When he saw my military ID tags, he knocked me on the head for being so stupid. He offered me a job on the spot, told me I could be his driver for as long as I wanted to be. *If* I did everything he asked. Your father paid me more money than I'd ever seen, just to drive him wherever he wanted to go. Then, a couple months later, when I guess he figured he could trust me, he offered me even more money to take on other responsibilities, ones that weren't as simple as driving him around. In a very short time, I went from being homeless to being head of security for your father's company."

As Adam absorbs Mr. Devine's words, a troubled furrow forms between his eyes.

"What I'm saying is…I know all of your father's secrets, Adam. Everything he did and said for the last seventeen years is right in here." Perry Devine taps an index finger against his own temple. "And a lot of it isn't very nice. But, I also got a lot of memories of you up in there, too. Because while I was doing everything your father asked, I was also watching you. You deserved better than what you got from your dad. But, I couldn't do anything about it, you know? I couldn't speak up for you because I didn't wanna lose what I'd worked so hard for. So, I just tried to do right by you. I tried to be there when your father wasn't."

"You *did* do right by me." Adam's words are spiked with admiration for this man, a man I never would've considered admirable. "Why didn't you quit? Especially after I went to college."

Perry Devine gently shakes his head. His gaze shifts down the row of cars, right to the glass doors of Pine Manor. He thinks hard before he answers. "You don't walk away with another man's secrets in your hands. At least not alive."

What the hell is that supposed to mean?

The ounce of admiration I might have felt for him immediately morphs into fear, and then multiplies itself lightning-fast, over and over again, until my body is brimming with anxiety. I'm confused and suddenly scared for Adam's safety. Is Mr. Devine talking about Bradley? Are his boss's secrets *still* worth protecting, even though the man is dead?

Fear swirls around inside me.

Does he know what Adam might have done to his father?

Adam is quiet for a long minute, his hands pressing against the sides of his thighs. I'm frozen, reeling with uncertainty.

"So what happens now?" Adam asks.

Mr. Devine centers his weight as his eyes backtrack along the row of cars until they meet Adam's again.

"I walk away."

Adam slowly bobs his head in understanding, not taking his eyes off Perry Devine's. I exhale all the air that's been pent up in my chest since I took the envelope of money. It whooshes out of me like a long, slender train of relief.

"Your father once told me life is full of hard choices," Mr. Devine continues. "You can tackle those choices head-on, like a man, or you can second-guess your decisions and end up being nothing more than a powerless over-thinker." His hands move to Adam's shoulders, resting on them with gravity and purpose. "But what I'm doing now isn't a hard choice. There's nothing to second-guess. I'm walking away with every one of your father's secrets in my hands, and someday, when I get to hell, I'll drop them right into the fire and watch them burn." He lifts his hands and uses one of them to plant a light, fake punch on Adam's chin before putting them back into the pockets of his trousers. "Have a good life, Adam. Tell your mother I said goodbye."

Without another word, Perry Devine turns his back on us and walks away. Adam stays completely still and watches him disappear down the street. When Mr. Devine rounds the corner, Adam turns back to me. His eyes are watery and clearly full of private memories. He doesn't say a word as he pulls his car keys from his pocket, presses the unlock button on the fob, and walks around to the driver's side of his car.

As I tug the passenger-side door handle, I glance at the envelope in my hand. It's bulkier than the last one was, making me wonder if there's more in it than there should be. Before I climb in the now open car door, I peek inside the envelope. It's full of cash. Hundred-dollar bills. Whether or not it's more than it should be, I don't know. But the sight of it brings Charlie and her little one to the forefront of my mind. I picture her face as she opens the envelope and sees another cashier's check inside. Her Blue Cliff tuition can be paid in full. And she'll have enough left over to pay a half-year's rent, either to Tasha or to a landlord of her own. The thought spikes my blood with a heady rush of pleasure. I'm inundated by peace and happiness, believing beyond a doubt that, this time, Charlie will make our daddy proud. She'll finally have the perfect life she deserves. For herself and for her child.

I tuck the envelope full of Charlie's future into the pocket of my scrubs and climb into the car.

My seatbelt is buckled before I notice Adam hasn't started the engine. I look over to find him sitting quietly in his seat, staring at a large, bloated manila envelope on top of the car's dash. Something is written across the front of it, in bold, black marker.

"For K'acy McGee Only" it says.

Adrenaline gallops through me.

CHAPTER 38

Evelyn Sinclair—Room number 112

I spent most of my life raising little boys. Three of them, to be exact. One grew up to be a scoundrel and another never got to grow up at all. The third one, though, he's the one I'm the most proud of.

Winston never knew his father, and maybe that was part of the problem. I lost Carl when Winston was just a month old. He had a massive heart attack and that was that. Some might say I babied Winston too much, letting him get away with things another mother may not have. But he was all I had, and I didn't know what I'd do if I lost him, too. I just wanted him to be happy.

When I found the dead, half-rotted canary in the bushes beneath Winston's bedroom window, its wings broken and twisted, I didn't say a word. I figured he'd hurt the bird by accident, and he'd only lied to cover it up so I wouldn't be disappointed in him. I learned soon enough that I was wrong. Winston didn't care about disappointing me. He only cared about saving his own hide.

When he grew into a teenager, full of more stories and lies, I kept thinking it was just a phase. I thought he'd grow out of it, but the lies kept building and the mountain he'd become grew too tall for me to manage. It was easier to pretend. Mothers always want to see the best in their children, and I kept believing someday he would change.

I really thought he'd turned a corner when he married Heather. She was good to him, and she gave him a beautiful son. When Adam was born and they asked me to help care for him, I was more content than I'd ever been. He was my sweetheart. I loved him more than I'd loved anything in my entire life, including my own son. Adam and I were best friends. I took care of him almost every day, and I'd often stay over at Winston and Heather's at night, too, when they needed someone to stay with Adam for one reason or another. We'd go to the playground, build Lego castles, and eat chocolate pudding every day for lunch. He was my everything.

The instant Winston showed up at my door with a pudgy baby Bradley, I felt the noose tighten around my neck. My own son was forcing me to give up what I loved the most in order to help him hide the biggest lie of his life. But I knew if I didn't, Heather and her lawyer would take *all* of my boys away from me. If she found out about Bradley, she'd leave Winston, and he'd blame it on me and never speak to me again. I could handle that part, but I'd also never be allowed to see Adam, and my new grandson would probably wind up in the foster-care system, and that's the part I *couldn't* handle. Heather was not mean and vindictive, but I knew her hurt would make her want to fight back the only way she could. Bradley and Adam would be the collateral damage in their divorce.

I only saw one way to stop it from happening. So, I let the mountain swallow me whole. I took Bradley to save us all from complete devastation. Winston had already moved Adam and his mother to the other side of the country and now I knew why. I figured I'd still get to see Adam from time to time, and I knew Bradley would be safe with me. I thought I could handle everything. I thought it was the only way.

I should've known Winston was lying.

Bradley grew into a sweet boy, too, though he was far more stubborn than his half-brother. I came to love him as much as I loved Adam. I sent Winston pictures of Bradley as he grew, hoping someday he'd want to meet him in person, but I never heard back from him. For all I knew, those photos went straight into the garbage.

As he grew, I'd tell Bradley stories about his father and mother, just to make him feel like he was part of a larger family. I told him his parents couldn't take care of him because of issues he'd come to understand when he was older, but he died well before he could understand. He died a week after his ninth birthday.

When Marissa showed up at my door, she already felt like an old friend. Even though almost nine years had passed, I recognized her from the playground. I didn't know she was my son's lover back then, but when she stood on my front porch looking for Bradley, I knew she wasn't just the one-night stand Winston made her out to be. I knew my son had loved her and then discarded her when she got pregnant. I knew it because I'd heard the entire story from her own lips, nine years ago, in Canterbury Park. Only I didn't know the man she was talking about was my own son.

I felt so much shame. Shame that it was *my* son who had hurt her so much. Shame that I didn't recognize baby Bradley as belonging to the girl from the park when Winston came to the door with him. Shame that I believed my son when he said Bradley's mother had chosen drugs over her own baby.

I knew there was more to her story, and I figured if I let her get to know Bradley, someday I might find out the truth and Winston's mountain would collapse.

Only it didn't happen that way. The next morning, I had to call my son and tell him about the car wrapped around the phone pole.

After that, I was alone. I spent the next eight years falling into a hole. That's what Alzheimer's is, really. A hole. You can feel yourself falling, but you can't stop it. You just keep getting sucked in, and eventually, you're too far down to know where you are. Too many memories disappear and it changes you. You forget who you are.

By the time Adam came to Pine Manor, the real me sat at the bottom of the hole, inside my own brain, waiting for something to lift me out, even just for a moment. Occasionally a memory would crash down on me and I'd be hoisted up out of the hole. But it wouldn't last long. Just when I'd recognize myself, the memory would leave and I'd be dropped back down into the hole again. Alone. It made me sad, and I knew there was nothing I could do to change it.

I also knew that one day the hole would swallow me up entirely.

Adam tried to lift me out of the hole. I know he did. He wanted more memories to come and raise me out of there, and whenever one would, it was shiny and brilliant and amazing. But he couldn't make them come any more than I could. So, most of the time, I just sat in the hole and waited for it to swallow me completely.

But it never got the chance.

I died before the hole closed, before I lost all of myself to Alzheimer's. The girl—the one Adam loves—came in to my room one afternoon, when things got bad. She lifted me up out of the hole one final time.

They never told me, but I now know my son died six weeks before I did. His mountain had crumbled to nothing more than a pile of burned-up metal and skin. I'm glad they didn't tell me, because I wouldn't have understood. The hole kept me from fully comprehending a lot of things, and Winston's accident would have just been another one of them.

Some people say ignorance is bliss. And that just may be the only good thing about the hole they call Alzheimer's.

K'ACY'S EPILOGUE

Evelyn Sinclair left this world looking like a million bucks. I made sure of it. Her owl brooch—the one now pinned to the leather strap of my Music Man StingRay bass guitar—twinkled in the light of her bedside lamp. She was wearing her favorite bubblegum-pink sweater set with matching polyester pants. I dressed her that morning, almost two months ago, knowing it would be the last day she'd get to spend in this world. Things had gotten bad. She'd fallen and hit her head shortly after Mr. Sinclair died, and she hadn't gotten out of bed since.

I knew it was time, because her eyes told me so.

She died with all the dignity and compassion she deserved. It wasn't as hard as I thought it might be. Adam was ready, too. Even though those words never came out of his mouth.

As the stage lights whirl around me, tiny specks of radiance spread over the audience, moving and swirling across their skin. The dots are only reflections of light, bouncing off the owl's rhinestone eyes, but I like to think of them as little pieces of Ms. Sinclair. Every time I move, she's shuttled in a million different directions, spreading herself around the room in erratic prisms of radiance and light.

My bass notes vibrate their love through everyone's chest as the bits of Ms. Sinclair dance with joyful exuberance. It seems that tonight, there's no better place for a person to be than right here. At Crackerjack Townhouse's feet. Jarrod's voice pours over the audience like icing over a still-warm cake.

With me thumping inside his heart and his grandmother's light dancing around him, my bed-headed swooner looks more than happy. He's encased in Jarrod's voice, too, and as I look down at Adam, standing at the corner of the bar with a shot glass in his hand, I know everything there is to know about forgiveness and love. I know about perfection. He smiles up at me as numbness settles into my fingertips, unstoppable music rushing out of them. Naysayer Records may not have been impressed by what they saw at Bartholomew's three months ago, but it doesn't matter. Crackerjack Townhouse will keep doling out the panty-dropping feels for as long as Philadelphia thinks funk deserves a home.

As the notes of Marquis's trumpet solo cut through the air, yesterday returns to my mind. Jarrod sang the National Anthem at the groundbreaking ceremony, and it was absolutely beautiful. Adam insisted on it, saying the Evelyn Sinclair Alzheimer's Center deserved one hell of a welcome reception. I've heard Jarrod sing a million times before. But, I've never heard him sing like *that*. It was breathtaking. Ms. Sinclair would've loved it.

After Jarrod sang, Adam's mother gave a touching dedication to her husband, reminding us all that, sometimes, money can do a lot of good. Even when it comes from a giant dickhead. She and Adam fully funded the Center's construction using his trust fund and some of her inheritance from Mr. Sinclair's life insurance policy. She flew back to Seattle this morning, leaving Adam to oversee the project and represent their family on the Center's Board of Trustees. As I see him out there tonight, dressed in his favorite hoodie and slurping down a shot of vodka with Grace and couple of her friends, I'm so proud of him. Of *us*.

After a few more measures, Crackerjack Townhouse ends the song with a deafening punch of horns. The sound ricochets around the room for a hot instant before the audience erupts with appreciation. We don't stop very long to let it soak in, because a moment later, Liam delivers the first tight chords of "Break It Out," quickly turning the crowd into a fresh frenzy of drunken exuberance. I've come to realize they're watching *all* of us move around the stage, not just Jarrod. They're soaking in our music, but also our presence. It's the part that makes it a live show, instead of a bunch of songs coming out of an iPod. I'd never thought about it before, about how much the actual performance makes us who we are. Not until I saw the pictures from Perry Devine.

I waited until I got home to open the bloated manila envelope he'd left on Adam's dash that night, and as I sat alone in my bedroom sorting through the contents, things became clearer. There were dozens of photos of me, surveillance shots likely taken by Mr. Devine himself. Images of me on the street in front of Wicked Mocha, on stage at Bartholomew's, slapping my bass at The King's Court, opening the door of a twenty-four-hour pawnshop, walking into Pine Manor, stepping onboard the 61A on my way to work and off the 43D at one in the morning. There were pictures of my empty apartment and some of the things he'd found there while I was at work. There were also plenty shots of Adam and me together, too, taken at the Mexican restaurant, the coffee shop, my place, and his.

But the image that probably made the biggest impact was of the vial of pentobarbital from the dealer on Latham Street sitting inside the small wooden box of syringes in the back of my closet.

348 | CLAIRE WALLIS

The photo was obviously taken before I threw the contents of the box down the garbage chute.

Also in the envelope were pages and pages of handwritten notes, filled with information about my childhood, my father, and Charlie—including her pregnancy. There were even notes about Jarrod, things that happened well before we even met.

I burned every one of the photos—and every last page of Perry Devine's handwritten notes—in a metal trashcan in the alley behind my apartment building. And when I was done, I called Adam and told him about everything that was in the envelope. Everything except for that one photo. He said he was angry but not surprised. Then he apologized again for having the kind of father that would do such a thing.

A small river of sweat makes its way down the front of my neck as the last few notes of "Break It Out" spring from my fingers. Sometimes, I can still feel the downy head of a mourning dove nestled between those same fingers, and if I listen hard enough to my own thoughts, I can hear the snap of their small, brittle bones. Ever since Mr. Sinclair died, I've been dreaming about my daddy's quarry and the flocks of mourning doves flying overhead. In my dreams, there's always a single bird sitting in my lap, its dark eyes watching me without fear as it waits to die. And in my dream, just as in my life, I'm swift and sure. I end the dove's suffering exactly how my daddy showed me. In the dream, when it's over, I cry. I only remember having cried once in real life, on the day I met a dying Lindsay Chapman in the parking lot. After that, I don't remember shedding a single tear in that quarry. I only remember feeling thankful and necessary and right.

Soon after "Ecce Homo," our final song of the night, comes to its always-rousing end, Crackerjack Townhouse leaves the stage, overflowing with satisfaction and energy. I step off the stairs and follow Jarrod down the narrow hallway toward the back room, knowing my Mr. "Soul to Squeeze" is headed there, too. With a quick snap of his fingers, Jarrod turns on his heels, cursing about leaving his cigarettes on Liam's amp yet again. As he slides past me in the slender hall, he gives me one of his sly smiles.

The moment he does, a stampede of happiness washes over me and weaves its way through my scarred heart. I suddenly know without a doubt that we're both going to be okay. Because for the first time ever, I see hope in Jarrod's eyes.

The End

ABOUT THE AUTHOR

In addition to THE SOUND OF LIGHT, **Claire Wallis** is also the author of the novels PUSH and PULL. Her "day job" as science writer allows her to share her love of rocks, plants, insects, and microbes.

She lives in Pennsylvania with her amazingly awesome husband and son.

Sign up for Claire's Newsletter
Follow Claire on Twitter: @ClaireWallisNA
Become a fan on Facebook: Claire Wallis
Hang out with Claire on Goodreads: Claire Wallis
Stop by her website: www.clairewallis.com
And, last but not least, please help other readers find this book by writing a review.

OTHER TITLES BY CLAIRE WALLIS

Push
Pull

Praise for Claire Wallis's Novel PUSH

"PUSH was an intoxicating book, leaving the reader spellbound from the very first page. The twisted plot, brilliantly conceived and executed, had me on the edge of my seat with every word, wondering how it would all play out."—**JM Darhower, author of** *Monster in His Eyes, Torture to Her Soul, Sempre, Made,* **and other titles**

"Wallis' first New Adult title reads more like a psychological thriller along the lines of a Gillian Flynn novel with New Adult elements thrown in. Sure, it has the requisite hot bad boy and loads of steamy scenes, but there are also extraordinary twists and missing pieces revealed, guaranteed to surprise readers... Definitely one of the most unique NA books out there!"—*RT Book Reviews*

"Now that was an exhilarating read indeed. Excuse me, while I pick my jaw up off the floor. I'm just sitting here. Stunned."—**Maryse's Book Blog**

www.ingramcontent.com/pod-product-compliance
Lightning Source LLC
Chambersburg PA
CBHW031506210626
46816CB00019B/1516